STRETCHING HEAVEN

by Keith R. Clemons

"In the begining - God"

GEORGE COLTON
PUBLISHING

George Colton Publishing, LLC.
For information email:
GeorgeColton@att.net

Churches, schools, charities, and other not-for-profit organizations may acquire George Colton books by writing to the above attn: Ministerial Markets Department.

This book is a work of fiction. The characters, incidents, and dialogues are products of the author's imagination and are not to be construed as real. Any resemblance to actual events or persons, living or dead, is entirely coincidental.

Published by George Colton Publishing LLC

Clemons, Keith R. 1949-
    Stretching Heaven / Keith R. Clemons -- 1st ed.

Library of Congress Control Number: 2015921344
ISBN   978-0-9731048-4-4

Printed in the United States of America

First Edition

16 17 18 19 21 22 23 – 10 9 8 7 6 5 4 3 2 1

Also by Keith R. Clemons:

If I Should Die

Above the Stars

These Little Ones

Angel in the Alley

Mohamed's Moon

Mohamed's Song

"He has made the earth by his power, he has established the world by his wisdom, and has stretched out the heaven by his understanding." —Jeremiah 51:15

Prelude

The trees bending and twisting looked like grass skirts on hula dancers tousled by the wind.

The glass wall kept him apart, safe and dry. He sat watching dead leaves tumble across the lawn in uncontrolled frenzy. Out over the ocean waves frothed green and white, swelling as strobes of electricity pulsated in the clouds. The storm would hit land soon. His fingers drummed the table.

Wallace is a leech, taking but not giving back, a man whose accomplishments are in the past. He should have quit long ago.

They shoot horses, don't they? No one complains when you swat a fly. A pest is a pest.

A torrent of rain pelted the window distorting his vision.

The question was no longer if, but when.

One

In the beginning God created the heavens and the earth. —*Genesis 1:1*

The rain sounded like gravel poured on a sheet of tin.

SARAH STARED at the long stream of red taillights blurred by the downpour. She was stuck. Traffic wasn't moving. *Honnnnnnnnnk.* She flinched and turned. The guy in the truck behind her flicked his hands erratically. *Really, like it's my fault.* Lightning crackled, rumbling through the van's interior.

She reached for her phone and shook it, trying to wake it up. The battery was dead. The screen was as dark as the sky. The rain continued to pummel her windshield obscuring the world on the other side of the glass. Dr. Summer wouldn't wait. *Phooey.* She leaned on her horn joining the cacophony created by the snarl of commuters struggling to get home.

This was San Francisco at its worst—foul weather and traffic—especially when she had somewhere to be.

She *loved* the city—*most of the time.* She had arrived on a one way ticket from South Dakota thinking she was living the dream: sipping clam chowder from a fish market on the Wharf; sharing hot chocolate with Buddy at Ghirardelli Square; and listening to the sound of cable cars jerking their way up Nob Hill with bells clanging.

She loved strolling through Golden Gate Park, the painted ladies with their Victorian architecture shining in the coral glow of the sun, and standing in Union Square staring up at Macy's eighty foot tall Christmas tree with its twenty-two thousand lights—and the art—the art was everywhere. But when late for an appointment, the slow grind made San Francisco the most undesirable place in the world to be. *Ah! At last*, the car in front of her pulled around. A vehicle was stuck in her lane. All she had to do was—*there*—she saw her chance and took it. The stalled driver looked away, mortified.

Sarah gunned her minivan and swerved to avoid a wave of water sprayed by a passing vehicle. She checked her watch. Barring another incident, she'd only be a half hour late. He might still be there.

The traffic loosened and began to move. The river of cars flowed down U.S. 101 in a rebellious mix of oil and water.

Now her only obstacle was the rain. *Waa-fump, waa-fump.* Her wipers whooshed back and forth. Shrubs along the highway blustered in the wind. She flicked on her blinker and moved over. The exit was just ahead.

Her heart quickened as she rolled past the rows of palm trees guarding the entrance to CellMerge. The three towers were made of gold glass. In the sun they looked like brass harmonicas standing on end but under the clouds resembled dirty combs. She pulled up to the garage and rolled down her window handing the attendant her keys.

Her neatly stacked proposal had come undone. She unclasped her seatbelt and reached out scooping the pages into a pile which she clutched to her breast. The door swung open. She tugged her red hoodie over her head and launched herself into the storm splashing water as her tennis shoes slapped the pavement.

She was almost to the building rushing forward with her head down—*Ohhfffff.*

The man stumbled backward, his sunglasses knocked askew, his sensory perception fouled by the iTune playing in his ear. Sarah's hand jerked away sending her report into the wind like a cyclone of paper.

Her eyes went wide, her mouth ajar as she watched her work blowing across the parking lot, the pages tumbling through the air, sloughing in puddles and getting pinned to the asphalt by the rain.

"*Noooooooo!*" she said.

Two

Then God said, "Let Us make man in Our image, after Our likeness; let them have dominion over...all the earth." —Genesis 1:26

OF THE THREE towers that comprised CellMerge, only one housed the corporation. The other two were staged for future growth. They had been built on investment capital and in the interim were leased to other firms. The rent money was channeled back into the corporation to finance further research. In good times, it worked well, but with the faltering economy many of the tenants had either downsized or folded completely creating a deficit.

The pinnacle of the CellMerge tower was reserved for executives. This was where the company's CEO, Jack Landon, and his corporate vice presidents had their quarters. Jack's own office was a statement of privilege. A library of books ran along one wall with hundreds of polished leather bound, unread volumes. The wall opposite was made of glass providing a panoramic view of the Bay. A door at the rear of his office led to the corporate boardroom, giving Jack private access to meetings.

The boardroom was the inner sanctum, the holy of holies, where only key investors and heads of kinship corporations were permitted. Meetings were always behind closed doors. This was where the corporation's deepest secrets were disclosed.

Jack sat at the head of a table big enough to seat twelve but where only seven were assembled. These were the corporation's Board of Directors, an illustrious group of equity builders, power brokers, and financial movers and shakers.

Lightning crackled the sky followed by a thunder-boom so loud it made the lights flicker, but to the men in the meeting it was hard to tell which was worse, the storm outside, or the one brewing in the room.

"I don't see enough here Jack," the president of Aztec Microbiology said. "You keep talking about advances in research but in terms of a product we haven't seen zip."

"I agree," said the retired former head of Colorado Industries. "Our share price has never been lower. We've lost capitalization. Six more months of this and we'll go under."

"Research takes time. Development takes time. Things don't happen overnight." Jack raked his hand through his hair, then slipped his fingers into his pocket for an antacid.

"Same old song and dance, Jack. We all understand how business works but we have to be realistic. Our shareholders won't stay with us if we can't offer them something. We've been at this, how long, nine, ten years? We should have a product by now. At least one."

"We wouldn't be here if it weren't for Summer. He killed us. I wanted him off the books then, but you guys tied my hands."

"Old news, Jack. We still need a viable product."

Jack squirmed in his seat, looking for a way to get the chalky tablet into his mouth discretely. "We need to make an announcement, shoot a few rockets in the sky with pinwheels, anything to get the market's attention. I still think we should have invested in Tecnologias Celulares. The release would have made good press."

"The financials weren't good," quipped George Fishman, the only African American at the table. "We sanctioned your investment, what you do privately is your business, but to risk corporate revenues would be fiduciary irresponsibility."

"I still think it's a sound investment, but that's not the point. It would have given us something to brag about. Make an announcement with a lot of fanfare and hoopla to get the market excited again."

"Until someone checks their books." Fishman shook his head. "No thanks."

"No one can check into it. It's a privately held corporation. They don't release their financials."

Dressed in a three piece suit, the manager of Millbrook Investments swiveled in his chair and brought a hand up to end the discussion. "I'm sorry, Jack, but we've decided to cash out. We're putting our eight-hundred thousand shares on the market. We just can't sustain further losses."

"You can't do tha..."

"I'm sorry, the decision's been made. Our investment group met yesterday. I was told to sell if you didn't have something new to offer, and you don't." He put his hand on the table pushing himself up.

"Wait! Look, there *is* something but I've been holding it back. Several months ago we applied for a patent on a new process and it's just been approved, only it's covered by a nondisclosure so I can't talk about it yet. But it's big, in fact it's a major breakthrough. Over the next month I plan to make several announcements guaranteed to turn us around." Jack paused for emphasis. "If it doesn't, you'll have my resignation."

The man stood, picked up his briefcase and headed for the door. "Thirty days, Jack, that's all you've got. I can't hold my investors off any longer than that."

Three

Then God said, "Let there be a firmament in the midst of the waters, and let it divide the waters from the waters." —Genesis 1:6

SARAH'S PAPERS rode the maelstrom across the parking lot, some sticking to bushes and trees and others driven by rain to the ground. *Ohhhhhhhh.* She spun around chasing after, running from one to the next plucking wet pages from the asphalt and grass. The faded red hoodie flopping over her head made her look like a cardinal pecking seeds. Dark clouds roiled above the towers of CellMerge pulsating with electricity.

Dr. Aaron Rose, one of many young scientists upon whom the company was pinning its hope, shook his head still trying to grasp what happened. He straightened his misaligned sunglasses over his nose and removed the ear buds leaving them dangling over his shoulders. Music blared from the tiny speakers. He cocked his arm over his head like an umbrella and ran to peel several pages from the side of a car, and another from a tree. "Here," he said, handing the soggy paper to Sarah.

"All that work—it's ruined." Water ran down the side of her cheek and dripped off her chin.

"You should watch where you're going."

"Me! *Ohhhhhh.*" Sarah took the wet glop, slopping it onto the pile she'd collected. Half the folio was missing. A gust of wind caught her hood and pulled it back. Her hair, usually flipping out in short erratic lengths, hung limp, its auburn sheen turned to rust. She wiped her brow with her sleeve, raking strands across her forehead. Her mascara was beginning to run giving her the appearance of a sad clown. Rain continued to pelt the ground.

"What is it?"

"What's it matter?" She checked herself. "It's a proposal for Dr. Summer," she answered, her voice muffled by the wind and rain. Lightning lit the dark sky followed by a peal of thunder. She tugged her hood up and ran off to salvage more paper.

Aaron turned to help. There had to be a dozen sheets still drowning in puddles. He was soaked by the time he finished, his cable knit sweater sticking to his skin. He retrieved one last page from a patch of lawn and held it by the corner, shaking it. "'Justification for the Continuance of Adult Stem Cell Research.' Good luck with that," he said, holding the dripping sheet out for Sarah.

She took the wet sheet and slapped it onto her pile. A gust of wind pulled her hood back again exposing her to the downpour. She struggled to drag it back over her head. "Thanks, but I know what I'm doing." She turned and ran off toward the building to find shelter from the rain.

Aaron swung around and hopped up alongside but she didn't acknowledge him. He reached out to swipe his card and pulled the door back allowing her to enter. The vinyl floor reflected the overhead fluorescent lights as they shuffled down the corridor leaving trails of water.

"Weren't you just leaving?" she said.

"I'm curious to know why you're doing that."

"Doing what?"

"Hey, try to lose the attitude? I'm not the enemy. Why are you bucking policy? Aaron raised his chin toward the glob of papers. "They'd probably let it slide if you had tenure, but not while on probation."

9

"Bucking what? *Really?* I thought our policy was to find cures. Anyway, it's just a plausible alternative. Why do you wear sunglasses when it's raining?"

Aaron shrugged. "Forgot I had them on."

Stepping into the main research facility was like entering a transparent maze. The corporation believed in an open work environment. There were few walls and except for private offices the partitions were made of glass. Scientists and lab techs bustled about looking to find cures for one disease or another. Sarah could feel their eyes watching her. She hugged the papers to her chest and shivered. Dr. Summer's office was just ahead. *Why'd he insist on paper, anyway? Ever hear of a flash drive?*

Aaron placed his hand on her arm, turning her to face him. "Look, you're new here so I should probably give you warning."

Sarah stiffened.

"Summer's on the company's blacklist. He published a paper that made investors nervous and put our shares in a tailspin. The only reason they didn't fire him was his name still carries weight, but he was censured. Suffice it to say, he's being watched. I doubt he'll do anything that doesn't toe the party line. Understand?"

Sarah looked down at her proposal and wiped a drop from her chin, but nodded. She moved away slogging the last few feet. The door had a large window. The lights inside were off. She reached for the knob but it was locked. Her shoulders sagged.

Aaron squeezed water from the elbow of his sweater. "Let me make it up to you," He said. "How 'bout a cup of coffee? It'll warm you up."

Sarah's eyes filled with rain. She shook her head. "Thanks, but I have to go." She turned and walked away leaving Aaron standing in the hall with a puddle forming at his feet.

Four

These are the generations of the heavens and of the earth when they were created, in the day that the Lord God made the earth and the heavens. —Genesis 2:4

"YOU'RE WELCOME," Aaron murmured as Sarah sauntered down the hall toward the exit. He removed his sunglasses and shook his head, spinning water from his hair, then combed it through his fingers and propped the Ray-Bans over his forehead. His tennis shoes squished as he turned and trudged down the corridor toward the lab.

The room was filled with stainless steel tables, rolling trays, and clusters of petri dishes all glaring under banks of fluorescent light. Researchers in white lab coats stood at stations mixing viscous fluids and taking notes. A guy the size of a linebacker sat on a small stool staring into a microscope.

"Hey Larry, still trying to make fat cells turn skinny?"

The man's body jerked but he kept his eye to the scope continuing his observation. "It's not about that. Besides, it's after five. I'm on my own time. I can work on whatever I want."

"Which is?"

"I'm trying to ascertain why some cells seem predisposed to absorbing more fat than others." He rolled his head around, his cheeks flushing red. "Oh, hey, what happened to you? Looks like you fell overboard."

11

Aaron raised his hands. The nap of his bulky sweater drooped under his arms. "It's raining a storm out there." His iPhone was still playing music through the ear buds. He reached into his pocket snapping it off, and then grabbed Larry's notebook, scanning the pages. "No, I get it. Why exercise when you can take a pill."

"Go ahead, laugh, but imagine what people will pay for an enzyme cocktail that keeps them slim and trim. I'll be rich."

Aaron felt a tug on his shoulder and turned. "Oh, hey Jen."

The young woman was tall and blond with long tresses that fell in loose waves over her shoulders. She raked her fingers through her hair bringing it to the front and placed her hand on her hip, discretely pushing out her chest. "Lose your umbrella? I think they have towels in the gym. Why haven't you returned my calls?"

"What?" Aaron reached for his iPhone. The display showed four unheard voice messages. "Sorry, I've been busy. What's up?"

She wore her lab coat open revealing her street clothes underneath, a yellow T-shirt and tight denims that emphasized her figure. Her lips, glossy pink, puckered into a pout. "We're going tonight, aren't we? Jack's party. Don't look so clueless."

Aaron shook his head. "Haven't made up my mind if I'm going or not. And as for *we*, there is no *we*. There's just you and me."

"But…"

"Look, Jen, I'm not into relationships."

Jen's mouth popped open forming a little pink O.

"It's nothing personal; I think you're great but I have rules."

Jen tilted her head tossing her hair back over her shoulder. "Well, Mr. Ego, if you'd waited for me to finish I was about to say I'll probably be going to the party with friends. I just wanted to see if you needed a ride, that's all." She spun around leaving Aaron to watch her walk away, her lab coat flapping as she sashayed down the aisle.

Aaron shrugged and looked at Larry.

"Dang, you're wet as a frog in a marsh. Must be bad out there."

"Dr. Jaeger, I was hoping to see you." Aaron had to look down on the man, but not without respect. Carl Jaeger was only five foot six and was just about as round as he was tall. He wore cowboy boots to lend a few extra inches of height, and often a cowboy hat too. His white lab coat covered a plaid pearl button shirt and, in keeping with his western motif, a bolo tie. His face was circular, his head bald, and his eyes small behind his spectacles. A short goatee decorated his chin. He leaned in toward an incubator but his girth got in the way. "My appointment schedule is posted on my website," he said. "I didn't see your name on it."

"Just a quick question."

Dr. Jaeger straightened himself and folded his arms over his clipboard bracing it against the shelf of his stomach. "Go on."

"It's about the cancellation of our adult stem cell program."

Jaeger's lips grew taut. "Wally put you up to this?"

"What?"

"Wally…Wallace Summer…Dr. Summer. He hasn't stopped whining about it since the memo came down."

"No. I haven't seen Dr. Summer. It's that new girl, Sarah. I gather she wants him to let her continue working in that area."

Dr. Jaeger brought a hand up to stroke his goatee. "That would be a serious breach of corporate policy," he said, rubbing his chin. "Know what? I hope he lets her do it."

Dr. Wallace Summer entered his house closing the door against the wind and rain. He stopped in the foyer sweeping water from the weave of his tweed coat before throwing it over the sofa. Limping to the kitchen, he opened the refrigerator and placed the remainder of his lunch inside: a partly eaten ham sandwich, two sticks of celery and a half dozen prunes. He turned, leaning heavily on his cane. His foot always hurt more in wet weather. He shivered and moved to the table, easing himself onto a chair. The party didn't start for a few hours. He had time to prepare. He ran his fingers through his moist white hair, matting it down.

The folder was still on the table. He should put it away; lose it in a file cabinet somewhere. It had caused enough trouble. Instead he pulled it over and flipped it open. The journal was right on top covering reams of articles and technical papers.

He puckered his lips. His questions had become doubts, unresolved issues he hoped to one day reconcile. *Should have let it go,* he thought, thumbing through the pages. But he couldn't. Searching for answers, he'd found little to curb his growing uncertainty.

Where does it say we all have to think alike? Where's the inquiry, the innovation, the discovery in accepting what everyone already believes? Nuts, if science is about anything, it's about killing sacred cows.

He flipped through a few pages, one a note about the human eye, another about the structure of our DNA, and one outlining his views on reproduction. *What's everyone so afraid of? I'm not out to prove anything, I just want an open discussion.*

He'd gone and expanded his journal into a full blown thesis, assembling references and charts, and then published his findings for peer review. *Maybe I am crazy.* He flipped back to the first page of his notes.

My Struggle With Intellectual Honesty
The Journal of W.L. Summer

I intend to put my thoughts on paper. I don't plan to write a thesis, at least not at this point. I haven't time or inclination to include everything I've learned; I just want to clarify my position.

It's time to admit that I'm no longer an atheist; in fact I never really was. I pretended to be, even wanted it to be true, but there were always those nights when I'd sit gazing at the heavens and question how so many stars could evolve from nothing; then I would recall a verse I learned as a child, "The heavens declare the glory of God," and I would know the answer.

Some would say their doubts about God turned them to evolution. As for myself, I believe my doubts about evolution turned me to God.

It feels strange to stand on the other side. I once would have argued evolution was the only possible explanation for the origin of life. I was predisposed to accept things no one could prove simply because I wanted them to be true. I refuse to do this any longer.

Science, by its very nature, should welcome the expression of unconventional ideas and be open and willing to investigate their merit. It's the job of scientists to observe the macro and microcosms of the universe, gather information, and then place the evidence on a scale and see which way it tips. It's all about believing what best fits the facts. After several decades of study I'm left to conclude our universe, from atom to man, could only have come about by design.

Five

Rain down, ye heavens from above, and let the skies pour down righteousness: let the earth open and let them bring forth salvation, and let righteousness spring up together; I the Lord have created it.
—*Isaiah 45:8*

SARAH PULLED off US 101 onto the central freeway heading for her apartment in the mission district. A hot bath would take the edge off but for that she needed the right body oil. She checked her watch. It was still early. She had plenty of time. She was supposed to be meeting with Dr. Summer. Buddy wouldn't be expecting her till around six.

A truck on her left trundled through a puddle creating a wave that buried her windshield in water. *Waaa-fump, waaa-fump, waaa-fump* went her wipers clearing the deluge. She swung around onto Duboce backtracking under the freeway to Folsom. The Rainbow Grocery stood on the corner but the lot was full, even the handicap spaces. Parking was always difficult but especially on rainy days when people weren't so inclined to walk or ride bikes.

A lady holding her umbrella over a bag of groceries hurried by. Sarah watched as the woman stepped off the curb and bustled to a waiting car. *Perfect, thank you Lord.* She flipped her blinker on and waited, pulling in as soon as the space was vacated.

The store was a co-op started by hippies in the 1970's with the idea of selling vegan foods commensurate with their ashram spiritual beliefs. Sarah wasn't a vegan, she wasn't even a vegetarian, but she did like the store. They had a fabulous bath and body department. It was a veritable ocean of lotions. She slammed through the door, pushed her hood back and wrapped her arms around herself, shivering. Soaking in a hot tub was sounding better all the time—anything to remove the chill.

The walls were covered with brightly colored murals depicting farm laborers tilling the soil and harvesting a bountiful crop. She found the bath oil she was looking for—a substance squeezed from a Jojoba cactus but given an aquatic name to neutralize its parched desert image. *OceanAir?* Grabbing a bottle, she made her way to the register and handed it to the clerk.

"Would it be possible to use the phone?" she asked. "It's kind of an emergency. Just for a second."

She began fishing in her purse and looked up just in time to see the girl behind the register shrug. "We don't have a public phone but if it's an emergency you can borrow my cell."

Sarah handed the girl a twenty and received the phone along with her change. "Thanks." She stepped back to avoid being overheard and dialed Dr. Summer's number but the call was picked up by the department secretary.

"Hi, I uh," Sarah glanced at her watch, "I guess I wasn't expecting anyone to be there. I was hoping to leave a message for Dr. Summer."

"He's gone for the day, as am I actually. I forward his number after hours."

"Oh, okay, *ah*, my name's Sarah Hunter. I had an appointment with Dr. Summer but I got caught in traffic and missed it. I need to reschedule. Do you know if he has any time open Monday?"

"I'm sorry, Dr. Summer's in Europe all next week, and I'm afraid his calendar's completely full the week after that."

Sarah sighed. "*Rats!* I was supposed to give him something. Will he be in at all before he goes?"

"No, not likely, but if you leave it on my desk I'll see he gets it as soon as he returns."

Sarah paused, letting the silence build for a moment.

"Or you might try giving it to him at the party tonight. I think he plans to attend."

"*Uhmm*, that's a thought. Thanks, I appreciate the help." She cancelled the connection and handed the phone back to the clerk.

"Everything all right?"

Sarah nodded and picked up her bag, a paper bag she noted, because plastic wasn't biodegradable. "Uh, yes, I think so...I'm fine, thank you." She turned and scurried for the door.

Aaron slid the knot of his tie up and drew it snug around his collar. The silk shone in the light. His shoes were mirror polished, his expertly tailored Hugo Boss suit designed to make an impression. It was pretentious but that was his mother's fault. *If you want to be a professional, look the part.*

He pulled his cuffs into place and stood back, admiring himself in the mirror. He had his father's looks, dark and brooding with thick brows and a chiseled face. Every photo he'd seen confirmed the resemblance, but they'd never actually met. He was only three when his father worked his way to the grave, a heart attack at age thirty, just after he'd increased his net worth to over a million.

The keys to his black-sapphire Beemer were on the bed. Aaron snatched them up and headed for the door, his Florsheims clapping the polished tiles.

Sarah felt the tension melting into vapors of steam as the water massaged her skin. She pulled her leg up and lathered it with soap glancing at the small white vanity, its multilayered paint chipped and scarred, the oval mirror covered with steam. Buddy was waiting in the other room. "I'll be out in a minute, hon." She wiped suds from the end of her nose and reached for her razor.

Three rooms: bath, kitchen and living room, comprised her tiny apartment. The bath featured a claw-foot cast iron tub with a showerhead mounted atop a vertical pipe that thudded against the wall when she cranked the taps; the living room came furnished with a hide-a-bed that served both as a place to sleep and a couch for entertaining; and the kitchenette included a sink, refrigerator, stove and table. Not chic, but functional, and all she could afford.

Grabbing her towel she stepped out of the tub, dripping water. Her toes curled on the cold floor. Pulling the plastic cap from her head, she leaned in wiping a circle in the steam on the mirror and stood back. Same-ol' same ol', the shaggy auburn hair that she'd never liked, though better now, not as blazingly red as it had been when she was a child, and a simple face with impish green eyes that made her look like a pixie. She hated being called *cute*. It made her feel like a bobble-head. They only said it because they were searching for something nice to say and the word *pretty* didn't fit.

She slipped into her dress, an ugly maroon velveteen that clashed with the color of her hair, but it was the only full-length gown she owned and the gathering was supposed to be formal. She didn't want to go to the party anyway, wouldn't go if it weren't her only hope of seeing Dr. Summer.

The sound of the TV blared from the living room. Buddy was using it to avoid talking. He was upset, and rightfully so. Rushing out to meet with Dr. Summer and then skipping out again at night wasn't fair but she had no choice. Her work had to continue. She was running out of time.

Six

The rich and poor meet together: the Lord is the maker of them all.
—Proverbs 22:2

THE HOME of Jack Landon shone like a beacon on the edge of a cliff overlooking the Pacific Ocean. The coastal region was one of affluence. Multi-million dollar mansions lined the shores, but as president and chief executive officer, Jack could afford it. It was the perfect setting for a party. Those with an addiction to nicotine stood on the deck enjoying the floodlights that illuminated the waves crashing on the rocks. Ladies pulled their arms into their wraps and the men held their lapels closed with their hair whipping in the wind. The roar, glop, and sucking of water being dragged through tide pools echoed below.

Inside, the rooms were filled with light and laughter. Researchers, management, and a few key investors milled about with drinks and crab cakes in hand expressing goodwill. Larry was going for his fourth helping of shrimp and oysters. Cocktail sauce dripped off his dish onto the pristine white tablecloth as he slurped down another slimy mollusk.

"Better ease up on that or you'll have a bellyache in the morning," Aaron said.

"Are you kidding?" Larry turned his head and lowered his voice speaking into Aaron's ear. "Oysters are an aphrodisiac. I'm going for all I can get."

Jen leaned in, taking Aaron's arm. "Come on, danch with me."

Aaron turned. Jen's black dress was so tight it looked like she was about to bust out of her brassiere. Her blond hair was pinned to the top of her head but she removed the clip letting it fall free as she pulled Aaron toward the dance floor plucking a rose from a vase along the way which she clenched in her teeth. *Clack, clack, clack,* her high heels tapped as she clapped her hands overhead.

"Oh no, none of that." Aaron raised his hands palms outward and backed into the crowd. The trumpeter picked up the pace, spurring Jen on with a *root-toot-toot, cha, cha, cha.* She grabbed the arm of another man, one of the security staff, pulling him onto the floor and they began doing a bizarre imitation of the Fandango with steps from the Salsa and Tango thrown in for good measure.

Aaron squeezed back through the crowd and found Larry at the dessert table filling his plate.

"I think Jen's had one too many."

"Fine by me," Larry said. "I brought her, so I have to take her home. The more she drinks the better." He winked to emphasize his point.

"*Yeeeeehaaaa,*" came a scream from the dance floor. They turned but couldn't see beyond the wall of people. "Shouldn't you be with your date?"

Larry shoved a slice of chocolate cake into his mouth. "Oh, I will, my man, I will." A small crumb stuck to the corner of his lips as he chewed. He poked at it with his thumb. "I got her right where I want her, where she's too weak to resist."

"How'd you get her to come with you?"

"Easy. She expected you to take her. By the time you turned her down, everyone else had a date. I just happened to be in the right place at the right time."

The band finished the number and stood to the side holding onto their instruments. Jen staggered back over to Aaron and Larry with her hand held to her chest. She began fanning herself. "Whew, I'm shready for another drink. Larry, whoosh you be so kind?"

Larry looked at Aaron and gave him another over-exaggerated wink. "One Crantini coming right up."

Jen snuggled in close to Aaron taking his arm. He could feel her warm breath in his ear. "How 'bout we ditcsh this party and you and I shake a wittle drive?"

A bell was sounding. Jack Landon in a tux with wing collar and bow tie was clinking the blade of a knife against his glass. Aaron straightened himself, slipping Jen's hand from his arm. The company president was standing at the microphone.

"I'm delighted everyone was able to make it out tonight. We've had some tough times but I'm pleased to announce we've been granted several new patents which should help turn things around, so here's to a bright future, and to all of you who helped make it possible." He raised his glass to vigorous applause.

Larry squeezed back through the crowd handing a martini glass filled with a ruby colored drink to Jen. His other hand held a bottle of beer.

"Please join me in a toast." The company president raised his glass to the sky, as did everyone except Aaron. He hadn't had a drink yet. He looked around for a waiter. "This is for all of you. To the people to whom we owe our success, from the company with heart." Mr. Landon brought his glass to his lips.

Aaron looked around feeling self-conscious about not joining in, but he wasn't alone. Dr. Summer, wearing a herringbone tweed, was standing in the periphery. He set his glass down declining to raise it or take a sip. *What's that about?*

Jack Landon stepped down from his rented podium, allowing the band to resume their positions. The music began as the guests fell into small pockets of conversation.

Jen downed the rest of her drink. "Come-on Aaron, I wanna danch." She tried reaching for his hand but he pulled back and she stumbled forward forcing him to catch her shoulders to prop her up.

"Whoa, I think you should sit this one out." He put his arm around her waist, walked her into the den and settled her on a soft leather couch. Larry lumbered over and plopped down beside her, the air elevating Jen as it squeezed from the cushions. He tipped his bottle back finishing his beer and set the sweating empty on an inlaid teak table without a coaster. "So what do we do now?"

Jen laid her head back and closed her eyes.

"Maybe you should get your date home."

"Home? It's early."

A conversation was taking place in a recessed alcove. The lights were subdued but Aaron could see Dr. Summer waving his arms in front of Jack. Both men seemed agitated. Aaron glanced around to see what Larry thought. Jen had her head resting on his shoulder. Her mouth was open snoring softly with her glossy red lips shining in the light.

Aaron turned back to the quarrel. Jack was shaking his head. He brought his hand up pointing to the vestibule. Dr. Summer swiveled around and limped off in a huff, the rubber tip of his cane leaving smudges on the polished hardwood floor. Aaron felt a rush of cool air as Dr. Summer exited, slamming the door behind him.

Sarah pulled up in front of Mr. Landon's house. The cars lining the street stretched for a quarter mile. She sighed. She'd tried to put some curl in her hair, but looking across the palatial lawn, she knew by the time she made it to the door it would be limp. Rain had a way of doing that. Not so much the water itself, she had her umbrella, but the moisture in the air would flatten her hair like a board.

Mr. Landon's mansion looked brighter than Macy's Christmas tree in Union Square. Every light in the house had to be on. She didn't track real estate but she was savvy enough to know homes overlooking the ocean were for millionaires. The windshield wipers flapped streaking the image. Her hand came up taking hold of her necklace, the string of cultured pearls feeling cool and smooth as she rolled them between her fingers. The van gave a shudder. With so many people the odds of getting Dr. Summer alone were slim anyway—*wait*—taillights up ahead, someone was pulling out, someone very close to the front—*Thank you Lord!*

Sarah waited until the car pulled into the street and was rolling down the road before claiming the vacated space. There was no turning back now. If Jesus had opened up this space then she needed to take advantage of it. She started to grab her proposal, but pulled back leaving it on the seat. Others would want to know what it was. Better to get Dr. Summer's interest first. The rain was lighter than before. She opened the door and stepped outside, her heels clicking the pavement as she hiked up her dress and with the umbrella bouncing along overhead ran for the door.

The din of party revelry could be heard even before she stepped inside, laughter, boisterous conversation, blaring music and clinking glasses all creating a dissonant clatter. She stood in the vestibule, an image of herself caught in a gold filigreed mirror mounted by the door: a wilted flower with hair the color of a soiled copper penny. She pushed her bangs back wishing she could turn around and leave. Eyes turned her way as she squeezed into the crowd but no one said anything. That was to be expected. She hadn't been with the company long enough to make friends. It was her dress. Everyone else wore slinky black evening gowns. Her maroon velveteen flashed like a neon sign.

Aaron stepped onto the balcony outside, seeking a break from the noise. A gust of wind peeled back his jacket and ruffled his hair. He rolled his shoulders in, tucking his tie into his coat before buttoning up. Airborne moisture spat in his face, but the rain had stopped—at least for the moment.

He'd seen smokers out here earlier but they'd fled indoors to find shelter which was fine by him. He welcomed the solitude. The deck was large and made of simulated wood. He walked to the rail and peered into the darkness of a starless night. The wind and water swirled and churned. Spotlights illuminated the white foam of the ocean below. Waves crashed against the shore, the pounding surf washing up on the rocks and dragging back in a never ending cycle. Like life itself.

A squall picked up his hair and sent his tie flapping over his shoulder: *Poseidon, Neptune,* some other god? *To be or not to be—* the unanswered question of the universe. That's what led him to choose the field of molecular and cellular biology. No, that wasn't it. His mother had made the decision. He'd wanted to pursue atomic theory. It fascinated him that something as large as our solar system, and the billions of galaxies beyond, could be made of something so small.

But his mother was adamant. There wasn't any money in the study of atoms. Only intellectuals on a quest for discovery were interested in such pursuits. Science should benefit everyone. If he wanted to understand the marvels of life, cellular biology was where to start. Pharmaceutical companies were offering six figure incomes to those able to find ways of increasing man's longevity. "If you want to learn about life, follow the money," she said. She'd selected which college he should attend and paid his ticket.

Another blast of cold air sent a chill down his spine. He shook it off. The stairs at the other end of the deck led down to the sand where he would be out of the wind. He wasn't ready to go back inside.

Sarah made a loop of the party looking for a head of bushy white hair while trying to avoid eye contact. If Dr. Summer was there, he was in a room behind closed doors. A penguin suited server held out a tray of glasses filled with bubbly champagne but she declined. She felt more than saw the cynical looks of people shaking their heads. She wasn't one of them. She didn't belong, the proverbial fish out of water. She shouldn't have worn the dress. She shouldn't have come.

She thought about the folder on the seat of her van, the hours she'd spent preparing it and the last minute effort to print it again—*Lord, I thought you wanted*—but it wasn't to be. There was a tug at her arm.

"You're that new girl, aren't you?" The voice was nasal and high-pitched.

She turned to see a quirky young man with his hair parted in the middle and combed straight back, obviously held in place with a gob of Crisco.

"Hi, I'm Danny, pleased to meet you," he said, extending his hand, but Sarah didn't take it. He was wearing a dark blue coat, black slacks and a wide candy striped tie. His magnified eyes bulging from behind raccoon glasses appeared to be undressing her. "Want to dance?"

Sarah shook her head, looking at the people bopping up and down. "I...I...I can't, sorry, no thank you."

"Ah come on. It's no big deal. I don't dance so good either." The young man grabbed her arm and began pulling her toward the dance floor.

"No!" Sarah jerked free. She stood, her heart beginning to pound. They were gawking at her, staring at her neon dress, her freaky hair. She took a step back and turned. The crowd parted as she pushed her way through. She reached the front door and exited without looking back. She was half way down the steps before she realized she'd left her coat and umbrella behind. She paused, shivering.

Dr. Rose stepped around the corner.

Oh.... She pulled back into the shadows hoping to avoid being seen, but it was too late.

"Hey, Sarah," Aaron said with a brisk wave. "I didn't expect to see you here. What's up?"

Sarah chafed the goosebumps on her arms, shaking her head without lifting her eyes.

"Hey, you'll catch your death out here. Where's your coat?"

She turned toward the door, her face red in the veranda's dim light. "In there," she said, tilting her head.

"What's wrong? You okay?"

She began fidgeting with her string of pearls, looking down at her shoes. "I'm fine. I just…I thought, I mean…I was hoping to see Dr. Summer, but I guess he didn't come. I'm just disappointed, that's all."

Aaron nodded. "He was here but he didn't stay long. Still want to show him your paper, huh? Look, if it's that important, why don't we just run it by his house? He only left a few minutes ago. I'm sure he's still up."

Sarah rubbed her arms, shaking her head.

"Come on, I'm the reason your presentation got ruined. I owe you. Wait here, let me grab your coat." The young man took the steps two at a time heading for the door.

"It's the red one…and my umbrella…" Sarah stammered as he disappeared into the house leaving her shivering in the cold. She would have said no, perhaps should have, but she was too embarrassed to go back inside herself. And it appeared she was being offered another opportunity to get her proposal into the hands of Dr. Summer.

From the Mouth of God
The Journal of W.L. Summer

The scientific consensus is that all the elements of our universe were once couched in nothing, then this nothing exploded and became the innumerable number of stars and planets that comprise our cosmos.

I'm being simplistic, but if I took the time to explain this theory in detail it would still sound farfetched. We know that before the beginning of time there was nothing, but we don't know what nothing is. Everything we know of is composed of something: atoms and subatomic particles like quarks, leptons and bosons.

Physicists tell us if you trace the expansion of our universe back to its beginning it becomes a subatomic particle billions of times smaller than an atom. There's no empirical evidence for this, but even if we assume it's true you still have to ask where this micro-speck came from? Did it invent itself? It supposedly contained, in densely compacted form, all the material required to build our universe. If so, what was the composition of the space in which it existed? Atoms hadn't yet been formed so it had to have rested in a void. Our universe literally sprang forth out of, "nothing."

Unless of course you believe in God. We know there had to be a causation, but it couldn't have come from materials that didn't exist before the universe began. The means of causation would have to come from something that transcends space and time, like information, or words, or thoughts. These are mass-less. Thoughts, words and ideas aren't made of atoms. They have no weight or substance and as such don't exist in the physical realm. I submit that pure intelligence put forth information, like the if-then of a computer program, and worlds were formed. It's a plausible explanation and one that satisfies all natural laws. Isn't it time we at least consider the possibility that God might have spoken the universe into existence?

Seven

By the word of the Lord were the heavens made; and all the host of them by the breath of His mouth. —*Psalm 33:6*

THE BEEMER hummed down the highway with its wipers on intermittent, blinking away the mist. Sarah sat in the passenger seat trying to feign interest as Aaron rambled on about his fancy car. The music from the eight speaker sound system was low and unobtrusive, the cushy leather seats warmed by heaters, and yes, it probably was powered by a 300 horsepower turbo inline six-cylinder engine, but if he was fishing for a compliment he wasn't going to get it. As far as she was concerned, any car that got her where she was going was good enough. This was taking too long. She needed to be home with Buddy.

They were rolling down a tree-lined street on the south side of Redwood City. The homes, though expensive, were far less ostentatious than the multi-million dollar estate they had just left.

Aaron pulled to the curb. "That's his place," he said, nodding at a brick and ivy home with a coach lamp illuminating the front lawn. A flagstone walkway slick with rain meandered up to the porch. "Lights are on, looks like he's here. That's his car parked across the street."

Sarah opened her door and climbed out. Taking the folder in her arms she turned and stepped onto the sidewalk, thankful the downpour had stopped. Aaron bounded up alongside.

He leaned in close and whispered, "I don't think it's wise to get too friendly. Like I said, Dr. Q's a bit strange."

Sarah nodded, her heart thumping as they stepped onto the porch. Aaron poked the doorbell and knocked. They stood back in silence, waiting. Somewhere inside a dog barked. A few moments later a shadow appeared behind the translucent curtains. The door opened and there stood Dr. Summer.

He was tall and thin, with a full head of snowy white hair and an equally white beard that came to a point at the end of his chin. When one of her colleagues referred to the doctor as "Q" Sarah inquired and was not overly surprised to find it was a nickname given to him by those who thought he looked like a walking Q-tip. He leaned forward, propping himself up with both hands on a cane. His jacket was open and his tie hung loose with his collar unbuttoned. His brows furled in. "Dr. Rose. What..?" He stepped back, opening the door wide. "What brings you here? Don't just stand there; you're letting in a draft; come inside."

"I brought Dr. Hunter with me."

Q blinked as though seeing Sarah for the first time. He turned and hobbled on his cane leading the party through the living room to the breakfast nook. They couldn't have sat in the living room even if they wanted to. Every piece of furniture was covered with books and magazines and journals. There were piles on the floor, and the coffee and lamp tables were littered with paper. The dining room was the same. The table appeared to be overspread with maps. A smaller table at the back of the kitchen was the only one reasonably clear and it was cluttered with newspapers and junk mail along with a toaster and a scattering of crumbs. A small white dog, fluffy as a cotton ball, ran over and began sniffing Sarah's feet.

"I'm afraid you've caught me at a rather bad time. I'm leaving tomorrow, and I still have work to do before I pack. Can I get you anything, perhaps a cup of coffee?"

Sarah shook her head. "No, thank you, I'm fine."

Aaron looked at the counter and nodded. "Sure, I'll have a cup, if it's already made."

Dr. Summer reached for the pot and turned to remove a cup from the sink placing it under the tap to rinse it off. From where Sarah sat, it still looked dirty. He shook off the remaining water and filled it to the brim, setting it in the microwave. The unit hummed for a minute and then beeped. Steam rose from a rainbow colored sheen that swirled about the coffee's surface like oil on water. He handed the cup to Aaron.

Aaron took a cautious sip, grimaced, and set the cup down.

Dr. Summer stood with his cane propped in front of him. "Now, what can I do for you," he said.

Sarah placed her folder on the table. "I'd scheduled an appointment to meet with you this afternoon but the rain held me up and by the time I got there you were gone and when I tried to reschedule, your secretary said you were going out of town. Anyway, I was hoping I could get you to read this." She slid the document across the table. "Not now, just take it with you and read it on the plane, or maybe in your hotel."

Dr. Summer's hands remained perched on his cane, declining to reach for the folder. "And what am I supposed to be reading?"

"It's a proposal. When I was doing my graduate studies we had several groups working to cure muscular dystrophy with adult stems but here everyone pooh-poohs the idea. I believe we'll find a cure faster if we stay the course." She tipped her chin toward the document. "That's a summary of my results to date. If you'll just look at it, I…"

But Dr. Summer was already shaking his head. "I'm sorry, I can't help you," he said.

"But…why?"

"This isn't academia. You've left that behind. This is the world of business, and here, money drives the machine, not finding cures."

"What?"

"Adult stem cells are readily available. They can be harvested from every adult human being. There's no engineering involved, no training the cell to become the kind of cell you want it to be, no proprietary process. And if there's no proprietary process, there's nothing to patent. You could spend years coming up with the perfect cure but in the end, about the time the company takes the product to market another company steps in and capitalizes on your research and develops a generic. No, in order to satisfy the czars of capitalism you have to have a proprietary process, one you can protect with a patent. Trust me, I know something about patents. I recently had one of mine denied and Landon, that old crow, took me to task for it."

"Was that what the fight was about?" Aaron joined in.

Dr. Summer looked up sharply, his eyes narrowing.

"You and Landon exchanged words at the party."

The doctor nodded curtly. "That and also about my censure. It seems I keep crossing the line."

"Still trying to debunk evolution?"

Dr. Summer straightened himself, taking the weight off his cane. "I never tried to debunk anything. My call was for intellectual honesty."

Aaron felt something bump his leg. It was the dog sniffing his cuff. He reached down to scratch its head "Maybe, but with all due respect, how is it intellectually honest to suggest we got here any other way? There's no logic to it."

Dr. Summer frowned. "I have no intention of getting into a debate with you, but you're wrong. Logic, plain simple logic, dictates that everything has a designer. Someone made this table, a contractor built this house. I'm leaving for Europe on a Boeing 787 tomorrow and logic tells me those jet engines, the aerodynamics, the navigation systems didn't just come together over billions of years and bingo, a plane. Yet if I took a poll of the passengers a whole lot of them would say man evolved, or just came together over billions of years by chance. Talk about illogical. The human body is a machine, infinitely more complex than any plane."

"Yes, but arguably…"

"I'm just looking at the facts, and the more I look, the more I find that suggests our origin required some kind of design. I want free inquiry. I think all avenues should be explored."

"But that's just what I'm saying," Sarah chimed in, her voice squeaking with excitement. "Dr. Summer, I'm like you. I don't believe in evolution. I believe all life comes from God and I don't want to work on projects that are designed to destroy human embryos because it puts us in the position of destroying a life God has made. Besides, we can reach a cure faster using adult stems. Please, you have to read my paper. If you don't, you're just doing what you say you're against. You're investigating only one side of the issue without giving thought to the other. *Please?*"

Aaron rolled his eyes and sighed discretely.

The dog began whining and scratching at the door. Dr. Summer leaned on his cane and made his way over to let the critter out. Cool air rushed in along with the pungent musk of seaweed. They had to be by the ocean. Wallace closed the door and turned back to Sarah. "I'll make you a deal," he said. "I've got a million things to do and one of them is to find someone to take care of Snowball. That's the dog's name. Anyway, I should have taken care of it but I've been busy. You take care of Snowball while I'm gone and I'll read your paper. Fair enough?"

Sarah balked. Her apartment didn't allow pets. "No, I couldn't possibly, I…"

"You're right, I've got far too much reading to do on the plane already." Dr. Summer waved his hand dismissively and turned to let the dog back in. "Now, if you'll excuse me, I have a lot to do before my flight."

Aaron pushed himself away from the table and stood.

Sarah rose from her chair staring at her proposal. She reached across the table to pick it up and hand it to Dr. Summer. "Okay, you've got yourself a deal."

The doctor frowned but nodded leaning on his cane. "But remember, I'm not making any promises. The corporation dictates policy, not me."

"I understand. I'm only asking you to consider it. Ah, could I just use your bathroom before we go?"

The roads were wet, the wheels spraying water as the Beemer rounded the corner. Aaron wasn't saying much, which suited Sarah fine. The dog tried to lick her face but she pushed him away.

She brought her wrist up to check the time. It had taken thirty minutes to get back to Redwood City. They slowed as they rolled down Mr. Landon's street again. There were more open spaces now, though enough cars remained to suggest the party was still going strong. Aaron pulled into an empty spot and killed the engine. Sarah opened the door and the dog jumped out immediately setting about to mark its territory.

She grabbed her umbrella and purse, thinking once again about the sample she'd collected from Dr. Summer's brush. Now she'd know for certain one way or another. She pulled herself out, anxious about saying the obligatory thanks and good-night. Aaron hurried around to her side of the car.

"You want to go back inside?" he said.

"No, I can't. I have to be getting home." She took a step back but her heel sank into the wet grass causing her to trip backward. Aaron reached out to keep her from falling, catching her by the arm and pulling her in. For a moment the fog of their breaths merged in the chilly night air. Then her eyes grew wary and she pushed him away. "I have to go," she said. She twisted free, yanked her heel from the muck and with her purse under one arm and umbrella under the other she raced to her van without looking back. The door slammed, the lock clicked and within a matter of seconds the lights snapped on and the van pulled away.

Aaron caught a streak of white running across the lawn. He cupped his hands around his mouth. "You forgot your dog," he yelled. *Oh brother.* He raced to catch Snowball and with the dog in his arms hurried back to his car. *Stupid!* He pursed his lips. She wasn't that far ahead. He slammed the car into drive and punched it, his tires skidding as he peeled away from the curb.

He didn't catch sight of her until they were on the highway. He could have overtaken the van easily but for some reason he held back keeping a car between them to avoid being spotted, which was silly since he had a perfectly good reason for tailing her. The dog tried to climb into Aaron's lap but he held it off. She was the one supposed to be taking care of the animal.

It surprised him when she continued over the bay bridge heading into San Francisco. He liked living in the city, but there weren't many at CellMerge that did. Most thought it was too far to drive. The wet pavement glowed with a rainbow of neon colors as they sped by the buildings.

Sarah slowed and pulled to the side in front of a two story apartment. Aaron hit his brakes and slid to the curb a few cars back.

She stepped out and stood for a moment mirrored in a pool of rain. Then her fist banged the side of the door as though just realizing she had forgotten the dog.

Time to be the hero. Aaron reached for the animal but it had disappeared. He began groping in the shadows under the dash. No dog. A muffled whine came from the back. He brought his arm around breathing a sigh of relief. "Gotcha."

He looked up but was too late. Sarah was already gone.

Eight

My hand also has laid the foundation of the earth, and My right hand has spanned the heavens. —Isaiah 48:13

ARON GROANED and drug his pillow over his head. "Stop licking me, dog." Snowball hopped off the bed dancing in circles. Light streamed through the window in bands of yellow. Aaron pushed the duvet aside and rolled to a sitting position. Yesterday had been all clouds and rain. It looked like today held more promise. The dog ran to the door and began whining.

Quiet, Snowball, whatever your name is. He pushed himself off the bed and shuffled to the window, opening it to let in air. His Mother's condo, the one she insisted he use, offered a panoramic view of the bay. A crisp breeze whispered against his skin. The sky was turquoise and the waters blue with a gray ribbon of clouds resting on the distant horizon. He drew his shoulders back placing his hand on his chest to scratch, pausing for a moment to enjoy the briny smell of the ocean. A cyclone of seagulls circled endlessly over the wharf. Out on the water the low drone of a tugboat could be heard chugging across the bay. He couldn't see his own boat, the berth of the Rover Moon was around the bend hidden from view. The dog continued to whine.

"Yeah, yeah. I hear you, but you're going to have to wait until I'm dressed."

He spun around and went to his closet. More than two dozen shirts lined the walk-in. Aaron thumbed through his wardrobe trying to make a decision. Seemed no matter how many shirts he owned, nothing ever seemed right. He picked out a Chaps knit brown turtleneck, a pair of tan Docker slacks and his Sperry beige Top-Siders and tossed them on the bed. He would be seeing Sarah later. She only lived ten minutes away. Last night he'd dialed information for her number, and then called to let her know the dog was safe. She'd been effusive in her thanks, thrilled that he'd captured Snowball. He'd saved her from going back to find the animal. He'd thought it best not to let her know he was parked just outside her apartment and instead arranged to meet her today.

The phone rang. *Was she calling to cancel?* No, the caller ID revealed his mother was on the line. He punched the speaker button, talking while he continued to dress.

"Yes, Mother, what is it?"

"That's no way to greet your mother."

"Sorry. I'm in a rush. What do you need?" He slipped into his pants, tugging them up around his waist.

"Do I need a reason to call? I haven't heard from you lately. I just wondered how you're doing."

"Everything's fine."

"So…what's new in your life?"

"Nothing, Mother. Same old thing." Aaron slipped his hands into the sleeves of his T-shirt and brought it down over his head. The dog was pawing the door. "Be patient, I'll get to you in a minute."

"Sorry, I didn't know you had company. I'll leave you alone, but Airy, do promise to fill me in later."

Aaron let out a sigh. "First of all, I'm not with *someone*. I'm taking care of a friend's dog and it wants to be let out. Second, don't call me Airy. I hate that name, and third, you're on the speaker phone so if I was with someone you'd just have embarrassed the heck out of me. I'm thirty years old, Mother. I'm not your little boy."

"What dog? Get rid of that thing, and I mean right now! I won't have an animal in my house."

"Calm down, Mother. As soon as I leave, it's gone. I was only taking care of it overnight."

"Be sure you do. And I didn't mean to be presumptuous but the thought of you being with someone...and why shouldn't you? What about that girl you brought to the exhibition—tall, blond, terrific figure. Jen, I think you said her name was."

Aaron went back to the closet for a belt. "What about her?"

"I thought she was adorable. Are you still seeing each other?"

"We never were. I just needed a date for the expo and she was available."

"Well you should pursue that. She likes you. I can tell. You keep going the way you are and people will think you're gay. I mean, you're not are you? Because I suppose I could handle it if you are, but..."

"Gay? *Really?* No, Mother, I'm not gay. And I can't help what people think." He tucked in his T-shirt and slipped his belt through the loops buckling up, then sat on the edge of the bed to slip into his shoes. Snowball was whining at the door. "Hey, Mother, while I've got you, I have a question."

"Yes?"

"Do you believe in God? I mean, do you think there's some kind of Divine power out there watching over us?"

"Goodness gracious, Aaron, whatever brought that on?"

"Nothing. It's just, I was with one of the senior researchers at our company last night, and I got the distinct impression he thinks there is one. He didn't say it, not in so many words, but he says there are too many things pointing that direction to just ignore. And there was this girl there too, and she flat out said she believed in God. Kind of weird. What do you think?"

"Well, I suppose there is. My psychic talks to spirits and that's the same thing. You know, like we all go somewhere and become gods of a sort, know what I mean?"

"No, that's not it. She was meaning a more biblical kind of God."

"*Ohhh,* I see. Like the God of our fathers. No. We got out from under all that when we changed the family name. Be careful. That girl's one to avoid. Last thing you need is a Bible thumper breathing down your neck. Been there, done that, and believe me it's no fun."

Aaron reached up to close and lock the window. "You're right. That's not where I'm at. Mom, I gotta go. If I don't get this dog outside, I'm gonna have a mess to clean up."

"Alright, but don't be such a stranger. If you can't drop by, at least give me a call."

"Okay, talk to you later. Bye." Aaron tapped the disconnect and went to the bed for his sweater. He pulled the brown turtleneck over his head feeling his shoulders itch as he rubbed his scalp and combed his fingers though his hair. The shower would have to wait. "Come on Dog, let's get you outside."

Dr. Jaeger flopped into his chair and swiveled around, turning on his computer. The image of Aaron appeared on the screen, not in the matrix that made up the picture, but as a reflection.

"Well bless my boots." He swung his chair around. "In on the weekend? To what do we owe the honor?"

"Not much. I was bored so I thought I'd drop by and catch up on my reading. I didn't expect to find you here either."

Dr. Jaeger shook his head, his bald dome shining. "I'm here most every day. You should try being bored more often, then you'd know. On a day like this, I figured you'd be out on your boat."

"I would, but I'm supposed to meet someone later. Speaking of which, I had a strange meeting with Dr. Summer last night." Aaron walked around and slipped into the chair in front of Dr. Jaeger's desk.

"Dr. Summer? At the party?" Carl said, swiveling in his chair to follow him.

"No, after that." Aaron sat back with his hands behind his head. "That new girl, Sarah, she wanted to pitch him on her adult stem idea but he'd already left so I drove her over to his house. You would have loved it. The man was talking crazy, about evolution and God. Kinda blew me away."

"He was told not to spout that stuff anymore. He could get himself fired."

"It wasn't like that. I brought it up. He just defended his position."

Dr. Jaeger leaned forward placing his elbows on the desk with his fingers propped under his goatee. "Just between you and me, it's time for him to go. All his accomplishments are in the past. If he weren't a Nobel Laureate they would have fired him long ago. They just like having his name on company brochures because it builds shareholder confidence, but he's a dinosaur." Dr. Jaeger cracked a smile and leaned back again. "I call him 'dinosummer', you know, like dinosaur, only summer." He paused, waiting for a reaction but his smile faded when none came. "Anyway, the sooner he's gone the better. What did Dr. Hunter think? I'll bet all that craziness freaked her out."

"Actually, I think she agreed with him."

"That's nuts, but I guess women are like that, more inclined to be gullible. I will say she's got drive, though. Look at her, chained to her work even on a Saturday."

Aaron spun around. "Here?" He stood, looking through the glass to find Sarah across the room. "I'm supposed to be meeting her later on, but she said she had something to do this morning."

"I guess so. She's been in every Saturday since she started working here."

Aaron moved down the hall, slowing as he approached Sarah's station. Her back was to him as he stepped into the lab. She didn't bother to turn even though he was sure she'd heard him crossing the floor.

"Sarah?"

He was standing just over her shoulder, but she seemed completely absorbed in her work. She pulled a petri dish in closer, examined its contents, and made a note in the tablet at her side. "I thought our meeting wasn't till this afternoon," she said without looking up.

"So did I. I just came in to kill some time. You're the one who said you had something important to do, but here you are, doing what you do every day."

"You don't think this is important?"

A groan came from behind causing Aaron to turn. *A wheelchair?* A young man strapped to the chrome apparatus tried to lift his head but it appeared he didn't have the strength. The boy's head rolled side to side.

Sarah rushed over taking the boy's hand. "You okay, honey?" She leaned in to kiss his cheek, then raised herself, fondling the young man's hair. "I guess I should make the introductions. "Aaron, this is Buddy, my son," she said, glancing down at the boy.

Buddy's thin chest raised and sucked air like he was struggling to breathe. He had shadows under his eyes, and his skin was as white as someone who never went outdoors.

"And Buddy, this is Aaron." She turned eyeing Aaron again. "He's going to help us find you a cure."

God Before the Dawn of Time
The Journal of W.L. Summer

According to Stephen Hawking it's difficult to accept the idea that time had a beginning because it argues for the existence of God. I would agree. But then this is refuted by suggesting that God could not have existed before our universe materialized because that's when time began and without time there's no framework in which for God to exist.

There's no justification given for why time is necessary, it's just assumed, which is circular reasoning. Any concept of God as creator would have to infer that God isn't confined by His creation. In other words, if God created everything, including all natural and physical laws, as well as the properties of time, He is beyond their scope and therefore not subject to their limitations.

The God of the Bible is always said to be outside time, without beginning or end, forever and eternal. When St. Augustine was asked what God did before creation he answered: "Since God created time when He created the universe, there was no before," a rather astute answer for a fourth century theologian. Before and after are terms used to describe points in time, but with God there can't be a before or after because He exists in the eternal present.

Any argument that suggests God could not have existed before the creation of time requires we believe the physical properties of our universe comprise everything, and that there can be no other dimensionality in which the rules do not apply. I suggest we open ourselves to the very real possibility that there's more outside the realm of our human experience than our limited minds could ever comprehend.

Nine

I have made the earth, and created man upon it: I, even my hands, have stretched out the heavens, and all their host have I commanded.
—*Isaiah 45:12*

CARL WAS ONLY a few steps out the door when he pulled up short grabbing his Stetson to keep it from blowing away. That was Jack's car. It had to be. No one else drove a Jaguar XJ. Its molten silver paint mirrored the overhanging clouds, as did Aaron's black BMW. He glanced at his own set of wheels, an oxidized green Jeep Cherokee that looked like it had been driven through the jungles of Ecuador. Anyone peering into the back could see the old magazines and hamburger wrappers that summed up his life. He turned and headed back inside.

He took the elevator up, perspiring as he thundered down the hall. With any luck he could catch the president before he left. The door to Jack's office was closed. Carl stood outside, pausing to remove his ten gallon hat and mop his forehead. He pulled on the strings of his bolo tie making sure they were straight. Jack's secretary was off today. Should he knock? Nonsense, he and Jack were friends. He pulled the door open and stuck his head in.

Mr. Landon's desk was polished to a mirror shine reflecting the framed photograph of his now deceased wife. He closed the file he'd been leafing through. A pipe hung from his lips sending swirls of smoke up into the space above his head.

"Hey, Jack, got a minute?" Carl said, his voice betraying uncertainty.

Mr. Landon looked up removing the pipe from his mouth. A soft whoosh escaped from the leather as he leaned back in his chair. He nodded. "Come on in, Carl. My door is always open."

Dr. Jaeger stepped forward. "I uh, I don't mean to bother you but I just heard something I thought you should know."

Mr. Landon removed a cork pedestal ashtray from his drawer and tapped the remaining tobacco from his pipe. "And what's that?"

"It's about Dr. Summer."

Jack's eyes narrowed, but he nodded. "Go on."

"It's just that, you recall that paper he published, the one that got everyone talking? I just heard he's still at it. Wasn't he supposed to be censured?"

"He was, yes; we were very clear about it. Either cease and desist or face dismissal."

"Good, well, he's still doing it. If I were you I'd fire him." Dr. Jaeger caught his breath realizing he might have stepped over the line. He fidgeted with the brim of the hat in his lap.

"So would I…"

"You would?"

"…but it's not that easy. Having a Nobel Laurate's good for the company's image. People invest because of him."

"He's a joke. He's putting a smear on our corporate name."

"Yes and thank you for bringing it to my attention. I'll look into it, but other than mentioning it to the board, I'm afraid there's not much I can do."

Sarah looped Alamo Square looking for parking. She'd excused herself from Aaron saying she was running a series of tests, but agreed to meet him here at three o'clock in keeping with the original plan. He had to return to his condo to collect the dog anyway, but she hadn't meant to stay so long; she'd simply got caught up in her work. He should be here by now, but she didn't see him.

The van surged up Hayes Street. If San Francisco was anything— it was steep. She dialed down the radio. A mother and her three children stepped off the curb and gathered around a parked car, climbing inside. *Finally.* Sarah stood on her brakes and reached out to catch her son. His wheelchair occupied the space usually taken by the passenger seat. Buddy turned his head to his mother and tried to smile.

Sarah pulled into the empty space and once again looked around for Aaron. One of the reasons she picked this park was its size, only four square blocks, as opposed to the three-mile long Golden Gate Park which covered more than a thousand acres. Her head turned at the sudden rumble behind her. Several motorcycles roared by, one after the other followed by a few more and a dozen more after that. She climbed out of the van and went around to fetch Buddy.

She slid the side door open and pushed the button to deploy the automatic ramp. Then she moved to the front, disengaged the wheelchair, and rolled Buddy down to the ground.

"So that's how it's done."

She turned to see Aaron standing behind her. His voice was raised so he could be heard over the rumbling engines.

"I was wondering how you managed to move Buddy around."

The small white wad of fluff that Dr. Summer called Snowball was jumping up and down at Sarah's feet begging for attention. She took the dog in her arms and placed her cheek against its fluffy fur, her eyes watching the parade of motorcycles as they passed.

Buddy was trying to lift his arms but didn't have the strength. "Leme see…" he slurred in a voice liquid as water.

Sarah placed the dog in her son's lap. "Be careful. This dog's a little hyper."

Snowball began licking Buddy's face. Aaron reached over to keep the dog from jumping down but it made no attempt to leave. "Looks like you've made a friend there Bud. Yep, it looks like he really likes you."

Sarah put the chair ramp back and closed the van door. "His name's Buddy, not Bud." She said over her shoulder.

Buddy giggled letting the dog lick his neck. Aaron turned the wheelchair to face the street. "Hey Buddy, what do you think? How'd you like to ride one of those?"

Buddy grinned broadly, "Yeah!" but his mother took the grips from Aaron's hands and brought the chair back around. "Do you mind? I'd appreciate you not filling my son's head with nonsense."

Aaron fell in alongside as she began strolling down the sidewalk, pushing her son ahead of her. Her Levis were a loose fitting men's style, stonewashed, and her purple flannel shirt was covered with a blue nylon jacket, a collection of odds and sods from the neighborhood thrift store.

"What's so crazy about wanting to ride a motorcycle? Buddy could do it. They have sidecars and things like that."

Sarah paused to stare at Aaron, her expression flat. "Seriously?" she said.

"Come on, you've never wanted to ride?"

"Doesn't matter what I want. I have a child and he comes first. Anyway, I couldn't balance one of those if I tried." Sarah resumed walking again. They were headed in the direction of Steiner Street and the Painted Ladies, a row of Victorian houses painted pastel blue, green, yellow and pink.

Aaron shook his head. "I guess I just want to feel all that power at my fingers, to be able to ride off into the sunset with the wind in my hair. Maybe it's kind of silly but it's always been a dream of mine."

"Boy, that's a side of you that doesn't figure. You seem more like a spoiled rich kid."

"What?"

"You drive that fancy car, you wear a Rolex, and you've got a yacht…"

Aaron's head jerked around. "Who said I had a yacht?"

"The Rover Moon. Come on, it's on your Facebook page."

He nodded, trying to suppress a brief smile. She'd been checking up on him. "It's not really *my* yacht, it belongs to my mother, though I have full access, and she never uses it so it's mine by default. Same goes for my car, but the watch is mine," he said holding up his wrist, "not top of the line but a real beauty all the same. She gave it to me for my twenty-first birthday. So, as for being a spoiled brat, guilty as charged. My mother likes to spend money on me and I see no reason to stop her."

The dog spun around in Buddy's lap. The free end of its leash dropped and quickly became tangled in the wheels of the chair.

"Here, let me get that." Aaron stooped to free the leash and remove Snowball. He set the dog on the ground and kept the leash in hand.

"At least you admit you're spoiled."

The dog was tugging at its tether. Buddy reached out to take it from Aaron.

"Whoa, I'm not sure you're ready to hold this. Why don't we just tie it to the front of your wheelchair, like this," he bent over looping the leather strap around the wheelchair's armrest, "then you can hold it anytime you want." Aaron took Buddy's hand, placed it over the leather knot and straightened himself. "My mother's okay, but she has her ways. I found out long ago it doesn't pay to try to change her mind. Like the motorcycle thing. She once told me if I ever bought a bike, it would be the last of her money I'd see. She's a control freak in that kind of way. But I like her money, so I guess I can do without a bike."

"I like your mother already."

"Okay, so where do you get your money?"

"Beg pardon?"

"That rig you drive isn't cheap. Not something you could afford on your salary."

"Oh that. I'm part of a support group, PCMD, Parents of Children with Muscular Dystrophy. One of our group had a child who died and when they saw how I was struggling they passed some of the things they no longer needed along to me. One of them was that van, but I don't get to keep it. When Buddy's time comes, I've agreed to pay it forward."

"Sorry, I didn't know."

"Don't be. Buddy knows he's going to die. All the kids do. We talk about it openly, though I'm the only one hoping to find a cure." She looked down at her son and leaned in to say something. "How much time do we have left, Buddy?"

Buddy smiled and rolled his head in her direction. "D…don't know, but weee've got today."

Sarah looked back at Aaron. "It's a routine we go through all the time."

"I'm a…an astronaut."

"What's that?" Aaron bent down to hear what the boy said.

"I'm go…nna fly."

"He means when he dies, God's going to take him to heaven. He likes to think of it as flying a spaceship, you know, like out of this universe into the next."

"Oh."

They were standing on a hill overlooking the Painted Ladies. The grass was a shadowy green and the trees reached out with limbs that coiled and twisted like snakes. The cityscape spread before them under a pink afternoon sky. Lights were beginning to twinkle in the distance. An onshore breeze swept across the park scattering scraps of paper and fallen leaves. Sarah shivered and wrapped her arms around herself, her nylon jacket rustling in the wind. She began humming an old church hymn. "Do you like to sing?"

"What?"

"Sing, you know, like Christmas carols and stuff like that."

Aaron shook his head. "No, not so much, I really don't know any songs so I couldn't even if I wanted to, but I'm guessing you do."

Sarah nodded. "It's one of my favorite things. Sometimes when I see a beautiful scene like this it makes me want to take off running, you know, like Maria in the Sound of Music dancing through the flowers. She closed her eyes and began singing softly, "*The hills are alive*," but she stopped abruptly.

An awkward silence settled between them. Sarah pulled her jacket's collar tight to keep the wind off her neck and leaned over to tuck a blanket around Buddy's waist. She felt her hair fluttering around her cheeks, a rich auburn color in the dusty rose light.

"Beautiful," Aaron said.

Sarah straightened herself and followed his gaze out over the horizon. "It is," she agreed, and then shivered as she folded her arms again. Aaron was standing close—too close. She felt more than saw his arm coming up. "Don't!" she warned, twisting away, her voice terse, her body stiff.

His arm dropped to his side.

She tried to relax. "It's getting late. I think we should be going," she said.

Ten

Thou, even Thou, art Lord alone; Thou hast made heaven, the heaven of heavens, with all their host, the earth, and all things that are therein, the seas, and all that is therein, and You keep them all...
—Nehemiah 9:6

H E WAS ON the water in time to see the sun cresting the horizon. A crimson dawn painted the shoreline casting the morning fishermen in long black shadows. The winds had blown the clouds out to sea leaving the earth languishing under a gray-blue sky. Aaron stood at the helm of his sixty-five foot Viking motor yacht feeling the wind course through his thick brown hair. This was it. As far as he was concerned, this was his motorcycle on water. He loved the sound of the twin diesel engines and the expanse of the open sea. It was the one place he could come and think without distraction.

He welcomed the solitude. There was much to consider. Sarah hadn't said a word all the way back to the van and then she'd loaded up her son and the dog, said some quip about seeing him at work on Monday, and raced off leaving him standing at the curb eating dust. All he'd wanted to do was help her keep warm.

A wave rolled against the boat's port side washing foam across the deck. Plowing through the swells at that speed wasn't safe. He notched back the throttle. The boat rocked as it dropped off the crest and slipped into the receding wake.

So she'd been to his Facebook page. He couldn't recall friending her, but he routinely friended people he didn't know without checking to see who they were so it was possible. Most of those photos were old, posted during his university days when the Rover Moon was a floating party. But the one of him and Jen, *yeah,* that one he should probably take down.

He felt a gust through the window as the boat dipped into another trough, a wave sweeping over the bow. The wind was picking up. The brass bell outside the galley was clanging.

God? *To be, or not to be?* It was the kind of thing he liked to think about as he stood at the helm bounding over the swells with the wind channeling through his hair. Contemplating the minuscule size of man when compared to a universe of unlimited scale had a way of putting things in perspective.

Man was just a collection of atoms, but so was everything else. But man was carbon based life with a brain that could think and process information. What did that make God? A force that preexisted time? A spirit without form or substance? A man sitting on a throne in the sky throwing lightning bolts at people on earth? Had God created man or had man, in his need to explain his existence, created God? And what was it about Sarah that caused him to consider what could never be explained. He didn't need some mousey little girl with a dying son—*however heart wrenching*—making him feel uncomfortable with his thoughts.

"NO! No, no, no, no, nooooooo. Not now Buddy, We'll be late for church." Sarah threw her towel down. The counter held puddles of water and wet dishes. She rushed to her son's side. "You should have said something! *Ohhhhh…fudge!*"

"I…I didn't feel it coming."

"Look at that! You're soaking wet. How could you *not* feel it?"

51

Buddy's forehead wrinkled, his eyes filled with pain and embarrassment.

Sarah took a breath and patted her son's shoulder. "It's okay, we'll take care of it. It's all right."

The dog was whining at the door. She sighed. "Snowball, *shush*, be quiet! You had a walk this morning. You're going to get us in trouble. *Quiet!*" Sarah took hold of Buddy's wheelchair and spun it around pushing him toward the bathroom. She had to get him out of his clothes, get him cleaned up, and get him dressed again, working her way backward in time to start over.

Her eyes were jittery, her skin felt tight. *Chill!* She began to hum, and then to sing…

> *"When peace like a river attendeth my way*
> *When sorrows like sea billows roll*
> *Whatever my lot, Thou hast taught me to say*
> *It is well, it is well, with my soul…"*

She sang loudly not caring that she might wake the neighbors on the other side of the paper thin wall. They always played their TV too loud and she didn't complain about that. She tugged Buddy's shirt over his head.

"*Owww.*"

Sarah tousled her son's hair and leaned over to kiss his cheek. "Sorry." She said. She didn't spend enough time with him anyway. It was a conundrum. Except for Saturdays, when because there were fewer people around, she was able to take him with her, spending time with her son meant time away from the lab, and finding a cure meant spending as much time in the lab as possible.

> *"Though Satan should buffet, though trials should come,*
> *Let this blest assurance control,*
> *That Christ has regarded my helpless estate,*
> *And hath shed His own blood for my soul."*

Even if they found a cure it would take years of clinical trials to obtain FDA approval. Buddy didn't have years. According to his doctor, he didn't have months, probably only a few weeks. Buddy would die and she'd be left feeling guilty about being away from her son during those final days when he needed her most. It was a lose/lose proposition.

She finished getting Buddy out of his clothes and set him in the tub to keep water from dripping on the floor. Cranking the taps she began working the soap into a lather giving him a sponge bath. Sarah stooped down to kiss his cheek. "Hey, little man, what day is it?"

Buddy's head didn't move but his eyes shifted to where he could see his mother. "Fi...rst day of the rrr...est of my life," he said, his voice little more than a breath.

"You bet it is, and how many days do we have left?"

"Do...n't know, but...but we have today."

Sarah leaned in to kiss him again. "I love you, little man." She lifted her son from the tub and toweled him off, then dressed him and put him back in his wheelchair before heading for the kitchen. "You know we may beat this thing yet. I have an idea that I think shows promise. It's a new way of making adult stems emulate other cells." She reached into the refrigerator removing two eggs which she placed in a pan of water to boil. Snowball was dancing around her legs begging for a treat.

"Do...do you...like Aaron?"

The question caught her off guard. She turned the burner down and wiped her hands on a towel. "Yes, I mean he works at CellMerge so were acquainted but we're working on different projects so we don't have much chance to talk. Why?"

"I...I like him."

Sarah took a knife and swirled a pat of margarine on her toast. She kept her eyes focused on the bread to keep from looking at her son. "Oh," she said, "well don't get any ideas. I don't have time for a friendship, or relationship of any kind. Every minute I have is split between the time I spend with you, and trying to find a way to make you better."

Buddy squirmed in his chair. "I'm not get…ting better, Mom." He paused for a breath, *uh-huh, uh-huh,* "You know th…at. I want you…happy, *uh-huh,* when I'm gone. Ca…can we see him again?"

"I don't think that would be wise." She placed her toast on a saucer and went to the refrigerator for a glass of milk. Snowball was bouncing at her heels. "Settle down dog. I'll get to you in a minute." Aaron had tried to put his arm around her but she'd rebuffed him. She didn't need to feed another illusion.

She's standing by the side of the road in the middle of nowhere, the tire of her car flat, glued to the asphalt, and while she does have a spare, she can't seem to find the jack. She's waited forty-five minutes. Her cell phone is out of range and looking down that long straight road as far as the eye can see, there's no one in sight. The sun beats down on her with a vengeance making ripples on the hood of her car. She regrets not buying that bottle of water at the gas station, but it would have cost a dollar.

She walks around to the passenger side and kicks the tire. Ohhhhh! She'd meant to get that thing replaced long ago. Food needed to be bought and bills to be paid. There was never enough.

You'd think a first year college student would be smarter. She looks at her watch for the umpteenth time. Or not!

What's that?

A sound in the distance, a rumbling sound, a—car? She stands on her tiptoes and begins to wave even though she can't see anything. A thick corrugated heat is bouncing off the pavement. There, there it is, a pickup by the looks of it. Her heart starts to pound. Not a family car. She needs to be rescued by a family, not some lone stranger in a truck. Is that a gun rack in the back window? She slips around her front bumper and steps off the road sliding down a steep embankment with gravel pouring into her shoe. She hits the bottom in a cloudy plume, but she has no time to think. She vaults forward hobbling along with sand in her socks until she stumbles upon a huge flood control pipe. She ducks inside panting like a fox weary of the chase, sure she can no longer be seen. She hears the truck and the screeching of brakes as it pulls to a stop.

"Hey lady, need some help?"

Beep, beep, beeeeeeeeep!

A door slams. Maybe he plans to steal the car. The keys are in the ignition. How will she get home? She pleads with God to keep her safe.

She waits. A half hour passes, maybe an hour. An engine turns over. She hears the truck enter the road and listens as the sound tapers off in the distance until it can no longer be heard.

Her heart is still hammering as she makes her way back to the highway, climbing the embankment until she can see over the top. She's cautious about stepping into full view. It might be a trick. He might have parked up ahead and circled back on foot. Her car is still there, thirty yards down the road, no other vehicles in sight. She decides to chance it. Each step is taken with foreboding, the soles of her feet pinched by the pebbles in her shoes. She can't seem to control the pounding of her heart. If she spots anything unusual, she should be able to duck back into the gully and make a run for it. But as she approaches, she finds her car abandoned and...is it possible? Her tire has been replaced. The spare is now where the flat tire was. The man did her a favor, but he also scared her to death.

Sarah took a bite of her toast and set it down, her fingers combing through Buddy's hair flicking it in place. She stood back, admiring the courage of the boy who had to endure so much. He was twelve years old but with weight loss and slow development he looked about seven. His eyes found hers. His head lolled to the side like it was too heavy to lift but he found the strength to offer her a smile.

He didn't look like Dr. Summer, but then again, neither did she. She'd know one way or the other soon enough. She reached over and slid back the drawer of the nightstand to make sure it was still there. She removed and unfolded the tissue revealing a few strands of white hair taken from the brush in Dr. Summer's bathroom. Finding someone to make a genetic comparison wouldn't be a problem. DNA was a mainstay at CellMerge. Never before had she felt such certainty but she needed proof. These few hairs would tell her whether or not Dr. Summer was her father. She felt a twinge of excitement. It had to be him. *Thank you, Lord.*

Chances Are We're One of a Kind
The Journal of W.L. Summer

In order to sustain life on our planet more than a hundred interdependencies must be maintained, each operating with little or no margin for error. When using the random accident scenario, we have to explain how the tilt of the earth's axis, our distance from the sun, our planet's surface gravity, the speed of the earth's rotation, carbon dioxide and water vapor levels, the distance our sun is from the center of the galaxy, and a myriad of other principles at the atomic and chemical levels, all came together at the right place and time with such precision. The accuracy of our planet's fine tuning is critical. Even the slightest variation would mean a cessation of life.

Probability statisticians have calculated the likelihood of all the parameters coming together in one place to be the number one followed by a thousand billion, billion, billion zeros. The number is so great it eliminates any possibility of a random chance hypothesis. Since the only other alternative is the miraculous, and modern science can't allow for that, we've had to bend the rules to improve the odds. The current theory suggests we exist as part of a multiverse, that there are actually trillions of universes out there coexisting with our own, only we can't see them. With so many universes from which to choose, chances are one of them would have to contain a planet that meets all the necessary life sustaining criteria. Earth just happens to be the one.

It's sad when brilliant men indulge such fanciful notions to account for the infeasibility of one planet having all the right variables to support life. Occam's razor says the simplest solution is usually the one that's right. Wouldn't it be more logical to employ this precept? If we did we'd conclude that our earth is the product of design. Yet instead of welcoming research in this area, we reject it out of hand and do our best to marginalize and discredit anyone who dares come to that conclusion.

Eleven

…We preach that you should turn from these vanities unto the living God which made heaven, and earth, and the sea, and all things that are therein. —Acts 14:15

ARON LOOKED at his watch again. He'd arrived a few minutes late expecting to find Sarah already hard at work but her station was empty.

"Didn't see you at the party. Where were you?"

Aaron turned to see Jen standing behind him. Her hair was bound in a ponytail that bobbed as she tilted her head waiting for an answer. Her posture, with her arms folded and her back straight, implied a challenge.

"I was there. You asked me to dance, remember?"

She shook her head, her ponytail swaying side to side. "No way. I'd remember that. I wasn't that smashed."

"Ask Larry. We had a nice chat. He said he was taking you home."

Jen's face reddened, her hands gripping her arms so tight it left white marks in her flesh. "*Ouuuuh*, the creep. I woke up with him lying next to me—in my own bed! *How gross.* I had to forcibly toss his fat butt out onto the street the next morning."

Aaron smiled. "He said you asked him for a date."

"*Arrrrugh!* That does it. If I hear one word about how we slept together, he's dead meat!"

Aaron glanced up and saw two people coming down the hall: Sarah, accompanied by the president's secretary.

"Who's that?" Jen said.

"New girl."

Sarah didn't acknowledge them. She passed by with her eyes focused straight ahead looking distraught.

"Poor thing needs a new wardrobe," Jen said, "taffeta went out in the eighties and *oh-my-gosh*, look at that hair."

Aaron shot her a look.

"What?"

Mr. Landon's secretary turned to address Aaron. "Doctor Rose, the president would like a minute of your time."

"Now?"

"Yes, right now." With that she turned and walked away expecting Aaron to follow.

Aaron looked at Jen and shrugged. "Catch you later," he said, and fell in behind.

They rode the elevator up to the ivory tower, the top floor where the CEO and a cadre of vice presidents had their suites. Aaron couldn't help but feel intimidated, but that was because he'd figured out why he was being called to the president's office. Sarah had ratted him out. In that scrambled little brain of hers she'd obviously concocted some allegation of sexual harassment. It was the only explanation. They'd heard her side of the story, now they wanted his.

He'd only touched her twice. *Not even.* The first time he'd just tried to keep her from falling and the second time she'd stopped him before his hand reached her waist. He could explain it away, he hadn't done anything wrong, but why should he have to? He squared his shoulders, straightening himself. *Women!*

The secretary opened the door and ushered Aaron into Jack's office, then turned away closing the door again. Mr. Landon looked grave but that was appropriate given the circumstances.

Aaron's heart was pounding, pinpricks of perspiration forming on his brow. "I don't know what she said, but it's not like that. I didn't touch her, at least not in that way."

Mr. Landon raised his eyebrows quizzically. "Beg your pardon?" Jack folded his hands on his desk as he leaned forward.

"Sarah. You had her in here. If that…if she said I touched her inappropriately, it's a lie. I didn't."

"Dr. Rose, I don't care about your personal life, or hers. What you do in private is your business, and if you misbehave on company time, it's a matter for HR. That's not why you're here."

Aaron exhaled a puff of air and dropped into the wing back chair in front of Landon's desk. "*What?* Why then?"

"Dr. Rose, it has come to our attention that prior to his leaving for Europe, you and Dr. Hunter had a meeting with Dr. Summer. Is that correct?"

Aaron had to think for a minute but slowly began to nod. "It wasn't exactly a meeting but we did speak with him before he left, yes."

"And is it true that during that meeting Dr. Summer suggested the science of evolution has been brought into question?"

"He mentioned that he no longer saw things in black and white the way he once did, yes, that would be correct."

"Did he ever out and out say he believed in God?"

"I think it was more like he wants to keep the door open."

"But he did express that the origin of man might be more metaphysical in nature than scientific, is that not correct?"

Aaron nodded. "Not in those words, but yes, I guess he suggested something like that, why? Everyone knows he wrote a paper about it. It's no big secret."

"Thank you, Dr. Rose. My secretary will show you out." Looking over his shoulder Aaron saw Mr. Landon's secretary already standing at the door. He hadn't noticed her being summoned. She turned to the side as he glided past. "Can you find your own way back?" she said.

"Sure, no problem."

He stepped out of the office but paused for a second to listen.

"...I want you to call an emergency session of the board. Try to reach everyone you can...ah...everyone but Fishman, he's out of the country, but get me a quorum. This has to be a board decision."

Sarah took a breath and sighed. The air smelled like rubbing alcohol. She drank it in. She loved the antiseptic smell of sterility, the undefiled purity, the sense of being clean. This was her world, a shelter from the chaos outside. She loved every test tube, petri dish, and stainless steel tray. She loved the freezers where they stored specimens and the incubators where they harvested cells, because they contained the answers that could ultimately save Buddy's life.

There were two kinds of researchers. Half were in it for the money, the lavish salaries paid by pharmaceutical companies, but the other half were in it for the discovery, those who wanted only to benefit their fellow man. She was among the latter.

The downside was that it robbed her of time with her son, but at least he had Beth. Thank God she'd found a caregiver who loved Buddy almost as much as she did, someone willing to do almost anything, including taking care of a dog that had to be smuggled outside to relieve itself even in the wind and rain.

She looked up. Aaron was meandering down the long glass corridor. Someone spoke to him and he stopped. He'd cautioned her about getting too close to Dr. Summer. It appeared he was right; they *were* building a case against the man. *Don't let it happen, Lord; I need time to introduce him to his grandson.*

Twelve

Let them praise the name of the Lord, For He commanded and they were created. —*Psalm 148:5*

LIGHT REFLECTED off the wings of the plane as it screeched and bounced, landing at SFO. Dr. Summer stared out the porthole. The field of genetics was exploding; it was far too much to assimilate in one short week.

At least he'd had the good fortune of running into Dr. Alex Lamar. They'd had lunch every day. It wasn't the first time they'd met but certainly the most enlightening. Wallace now had more information than he knew what to do with, all of which supported his own thoughts about the origin of life. It flew in the face of everything he'd been taught, and yet it was logical and made perfect sense. More importantly, it affirmed the faith he'd had as a child.

Science said the beginning started with a Big Bang where in one cataclysmic explosion the worlds were formed as they were flung into space. Alex said that lined up with what the Judeo-Christian Bible said all along. The difference being that the random chance scenario claimed the expansion took billions of years while Alex believed it was instantaneous, and those who ascribed to the cosmic accident theory held that something popped out of nothing, where the Bible claimed it was initiated by a primal cause, or preexistent being. He'd pointed to the classic logic *Ex nihilo nihil fit*—nothing comes from nothing—the very same premise Wallace had struggled with. On the one hand the scientific community belittled those who believed in God. The supernatural could not be proved. Science, on the other hand, could explain everything. But when it came to the origin of all things they reversed themselves and resorted to magic so that *poof*, out of nothing, something came, like pulling a rabbit from a hat. How could they say creation was a myth invented by early man to explain his existence, and then try to explain it themselves by presenting their own imaginary ideas? It was the height of hypocrisy.

That didn't mean he didn't have doubts. "How," he'd asked, "can God, who is supposedly big enough to hold the universe in the palm of his hand, create something as small as an atom, not to mention subatomic particles? How could he design something as marvelous as our DNA or the neural network of our brain?"

Dr. Lamar had simply snapped open his laptop.

"See this," he said.

"What? Sure, it's a computer, so..."

"You bet it is. This thing has a chip with a couple of terabytes of memory, not that I'll ever use it, but it's there. With this I can do a complete blood analysis. I can locate any anomalies a person might have that could lead to future health problems and have the results in just a few seconds. And see the brightness and clarity of this screen. It may not be as complex as the human eye, but you wouldn't know it by looking. But here's the best part. It was designed and built by humans. We did this, and I have to say it's a marvelous achievement, wouldn't you?

"Now imagine another dimension, one that's not subject to our natural and physical laws, in which exists an entity with a brain, or thought processing center, infinitely bigger than our own. We know even with our limited capability we can engineer the micro-circuitry of computers, yet we find it hard to imagine how a vastly superior being could create something as complex as us. And there's good reason for that. We're just too small to conceive of something so awesome."

They'd been sitting in an outdoor café with a mild breeze ruffling the fringes of Dr. Summer's hair. He shrugged and reached for his coffee.

"Okay, maybe I can find a better example." Dr. Lamar twisted around and began poking through the leaves of a nearby potted plant.

"What are you doing?"

"Looking for something. I saw one a minute ago. Where'd you go little fella. Ah there you are, gotcha." He plucked a snail from the plant and set it on the table.

Dr. Summer flinched.

"You think this snail can understand this computer? You think it can comprehend the circuitry, the resolution of the display, or the software that processes the information?"

"Okay, I see your point."

"That's right. This snail could never understand man's ability to design and create. When you think about man in comparison to God, you have to realize we're a lot further away from God than this snail is from us. We'll never understand His mind or His limitless capability. We're just too inferior. But God has made us in His own image, so, like Him, we have the ability to think and create. Perhaps we're better than the snail, but we're not in God's league. When you see His creations, don't question how He did it, just appreciate how much greater He is than us..."

The jet taxied past cargo loaders and fuel tankers and a dozen other aircraft on its long run to the terminal. They sidled up to the gate and a hundred people jumped up all pulling baggage from the overhead compartments in a rush to deplane.

Wallace didn't move. He sat furthest in by the window. He had no intention of being poked and prodded as he made his way down the aisle. Let everyone else go first. He had no family or friends waiting to meet him, no one to welcome him home, all he had were the same unsettling feelings he'd been wrestling with for the past few years. Only now he knew how to respond.

He gathered his papers and slipped them into a scuffed leather satchel, squeezing them around the Bible he was now prone to carry. He checked his watch, eight AM. He had to get moving. He didn't want to be late. Only a few people were left on the plane. He squeezed into the aisle and shuffled toward the door with his satchel in one hand and his cane in the other. His tall frame nearly scraped the top of the fuselage. He'd received an email from Jack saying they should meet first thing. His stomach felt queasy.

The few moments of sun had yielded to the clouds forming another gray day in San Francisco. Dr. Summer pulled away from the terminal with his windshield wipers flapping, his overcoat spotted with rain and a paper cup of hot black coffee in his hand. He didn't like confrontation but Jack had stepped over the line. It was time to put a stop to this nonsense. His satchel contained the evidence, circumstantial perhaps, but enough to build a case.

The clock on the dash read 8:48 AM. Traffic was heavy on southbound 101 with commuters weaving in and out vying for position. Fortunately his exit was just ahead. He pulled onto the ramp and took a right. The three gold towers of CellMerge loomed before him speckled with rain. He swung into the garage, stopping to show his parking pass and hand over his keys.

Ouch! He grimaced as he pulled himself from the car. His gout was bad this morning. He gritted his teeth, leaned heavily on his cane, and limped to the door with his satchel over his head like an umbrella. It was of little use. By the time he got inside his tweed coat was moist and smelled like a musty barn.

He glanced at his watch. Jack had little tolerance for those late to meetings. He didn't want to give the president the upper hand by giving him something to criticize. *Nuts*, he was supposed to be taking the day off to recover from his jet lag. If Jack wanted to call an unscheduled meeting he could just wait. He stepped off the elevator and limped quickly down the hall to Jack's door. Just outside, Jack's private secretary sat typing at her computer.

"Morning, Helen. Is Jack here?"

"Yes, he's expecting you." She continued pecking at her keyboard without looking up. "You can go on in."

Wally retrieved his satchel and coat and, using his cane to ease the pressure on his foot, sauntered to the door. It was an imposing barrier, floor to ceiling solid oak. He reached for the handle, pulling it open. The inside was even more commanding: three walls of dark paneled wood containing the library and photo gallery with a fourth of solid glass overlooking the ocean.

"Come in, Wally, don't just stand there."

Wallace saw Jack seated behind his giant desk. It made the man look small. He pushed forward dragging his hurting foot.

As Wallace sat down, Jack reached in his drawer for a file.

Wallace unzipped his satchel and began shuffling to find the documents he'd brought but they'd become lost between the pages of literature he'd collected at the show.

Jack tapped a finger on the folder. "Wally, Dr. Summer, I don't want to drag this out, so please, here," he said, sliding the file folder across the desk.

Wallace looked up, saw the file and then Mr. Landon's face. It was pulled back taut, the expression grim. "What's this?"

"I'm afraid it's your termination. Your contract with CellMerge is revoked, effective immediately."

"What?"

"I don't mean to be harsh, but you were warned. Any further debate about man's origin was to be completely avoided."

Wallace sat up straight. "What? I haven't, I…"

"Don't deny it. Your staff heard you firsthand. We simply cannot afford to let you embarrass us again. Our shares took a nosedive last time. It took months to recover. Believe me, the board's behind me on this. No one wants to see you leave. Your name carries a lot of weight, but when you were censured, you lost credibility. Heck, you made a laughingstock of yourself. How do you expect our shareholders to have confidence in us when our most senior scientist goes on record and, in spite of all scientific evidence to the contrary, says he thinks we were made by *God*?"

Dr. Summer's face reddened. He rose from his chair and leaned forward towering over Jack. "That's not what happened, and that's not what this is about and you know it." He pulled his satchel up and began rummaging through it as he plopped it on Jack's desk.

Jack sat back in his chair, unfazed. "It *is* what this is about. You were warned."

"Men used to think the world was flat, too. And Galileo was forced to deny heliocentrism when he knew the planets revolved around the sun. Drat, where are they?"

"Look Wally, we're not here to debate. I have no control over this. It's a board decision. You've been given fair compensation, and we've agreed we won't say why you were let go. We don't want to limit your ability to find another job. Now I'm giving you the opportunity to leave in a dignified manner, but if you refuse, I'll call security and have you escorted out. You're not to return to your office. All your personal things were collected over the weekend and will be sent to your home. Now just sign your termination papers and go."

"I'm not signing anything. Not until I talk to a lawyer."

Jack reached for the file, shaking his head, though a light smile played on his lips. "Okay, I tried. Your refusal to sign means our offer is off the table. Our lawyers tell us your breaking censure constitutes insubordination and since your actions are detrimental to the corporation, we have every right to dismiss, so I guess we'll see you in court."

Dr. Summer shook his head, faltering, unable to process what was happening. How could he be fired? His face was red, his skin itchy, and his foot was starting to throb. He wanted to say something but couldn't find the words. He took his satchel and cane in hand and with shoulders heavy as sand, turned to go, but he stopped just short of the door and caught Jack's eye. "Show me just one," he said.

"One what?"

"One irrefutable proof that man evolved, or that the planets came out of nothing, or that the coded information in our DNA wrote itself. Just show me one."

Jack shook his head. "And you wonder why we're letting you go."

An electric buzz was running through CellMerge. The employees were being gathered to hear an announcement and speculation was rampant about what the company had to say.

Sarah didn't like being pulled away from her work. She didn't have time to waste. She glanced around the room and caught the eye of the guy she'd met at the party, the one that had asked her to dance. He was staring at her. He grinned and raised his hand to wave. Sarah nodded to acknowledge him and turned edging deeper into the crowd hoping to avoid a meaningless conversation. She didn't want to be rude, but this was exactly the kind of thing she didn't have time for. She squeezed by several men and women, all in white lab coats, until she felt safe.

A loud *tap, tap, tap,* echoed though the building followed by screeching feedback.

"Is this thing on?" Dr. Jaeger's magnified voice boomed throughout the room. "*Hrrumph,* good." He leaned toward the speaker and received another ear-shattering jolt of feedback. "*Oooouch! Whoooeee.* Sorry about that."

"Okay, thank you all for coming. I've been asked to make an announcement, and I know you're all busy so I'll try to be brief, but we thought it best if we corralled the herd so we could announce this to everyone at the same time rather than wait for people to hear it through the grapevine. Anyway, this is it; as of this morning, Dr. Summer is no longer with the company."

The room erupted in murmurs. Dr. Jaeger put his hand up and waited for the whispers to die down before proceeding. "I know everyone appreciates Dr. Summer's contribution but sometimes you have to let a horse run. In any event, Dr. Summer and CellMerge have decided to part company. Obviously, this will necessitate a few changes. I will be assuming the position of department head while looking for someone to fill my former position. Those of you who reported directly to Dr. Summer know he managed at arm's length. I think you'll find me a little more hands on…"

Sarah sipped in her breath. She was waiting to hear what Dr. Summer thought about her proposal and…

"…now, I'm going to have to ask you to hold onto your questions and wait for the memo. I'm sure it will have more information."

Sarah turned to leave, pushing through the glut of arms and elbows once again. "Excuse me, excuse me, could I just squeeze by?" But it was futile. The crowd was starting to break up. It was easier just to move within the flow. She reached the periphery and there was Danny standing in a white lab coat with glasses that made him look like a raccoon. She turned to go the other way, but he stepped into her path.

"Hi, remember me? Danny, from the party, remember? I've been looking for you. Is this your department? Say, that was some announcement, huh? Boy, things really change fast around here."

Sarah nodded. "Yes, nice to see you again." She paused, and then said, "Well, I have to get back to work. Bye." She turned to go the other way but Danny jumped in front of her again.

"What's your hurry? We've got plenty of time. They're not counting heads or anything."

"No, it's just that…" Sarah's eyes fell on Danny's ID badge— *Section 4 DNA*. She glanced at her watch "Well I guess I can spare a few minutes, but only a few. I need to be getting back to work."

Computing and the Advent of Information
The Journal of W.L. Summer

It was the mystery of the human genome that first called me to question the evolutionary paradigm. There's nothing else like it. Even a simple cell is like a fully functioning city with robotic assembly plants that manufacture hundreds of thousands of modules. There are machines programmed to make other machines, machines that use molecular cables and pulleys to load freight, control systems for the assembly of parts and components, machines for delivering chemical products, solar powered machines that absorb light and store energy in chemical warehouses, machines that send electrical current to our nervous systems and switches for turning the processes on and off.

The software for the operation of these machines is composed of chemical letters that instruct how the machines are to be built and what function they're to perform. The machines can't operate without software. One has to ask where the programs for these machines came from. Software can't design itself. It requires intelligence to both write the program and to assign meaning to that which is written. Language doesn't make sense until there's agreement as to what each word, composed of individual letters, means. Even if the letters stored in our DNA had arisen by chance, they would serve no purpose without an intelligence to define their meaning.

In a computer, information is presented as binary code made of ones and zeros. Similarly, the code in every cell is composed of the chemical letters A, T, G, and C. There are six billion such letters in the average cell, all of which have to be paired in perfect sequence to work. Evolution calls the paring and alignment of these six billion letters an accident. I call it a miracle, definitely not something that could come about by happenstance.

But the real enigma is that information isn't made of matter. It isn't the chalk on the blackboard, the ones and zeros of a computer program, or the iron atoms on a hard drive. Information is thought, and like thought, information is without mass.

It would be impossible for information to evolve because it's ethereal; it lacks tangible substance. There's simply nothing to start with, yet every human cell contains about three billion pairs of chemical instructions that tell every part of the body how it's to grow and what it's to do. The challenge men of science face today is identifying the source of this information. As for myself, I can only conclude that the code must have been written by a superior intelligence. That is, it must have come from God.

Thirteen

You are blessed of the Lord Who made heaven and earth. —Psalm 115:15

SARAH CRASHED through the door slinging her backpack over her shoulder as she scurried down the hall. It was a new day, filled with uncertainty. Dr. Summer was gone. She now reported to Dr. Jaeger. Buddy had soiled himself again and she was late.

She plowed into a room divided by glass into work stations. People were busy tottering around the labyrinth like mice in a maze. No one looked at her. She made a beeline for her cubicle holding her breath until she was safely inside, and stopped.

Where was everything? Her computer was gone, her file cabinet, her microscope, her petri dishes and the small specimen refrigerator, the mice and their cages, all gone. She shook her head. The incubator was still where it should be, the bathrooms were just down the hall. She was in the right place. Her heart stuttered. Was she being let go? In defending Dr. Summer she'd let the president know she held similar views. Maybe she should have kept quiet.

"Dr. Hunter, glad you could make it." She spun around and there stood Dr. Jaeger. The rotund little man reached out a hand and flicked his fingers. "Please, I'd like to speak with you in my office. It'll only take a moment."

Oh boy, here it comes. Sarah fell in behind Dr. Jaeger. Her shoulders slumped, her feet doing the slow shuffle as though attempting to increase the length of her employment. They passed Dr. Jaeger's cubicle. Instead, she found herself in Dr. Summer's old office. Her temples were pulsing, her heart thudding in her chest. Dr. Jaeger rounded the desk and took the chair where Dr. Summer used to sit. He scooted up, placed his elbows on the desk and clasped his fingers in front of him. His round glasses reflected the overhead lights.

"I confess I don't know much about your work, Dr. Hunter," he said, raising an eyebrow and twiddling his thumbs, "but I guess I'm not alone. I asked around and no one seems to know what you're working on." Leaning forward he struggled to reach over his belly and retrieve a folder. He flopped it open, shuffled through several sheets of paper, then settled back in his chair, lacing his fingers again. "Those few pieces of paper there," he said, raising his chin to indicate the file, "that's all Dr. Summer had on you so, other than knowing your focus is muscular dystrophy, I'm clueless. Man can't ride herd unless he knows where his cattle are, if you get my drift."

Sarah opened her mouth to answer but he raised his hand stopping her.

"That may have been the way Dr. Summer managed things, but it won't do for me. There will be no more working in a vacuum. Your equipment has been moved to the other side of the hall. From now on you'll be reporting to Dr. Rose. I want you on his team. I understand you have a personal incentive for succeeding with your research. That's good, but I can't allow you to play the Lone Ranger. Not in this outfit. From now on, you'll be required to contribute to the group's goals and objectives. If there's something of a personal nature, you'll have to do it on your own time. Any questions?"

Sarah felt like a yo-yo, snapped to the bottom only to be jerked to the top and thrust back down again. She wasn't losing her job, that was good, but she had to work for Aaron on whatever project *he* assigned. Her eyes flicked across the room searching for Dr.

Rose and his team. Her lips pursed tight. God help him if he tried using her work as leverage to get favors. She resumed staring at Dr. Jaeger who was busy tugging his white lab coat over his rotund belly. He leaned back in his brown leather chair looking like a dab of whipped cream on a chocolate donut, his smugness implying he was waiting for her to object. *Sorry to disappoint.* She shook her head. "No, I'm good," she said.

Sarah made her way over to Aaron's work area. That other girl was there, the one she'd seen on his Facebook page—*Jen*—who turned away feigning disinterest. Sarah took it for what it was—*a snub*. Maybe Aaron would assign her to complete the work she was already doing. She looked around but didn't see him. Her personal equipment, her computer, microscope, cultures in their petri dishes and mice in their cages, were in the corner of a cubicle. She assumed it was where they wanted her to sit. She shuffled over, removing her coat and scarf and lay them on the counter as she took a seat. It looked like everything was there. She reached for the file containing her notes but didn't see it. She started going through her desk, shuffling paper. The mice looked at her with wide beady eyes as she bumped their cages. She had to have her notes.

"Glad to see you're getting settled in."

The voice made her start. She turned to see Aaron standing behind her holding the folder she was looking for. "Give me that!" she demanded reaching to snatch it away.

But he snapped it back. "Ah, ah, not so fast."

She swung her hand up and stood trying to reach it. "Give it back! It's mine."

"Actually, it isn't. Any work you do for the corporation is company property. I needed to see it to evaluate your progress. Now if you'll just calm down, I was about to suggest we go somewhere and talk." Aaron leaned toward Sarah lowering his voice. "You're on thin ice here. They mentioned letting you go but I said I needed you on my team. Now be good, and let's go someplace we can talk in private."

· ☆ ★ 🌍 ★ ☆ ·

Dr. Summer paced the floor limping. At least he had two feet. He kept his weight on one while using his cane to relieve the pressure on the other. It was a conundrum really, one of the unanswered questions: how did we end up with perfectly balanced pairs of eyes, ears, hands and feet? Obviously it was necessary. It took two feet to walk, he grimaced, and it took two hands to embrace things, but there was no logic to the evolution of pairs. One appendage might begin its evolution on one side of an organism while another could begin evolving on the opposite side but the appendages would be on separate evolutionary paths, each subject to their own mutations. Evolution couldn't explain how the two could reasonably be expected to turn out the same. It was far more likely we'd end up with a hand on one side and perhaps a club, or maybe a claw, on the other. Of course it wasn't a problem if we were created by design. *Ouch!* His gout was acting up. He put more weight on his cane to ease the pain as he shouted into the phone.

"What do you mean? Did you tell them I hold two doctorates and a Nobel Prize? Surely there's a position open somewhere."

"I wish there were, but I've called pharmaceutical companies as far away as New York and there's just nothing out there."

"That's impossible. At CellMerge we were hiring researchers all the time, and losing them just as fast to the competition."

There was a momentary pause followed by a sigh and when the caller began to speak again there was a certain amount of gravity in his voice. "Dr. Summer, I'm only telling you what I'm hearing out there. I wish it were otherwise, but it's not. I can only say I'm sorry."

"Sorry! What the heck does that mean? Something's wrong here. If CellMerge is out there badmouthing me, I'll have them in court. They said they wouldn't do that. I have their word."

"That's up to you, though it might be worth looking into. I admit I've spoken to H.R. managers who seemed excited when I first mentioned your name only to come back with regrets saying there was nothing available. Anyway, all I can do is keep looking."

Wallace placed the receiver back on its cradle and sank into his chair. He didn't need the money. They'd withheld his severance pay but he had enough to tide him over for a few years, and there was always his pension, they had to pay that, and unemployment. In retrospect, it probably wasn't the best idea to reject their offer. That alone would have amounted to at least a year's salary, plus benefits.

He'd threatened to sue but the prospect of winning a suit against the corporation was iffy at best. His lawyer explained what they were up against. By ignoring his censure, the corporation would claim he'd violated a trust. If they could show his actions would have a negative impact on their share price, as it had done previously, then his dismissal would be justified. According to his lawyer, he would be ill-advised to take CellMerge to court. They would probably countersue claiming the bad press brought by his lawsuit was hurting them even more and then make him not only responsible for court costs, but damages as well.

Mr. Landon was acting out of spite, of that he was certain. That little pipsqueak Jaeger was gloating, too. A small man in a big hat is still small. He was pretty sure Jaeger was orchestrating the whole thing. How else would Jack have learned of his meeting with Aaron and what's her name, that girl he'd brought with him, the one taking care of Snowball? Actually, he kind of liked her, full of spunk and her ideas had merit. He needed to call and ask her to bring his dog back. At least he would if he could find her number.

This was nonsense. Jack was a reasonable man. Maybe they

could resolve their issues in an equitable fashion. He reached for his overcoat. At least it was worth a try.

A bitter cold raked across the bay as Wallace drove his Saturn down US 101. The wind came in gusts nearly ripping the wheel from his hands. He struggled to keep the car from being pushed out of its lane. The heater was turned up with the fan circulating hot air to keep the interior warm. He pulled at his tie and reached beneath his seatbelt to unbutton his coat. He was being blackballed. *Would Jack really do that?* Jack had lied about the patents. One lie upon another. *Oh what a tangled web we weave...* He needed to explain that he no longer cared what happened to the company, then maybe Jack would stop spreading lies and let him get on with his life.

Through a hole in the clouds the sun hit the CellMerge triplex making the buildings look like bars of gold standing on end, especially against the steel gray sky. Dr. Summer pulled up to the garage. Specks of rain stung his face as he rolled his window down. "Afternoon Charlie, I'm here to see Jack Landon."

"Dr. Summer. It's nice to see you, but, ah, I hate to say it, but I have orders not to let you on the property. It's none of my business, you understand. When I read the memo, I said, 'this is wrong', but I don't make the rules, I just obey them. I guess I'm gonna have to ask you to turn around."

Dr. Summer shook his head. "That's ridiculous. Just call up to the office. I'm sure they'll make an exception. I really need to see Mr. Landon. It's important."

"No can do," the officer said, shaking his head. "The memo said your access to the property is irrevocably denied, no ifs, ands or buts. Sorry about that."

Wallace nodded and rolled his window up to banish the cold again. The car inched forward as he looked for a place to turn around, his grip tightening on the wheel. He'd never get into the building anyway. His access card no longer worked so he couldn't use the employee entrance, and he'd never get past the guard stationed in the front lobby. Then he saw his answer. A custodian rolled out a plastic bin filled with garbage. He would empty it before going back inside. All Wallace had to do was time it so he arrived just as the man was opening the door. It was doubtful they'd told the maintenance staff to keep him out. He gunned the gas, raced to the side of the building, and slammed his car into park. The worker shuffled by pushing his empty bin in front of him. Dr. Summer fell in behind and waited as the man swiped his card. "Whew, it's cold out here," he said, shivering as he followed the man inside.

He turned and limped down the hall passing several people dressed in white lab smocks but they didn't seem to notice. He looked up and saw a camera. What's the use? They were watching him by now anyway. The elevator sounded a *ding*. Wallace turned away looking the other direction as several men in business suits exited. He waited until they passed and caught the elevator just before the door closed. His heart felt like a ping-pong ball bouncing in his chest. This was ridiculous. What did he expect to accomplish? The door opened again. He stepped out and was immediately grabbed, spun around, and forced against the wall. Someone wrenched his hands behind his back and slapped a pair of cuffs on his wrists.

"Okay, boys, not so rough. No need to hurt him."

He was grabbed by the elbow and yanked around to face Mr. Landon.

"You must have known the garage attendant would tell us you were coming. Frankly, I have to admit, I'm surprised to see you, Wally. I thought you understood your coming here would constitute trespass."

Dr. Summer's heart was racing. Beads of perspiration rolled down his cheek. He looked back and forth at his captors feeling their grip tighten on his arms.

"You want us to call the police?" one of them asked.

"No, there's no need for that, just escort him off the property. And Wally, I trust we won't have another incident like this."

Wallace was trembling as he pulled his car into the street. His grip on the steering wheel made his knuckles white. They had actually handcuffed him. He shook, more from humiliation than the cold, his cheeks flushing with embarrassment. They had reduced him to the level of a common criminal. All he wanted was for them to lift the taboo. This was crazy. He'd talked to two junior researchers. That's all. Two people! What possible harm could come from that?

Carl! Had to be him. That half-pint cowboy had been trying to unseat him from the start. Envy and jealousy were twisted sisters. The man would have seized any opportunity to have him fired.

A car behind him honked. He checked his speedometer and hit the gas as the angry driver pulled around with his horn blaring. Maybe he deserved to be fired. His brain was getting addled. You get old and you start to wonder what comes next. Confound it all, it did seem like the world had design.

Another horn screamed as he squeezed over leaving only inches between his rear bumper and the car to his right. He'd nearly missed his exit. The man slammed on his brakes, squealing rubber.

Sorry!

He had to get hold of Fishman. It was risky. The man might be involved in the company's malfeasance, but then again, he might not. He was depending on CellMerge to find a cure for his wife, not as a means to increase his wealth. He was probably out of the loop. If so, it was time to bring him in.

The tall blond in her too tight pants and her hefty friend with his lab coat hanging loose, were huddled close, talking in whispers. The girl looked up as Sarah and Aaron approached. Her eyes widened for a moment but she recovered feigning disinterest. She nudged her co-conspirator who tucked his hands into his lab coat pockets and returned to his own work station.

So that's how it's going to be, Sarah mused. She would always be the outsider, the one they kept secrets from. She didn't like it, but she'd try to get along. Aaron was right, she needed this job.

"I don't think you've met everyone yet," Aaron said, leaning into Sarah with his hand raised to wave the others in. "Hey you guys, come here. I want to introduce you to the newest member of our team."

The big guy turned around and headed back toward Aaron. The blond crossed her arms raising her chin slightly as she stepped forward followed by a third person, a tiny Chinese girl who Sarah hadn't seen before. Aaron began the introductions.

"Group, this is Sarah," he said. She'll be joining our team as part of the reorganization."

"Why?" Jen said curtly. "We're not behind in our work." She turned, looking directly at Sarah. "Not that I don't think you're cute and I'm sure your PhD from, where was that, somewhere in South Dakota, is top drawer because everyone knows South Dakota is a bastion of intellectual advancement, but we really don't need another hand."

"Lay off, Jen." The guy was big, but had a boyish face. "Don't pay her any mind. She's like that with everyone. I'm Larry," he said extending a hand. Sarah shook it feeling her fingers get lost in a cushion of moist flesh, then quickly looked away, hoping the burning in her eyes would go unnoticed.

Her tongue was caught in her throat. Such hurtful words, *why?* She didn't even know the girl. She flashed back to the picture on Facebook. Dr. Rose was supposed to be the boss; *he* should have come to her defense, but it was obvious he and the blond had history. She drew in a breath, her timorous heart bleeding softly. "I…I didn't catch your name," she said, turning to the tiny Chinese girl.

"I May Ling," the girl said with a demure smile and an almost imperceptible bow. Her hair was cut in a pageboy with bangs so black they glistened. She was probably wearing the smallest smock provided by the lab, but it looked like it was wrapped around her twice.

Sarah nodded. "Is that everyone?" she asked, trying to keep a tremor from her voice.

"Yep, pretty much, though we lean on scientists from other departments from time to time." Aaron took Sarah's arm and pulled her along with him. "Over here we're working on understanding why mice with faulty dystrophin aren't as susceptible to muscle wasting as humans. Our hypothesis is that the mice have something that enables them to replace muscle cells damaged by the mutant dystrophin and we think it has to do with the enzyme telomerase. May will bring you up to speed. She's working on injecting mice with flawed telomerase and dystrophin to prove our theory. Once we do that, perhaps we'll be able to create an enzyme, similar to the one used by the mice, to improve the condition of children suffering with Duchennes." He leaned in close lowering his voice. "That would be good news for Buddy, wouldn't it?"

Dr. Summer parked across from his house and sat with the engine idling. He wasn't anxious to face the cold anyway. Getting hold of Fishman might not be so easy. The rich valued their privacy. He might refuse to take the call, though it wasn't like they were complete strangers. They'd spoken several times over the years, mostly during the discussion periods that followed presentations Wallace had been called upon to make to the board.

He liked George, a tall man of African descent with close cropped hair and a robust baritone laugh. He liked him because he seemed down to earth, never flaunting his wealth. But most of all, he liked him because he'd been told Fishman was the only one on the board to vote against his censure after the scandal broke last year.

Now if he could only find George's number. He looked toward the house thinking about the piles of clutter. It would be like looking for a needle in a haystack. Except…what if the Board of Directors had their names and contact information published in the company's annual report?

Aaron sat across from Dr. Jaeger. The little man's ten-gallon hat was hanging on a hook behind the door along with his denim jacket, the one with lamb's wool lining. The outfit was designed to make him look like a tall Texas cowpoke but in his white lab smock he looked pretty much the way he was—small and round.

The desk formerly used by Dr. Summer had undergone a transformation. Gone were the stacks of reports and scientific journals along with dozens of notes written on loose scraps of paper. It was now free of clutter. Front and center on its polished surface was a brass name plate etched with the words, "Dr. Carl Jaeger – Department Head" in large dark letters.

Aaron found himself staring at the soles of Carl's pointy-toed boots as the man leaned back in his brown leather chair with his feet propped up on the desk and his little sausage-like fingers linked over his belly.

"I know it's not necessary, I just thought it might provide some additional incentive. Sales teams do it all the time."

"But we're scientists, Dr. Jaeger, not salesmen. You can't push results. It's a matter of trial and error."

"I know, I know," Carl said, raising his hand to dissuade further argument. "You can lead a horse to water but you can't make him drink. But people are people. And people like perks. Offer them something extra and you'll be surprised at the results that can be achieved. All I ask is that you give it a try."

Against his better judgment Aaron found himself nodding. The idea of doing a contest, of pitting one group against another to hasten results, was appalling. At best, it could make people sloppy, at worst, it might tempt them to falsify their findings just to improve their score.

"Excellent. Now, I just had another idea. How 'bout we saddle up and get on out of here," Carl said, rolling his feet off the desk. "One thing you'll find out about me is that I'm a team builder. Why don't you round up your crew and let me take everyone out for a drink? My treat. It will give us a chance to discuss the new program."

Aaron stood. "Uh, sure, fine. I'm good. I'll see what the others say, but I doubt the new girl, Sarah, can join us. She has a child to take care of."

Dr. Jaeger tossed his white smock over the back of his chair and stood on his toes reaching for his coat. "See, that's what I mean. She's not a team player." He snatched his hat from the hook and plopped it on his head, looking up at Aaron from beneath the brim. "I think you're making a mistake keeping her on, but we can talk more about that later. Come on, let's boogie. It's Roundup Night over at The Corral."

Fourteen

The fool has said in his heart, "There is no God." —Psalm 14:1

THE NOISE was deafening. Rockabilly music blared from six hundred watt speakers accompanied by the amplified voice of a line-dance step caller shouting into a mike, *"Step left to left, cross right behind, left to left, stomp right."* Several dozen boots pounded the wood dance floor in response.

Raucous conversation filled the rafters along with the clatter of clinking beer mugs and boisterous cheers. Over in the corner a bunch of wannabe cowboys were urging drunken fools to ride Bronco Billy the mechanical bull.

Aaron leaned in toward Larry's ear. "Not happening," he said. "You couldn't get me on one of those things."

"Come on, man, you can do it. You were born for the saddle. Yippi-yi-yo-ki-ay." Larry reached out to flag a passing server. A girl wearing cowboy boots, a fringed miniskirt and a white shirt with a star shaped sheriff's badge stopped at the table.

"Yeah, cowboy, what can I gitcha."

"Bring us another round."

She threw a quick glance at Dr. Jaeger who had his credit card at the bar to cover the tab. The stool upon which he sat made him appear taller than he was, and his ten-gallon hat made him look taller still but the effect was lost because in this crowd everyone wore a cowboy hat. He nodded his approval. He'd be putting the bill on his expense account anyway, all in the name of team building.

"Couple more of these and you'll be asking that cow for a date."

"Larry!" Jen broke in.

"I'm just trying to get Aaron on that bull."

"Ain't a bull that can't be rode, or a rider that can't be throwed," Carl said. His elbow was on the table with his palm propping up his chin and his fingers scratching his goatee.

Jen slipped off her stool and grabbed Aaron's hand. "Come on. I want to try line dancing. It looks like fun."

Aaron looked over his shoulder at the crowd of people high stepping, shuffling and sliding to the tune of *Boot Scootin' Boogie*. "I think I'll pass on that too," he said, emphasizing his words loudly so she could hear.

"But I wanna dance."

"Go out there by yourself. You don't need a partner. They're all doing the same thing. It's mostly girls anyway."

The server returned holding a tray filled with mugs of beer but before she could set it down, Jen leaned in and grabbed one, downed a few gulps, and shook her head, "Yee-Haw! All right dance lovers, here I come." She turned and staggered off in the direction of the dance floor.

Larry lifted his mug and said, "Bottoms up." Aaron swirled his dark honey ale around in his glass and took a sip. He was glad Sarah hadn't come but then wondered why he cared.

Dr. Jaeger was watching Jen. "Girl like that makes me wish I was young again."

"Girl like that will make you old before your time," Aaron responded.

"Doesn't matter." Larry chimed in. "One night with her and you'd be in heaven anyway."

"I doubt that's where you're going." Aaron smiled.

Larry placed a hand the size of a mitt over his heart. "*Oh*, you wound me, *Mon'Ami*. I got as much right to be there as anyone."

"The point's moot," Jaeger quipped. "There ain't no such place." He reached for his mug and took a long pull on his beer.

"How can you be so sure?"

Carl slammed the mug down and tipped his hat back. His face flushed red. "Because…there ain't no God, and without God there's no Heaven or Hell. *Sheeeech*. I knew the Q was rubbing off on you. Hey, that rhymes." He began drumming his fingers on the table. "I knew the Q was rubbing off on you. Kinda catchy, doncha think? Look, let's get this out in the open, right now. We're men of science. Science, understand? We don't deal in the supernatural. We deal in facts, and there's one fact we know, there ain't no God because there's no proof He exists. None whatsoever. All God has to do if he wants people to believe in Him is stick His big fat finger down here and touch the planet so we can see it. That's proof. Seems to me that's the least He'd do if He wanted us to believe in Him, but He hasn't done that, has He? No, He hasn't. All we have are myths and fairy tales. Santa Claus, the Easter Bunny, and Jesus. There's about as much proof of one as the other."

Aaron nodded but his face held a pout. "Yeah, but what if God has reasons for not doing that. I mean, He could be up there folding His arms and saying, 'I'm God, take it or leave it. I don't have to prove anything.' I just wonder if it wouldn't be good to keep an open mind."

"That's Wally talking. Good thing they fired him. The man's headed for a padded cell. And if you're not careful they'll lock you up with him. Dang straight. The world won't be safe until that man's six feet under." Dr. Jaeger looked at Aaron; his eyes behind his misty glasses were wet and red. "Hey look, I'm not against the concept of God. For centuries it was the only thing society had to keep people in line. Better not do that, God's watching. But we've evolved beyond that. Now were smart enough to know we're our own gods. We don't need some ancient book telling us how to live. We use reason to discern right from wrong and intelligence to decide what to do. Larry, I promise you, you're not going to hell for wanting to sleep with Jen. Heck, every time I see that little filly bending over the sink I think about it myself.

Aaron drew back shaking his head. "*Really?* This is crazy. You think everyone should do whatever they want? That's anarchy. No way."

"Absolutely! We're our own gods, we make the rules. There's no eternal punishment. Go out and have fun. Eat, drink, and be merry 'cause we're all gonna die."

The server was back collecting glasses from the table. "Another round, cowboys?"

Aaron waved her off but Larry grabbed his mug and emptied it setting it on her tray. "Fill 'er up," he said, and then belched. He wiped his mouth with the back of his hand. Carl slid his mug across the table indicating he was ready for another as well.

"So what about murder?" Aaron asked.

"Depends on the situation. I can think of dozens of times when murder is perfectly acceptable. Say you got five people in a lifeboat that only holds four and it's sinking. If all five stay, all will die, but if you get rid of one, the remaining four stand a chance. Better one man die so that four can live, so you toss one overboard."

"Yeah, but who decides which one?"

"Draw straws. Doesn't matter. Maybe one is old and has little to live for. Toss him over. Or maybe one is sick and wouldn't survive anyway. Everything depends on the situation. What about mercy killing where a man is in horrible pain and wants to die to end his suffering? He asks his doctor to put him out of his misery. You'd do that for a dog but our laws, based on some sadistic idea that only God has the right to end life, won't let the doctor do it. I say Kevorkian was right. Either help the man kill himself or do it for him. That's when murder's the right thing to do. Same goes for those with disabilities who don't want to live. We should let them kill themselves instead of hanging around using up the planet's resources."

"Seriously?"

"Dang straight. There are people taking up space in hospitals that have no money so the state, read that you and I, has to pay their bills. What if a man is brain dead? He's robbing the planet of oxygen and not giving anything back so I say, let him go."

"Yeah, but you go through that door and where do you stop? Eugenics? Hitler did that. He started putting down the old and sick and look where it led, six million Jews stuffed into crematoriums. We're back to my original question, who decides who gets to live and who doesn't? If one group of people determines that another isn't fit to live, we could end up wiping out a whole race..."

"Hey guys, did you see me out there?" Jen was back squeezing her way up to the table. Her skin glistened under a thin film of perspiration, her hair moist around the temples. "I think I'm getting the hang of it. Come on, all of you. It's easy. Come on, I'll show you." She grabbed Larry's beer and brought it to her mouth, taking several deep gulps.

"Hey!"

Carl reached out and clutched her buttocks. "I gotta hand it to ya girl, you sure know how to dance."

Jen scowled, giving him *the look* as she swatted his hand away.

"What? This ain't the workplace, darlin'. You're on your own out here. See, that's what I mean." Carl glanced at Aaron, then at Larry. "Jen here's miffed at my patting her derriere. Why? It's just a lump of flesh evolution glued to her backside to give her a cushion for sitting. The problem is, about a billion years ago some dimwitted priest labeled it nasty so now she's offended. We really need to break free of those shackles. And for the record, I can see you're upset so I apologize. I really don't need to be accused of sexual harassment."

"Apology accepted," Jen said, though she continued to frown.

A lady in blue jeans, boots and a checkered shirt, approached the table with a camera in hand. "Howdy partners. It's picture time," she said, "but, oh my, you city slickers need some help. Can I get a conversion package over here?" She was shouting to be heard above the noise. Three cowboys seated at a table next to them swiveled around and plopped their Stetsons down on the heads of Aaron, Jen and Larry. Carl, who had his own, didn't need one. "That's better. Okay, everybody, snuggle in shoulder to shoulder, that's it, nice and tight. Alright, look at the camera and smile."

The photograph of four red bleary-eyed faces, three with lopsided hats that didn't fit, would appear on Facebook the next day.

Sarah sat in bed with her arms wrapped around her knees and blankets tucked up under her chin. The room was dark, but she couldn't sleep. Buddy's erratic breathing broke the stillness. At least he was resting.

She'd been awakened again. *Another nightmare.* She wanted to forget, she'd asked God to purge it from her mind, but it was an ever present memory. *Get over it. It was a lifetime ago. Move on.* She hugged her knees tighter, her head bobbing as she rocked back and forth.

Sarah rolled into the gas station and cut the engine. Her encounter with the flat tire had left her shaken but that was the least of her worries. Somewhere down the long, lonely stretch of Highway 80 her car had started knocking. She wasn't car smart, but she was smart enough to know something was wrong.

She looked around. As far as she could tell she was in the middle of nowhere, which was pretty much the same as everywhere in Nevada. The gas station was the first sign of civilization she'd seen and thankfully it boasted a garage and a coffee shop. At least it provided a place where she could rest while her car was being fixed.

Her vision was momentarily diminished as she stepped from the bright day into the dimly lit repair shop. She sipped in a breath. The room smelled of exhaust fumes. She approached the first person she saw, her shoes feeling sticky as she crossed the oil laden floor. The man nodded and went outside with her to inspect the car.

"You're the lady with the flat tire," he said, lifting his chin toward the red Dodge Colt.

"How'd you know that?"

"I fixed it. Name's Brian. Didn't mean to leave you stranded out there but you disappeared so there wasn't much I could do."

He was tall and lean, wearing Levis and a T-shirt that emphasized the contours of his frame. His hair was long enough to cover his ears but trim around his neck. His eyes were hidden behind a pair of aviator glasses.

"You work here?"

"Nope. I just stopped to fill my tank and use the facilities. My truck's around back. But I can look at your car if you want. I'm pretty good at fixing things."

"Can I help you?"

They both turned to face a man in coveralls, obviously the station mechanic. He had a baseball cap screwed to his head to shield him from the sun. His cheek, prickly with a two-day-old beard, bulged with a wad of chewing tobacco.

"Lady says her car's making a noise," Brian offered.

The garage man rubbed his whiskers and nodded. "I can look at it if you want."

Sarah didn't have a choice. She had to get home. The new semester started on Monday. "Alright," she said, "but don't fix anything without first letting me know how much it costs."

Brian spoke up. "I was just thinking about getting some lunch. Care to join me? It will give you something to do while you wait."

Sarah puckered her lips.

"My treat. Might as well wait inside, out of the sun. Besides I could use the company."

Sarah nodded. The guy seemed nice enough, and she needed to thank him for changing her tire, but she wouldn't let him pay. She'd insist on picking up the tab. Then they'd be even. "Alright," she said. She turned to the mechanic. "If you need me for anything I'll be inside."

They took a booth by the window. The table was chipped Formica and the yellow vinyl seats were cracked and held together with patches of duct tape. Brian sat across from Sarah and took a menu from the lady with a coffee pot in her hand.

"Java?" the waitress said, lifting the pot.

"That'd be good," Brian responded, but Sarah shook her head. She was looking out the window. The mechanic had found someone to help him push her car into the garage.

"I don't really need a menu. I'll have a Cheeseburger and fries with the works."

The waitress poured his coffee and nodded. She looked at Sarah. "And for you?"

"What kind of soup do you have?"

"Tomato or vegetable."

I'll have the vegetable, and a house salad, if you have one."

"You got it." The waitress collected the menus and turned away.

"So what brings you to Nevada?"

Sarah stared at the man seated across the table. If she had to guess, she'd say he was about her age, perhaps a year or two older. "What makes you think I don't live here?"

"Your car has South Dakota plates."

"Oh. Well, that's where I'm headed."

"You live there?"

"And go to school. What about you?"

The man shrugged. I'm just traveling and taking in the sights."

"Must be nice, but there has to be more to it than that. Travel takes money. What do you do for a living?" Sarah picked up her spoon and began polishing the bowl with her napkin.

"Right, well, up until just yesterday I lived in San Francisco but I quit my job and joined the Marines. I have to report for duty in about a week so I'm taking time to enjoy life before they ship me off to Afghanistan or Iraq or someplace like that. I just want to see what I'll be fighting for."

The waitress brought their food and put it on the table, sliding a bottle of catsup from the pocket of her apron to set it next to the burger. "Can I get you anything else?"

Sarah shook her head and looked at Brian. He did the same. "I guess we're fine," she said.

They ate making the kind of small talk strangers do at a party: "How's your food? Unusually warm weather we're having. Can you pass the salt?" meaningless conversation meant only to fill the empty space. When the check came Brian reached out and grabbed it.

"Hey, I want to pay. I need to thank you for helping me with my tire."

Brian pulled out his wallet, counted out several bills and laid them on the table. "Nope. I asked you to lunch, remember. And the way to say thank you is by saying, thank you."

"Okay, thank you. I appreciate what you did."

"No problemo. Let's go see if the man's had any luck with your car."

They stepped out into the bright light once again. Billowy clouds languished on the horizon, but elsewhere the sky was clear. The sun beat down lending warmth to a September afternoon in the high desert. Brian slipped his sunglasses over his eyes but had to remove them again to see Sarah's car parked in the shadowy recesses of the garage. The man they'd spoken with earlier was working at a bench. He looked up as they stepped inside.

"Fraid I have bad news," he said. "Your car's had it. There wasn't a drop of oil in the crankcase. She overheated and threw a rod. You're *lucky you got here. It was okay while you were driving but the minute you turned the engine off it seized. I couldn't get it to turn over."*

"But…can it be fixed?"

The man picked up a rag and began wiping his hands. "Sure, I can fix anything, but it would cost more than the car's worth."

"What do you mean?"

"I mean, it would cost upwards of a thousand to put this car back on the road, and if you tried to sell it, you couldn't get more than five hundred."

"But I need my car. I have to get home."

"Yeah, I thought about that. Look, my boy's got a Colt like this but it's a wreck. The frame's bent and the body's toast but the motor's good. I was thinking I could drop his engine in your car and put him back on the road. Tell you what; I'll give you two-fifty for yours."

"Two-fifty? You just said it was worth five."

"If it were running it would be worth five. Not as is. Like that it's just junk. Look, I'm only trying to help. I figure two-fifty should be enough to get you on a plane. Take it or leave it, but if you say no, it's your responsibility to haul it out of here. You can call a tow truck or do whatever you want but you can't leave it here."

Sarah looked at Brian.

"Make it three and you've got a deal," he said.

"You drive a hard bargain, but…"

"But how will I get home?"

"No problemo. I'll give you a ride. I was hoping to see Mount Rushmore anyway."

Men were such animals, well, maybe not all men…*yes all!* Mister nice guy was as bad as the rest, posting a photo of himself in the sack with Jen. Men only thought about one thing, and they spent half their time looking for it, and the other half figuring out how to get it. Buddy's father wasn't looking for marriage, not even a long-term commitment. With him it was *wham, bam, thank you ma'am*, and he was up and gone, leaving her with his child to raise and no support. She hadn't seen or heard from him since.

She could feel her heart thumping. Thirteen years and she couldn't forget. Maybe she never would. If that meant she had to live a solitary life, so be it.

Snowball pushed up, stretched, and jumped from Buddy's bed to Sarah's. She began stroking the dog's ears. "You're probably wondering when I plan to get you home, aren't ya?" she whispered. "I'll bet Dr. Summer's wondering too. Maybe after work tomorrow." She leaned over and reached for the drawer of the nightstand, jiggling the lamp. She turned the light to its lowest setting and retrieved an envelope from the drawer. The contents fell into her lap. The newspaper clipping had a number of words redacted. The story announced the hiring of someone new at CellMerge Inc. She didn't know who because the man's name had been scratched out with a ball point pen, and not lightly. Her mother had pressed so hard the paper had been ripped through so that no trace of the man's name remained. A photo caption with the name scratched out was there, but the picture had been cut off, again leaving no hint as to who the article was about. Sarah found the clipping buried underneath a pair of socks in her mother's dresser. She could only assume the article was about her father since her mother had no reason to be mad at anyone else. It proved her point: men were animals. Her father, just like Buddy's father, had abandoned them. Her mother had been left to raise her alone.

She needed to find out who her father was. As to whether or not it was Dr. Summer, she couldn't say. It was all guesswork at this point but that would soon change. She wouldn't make the mistake of asking him directly. Denial was too easy. Danny would be getting back to her with the results of his test and with evidence in hand she'd confront Dr. Summer and find out why he'd deserted her all those years ago.

Move Over E.T., We're Extraterrestrials Too
The Journal of W.L. Summer

The law of biogenesis states that all life comes from preexisting life. Or, *Omnis cellula e cellula,* which is Latin for, all cells come from other cells. Trying to get around this law and prove that matter, the stuff rocks and dirt are made of, somehow acquired life is one of the most difficult issues evolutionists face. Scientists long ago gave up trying to validate Stanly Miller's experiments. Life doesn't happen spontaneously. Chemicals floating in a primordial stew can't just receive an influx of energy and, like a Frankenstein monster, become alive.

The problem is so unsolvable some believe life didn't start here at all but rather began on an asteroid or comet that transferred life to us upon impact. This is usually the answer given to those who question how the earliest forms of life found on earth, the fossilized stromatolites of Australia, could at the outset be complex enough to have cell walls protecting their DNA.

But whether life originally formed here or elsewhere the question remains, how did it come to be? The truth is, science doesn't know. They assume the first form of life was an RNA or DNA molecule but how either came about they're at a loss to explain. All molecules are made of matter and as such are composed of atoms, but there's nothing in an atom or its subatomic particles that enables life.

Unless you accept that life was bestowed on us by an entity with an intelligence superior to our own, the question of how life began is the same as the question about the origin of our universe. Believing billions and billions of stars sprang forth out of nothing is no different than believing matter just one day started to wiggle and come alive.

Such is the realm of magic, not science.

Fifteen

...O man, who are you that replies against God? Shall the thing formed say to Him who formed it, "Why hast thou made me thus?"
—Romans 9:20

D R. SUMMER looked at his watch. It was two in the morning. He rarely stayed up past midnight, but much had changed. What happened to the man who used to spend hours poring over scientific journals? He hadn't read anything in days. He used to command the respect of his peers. Now they sniggered at the mention of his name. He wanted to scream, but he was too tired. His whole body ached.

He reached for the card and held it up, flicking it between his fingers. Dr. Alex Lamar Sc.D. It took more than a doctorate to earn an Sc.D. Europeans only conferred that title upon those who had made extensive contributions to scientific knowledge. The difference in time between London and California was eight hours. It would be ten in the morning there. Wallace picked up the phone and dialed.

"Lamar, here."

"Alex? This is Wallace Summer. We spoke at the conference."

"Wallace, yes, how have you been?"

"Healthy, I guess, well...actually I've been a bit down lately. I...uh...you know that talk we had over lunch, about the universe having design?"

"You mean, God?"

"Yes, of course. You read my paper so you know where I stand. I think I told you I was censured for that."

"Yes, you mentioned it."

"Okay, well, I guess I made the mistake of sharing my thoughts with a few of my colleagues and the next thing I know, I'm unemployed. They canned me Alex. My employer, CellMerge, decided my views might hurt them financially so they fired me."

The silence on the line was so pronounced Wallace began to think they'd become disconnected. "Dr. Lamar?"

"Unbelievable."

"*Oh*, for a second I thought I'd lost you. Yes, well, maybe, but that's what happened."

"I don't doubt you. Not one bit. I know a number of men who've lost their jobs for the same reason, some of them experts in their field. The good news is we've been able to find new positions for several of them. Some companies, especially start-ups, are seeing this as an opportunity to hire first-rate professionals they weren't previously able to attract. With your credentials I doubt you'll be on the market long."

"I have a half dozen rejection letters saying you're wrong about that. The inside track is, I've been blacklisted."

"*Humm*, are you willing to relocate? I don't know much about the American job market but I have a pretty good idea about what's happening over here."

The thought caught Wallace off guard. He hadn't considered moving, except maybe to another state, but why not? His only friends were his associates at work, and they'd disavowed him, and he didn't have family. There wasn't anything keeping him. The Europeans were making great advances in cellular technology. Why not? "Yes, anything's possible, depending on the offer."

"Fine. You still have my card?"

Wallace glanced at the small business card in his hand. "I do."

"My email address is on it. Send me a copy of your resume and we'll see what we can do."

Sunrise over the bay was glorious. Yellow beams fanned out over the water, stately palms stood in silhouettes against a rose-petal sky and seagulls danced across the sparkling coral sand. Perhaps it would rain later. The clouds might roll in to dampen his soul, but not now. Right now all earth, dare he say it, all creation, resounded with the good news.

Wallace took a sip of coffee and stepped onto the deck dragging his cane with him. The ocean was alive with sights and sounds and smells he hadn't known in years. *Dang*, he felt good. He hadn't slept, but he was wide awake and feeling fine, so good in fact he was buoyant. Shortly after speaking with Dr. Lamar, he'd received an email. Lamar had called a friend at a biotech firm looking for a senior scientist. Apparently the man listened and based on Dr. Lamar's recommendation had asked to set up a meeting. They were willing to pay Dr. Summer's airfare and expenses if he'd consider granting them an interview. *Consider?* He'd jump at the chance. He raised his cane and leapt forward realizing his mistake as his foot hit the ground. *Ouch! Dang it!* How do you limp when you're floating like a balloon?

He'd gone to the company's website and read their corporate profile and the more he read, the more excited he became. This was cutting edge stuff. They were cloning human body parts by building plastic models of needed organs, and then washing the model in a bath of stem cells. The cells adhered to the model, and after a period of growth and regeneration, became the part itself allowing the plastic mold to be removed and discarded. Rejection wasn't an issue because the newly created organ was made of cells originally taken from the patient's own body!

He had to get a haircut, polish his shoes, maybe even get a new suit and tie. The new girl would love it because it eliminated the ethical issue of using embryonic cells. Unfortunately, Muscular Dystrophy didn't involve the malfunction of any particular organ so the process didn't apply. *Too bad.* What had he done with her number? He needed to ask her to hold onto Snowball for a few more days. And perhaps for another small favor.

* * ⭐ 🌍 ⭐ * *

Sarah sat at her station reading notes penned in precise block letters by the Chinese girl, May Ling. She was trying to catch up with the rest of the team, hoping to contribute something worthwhile knowing in her heart that her own research was her son's best hope. Other than a cursory "good morning" Aaron hadn't said much. His eyes were mildly bloodshot, his hair tousled and his skin pale. He appeared to be distant and unfocused. Her own body ached from lack of sleep, so it was something she could relate to.

Jen was over by the incubator chatting it up with Larry who held a powdered sugar donut in one hand and a cup of coffee in the other. Food wasn't allowed in the lab, but no one said anything. He broke out laughing, spitting white crumbs into the air, and coughed as he wiped his mouth on his sleeve. Jen and Larry stole a look at Sarah but when she glanced up, their eyes slithered away. Sarah returned to her notes, pretending not to notice.

This was going to be hard. She'd arrived early enough to prepare a stem culture but wasn't able to complete her test before the others started to arrive. She'd had to slip it into the incubator without marking it, hoping to retrieve and examine it while everyone was on their morning break, but now Jen was moving the dishes around looking for something. She didn't want her experiment getting mixed up with the others. She slid off her stool and went to stand behind Jen. "Excuse me," she said.

Jen turned glancing over her shoulder, and then resumed rearranging things.

"Excuse me, I need to get something."

"You can wait your turn," Jen said.

"But I…"

"You what?" Jen spun around, glaring at Sarah. "You think this is more important than the work the rest of us are doing?" She held up an unmarked petri dish. Sara saw it was hers. "Well hear this, honey, the only experiments that belong in this incubator are those assigned by Dr. Rose and this isn't one of them. That makes this junk. She walked to the sink, turned on the water and flooded the dish washing its contents down the drain.

"*Ohhh,*" Sarah gasped.

"Better get with the program, sister." Jen shook the petri dish off and set it on the counter.

Larry stood looking down the sink while chewing on his second powdered donut.

Sarah felt her face flush. She turned and fled the room, passing Aaron on her way out.

"What's that about?" he said, looking from Jen to Larry and back to Jen again.

"Who knows," Jen replied. "I was just explaining our protocol and she turned and ran off. Go figure."

Sarah found herself seated on a cement bench facing a fountain in the courtyard of the three towers. The day was bright with only a few clouds and the jets of water shimmered in the morning light. Jen hated her, and the big guy, Larry, went along with everything Jen said. This wasn't going to work. She should start looking for another job… Her cell phone rang. She wrestled it from her lab coat pocket but didn't recognize the number. She swallowed trying to clear the lump in her throat. "Yes," she said, her voice quivering. She sipped in a breath and let it out slowly, trying to calm her jangled nerves.

"Am I speaking to Dr. Sarah Hunter?"

Sarah nodded. "Yes."

"Good, terrific, it took me awhile to find your number."

The voice was familiar, but she couldn't place it.

"I need to talk to you about my dog, I..."

Dr. Summer? "Oh, I apologize, Sir. I've been meaning to return Snowball, it's just that..."

"No, no, it's my fault. I lost your number and, as you know, a lot has happened what with my having to look for a new job and managing my other affairs. That's why I'm calling. Seems there's a position opening up, but it's based in Europe and I have to fly over for an interview. I was wondering if I could impose on you to watch Snowball for a while longer."

Watch Snowball? Sarah's first reaction was relief. Losing the dog would break Buddy's heart. "I don't see a problem," she said. "Did you happen to read my proposal?"

"I did, and I found it interesting, but, as you know, I'm no longer in a position to help. I'd like to talk to you about it, though. Perhaps when I get back from Europe."

"So you're thinking of moving?"

"Don't know. We'll see how it goes. This is just an interview. I'll only be gone a few days. I trust taking care of Snowball won't be too much trouble. Now, there's something else I was hoping you could do for me..."

The crystal blue water in the fountain's basin lapped against the sides distorting the few dozen coins tossed in by people seeking good fortune. A little luck might help right now...no, not luck—*God*. Was she really destined to lose her father so soon? Sarah closed her eyes feeling a chill as a cloud passed in front of the sun. "Lord, I can't do this. Please help, *please*." She glanced up sensing she was no longer alone. Aaron had slipped up behind her. "Trying to eavesdrop?" she said, her tone flat as she raised her phone for him to see.

"Eavesdrop? *Really?* I just came out to see how you were doing. You left in kind of a huff."

"Then why didn't you announce yourself?"

"Oh, I don't know, maybe because I was being polite and didn't want to interrupt."

Sarah stood, folding her arms across her chest. The mist from the fountain made the cement walkway sparkle. "It was Dr. Summer," she said.

"*Oh.*" Aaron raised his chin. "What did he want?"

Sarah began strolling toward the building. Aaron fell in alongside. "He wants me to watch his dog for another week. He's taking off for Europe again. There's a job he's looking into. Do you know how I can get a list of the CellMerge Board of Directors?"

Aaron thought for a second. "Sure, I think they're listed in the annual report." He swiped his card and held the door so Sarah could enter.

"Thanks," she said. "No, he tried that. What he really needs is their phone numbers. Actually he only needs one, some guy named George Fishman."

"Who?"

"George Fishman."

"No, I mean who needs the list?"

"What? *Oh.* Dr. Summer. That's who I was talking to."

Aaron shook his head. "You're going to get yourself into trouble. What does he want with Fishman?"

"Didn't say, but I got the impression it was urgent."

"Be careful. A few days ago they hauled him off in handcuffs. You heard about that didn't you? Next thing you know, he'll show up here with a shotgun blowing people away."

Sarah looked at him, squinting. "What?"

"Hey, it happens. Some guy gets laid off and goes postal."

"Not Dr. Summer. He sounded happy, not depressed. He has another job already lined up."

Aaron gave Sarah a sideways glance. "That's what he told you. For all you know, the trip overseas is just how he plans to escape. By the time the cops figure out who did what, he'll be gone."

They walked down a hall of glass cubicles all the way back to the lab. Sarah let her hand glide along the wall's smooth surface unmindful of the researchers on the other side engaged in the process of finding some miracle cure. "You want me to work with May Ling? she asked."

Aaron paused, his expression resolute. "No, I want you to work with Jen. You two need to learn to get along."

Carl's custom tooled boots and white lab coat were as incongruous as a tutu on a horse. He was pretending to relax with his feet propped up on the desk but it wasn't easy. Being short meant constantly defending himself against bigger men who were invariably thought of as smarter or more capable simply because of their size. Wallace Summer was six foot two. Dr. Jaeger wiggled his plump derriere as if settling in. They oughta shoot that varmint. He's not gettin' his chair back, no-sir-re-Bob. He chuckled. He was a cowboy, born and bred, but that didn't mean he had to think like one. The colloquialisms were a shield he used to deflect criticism, better to be thought of as a hick from the sticks than just plain short and fat, though he had to guard against their overuse. Every now and then an eyebrow would be raised letting him know it was time to dial back the clichés. Especially in corporate circles.

He reached up to scratch an itch on the side of his goatee. Dad-blame-it, Wallace was a burr in his saddle. Aaron had stopped by and, wouldn't ya know, aside from giving a routine progress report he'd asked the craziest question. Fortunately, Carl didn't know Mr. Fishman personally so he couldn't have provided the phone number even if he'd wanted to, but Aaron should have known better than to ask. He shouldn't be talking to Dr. Summer in the first place. Imagine Wally thinking Fishman could pull some strings to get his old job back. It was time someone took the old coot out behind the barn and gave him a good whupping.

· ★ ★ 🌐 ★ ★ ·

Sarah was finding it hard to concentrate, and not just because she was being forced to work with Jen. She'd returned to find an envelope at her work station and upon seeing it was from Danny, had excused herself and gone to the ladies room to read the note in private.

> Very Funny, ha, ha, ha, big laugh. I was only trying to be nice. You're new. I thought maybe you could use a friend. If you wanted me to go away, you should have just said so. You didn't need to embarrass me in front of my peers.

Sarah removed the report and immediately saw the problem. She had taken a few of her own hairs and put them with Dr. Summer's and asked Danny to compare the two and see if there was a paternal link. He had explained that, while it wasn't his area of expertise, he knew someone who could get it done.

She stared at the report. Her own hair had a diploid number of chromosomes of forty-six with the two X chromosomes typical of females, the other strands in the sample, however, were XY male, but the chromosome count was seventy-eight. The hair was identified as *Canis lupus familiaris*—dog hair. She could just hear the laughter as Danny's colleague slapped him on the back and said, "Yes indeed, this is for sure that little girl's daddy."

The hairs were white. How was she supposed to know they weren't Dr. Summer's? And why would Dr. Summer leave a brush he used on his dog in the bathroom anyway? She dreaded having to face Danny to apologize.

Sarah removed a slide from the microscope and placed it in a tray. *Whew,* she exhaled, her cheeks puffing out with her bottom lip protruding. Her logbook was filling with copious notes detailing her attempts to identify the agent carried by mice that enabled them to regenerate damaged muscles. She wasn't sure it was the telomerase enzyme, but she was doing her best to help find out one way or the other.

Jen was working beside her, her long blond hair fixed in a ponytail with an elastic band. Her lipstick was pink and freshly applied and her eyes a deep brown accented by mascara and lash extender. The lab coat she wore hung open revealing a white cashmere sweater and forest green slacks, and her high heels seemed to snap and click every time she moved causing, in Sarah's mind, a great distraction, but that was part of the intimidation.

Beneath Sarah's smock was a blue denim skirt with a rust colored patchwork top that made her feel like a woodsy bug looking for a leaf under which to crawl. She kept her coat buttoned. They'd hardly spoken two words since Aaron assigned them to be lab partners.

May sat to Sarah's right, but aside from being cheery when approached, she wasn't much of a talker. Across the aisle Larry, who by reputation was expert in genetic recombination, was busy going over the latest lab results. Everyone knew what was expected of them and each carried out the task to which they were assigned.

The silent treatment was driving Sarah crazy. It was one thing to feel like an extra leg on a centipede, but another to be totally ignored. She was the wallflower at a party where everyone wondered who she was and why she'd been invited. Jen and May had gotten along fine without her. She was there because Aaron was trying to save her job, and while she appreciated the gesture, it was obvious she was just in the way.

The arrangement was inefficient, actually making everyone's work more difficult. Jen, on the one side, was responsible for deciding the quantity and quality of the telomerase to be used, but it was May who injected the mice for observation, and because Sarah was in the middle analyzing and logging the results, Jen had to reach over or around her to hand things to May, but that was the seating arrangement Aaron insisted upon. It was doomed to disaster.

Sarah found leaning over a microscope tedious. She sat back and yawned bringing her arms up to relieve the stiffness in her shoulders just as Jen took a carefully measured serum and, holding it gingerly between two fingers, reached behind her chair to pass it to May. Sarah's elbow hit the vial bumping the concoction out of Jen's hand, sending it splattering to the floor.

Jen glared at her. "You…you did that on purpose, you…"

"What? No, I…I'm sorry I…"

"I just spent twenty minutes working on that!" Jen's pink lips puckered so hard they turned white, her eyes, darker than before, narrowed and her cheeks flushed red. Her hands balled into fists. She extended a finger and pointed to the ground. "Clean that up!"

"No…I mean, yes, but I…" Sarah heard the voice of her old friend insecurity calling. She stood, stumbling back as though she'd been shoved. She looked to May, then to Jen and turned to find Larry watching as well. She brought her hands to her face and fled the room.

"Where're you going? Get back here and clean this up!" Jen called.

"It was accident, Jennifer. You should not be so hard on her. She is new." May grabbed a towel and began wiping the floor. It wasn't much of a mess anyway.

"Not my fault she's a nut case," Jen said, turning back to her work.

Sarah paced the perimeter of the building taking deep breaths to calm the tremor in her chest. Her legs felt like rubber. She turned her face away from the windows making sure no one saw her tears.

Clouds roiled overhead darkening the gold glass and turning it a mossy gray. The wind picked up tossing her hair. Aaron would have recognized Jen's outburst for what it was—the tantrum of a spoiled child—but he hadn't seen it. He and Dr. Jaeger had wandered off to discuss some problem of meteoric proportions and hadn't returned.

Moisture thickened the air with bursts of light pulsating in the clouds. A curtain of rain was pelting the ocean and heading inland. She couldn't stay out much longer; a downpour was on the way. Was this how it was going to be? Was she destined to remain on the defensive with Jen confronting her at every turn? How could she go back inside? What could she say to make them understand? Jen hated her. She might as well quit and get it over with. She hadn't done anything wrong. Accidents happen, so what? She needed the job but instead of defending herself, she'd turned and run, and now the whole team would be talking about the incident. She wanted to earn their respect, instead she'd become a joke. Maybe God was mad about what she'd done to Danny.

Why, Lord, why? You know I asked for strength. Why am I still so weak? She raised her eyes and felt the devil spitting in her face. Drops of water spattered the sidewalk, increasing in size and number. She had only moments to decide. She rubbed the goosebumps on her arms. Either she had to find her car and leave never to return, or eat humble pie and go back inside. *Buddy?* It didn't matter that she was the victim in all this; she had to keep her job, if not for Buddy's sake, for the thousands like him who might be saved, which meant she had to go back and apologize—*to both Jen and Danny. Lord, help me, please.* She raised her arm over her head to shield herself against the rain as she ran for the door.

Carl sat across from Mr. Landon trying to get comfortable in a wingback chair that wasn't designed for comfort. He'd asked for the meeting but Jack's growing impatience made him edgy.

Lightning broke across the sky, followed by a sonic boom loud enough to rattle the windows. Rain slammed against the wall running down the glass in a torrent that turned Jack's magnificent view of the ocean into a smear of gray.

Mr. Landon's secretary closed the door, the *thud* letting Carl know he was now locked in.

Jack dribbled his fingers on the desk and then leaned back in his cushy leather chair. "Okay, Carl, you asked to see me. What can I do for you?

Carl took a breath, held it for a moment, and then exhaled. "Well, it's like this, I was just talking to one of my researchers and it appears Dr. Summer's trying to wheedle his way back into the company." *Ouch, nix words like wheedle.*

"Oh, how so?"

"He came to me asking for George Fishman's number. Imagine asking for that. As far as I'm concerned it can only mean one thing. He wants Mr. Fishman to persuade you to take him back. He wants to be reinstated."

Mr. Landon reached for his pipe and lighter and held the flame over the bowl sucking on the stem until the tobacco caught fire. Being top dog wasn't without privilege. Smoking in the workplace was illegal, but he'd never been challenged. Coils of blue smoke rose overhead. "That's interesting but I wouldn't worry about it. George keeps an unlisted number and travels a lot. I'm rarely able to reach him myself. But I am glad you brought it to my attention. You said Dr. Summer called one of your researchers. Who was that?"

"Aaron Rose."

"Dr. Rose? That young man's name has come up several times. Any reason to question his loyalty?"

"Nope, none whatsoever."

A haze of blue smoke wafted above Jack's head. He removed the pipe from his mouth, set it in an ashtray and fanned the vapor away, glancing at his laptop. CellMerge just went down a point to twenty-seven nine. He grimaced. "That's good, but I recommend you keep an eye on him all the same. You can't be too careful."

"You-bet-cha. I mean, yes *sir*."

Jack paused, thinking for a moment. He looked at his watch, gathered the papers on his desk into a neat pile, and stood. "You'll have to excuse me. Something's come up and I have to be going. Could you have Helen bring me my coat on your way out?"

"Sure, no problem."

"Oh, and if you hear anything else, please let me know. It's probably an isolated incident but we wouldn't want to let things get out of hand."

Sixteen

For thus says the Lord that created the heavens; God himself that formed the earth and made it; He hath established it. He created it not in vain, He formed it to be inhabited: "I am the Lord; and there is none else." —Isaiah 45:18

AARON STOOD just inside the door looking for Mr. Landon. The bar was bustling with the after five crowd, but Jack wasn't among them. Clusters of men sat at tables conversing about the wavering stock market, Uncle's Sam's attack on their pocketbooks, and their hope for a change in the weather so they could get back to golf and forget about everything else.

He continued scanning the faces until he located Mr. Landon sitting alone toward the back of the room. Their eyes met. Jack nodded, lifting a hand to wave him over. He did not look happy. Aaron glanced at his watch as he found his way through the tables. He had kept the man waiting.

A sign by the door said the country club was "For Members Only." He glanced around. The place settings were polished silver with fan folded linen napkins on bleached white tablecloths. He was curious to know why Mr. Landon wanted to meet him here.

He'd mulled it over all afternoon. He wanted to believe it had something to do with a promotion, or maybe a raise. Dr. Summer's leaving might have created an opportunity for advancement but that didn't fly because Carl, or rather, Dr. Jaeger, was his boss, not Mr. Landon. Carl would have been the one to pass along such news, not the president of the company. On the other hand, Carl was a jerk. Maybe they planned to let him go and wanted Aaron to step in and run the department, but that didn't wash. He was too young and inexperienced.

It would have been better if he'd spoken to Mr. Landon personally but the call had come from Jack's secretary who merely said Mr. Landon wanted to meet with him at five-thirty. It was now a quarter to six. Aaron sat down, his nerves popping like a hot wire.

"Sorry I'm late." He scooted his chair up to the table. He was a scientist, not a business manager, but he'd gone home to put on his Armani suit, wanting to look executive just in case. Now he was tardy. At least it made him feel more like he belonged. Mr. Landon was a sharp dresser, and this was a private club.

Ever the executive, Jack wore a virgin wool charcoal gray suit with a shiny blue pocket puff that complimented his blue silk tie. His hair was swept back and fixed in place with hairspray to give it a dry look with just enough gray around the temples to suggest maturity without looking old.

Jack made a deliberate show of turning his wrist to check the time.

A Concord Delirium, Aaron noted, a five thousand dollar watch, but only half what his own Rolex cost. He tugged at his sleeve. It wouldn't do to upstage the boss.

"I don't like to be kept waiting," Jack said, "but let's not dwell on it. Apology accepted. Now you have some catching up to do. I already ordered a cocktail, what can I get you?"

Aaron cringed. His hangover from the cowboy bar still roiled beneath the surface. "I think I'll just have water."

"Nonsense." Jack's hand went up with a flick of his wrist summoning a waiter to the table. "Bring my guest a gin and tonic," he said. Then settling back in his chair he eyed Aaron contemplatively. "Thanks for coming on such short notice. There's something I need to talk to you about."

Here it comes. "Oh, what's that?"

"I understand you're still in touch with Dr. Summer, is that correct?"

Aaron's smile faded, his face taking on a pensive look designed to mask his disappointment. "Not really. I haven't seen him since he left the company. Why?"

"No need to be defensive. Dr. Jaeger mentioned you were asking for George Fishman's number, that's all. He said Wallace put you up to it. You're not in any trouble. You can't help it if he calls you. Were you able to get the number for him?"

"No, and I haven't spoken to him since, nor do I plan to."

The waiter approached and placed a cocktail in front of Aaron who immediately took a sip.

"Good. Let's keep it that way. Did he happen to say what he wanted to talk to Mr. Fishman about?"

Aaron paused holding his glass in the air. He didn't dare tell Mr. Landon it was Sarah, not he, who spoke with Dr. Summer. Sarah's employment was tenuous enough already. He took another sip, grimaced, smacked his lips and set the glass down with eyes watering. He cleared his throat—*ahem.* "No, but Dr. Jaeger seems to think it has something to do with Dr. Summer wanting his job back. What really happened? The memo said it was his decision to leave but that doesn't mesh with his trying to get back in."

Jack frowned but nodded. "Wallace wasn't a team player. He emptied his glass and raised it to flag the waiter. "We'll have another round," he said without asking Aaron. Nor did Aaron think it wise to object, even though there was still plenty of gin in his glass.

"When it comes to theorizing new ideas Wallace is one of the best. He has an uncanny ability to think outside the box. But business isn't always about who has the best ideas. It would be great if we could be altruistic and find cures for every disease but unfortunately it takes money to pay the salaries of good scientists like yourself. As it is, we can only afford to find cures for diseases suffered by a good percent of the population. It's the only way we can guarantee our shareholders a payback on their investment."

The server brought two fresh drinks and placed them in front of Aaron and Jack. He turned to go and Jack resumed again.

"Business is a two-sided coin. On one side you need to create the right product, one people have a need for and want to buy, but on the other you need to raise the capital to pay for research and development until the product's ready for market. And to do that, you have to kowtow to investors." Jack raised his tonic, "Here's to doing what you have to, to keep the company afloat, even if it means reining in the efforts of someone you greatly admire." He paused waiting for Aaron to lift his glass.

Aaron did what was expected. He wasn't about to offend the president, and it seemed the president didn't want to drink alone. He smacked his lips and set his glass down. "You're referring to that paper Dr. Summer wrote."

Mr. Landon's lips drew taut, his expression flat. "In part, yes. But there were other things. Wallace never could understand that a corporation doesn't run on goodwill. If he had, he'd probably still be with us. He was a good man." He raised his glass again. "Here, join me in a toast to one of the finest research scientists to ever walk the planet. Here's to Wallace Summer."

Aaron's stomach felt queasy but he raised his glass. "To Wallace," he said and took another sip. "You'll have to excuse me. I need to use the bathroom." Aaron slid his chair back and stood, looking around.

"That way," Jack pointed.

His feet were unsteady as he found his way down the hall. The walls were too narrow, the ceiling too low. He reached out and caught the doorframe for balance. That was it. No more for him.

He took a deep breath determined to walk straight. He could hold his liquor. It just took willpower. He wasn't about to become a blathering idiot in front of the president.

The light in the men's room was glaring. He squinted, leaning in to wash his hands and slap cold water on his face. Water pooled on the sink and splashed onto the floor making a mess. A dark skinned man in a starched white jacket appeared out of nowhere to hand him a towel. He dabbed his face, squared his shoulders and reached for his wallet, placing a dollar tip in the attendant's tray.

By the time he got back to the table, Jack had bought another round. "I think I've had enough," he said sliding heavily into his chair.

"Just one more for the road," Jack replied. "You know, poor old Wallace's leaving hurt me as much as it did anyone. Maybe we weren't close, but I still consider him a friend. Here's another toast to Wallace," he said raising his glass.

And once again Aaron had to join in.

"Let me cut to the chase. Wallace is one of the best, a good friend and colleague but after we let him go he somehow got it into his head that I'm out to destroy him. I hate to say it, but I suspect he's suffering from early stages of dementia, a bit paranoid if you know what I mean. But one thing's certain, he's hurt. He thinks I betrayed him. I assure you, I did no such thing. Letting him go wasn't my idea. It was a board decision. Hey, don't let that sit there. Bottom's up." He waited for Aaron to take another drink.

Aaron hadn't eaten all day. Three drinks of gin on an empty stomach were taking their toll, but he sat up straight and did what he was told.

"As I was saying, Dr. Summer's termination was a board decision. He was refusing to comply with their demands so he had to be let go. I personally had little to do with it, you understand?"

Aaron's head felt like it was wrapped in a wet towel, like Jack's words were soft and far away. He sipped in a long, slow breath. His going home to change would be for nothing if he got up and fell flat on his face. Was his smile on straight? Last thing he needed was to look like a fool with a silly grin.

"He seems determined to lash out and hurt back," Jack continued, "so here's what I want you to do. The next time he calls or contacts you in any way, I want you to report back to me on everything he says. No matter how meaningless or insignificant. You think you can do that? I want to know you're a team player."

"Shuur, I can do that."

"Good. That's what I wanted to hear. I'm glad we had this conversation. I've been hearing good things about you. Last thing I want is for anything to come between you and your work. Oh, by the way, Wallace may try to bring a suit against us for wrongful dismissal. He'll lose, of course. His actions were hurting the corporation so I'm sure our decision will be upheld if it ever goes to court but in the meantime I don't want our staff feeling sorry for him or trying to come to his aid. You mind your own Ps and Qs and leave Dr. Summer to us." Mr. Landon reached into his vest pocket and removed his wallet, placing two twenties on the table. "Now, I don't mean to be abrupt, but we started later than I planned and I'm meeting someone for dinner so I'm afraid I have to excuse myself. Finish your drink, and I'll walk you to your car."

Aaron stood. His body felt numb and heavy. He let go of the table and tripped forward.

Jack caught his arm and held him up. "Whoa there. Maybe I should call you a cab."

Aaron straightened himself and stuck out his chest. "No sir, I'm fine," he said, but by the time they made it to the door he wasn't so sure. For once he welcomed the cold blast of air that hit his face.

· ★ ★ ✪ ★ ★ ·

Friday night and Sarah was home alone—*again*. Well, not totally alone, she had Buddy, but sometimes she longed for adult companionship, someone with whom she could carry on a conversation. Buddy, at best, could only struggle to say a few words and tonight she needed someone to talk to. Buddy's doctor had called her at work. The latest round of tests showed acute muscular degeneration. He needed to be placed in a hospice where he could be attended to twenty-four hours a day. The prognosis was that Buddy probably had less than a week to live.

Following the petri dish fiasco Sarah had gone back inside to face Jen, vowing to apologize and maintain her composure. Jen crossed her arms looking down on her and said: "I wouldn't ask a gay man to apologize for being gay, I suppose I shouldn't ask you to apologize for being clumsy. It's who you are." And with that she'd turned back to her work leaving Sarah to feel like a wad of gum stuck to the bottom of a shoe. They'd avoided speaking to each other the rest of the day.

Sarah remained stoic and in an effort to avoid further humiliation, decided to deal with Danny later. She'd made it to five and was slipping into her coat when she received the call from Buddy's neurologist, adding pain to an already injurious day. If clouds had silver linings, then this one was that the call came as she was getting ready to leave. Any sooner and she would have burst out crying causing her coworkers, who knew nothing of her terminally ill son, to think she was an emotional basket case. As it was, with her coat already on and backpack in hand, she was able to retreat out the door before anyone saw the floodgates open. The storm thundered as she ran to her car hiding the tears that poured from her eyes like rain.

They sat on the sofa together, the light from the television casting an eerie glow on the dark room. Buddy had his head in his mother's lap with his emancipated body stretched out on the cushions. His arms cuddled the little wad of cotton known as Snowball. A recorded version of *The Lion, the Witch and the Wardrobe* blared from the TV. "My Jesus is a Lion," Buddy murmured, but Sarah's mind was somewhere else. She combed her son's hair with her fingers. A tear, one she made sure Buddy didn't see, rolled softly down her cheek. It was times like these she wished she had a husband to share her pain.

Perhaps accepting a ride from a complete stranger wasn't the best idea but what choice did she have? Other students hitchhiked, and he was going her way. He'd already changed a flat tire and bought her lunch without asking anything in return.

Now as the truck rumbled through the endless miles of desert she found herself feeling relaxed, with the vibration of the road loosening her tension and the warm air channeling in through the open window. The sun had begun to dip behind the western hills drawing long shadows on the desert floor. Her skin felt numb where the air beat against her arm. She felt the truck slowing and the tires jarring across bumps as Brian pulled off the highway.

"Why are we stopping?" The rolling landscape of late evening was dotted with cactus that glowed yellow in the setting sun.

Brian steered the truck away from the road. "We need to rest," he said. "There isn't another town for fifty miles and frankly, I can't see the sense in paying good money for a room when we've got the great outdoors and it's free."

"But it's still light."

"That's the point. It's hard to set up camp after dark."

"But..."

"Don't get nervous. I plan to sleep on the ground. You can stay in the back of the truck."

Sarah rubbed the goosebumps on her arms. "You plan to sleep in the dirt?"

"I've done it before. Anyway, I've got a foam mattress and some blankets behind the seat. Once we get away from the road I'll build a fire and make you a bed. Nights haven't been too cold lately. You should do fine."

"What about you?"

"I'll have the fire."

Brian guided the truck around the side of a knoll. He climbed out letting the door slam, the metallic sound echoing against the low lying hills. *"We need to get firewood before it gets dark,"* he said, leaning into the window.

Sarah hopped down, pulled her light jacket from the cab and began scouring the hillside, gathering weathered branches. The scant few trees were old and gnarled. It took more than an hour to find enough wood to keep the fire burning all night.

Brian made a pile of dry grass and twigs. He struck a match and inserted the flame. It was smoky at first but as the fire began to catch he blew on it gently all the while adding more and more twigs and then a few sticks and finally, as the fire took hold, larger and larger pieces of wood.

The evening settled into a deep purple dusk. Brian went to the truck and removed the mattress, rolling it out in the truck's bed along with a few blankets. He slipped out of his jacket and folded it so Sarah could use it as a pillow.

"Won't you freeze?" she objected, but he insisted, saying he rarely got cold and with the fire he'd do just fine.

Reaching behind the seat once again, he came up with a can of chili and a small aluminum pot. *"Dinner,"* he said with a smile that made her complaint dissolve in her mouth. Somehow the meager offering seemed appetizing and right.

Brian sat on his haunches with the pot perched on two stones over the open flame stirring with a spoon until the sauce bubbled. He brought a bite to his mouth and tested it. *"Ouch, hot enough."* He stood again. *"Don't know about you, but I'd like to eat on the crest of that hill."* He pointed with the spoon. *"A motel might give you a TV, but here we have live theater."*

Sarah smiled. Such a great attitude. Nothing seemed to faze him. Have a flat tire, change it. Your car won't drive, hitch a ride. Can't afford a hotel, sleep under the stars. Brian seemed comfortable with *himself and that made her comfortable with him. She fell in alongside as they made their way to the top of the ridge. A rock with a reasonably flat surface provided the perfect seat. They sat rubbing shoulders as they shared the one spoon Brian owned and ate from the pot.*

The evening sky transformed into a stage with an orchestra of crickets, a hooting owl, and the far distant song of a coyote. Sarah tried to take it all in but there were too many constellations to see, too much music to hear. She felt like she was standing at the threshold of heaven. A shooting star burst across the sky leaving a trail of light so bright and beautiful it seemed like the visitation of an angel. Sarah put her hand on Brian's and squeezed. It was a moment she knew would never be repeated and one she would never forget.

"Mom, do you…think…Jesus will carry me around on His back?"

Sarah snapped out of her reverie, her fingers subconsciously twirling a lock of Buddy's hair. On the TV, Lucy was stroking Aslan's mane. "Of course, Buddy, but He won't have to. You won't be sick anymore."

Buddy tried to twist around, rolling his eyes up to see his mother. "I…hope He comes soon."

It was just what Lucy said about Aslan. Sarah swallowed the lump in her throat. "Don't be in too big a hurry, little man, I still need you here with me."

Dr. Wallace Summer closed the file and taped a note to the outside. The note read: "For Dr. Sarah Hunter." Pulling the data together had been cathartic, reaffirming that his decision had been right. The question was what to do with it now. Somehow, he felt Sarah would know.

The clock on the mantle chimed eleven times. He had to be going. Funny how a man's life could turn around so quickly. One day he was out of work with no friends and little reason to get out of bed, and the next there's a new job on the horizon, new friends in the making, and something worth waking up for.

Using his cane for support, he pushed himself up and began to hum, *Jesus loves me this I know, for the Bible tells me so…* He owed Dr. Lamar on so many levels, but especially for reminding him that it wasn't just about God—but also about Christ. Like the man said, you can't expect to know God any more than a snail can expect to understand man. Such a mystery, that God—so omnipotent He could create the vastness of the universe from particles as small as atoms—would make tiny little men and then give them the power to reason knowing they'd rebel and reject Him, and still love them enough to become one of them and be nailed to a cross to die in their place just so those who responded to His love could ask His forgiveness and have His death compensate for their mistakes. *Hallelujah!* Believe and receive. He opened the door and was greeted by a blast of cold moist air. He turned and went back for his coat.

The warmth of the thick wool jacket enveloped him as he tugged it up over his shoulders. He felt like a new man. He was ready. His car was on the other side of the street. Force of habit. He didn't like backing out of the driveway. Too many blind spots. Fog rose up from the ground looking blue gray under the glow of the streetlamp. He could smell the salt of the ocean and feel its briny spray.

He looked both ways and stepped into the road. About a half block down a car pulled away from the curb, just a black shadow he heard more than saw. It took a few seconds to realize it was bearing down on him. Suddenly the lights came on. He raised his hands to cover his eyes and froze.

Wham! Ooofff, flop, flop, flop. He lay on his back feeling nothing as a shroud of fog enveloped him, his body growing cold. A starless abyss swirled above, a giant black hole sucking him in and growing darker and darker until finally he caught a burst of white and found himself staring—*into the face of God.*

Death is but a Stop along the Journey
The Journal of W.L. Summer

If we submit that evolution accounts for life, what evolutionary process accounts for death? Particularly when we know our bodies are designed to forestall death as long as possible. For example, our immune system uses antibodies to identify bacteria and fight infection. When we cut ourselves, our blood coagulates allowing the body to heal. And there are millions of proteins produced every second that replace old dead cells with new ones, to name a few. So why hasn't evolution been able to eliminate death completely?

Every form of life: invertebrate, amphibian, bird, fish, reptile, mammal—even plants, billions of life forms and every one eventually self-destructs. Not one has been able to evolve a mechanism for staying alive. It's clearly in the best interest of every organism not to die. If life evolved through natural process, why haven't these same natural processes abolished death—at least in something?

This is problematic for the atheist because if death is all we have to look forward to, life has little meaning. One can rule nations, obtain great wealth, contribute to art and science, but death takes it all away, and then—*nothing*. A colleague of mine once said it would be enough just to have people remember him for the good he'd done. "Why," I asked, "once you're gone you have no cognition. Your brain will be dust so you won't know if they remember you or not. What's the point?"

I prefer the Biblical answer. Death entered the world through man's sin, and death will remain until the end of time. Neither natural process or science will ever overcome it. But death is not something to fear, not for the believer. For the believer death just opens a door to a better life, one that never ends, and to a reward for the things done while on earth.

Seventeen

Lift up your eyes on high and behold who hath created the stars and brings out their host by number. He calls them all by name...
—Isaiah 40:26

MORNING BROKE through the window like a quiet thief robbing Aaron of sleep. He groaned and rolled onto his side pulling the sheets up to shield his eyes from the intruding light but it was no use; a bell was clanging in his head. Tossing the covers off he drug his feet around and sat rubbing his temples. He tried to stand but wavered and quickly sat back down, then tried once more, this time successfully keeping his balance, though still a bit wobbly.

He swallowed. His tongue felt like sandpaper. "I will never do that again. *Never!" Aughhh.* He stumbled into the bathroom and began fumbling through the medicine cabinet to find the aspirin. His head *thump, thump, thumped like a drum.* Even the plastic bottles were irritating, the way they clicked clacked and bounced around. "Come on, where are you, come to Papa. Aw, gotcha." He slammed the cabinet door and flinched, thinking for a second he'd broken the mirror. *Auggggh.* Two weren't going to be enough. He'd have to take three.

He popped the cap off the bottle and poured the extra strength pills into his hand. *I don't know how you do it Mom.* Never a sober minute. The chances of her fifth marriage lasting were slim to none, but at least she'd married well. Each one had left her better off than before. *Down the hatch.* He tilted his head back, felt a surge of throbbing, tossed the pills into his mouth and leaned in to drink from the tap.

"*Ooo-whee!*" he said, slapping water on his cheeks. The basin felt cool as he gripped its sides looking into the mirror. A sallow face with stubble beard and bloodshot eyes stared back. Water dripped from his chin. He reached for a towel. His father never touched the stuff. He should strive to be more like him—*or not.* His dad's vice had been greed, an enemy much more formidable than alcohol. He'd left for work one day and had come home in a box leaving his mother to find solace in a bottle. He stumbled to the kitchen. He needed coffee.

What's with Landon anyway? There wasn't a thing they'd talked about that couldn't have been said at work. At least as far as he could remember. The details were fuzzy. What *did* they talk about? *Oh yeah.* Landon wanted him to rat out old Q. That wasn't a problem. Old Q wasn't talking to him anyway. Sarah was the one guilty of collaboration. She needed to be more careful.

Sarah was at her bench continuing the research she'd begun before the reassignment. She pulled back from the microscope. "Hey Buddy, look at this. I think the kidney is accepting the new cell as one of its own. If I can replace all the damaged cells this way, it might serve to repair the kidney. What do you think?" She leaned over and tousled her son's hair. "We're getting there, Buddy, we're getting there."

Buddy didn't respond. He lay with his head to the side, drooling onto his pillow. Every day he seemed weaker than the day before. *Please, Lord, don't let him give up.*

Sarah tugged back the sleeve of her lab coat and looked at her watch. Already four o'clock. She'd come in early and hoped to stay late, and since it was Saturday, she had Buddy with her. She would be in tomorrow, too, right after church. That was a given. The new arrangement meant weekends were the only time she had for testing her theory, at least for now. As soon as she could demonstrate her hypothesis had promise, she would go to Dr. Jaeger. Once he saw she had a real prospect for a cure, he'd have to let her continue.

Buddy stretched and squirmed, trying to get comfortable. She watched him struggle, his muscles too weak to lift his own weight. She wanted to help but he'd just push her away. Even in his weakened state he wanted the satisfaction of feeling self-reliant. She put her eye back to the microscope. "This is really showing promise, Buddy. I think we've got something here."

On the other side of the wall, at the end of the long corridor that led outside, a metal door closed with a *bang*. Sarah didn't look up. There were other people in the lab. It was just someone leaving for the day.

The sound echoed in Aaron's head. His brain was too fragile to handle loud noise and the lights were too bright, glaring at him with obscene intensity. He tried squinting as he sauntered up the hall dragging his feet, his malaise the result of spending two nights in a fog. Sarah's van was in the parking lot. He wasn't sure what he should say.

Earlier he'd thought about taking the Rover Moon out on the Bay but he'd stopped at Denny's for breakfast and while waiting found the smell of bacon grease frying in the pan making him nauseous. His stomach wasn't seaworthy yet. He'd settled for toast and coffee.

The light in the main lab was even brighter. He squinted, letting his eyes adjust. Sarah loomed closer with each step. He approached the edge of her station trying to ignore the throbbing of his temples. She appeared fuzzy, standing over by the counter with her eye glued to a microscope, her auburn hair a subtle flame. She didn't acknowledge his approach but Buddy did. "Hey, Aaronrrr…" he said, the air wheezing from his lungs, his body writhing as he reached out to take Aaron's hand.

Sarah turned. In spite of her misgivings, her son's excitement was a good thing. He still had a spark of life. Aaron had a positive effect on Buddy.

"So what brings you here?" she said.

"Just in the neighborhood. Thought I'd stop and pick up some work to take home. You?"

Sarah tilted her head toward the microscope. "It's the only time I have to work on a cure for Buddy. My new boss has me doing redundant tasks just to keep me busy."

"Sarah…"

"But don't think I don't appreciate it. I do. It's just that I'm very close to proving my theory and I hate to waste time where I'm not really needed."

Aaron leaned against the cubicle in his tan Dockers and Nike Air Force One sneakers. His casual looking sweatshirt was Champs, but he looked anything but relaxed. He ran his fingers through his hair, his eyes tinged with red. "Look, I'm sorry. I did what I had to do. So, how's your thing going?" he said nodding toward the culture Sarah had been examining.

"My '*thing*' as you call it, is doing just fine."

"Any rejections?"

"No."

"Any tumors?"

"No, none."

"Great." Aaron walked over and looked into the microscope for a second and then backed away. "I can see why Q let you run with this. You may be onto something."

"This from the brilliant microbiologist, Dr. Aaron Rose."

Aaron's stomach sloshed with too much coffee and his head still felt like it was wrapped in a rubber band making it hard to respond.

He wished he could turn down the lights. "Okay, I guess I deserve that. How late will you be working?"

"I was hoping to stay a little longer but Buddy looks tired and we haven't eaten so we'll probably have to leave earlier than planned. I want him to keep up his strength."

Aaron nodded and then smiled. "Hey, I know, how 'bout you let me take you and Buddy out for dinner. I know a great place..."

"I thought you came to get some work done."

"I did, I mean, I will, but like you said, you have to eat and," he glanced at his watch, "look at the time. I haven't eaten either."

Buddy's chest rose. He was pushing himself up as though trying to climb out of his chair. "Mom, pleeeeeeese."

"Just a second Buddy. Aaron, I appreciate the offer, maybe some other time, but we really should be going. My son needs his rest, and, well, frankly any free time I have I want to spend on getting him well..."

"M—om!"

Sarah jerked her head around. Buddy *never* raised his voice. He was breathing hard.

"Buddy?"

He tried to catch his breath. "I'm not...*uh huh*...going to live...*uh huh*...stop pretending."

"Buddy, no..."

"I'm...not afraid....*uh huh*...I'll....*uh huh*...I'll be with Jesus... you know..." His voice was raspy, barely above a whisper, his chest rising and falling. "Can't I have....*uh huh*...a...a little...*uh huh*...fun?"

Aaron smiled. *Way to go, Buddy*. "You heard the man," he said. He took hold of Buddy's wheelchair and for once, Sarah, seeing she was outnumbered, didn't argue.

"Not so fast. I still have to clean up and put things away." She turned and took the petri dish back to the incubator. "We like to eat healthy, and sometimes Buddy has trouble chewing so no burgers. You might as well relax. I can't leave until I log the results of today's tests."

When Aaron said he knew a great place, he wasn't thinking Chinese. That idea came to him when he realized Sarah wanted food Buddy could easily ingest—and what could be easier than noodles? His own stomach agreed.

The Grant Street entrance to Chinatown was further from the restaurant than necessary, but Aaron went that way because it gave them access to the tourist area. The narrow backwater streets where men sat in murky, smoke filled, opium dens playing dice while their women haggled over the price of bok choy, were for locals. He wanted to keep the evening light and entertaining, and Sarah might not appreciate Chinatown's seamy side.

Buddy's eyes lit up at the sight of the huge dragon that guarded the street's entrance. He reached out to touch it but his arm fell limp.

Aaron rolled his wheelchair right up alongside the mastiff statue. "Boy, that's one big dog, isn't it? And how do you like them teeth?" Aaron curled his fingers, pulling his hands up to his shoulders like paws. He made a Cheshire cat grin. "*Gurrrrrrrrrrrrr.*"

Buddy giggled as Aaron punched at him playfully. "*Gurrr, gurrrr, gurrrr.*"

Sarah was mesmerized by the sights. Signs hanging from brightly colored banners were ornamented with Chinese calligraphy, the lampposts were festooned with dragons, and strings of red, green, and yellow paper lanterns were strung across the road flickering in the blue twilight.

"Have you and Buddy been to Chinatown before?" Aaron asked.

"No. I've wanted to come, but we haven't had time and frankly it's hard pushing Buddy's wheelchair through the crowds, like swimming upstream against a school of fish heading the opposite direction." Sarah began to hum and then put words to the music but caught herself and stopped abruptly.

"What?" Aaron said.

"I forgot, you don't like singing."

Aaron shrugged. "Maybe I never had a reason to."

"Why do you need a reason?"

Something caught Sarah's eye. She grabbed Buddy's wheelchair and turned it into the nearest shop pulling Aaron along behind. Next thing he knew he was staring at everything from plastic Buddhas to white herons of sculpted ivory. The store, like others that lined the street, was a mishmash of bedspreads, tea sets, candles, silk robes and kites.

"Why'd you stop?" he said, picking up a Chinese puzzle box to search for the secret opening.

"I just wanted to take a look," Sarah replied, but her eyes were staring out the window. Aaron followed her gaze. She appeared to be watching a blue pickup as it lumbered down the crowded lane.

From the height of the mountain the sixty foot tall effigies of George Washington, Thomas Jefferson, Theodore Roosevelt, and Abraham Lincoln overlooked the Black Hills of South Dakota. Carved out of solid granite they stood shining in the sun like giant silver coins on a blue velvet sky.

Sarah stood beside Brian with her arm locked in his and her head resting on his shoulder. The sun on his shirt warmed her cheek, a feeling equal to the burning in her heart. Love wasn't supposed to happen so fast.

"Can you imagine one man carving all that," She said.

"One man didn't," Brian replied. "Says right here that…" he held up the brochure and read. '…Gutzon Borglum was commissioned to design the sculpture but it took a crew of more than four hundred to bring it to life.'"

"Still a marvelous achievement."

"That's why I wanted to see it, especially since it just happened to be on the way."

Sarah sighed. School started Monday, the second semester of her freshmen year, and there was much preparation to be done but now with Brookings and SDSU only a few hours away, she wasn't so sure she wanted to be home. Her arrival would signal the beginning of the end. Brian would be leaving for his tour of duty and she would remain and go to school. They might not see each other for several years.

"When do you have to report to the base?"

Brian raised his watch. "In four days, eleven hours and twenty-three minutes but who's counting."

"Here's your hat, what's your hurry?" Sarah let go of his arm and pushed him teasingly. "Come on, I know you're touring and all that but I was thinking, if you've got four whole days you might want to spend some of that time with me."

Brian had gone off to war never knowing he'd fathered a child. She'd been left to raise Buddy alone. It hadn't been easy, especially learning that her son, *Brian's son*, had a defect that would eventually take his life, but she'd refused to quit. She'd stayed in South Dakota another twelve years earning her undergraduate, her master's, and a PhD all the while hoping Brian would return. But he never did.

The truck disappeared beyond the traffic. Sarah turned around to face Aaron. "We can go if you like. I don't really need anything."

Buddy had his eyes on a kite. He was trying to point but he didn't have the strength. "Yes, I see it Buddy, but you can't fly a kite."

"Aaronrr...can!"

Sarah's eyes glanced at Aaron. "That's not fair..."

"That'd be great. I haven't flown a kite in years." Aaron reached up to take a bright red kite from the rack and winked at Buddy. "And I'm going to buy it myself so your mom can't say no. Hey, how about this? I'll bet your Mom plans to do research tomorrow. What say you and I go to Golden Gate Park and fly this baby ourselves? That way she'll have more time to work uninterrupted." He shot Sarah a glance looking for her approval, but she shook her head.

"Buddy and I are going to church tomorrow. You're welcome to come along."

"Yeah, but after that?"

Sarah crossed her arms, her lips forming a pout. Then she said: "If you're willing to meet us at church, I'll let you take Buddy kite flying, weather permitting, but not for more than an hour. I don't want Buddy getting tired. We're meeting with his doctor Monday to make some decisions about what's best for his health."

Buddy began slowly rolling his head side to side with a groan.

Sarah reached over and teased his hair. "I know, hon, I know. We'll see what we can do." Her eyes went to Aaron. "He doesn't want to stay in a hospice but the doctor feels its best."

Aaron nodded and turned to the counter to pay for the kite. They'd had enough distraction; they had to get to the Empress of China. His mouth watered with the thought of Sizzling Rice Soup and Dungeness Crab. He glanced at Buddy but the boy looked asleep.

"Wait till Buddy's sees what they have for dessert at this place."

"Dessert?"

"Yeah, Buddy's going to love it. Ice cream with lychee and *dragon eye*." He bent down over the wheelchair with his fingers spreading his eyes wide pretending to be a dragon, but Buddy didn't respond.

Sarah looked at her son, her eyes creased with concern. "Maybe we should skip dinner," she said. "Buddy's exhausted."

Aaron's mouth puckered, then he let out a sigh. He'd planned to take them to the Empress because it was his mother's favorite restaurant, and she had impeccable taste. *Let the Empress impress them*, she liked to say, but it wasn't to be. He knew the drill. Buddy was weak and Buddy had to come first. At least they had a kite to fly tomorrow.

It was completely dark by the time they made it back to Sarah's van. The hustle and bustle of Chinatown could be heard in the distance, but the sound was muted by the traffic in the street. Horns honked and tires whooshed and brakes screeched. Window lights were still on but the art stores along the boulevard were closed. Pedestrians in overcoats stopped to view the paintings of local artists through the glass, and then moved on.

Buddy's chest rose and fell with labored breath as he struggled to take in air. Aaron helped Sarah load the wheelchair and get Buddy settled. "You don't live far from here," he said, closing the door. "No point in your going all the way back to the lab for me. Just take Buddy home."

"How will you get back?"

"I'll catch a cab."

"Would you? I mean I can take you if you want, but that would be a big help."

"No problem. Buddy needs his rest. We have a big day tomorrow."

Sarah hesitated and Aaron sensed by her silence that she might be reconsidering. She reached into her purse and came up with a card, handing it to him. It had one of those fish logos and an address. "We'll see you at church," she said. Then she climbed into the driver's seat and pulled away leaving him standing by the side of the road with a residual hangover that made him feel both physically and emotionally drained.

Eighteen

As you do not know the way of the spirit, or how the bones grow in the womb of her who is with child: even so you do not know the works of God who made everything. —Ecclesiastes 11:5

THE CAB pulled around to the front of the building. Lights were on inside, a few in areas serviced by the cleaning staff, others in rooms occupied by those still working. The glass wall was a gold and black checkerboard shining in the night.

The valets didn't work weekends so Aaron had parked his car out front in one of the spaces reserved for visitors. The cab made a sweeping turn to pull up alongside, catching the Beemer in its lights as it rolled by.

What the? Aaron's brows furrowed. Someone had plowed into his car creasing the front bumper. *No way!*

"Metea say you owe floaty-flee dalla. Pay prease."

It looked like the grill was damaged too. His car was ruined. He cringed but reached for his wallet, slipped out his credit card and handed it to the man. He grabbed his kite and climbed out. The driver handed his card along with a receipt through the window. He signed and handed it back and the cab pulled away.

Aaron turned to examine his car. The damage was minimal, at least not as bad as he first thought, but an ugly dent nonetheless. How could someone have missed seeing a big shiny Beemer in an empty lot? He checked, hoping to find a note under the wiper. *Nothing.* He glanced up at the lamppost. Good thing they had security cameras. He'd find whoever did this.

Sarah had been able to get Buddy into the apartment without waking him, which was unusual, but to have been able to change his clothes and get him into bed without disturbing him was truly remarkable. Even Snowball, who had met them at the door jumping and pawing and whining to be let out, hadn't caused him to stir. She let the dog have a few minutes outside.

She hadn't said anything to Aaron—*why voice concern to someone who can't do anything?*—but Buddy had grown terribly weak, especially over the past few days. *God, please give me time to find a cure.*

Sarah stood in front of the mirror. The collar of her wrinkled polyester shirt flipped up at an angle. Maybe she should try getting some new clothes. She had an aversion to paying for trendy labels, but that didn't mean she couldn't find inexpensive clothes that at least matched. Who was she kidding? She began removing her makeup. The yellow light in the bathroom usually minimized her flaws, but not tonight. What she saw was the reality she lived with. She was plain. Her eyes were green and her skin pasty white. She reached for a lock of hair and held it up, hair that was stringy and mousy red and growing longer by the day. No fancy wardrobe was going to change that. Buddy was the only man she could trust with her heart. *Please God, don't take him away.*

Sarah went back into the living room, trading her clothes for a flannel nightgown. Buddy wasn't known for sleeping soundly, but he hadn't moved. Snowball was nuzzled against his side. It appeared they were both sound asleep *but*…she panicked, placing an ear to Buddy's chest. *Tha—thump…tha—thump…tha-—thump.* His heart was still pumping, but his breathing was labored and slow. *Please don't take him, Lord.*

She crawled into bed and pulled the covers up around her neck. Her head buzzed with worrisome things. She had to remember to get diapers for Buddy. Was there enough milk? And dog food, she had to pick up some dog food. Her budget didn't include feeding a dog—she slid a hand up under her pillow and closed her eyes.

"*Kufff, kuff, uh-huh, uh-huh…Maaa— Kufff, kuff!*"

Sarah's eyes popped open.

"I… *uh-huh, uh-huh*…I…caaaan't breath."

The covers went flying as she leapt across the mattress and began groping for her son in the dark. "What is it Buddy? Are you okay?"

"I…"

Instinctively, she placed a hand on his forehead feeling for a fever. He felt warm, but not more than usual. "What's wrong, baby? What's wrong?"

She could barely make out his features, but what she saw gave cause for alarm. His eyes were wide and his mouth was agape and he seemed to be choking. He looked like he was straining to take in air. *Oh, no! No, no, no, no, no!*

Respiratory failure was the final stage of Muscular Dystrophy. Even in the dim light she could see her son was turning blue. *No, Buddy, stay with me.*

"Mom…I can't…"

"Shush, Buddy, don't try to talk."

"Don't cry. I'm gonna…beee…be with Jesus." His voice rasped. Words came like air squeezed through the pinched neck of a balloon. "Prom…promise…me…"

"What, darling, what?"

"Marry…Aaron…shhhhhhhhh."

Sarah felt the breath wheeze from her son's body and not return. She looked for her phone and realized it was on the table next to her purse. She lay Buddy's head down and ran to get it, regretting having to leave her son's side even for a second. She flipped it open and dialed 911, racing back to be with Buddy.

"Dispatch. Please state the nature of your emergency."

"Myson ischoking; he's turningblue andcan'tbreathe!" She screamed.

"Maam, please, try to stay calm. Take a breath and repeat what you said slowly and clearly."

"My son can't breathe. He's…he's choking to death!"

"Are you able to perform a Heimlich maneuver? If not, I can walk you through…"

"No, no, no, it's not that! He's got Muscular Dystrophy. His lungs are too weak to breathe. I need help! Fast! Please!"

"I'm dispatching an ambulance. Give me your address."

Late night party goers returning home began to assemble in the street, curious about the commotion. They'd heard the sirens and saw the lights flashing. The street was painted in stroboscopic bands of red. The ambulance had raced to the apartment and screeched to a stop. The medical technicians flung themselves from the van and ran into the apartment with a stretcher. The crowd stood outside, their numbers growing, rubber necking to see if this was another case of spousal abuse, a drug overdose, or maybe even—*murder.*

But inside the building all was still. The paramedics stood silently, reverenced by what they saw. A mother seated amidst a swirl of blankets on an open convertible sofa held her child to her bosom, rocking back and forth with tears flooding her cheeks. She was singing, softly. So soft it was hard to make out the words.

> *"We shall rise, hallelujah, we shall rise,*
> *We shall rise, hallelujah, we shall rise,*
> *When the trumpet sounds and He calls us home,*
> *We shall rise…"*

Still Just a Penny for Your Thoughts
The Journal of W.L. Summer

Infinitely more complex than our most advanced super computers, the human brain is made up of more than 100 billion nerve cells, or neurons, that communicate over trillions of connections called synapses. The information to organize and build the brain originally came from instructions coded in the DNA, but there's nothing in our DNA that accounts for human thought. A computer program may carry out the functions inherent to its design, but it doesn't think. It can't obtain consciousness or self-awareness. It's one thing to have a brain which keeps our bodies functioning and allows us to respond to outside stimuli, and another to be given the ability to observe, study and acquire knowledge.

This capacity is unique to humans. Animals lack the ability, as do invertebrates, plants, and microorganisms. Humans are different. We're more than just alive, we think and make decisions. It was French philosopher, René Descartes who said, "I think, therefore I am." The phrase was coined to illustrate how it's our thoughts that make us who we are.

But where does thought, or the ability to think, come from? The truth is, no one knows. Thoughts are inherent to brain function, perhaps resulting from the rapid fire stimulation of neural networks or the activation of the areas of our brain that deal with perception, but what causes thoughts to arise, and where they originate from, remains a mystery.

Thoughts are magical, like life itself. We know thoughts could not have evolved because evolution requires hardware, or something of substance to build upon. Thoughts however are software; they are the product of intelligence. They can't invent themselves. So how did they originate? The best answer would have to be that we inherited them from the one who made us in His image.

Nineteen

*For in those days shall be affliction, such as was not from the beginning
of the creation which God created unto this time... —Mark 13:19*

IT WAS the dark hour of the soul, a time when God seemed
far away and oblivious of everything that mattered. In the
empty gloom of mourning, with the lights out and her
world blurred by tears, Sarah struggled to comprehend why all she
knew about God didn't line up with what she was experiencing.
God had designed the universe, created worlds, He was all-
knowing, all-powerful, giver of life, healer of the sick, and mender
of broken lives. He could have saved Buddy, but He chose to let
him die. *Why? Why let the innocent die, Lord? Why didn't You touch
Buddy and make him well? You've taken the only one who ever loved
me. Was it my fault? Did I do something wrong? Why, God, why?*

The darkness enveloped her. Through watery eyes she could
make out indistinct shadows, the shape of the open sofa-bed where
they'd watched TV, the table that held her computer layered with
scattered sheets of paper, the chrome contraption with wheels that
held Buddy captive so long, all shades of gray visible only in the
feeble light from the street. The constant drip of the faucet, *plop,
plop, plop,* assaulted her ears.

They had taken her son, ripped him from her arms—*You have
to let us take him, ma'am. The coroner can't come. We have to get him
to a pathologist as soon as possible, for the autopsy—arrruggggh!* And

they wouldn't let her attend and now she was alone—so utterly alone. Could they be any less compassionate? The little dog licked the tears from her neck but Snowball's kisses were no substitute for those of her son. Still she hugged the dog thankful for its presence. *You understand don't you Snowball?* Coming home to an empty apartment without Buddy was unthinkable. *I miss him Lord, I already miss him…What did I do wrong? I just wanted to save him. Are you mad because I was depending on science more than You? You could have healed Buddy. I begged You to heal him, but You didn't.*

She sniffed and wiped her nose on her sleeve. The air in her chest fluttered. Her world was out of focus. God never let anything bad happen that He couldn't turn into something good—*but what good could possibly come from this?*

Sarah hugged the dog again, his warm fur and breath a welcome relief, but then set him on the floor and stood. Snowball began pawing her leg, pleading to be taken in her arms. Ignoring the dog, she wiped her tears on her sleeve and pressed the palms of her hands to her cheeks. Where was Aaron when she needed him? Now more than ever she needed someone to hold. God was her refuge and strength but trying to hold God was like squeezing a vapor. She needed warm flesh and blood, someone she could feel, someone with a shoulder to cry on, someone to assure her everything would be alright.

The sleeve of her nightgown was wet. She pulled the cuff to straighten the material. She would make it. A sob escaped her throat. A tremble shook her body and her knees went weak. She collapsed onto the bed as her tears began to flow again—*Oh God, whyyyyyyy, uh-huh, uh-huh*—and didn't stop until her lungs rasped raw and her tears ran dry.

The ambulance pulled up short of the loading bay and stopped.

Oh Boy. Two other emergency vehicles were already there, blocking the lane. Now he understood why the officer had instructed him to take the body to the hospital's morgue instead of waiting for the coroner. The child's death wasn't the result of foul play, which was their primary concern, and with so many accidents the coroner's office would be backed up.

"Oh Man. What a mess."

"Hey Gus, you know I can't stay. My vacation started an hour ago. My husband's waiting at the airport with our luggage. If I don't go right now, I'll miss my flight."

"Right. Okay, I'll try to get us out of here fast as I can but…"

"No, I mean I have to leave right now!"

"How? I can't take you to the airport. We can't leave until we wrap this up and your car is back at the station."

"It's a hospital, Gus. I can catch a cab out front."

"Okay, gotcha. Help me get the corpse down and I'll take it from there."

"Great. Thanks, I owe you."

Gus took a deep breath, glad his shift was over. Heck, like Kerry said, it was over an hour ago. He rolled the gurney through doors that opened in front of him automatically just as his radio crackled to life. The speakers hissed with static.

"Unit Three, we have an accident at Gough and Vallejo. Can you respond?"

"Sorry, no can do. Kerry had a plane to catch. I'm alone here."

"Affirmative. Stand by." The voice disappeared. Gus relaxed thinking he was off the hook but then the radio popped and hissed again. "All other units are in transit. Need you to respond. Rochelle is standing by to assist."

"It's her day off."

"She's on call. Swing by her place. Pronto. We have casualties."

"I have to take care of this one first but I'll do my best."

"Copy that."

It was notably warmer inside. Gus struggled to loosen his coat as he rolled the gurney up alongside a metal table looking around for a doctor, or at least another medical technician, but the room was empty. Four of the five benches were already occupied. A woman, two men, and another young boy. Two boys in one night? Man, that's bizarre, but the other boy wasn't his concern. He needed the death certificate signed for this one. The paperwork was attached to the gurney. He picked it up and shuffled through the pages. All he needed was someone to say the boy was dead. The cause of death, acute muscular dystrophy, could be verified later, but you could tell that just by looking. The kid was shriveled to half his normal size. He glanced up. Then again, the other boy was skinny too. Not his concern; just get the certificate signed.

Where is everybody? He unclipped the paperwork, set it on a desk, and went looking for help. The hallway on the other side of the double metal doors was empty too. A nurse turned the corner.

"Excuse me. I need a pathologist to verify a death."

The woman looked toward the still swinging doors shaking her head. "That would be Dr. Jameson, but if he's not in the morgue I don't know where he is."

"It's kind of important I find him."

"You might try the cafeteria. He could be on his break."

Gus stepped back into the morgue. *This is ridiculous.* People were injured, people he might be able to help but he was stuck here wasting time with someone that was already gone. He glanced at the child. A small foamy bubble had formed between the cadaver's lips. *That's impossible.* He leaned his ear down toward the boy's chest and heard a faint *thump—thump—thump.* His eyes widened. The child was alive!

Gus swung the gurney around and plowed through the swinging metal doors into a maze of fluorescent lit corridors heading for Emergency, turn left, turn right, every passage looked the same, but he'd been there before; he knew the way.

The emergency room was a madhouse, filled with more people than could comfortably fit in such a small space. He looked for the intake nurse, weaving the gurney in and out as he raced to her station. He found her filling out a form for a man whose hand looked damaged. Twenty minutes had already passed. People could be dying. He reached for her arm. "Excuse me, we thought this boy was DOA but he's still alive. He needs to be looked at ASAP."

"Is he bleeding?" the nurse responded.

"No."

"Diabetic coma?"

"No, I don't think so."

"In cardiac arrest?"

"No, but he almost died."

"Leave him here. I'll get him checked out as soon as I can."

"He needs attention, now!"

"Look, we're code black. I've only got two doctors on shift and both are handling major traumas. Just leave him here. I'll see he gets looked after."

"Oh for the love of..." Gus looked at his watch. He didn't have time to argue; he had to get moving. He hustled outside to his ambulance and reached for the door when, *Aruggg*, he realized he'd left the paperwork for the boy on the pathologist's desk.

Gus raced back inside, his head swinging right and left looking for the nurse, but she wasn't there. The patient she'd been attending was holding a hand with a black-and-blue finger. He nudged the man's shoulder, getting his attention. "Sir, I need you to do something. You know that nurse you were just talking to, the one helping you fill out forms?"

The man looked up with half lidded eyes and nodded. He looked stoned. Of course he was stoned. At any given hour of the day half the population of San Francisco was stoned.

"Good. See that boy right there? You have to let her know his paperwork is on the pathologist's desk, back in the morgue. Have her send someone to get it. This is important. I have another emergency to attend. Think you can do that?"

The words came slow and slurred. "Uh, *shurrrre.*"

"Great. Tell her I'll explain soon as I get back."

Gus raced out and hopped into his truck. He flipped the switch to get the light bar flashing and sped away with the siren screaming. The van raced through a labyrinth of blinking storefront signs. The intersection of Gough and Vallejo wasn't that far away, and Rochelle lived only a few blocks off the route. He'd gone more than a mile before he thought to pick up the mike and report in. "Unit Three in transit. ETA five minutes."

"Belay that Unit Three. We have someone already on site, minor injuries only. Return to base. Rochelle and Mike will take it from here."

Gus breathed a sigh of relief. "*Whew*, copy that."

Back at the hospital the man Gus requested help from was asleep. He'd slammed his finger in a car door and had taken Tylenol and a few prescription sleeping pills to ease the pain. By the time they finally got around to seeing him he was so groggy he no longer remembered anything about the boy, or the message he was supposed to convey.

A half hour later the Chief Pathologist finished his break and returned to the morgue. Four dead bodies, not a good night for his intern to call in sick. There was no way he'd be able to process them all without help. The tox screens were already back. One man was an OD but the rest were free of drugs and poison. Might as well start with the child. He peeled back the eyelids, no hemorrhaging, the boy wasn't suffocated. No knife or bullet wounds, no trauma to the head or body. It appeared he'd died of natural causes. A street urchin, probably abandoned by his drug addicted parents, or maybe a runaway from a life of abuse. He needed to identify the child which, without dental records, DNA, or fingerprints already in the system, would be impossible. This boy was lucky to have survived as long as he did. He turned and saw a file on his desk. Odd, hadn't been there before. Picking it up he scanned the pages and found what he was looking for. *Cause of death—MD.* That would certainly explain the loss of weight. Not a street urchin after all. He tucked his chin looking at the boy over the rim of his glasses. *I thought you were a John Doe.* He went to his computer, typed in the boy's name and came up with a complete medical history. An easy one. From his drawer he removed a tag with a string and wrote "Buddy Hunter" on it. Walking over, he slipped it around the boy's big toe.

Twenty

*God, who made the world and all things therein, seeing that he is
Lord of heaven and earth, does not dwell in temples made with hands.
—Acts 17:24*

ARON PULLED into a parking space feeling antsy.
She was right, it wasn't what he expected. It looked
more like a strip mall than a church, and certainly not
like a synagogue, though he'd only been in a synagogue once to
attend the bar mitzvah of a childhood friend. He checked again.
Yes, he had the right address.

He stretched, easing the knot in his back. The night hadn't gone
well. The person that hit his car was probably a fellow researcher.
Who else would be in on a Saturday? Coward! Couldn't face the
music, had to duck and run. *Jerk.*

Then he had arrived home and in going through his emails
found one from his mother saying she was off on another one of
her adventures, globe-trotting, this time to some ashram in the
Himalayan Mountains. His holiness Guru Swami Omkarananda—
the embodiment of highest spirituality—was supposed to help her
find inner peace. *Really? Oh please.* But that meant she wouldn't
be around to fix the car. The pink slip was in her name, as was
the insurance policy. It chagrinned him to think he'd have to drive
around in a wrecked Beemer until she got back. And to top it off,
Sarah didn't seem to appreciate the courtesy. She'd left him standing

out in the cold, *as usual*. There had to be a word for people like him who took abuse and kept coming back for more—*stupid?*—or maybe just *weak*—either one fit.

Wisps of slow moving fog hovered close to the ground as he shuffled toward the building, a mist with a cold dankness that seeped through his skin. He yawned and scrunched his shoulders with a shiver. He'd gone to bed early but the two previous nights of drinking had drained him. By the time he opened his eyes and saw light coming through the window he was already late. Then he'd rushed out without grabbing the kite and had to turn around and go back. Music boomed through the walls. The service had already begun.

He reached for the door feeling his heart race. Sarah would be waiting inside, though she'd probably chastise him for interrupting the service. Perhaps it would be best if he just took a seat in the back and tried to connect with her after the meeting was over.

The congregation was praying. He slipped inside and found a chair at the rear of the sanctuary. His smooth cotton denims and Izod shirt were probably overkill but he deserved credit for at least trying to dress down, she'd said it was casual, but he didn't own a pair of denims as tacky as those worn by most of the men, and he couldn't imagine wearing shorts to church, though some did, *weird*, but then, he'd never seen a preacher with a ponytail either.

He didn't close his eyes. Instead he used the quiet time to scan the room for a thatch of red hair. He didn't see one. Sarah had to sit at the end of an isle to accommodate Buddy's wheelchair, but he went through the process of examining every head one at a time anyway. She wasn't there. He might fail to see her, but Buddy's wheelchair would be hard to miss. Come to think of it, he hadn't seen her van either. Something was wrong. He got up and slipped quietly out the back. Where was she?

If he left, and she really was there, it might jeopardize their already fragile relationship. He decided not to risk it. He began walking through the rows of cars. The sun, low on the horizon, looked like a fuzzy orange. The morning fog swirled around his feet like gossamer haze. He took one row at a time but it was becoming more and more obvious the van wasn't there. Both handicap spaces in front were empty. She would have used one of them. That said it all.

Aaron hustled to his car. The fog offered poor visibility but he flew like a jet, his fingers trembling on the wheel. Something was terribly wrong. He could feel it. His tires squealed as he skidded to the curb in front of Sarah's apartment leaving rubber on the asphalt.

He sat for a moment trying to think. It wasn't likely she'd welcome him with open arms, especially if Buddy was sick and he awakened the boy by knocking. Maybe she wasn't even home. He eyed the cars that lined the street. The van was parked about five cars ahead visible even through the fog. She had to be in her apartment. He shouldn't have rushed over in such a panic. She was probably fine. And if Buddy was sick, she'd have taken him to the hospital and her van wouldn't be there. He was acting pretty rash for a normally rational guy. Still, he had to know. There was no point in leaving without finding out. He let the door swing open and stepped into the street.

Calm down, he thought, *I do have a reason for being here. We were supposed to meet. She stood me up. I deserve an explanation.* He pressed the intercom button, hoping she'd *buzz* him in. He waited a few long seconds and then *buzzed* again. He could hear the dog barking in the background.

"Go away. Please, whoever you are, just go away." Her words were breathy and frail, like she'd been crying.

"Sarah, it's me, Aaron. We were supposed to meet at church. Are you Okay?"

"Aaron? Oh gosh, *sniff*, I'm sorry. I'm not feeling well. Can you come back later? I'm not in the mood..."

"What's wrong, Sarah? Something's wrong. What's going on?" He took a step back. Several seconds passed before he heard the click of the deadbolt. He reached for the handle before she could change her mind.

The door swung open and there stood Sarah wearing a long flannel nightgown. The material had a repeating image of Pegasus flying through the clouds but it had been washed so many times the print was barely visible. Her hair was unruly and her eyes wet and red. She bit her lip. Her whole body seemed to tremble. "Buddy died last night," she said.

Aaron's eyes widened. "What? Oh Sarah, no…" He took a step forward and pulled her into his arms. Her hair felt damp against his cheek.

She didn't resist. He could feel a shuddering in her chest as he held her tight, saying nothing because anything he might say would be inadequate.

After a few minutes the tears stopped, but the flutter in her breath continued. She brought her hand up balled with tissues and wiped her eyes.

"How? What happened?"

Her body shuddered, her head still buried in his arms. Her words were muffled by his shirt. "I was sleeping and…and he woke me up saying he couldn't breathe. I couldn't help him…I couldn't…"

"It's okay." Aaron looked around the apartment. Buddy's wheelchair was still there, sitting by the dining room table. There were dishes piled in the sink. The door to the bathroom was ajar. He could see plastic shampoo bottles and a hair dryer lying on the counter.

"No, it's not okay!" Sarah said, raising her voice as she stepped back pushing him away. "My son is dead and it's not okay! Whatever possessed you to say a thing like that? No, it's definitely not okay. I couldn't save him…I…"

147

"Sarah." Aaron reached out but she turned away. "You can't blame yourself. We're all trying to find a cure but there isn't one yet."

"Then you're at fault too. All of you are, you and Jen and Larry and May…everyone who worked on that stupid idea of looking for a missing agent in rats blood. A waste of time. And now my son's dead…"

"Sarah, no one's to blame. Sometimes, things just happen."

"Wrong. I blame…everyone. I blame God! Hear that God?" She raised her fist toward the ceiling. "I blame You. You could have saved my son. You could have healed him. And now he's dead and I can't…I can't…" She stumbled over to the bed, and dropped onto it sobbing again. The little dog nuzzled under her arm.

Aaron followed and sat down. Their legs touched. She opened her eyes, looking into his. "I'm sorry," she said. "I'm a mess. Would you…could you hold me?"

Aaron pulled her in tucking her head under his chin. The warmth of their bodies connected, though nothing was said. Suddenly she tipped her head back and looked at him. Her eyes were wet as rain and her lips full and moist. Without warning she brought her mouth to his and kissed him. Aaron felt the passion in her lips and responded and for an eternity that lasted only a second they melted into one.

Her eyes opened and her body tensed. Aaron sensed a pulling away.

"What?"

"What are you doing?" she yelped. "You're taking advantage of me aren't you? You're using my grief to hit on me." She scooted over and stood up, smoothing her flannel gown.

Aaron scrambled to his feet. "Sarah, I'm sorry. I didn't mean to, it…it just happened."

"I think you'd better leave."

"Sarah, don't."

"Leave," she said, pointing to the door, but she was interrupted by the ringing of her phone. She continued glaring at Aaron as she went to answer. "Hello…Yes, this is she…What? Can you repeat that? That's not possible. What? No, I heard you, I just…alright, no, I mean, I don't know. I'll do what I can."

She went back to the bed and dropped onto it again. "It was the police," she said, wiping her tears on the back of her hand. "Dr. Summer was in an accident. He was killed. They need me to answer a few questions but…I can't…It's just not…there must be some mistake. Buddy…and now Dr. Summer…" Tears began rolling down her cheeks; her fists balled into knots. "What's going on?" She looked toward heaven. "What did I ever do to You, God? What did I ever do?"

We've Lost the Race Against Time
The Journal of W.L. Summer

Those who dabble in statistical probability have calculated the odds of a single molecule being organized by chance are 1 in 10 followed by 161 zeros. When you figure the number of atoms in the entire universe is only 10 followed by 80 zeros, you get an idea of just how big a number that is.

Molecules, of course, coalesce into cells. There are about a trillion bits of information contained in a simple cell. That's equal to counting every letter in every word contained in about ten million telephone books. How long do you suppose it might take to assemble a cell and then amass the trillion bits of information it needs to function when the only way it has of acquiring this data is a series of accidents which frequently do the cell more harm than good?

The issue has always been time. Thomas Huxley, a man known to be a bulldog in the defense of evolution, argued that given enough time anything was possible. He used the example of ageless monkeys infinitely stroking the keys of typewriters until they had arbitrarily composed one of Shakespeare's plays.

The problem is we don't have an infinite amount of time. The notion of the Big Bang reduced the age of our universe to about fourteen billion years. I prefer the biblical account which says God compressed that time into a single moment, but even if you buy the Big Bang scenario, that's the most any competent cosmologist will allow. And they say the earth itself has only been around about 4.5 billion years. That isn't remotely enough time to evolve something as complex as a simple cell, let alone the billions of sophisticated life forms with infinitely complex substructures that supposedly evolved after that.

Twenty-One

It is He who sits above the circle of the earth, and its inhabitants are like grasshoppers, Who stretches out the heavens like a curtain, and spreads them out like a tent to dwell in. —Isaiah 40:22

LIGHT FROM the incandescent bulb of the sun was blocked by a sheet of gauze. The gray wall kept traffic on the Bayshore Freeway at a crawl, though it was apparent the fog was beginning to thin. Aaron's fingers tapped the steering wheel. He felt like he should say something but the barrier of silence was too thick to break.

Sarah sat beside him in the passenger seat, curled up in a ball with her Army boots on the leather cushion. Her knees were tucked under her chin and her head lying against the window, her breath clouding the glass. Aaron refrained from telling her how much he disliked people putting their shoes, and especially boots, on his leather seats, or that she should be wearing a seatbelt. In her state of mind, the information would not be well received.

He passed under a sign that announced the Seaport Boulevard exit. So far he'd respected her silence but now he had to say something. They were almost there.

"How you doing? You alright?"

He glanced to the side. She was shaking her head. "How am I supposed to be? I feel like a wreck. I want to scream." She straightened herself looking at Aaron for the first time since they'd started the twenty minute drive. "All I can do is pray. Of course you don't believe in God, do you?" She shook her head. "That's just sad. At least when I'm down I have someone to call on for help."

"I thought you were mad at God." He smiled, but the irony seemed lost on her. His eyes flicked back to the road staring into the distance, his fingers tightening on the wheel. "I don't know about God but I do know about me."

"What about you?"

"You say you need help and I'm helping, or at least I'm trying to."

"Thanks, but it's not the same. Look, don't think I don't appreciate it. I wouldn't be doing this if I had to drive myself, but that's the outward stuff. Only Jesus can heal my heart." Tears began leaking down her cheeks.

Outward Stuff? Aaron nodded trying not to be offended. "What about the funeral?"

"I don't know? I can't think about that right now."

"Perhaps you should, it's important."

Sarah's head fell back against the seat. "I haven't even bought a plot. I knew Buddy was dying but I couldn't because that would be like giving up. Know what I mean? It's still hard to believe he's…I keep thinking Buddy's at home, you know? I just can't get used to the idea that he's gone." She swallowed and dabbed a tear with the palm of her hand.

Aaron pulled to the curb. "We're here. Are you sure you want to do this? If you want to back out, I'm sure they'll understand."

Sarah braced herself stiffening her resolve. Her hand went to the door swinging it open. "I want to know what happened," she said.

The woman at reception pointed to a row of empty chairs but they didn't bother sitting down. Sarah felt she could cope better on her feet and Aaron, though he'd never been in trouble in his life, felt the way he did when he got pulled over for a traffic violation.

A man in a frumpy sports coat bounded into the lobby with an outstretched hand. "Hey, you must be Sarah Hunter. Thanks for coming in." He was a meaty package, tough fiber, not the kind of gristle you want to chew. His bulked up shoulders all but swallowed his neck. His skin was tanned and swarthy. His hair, the color of pewter, was cropped so short you could see his scalp peeking through.

He kept his hand out waiting for Sarah to take it, which she did, hesitantly. Her petite fingers disappeared into his meaty flesh.

"I'm Detective Irons. Hugh Irons. And you must be the husband," he said, turning to shake Aaron's hand.

"No, just a friend." Aaron winced in the man's grip and pulled himself free as he took a step back. "Sarah needed a ride so I volunteered."

"And your name is…?"

"Aaron Rose."

"Well Mr. Rose, I'm going to ask that you wait out here. Our business is with Miss Hunter. It's a police matter, I'm sure you understand. Go ahead and make yourself comfortable, we won't be long. Miss Hunter, if you'll step this way." He turned and charged back through the door from which he'd come.

The core of the police station was a beehive of activity. Uniformed officers with the patrol division and detectives in business suits huddled around desks or talked in small groups. A seedy young man with long hair and a scraggily beard was being interviewed by a female detective. He looked like a vagrant, maybe even a cat burglar, but who was she to judge. With her unkempt hair and rough worn Army jacket, she didn't look much better. She felt the eyes following her as she was led through the room.

Irons' navy sports coat was stretched tightly across his broad shoulders and the polyester of his tan slacks was rubbed shiny at the knees. His tie hung loose around an open collar which seemed appropriate in the absence of a neck. He pointed to an empty chair, indicating where Sarah should sit and went around to the other side settling into a chair of his own. His jacket swung open and Sarah noticed a gun holstered under his arm.

"Sit down Miss Hunter. I promise this won't take long."

Sarah obeyed.

"As I explained earlier, two nights ago Dr. Wallace Summer was struck by a car and killed. The driver of the vehicle didn't stop. We're doing our best to find the responsible party but, unfortunately, as with most hit and runs, we have little to go on. What I need first of all is to know more about your relationship with Dr. Summer."

"Dr. Summer? We worked together at CellMerge. He was my boss, at least until just recently."

Hugh shuffled through the litter on his desk looking for something and came up with a yellow legal pad. He began taking notes. He looked up, letting his pen drum the paper. "Until recently? How's that?"

Sarah's mind raced over the past few weeks. Under Dr. Summer she might have found a cure. Tears rimmed her eyes but she fought to hold them back. "Something happened. I don't know what. I just know they announced Dr. Summer had left the company...and now he's dead...and I still have his dog..."

"His dog?"

She nodded. "Dr. Summer asked me to watch his poodle, and I still have him and...I guess I won't be able to return him now." Tears began washing down her cheeks. "How am I supposed to look at that dog without thinking of Dr. Summer?" She paused and drew in a breath. It wasn't Dr. Summer she'd be thinking about, it would be Buddy. Detective Irons continued taking notes. "If you want to know about Dr. Summer you should probably talk to someone else because I'm new with the company. A lot of people knew him better than I did." She wiped her cheek on her sleeve and reached into her pocket for a tissue.

"Yes, and we'll talk to them in due course, but what we really need to do is locate his family or next of kin and..."

"You think I'm his daughter."

The detective's head snapped up. "No, why? Are you?"

Sarah's eyes dropped to her lap. Her chin fell. She folded her arms across her chest and crossed her legs. "No. I don't know, maybe." She managed to look at her interrogator without raising her head. "It's a long story."

Detective Irons waited, his pen tapping the tablet.

"I don't know who my father is but he's supposed to work at CellMerge, and I kinda thought maybe it was Dr. Summer."

Detective Irons was already reaching for his phone. "Hey Mike, this is Hugh. Can you send someone over with a swab kit? Okay. No, that's fine, see you in a few." He put the phone back down. "If you're Summer's daughter, it will save me a lot of trouble, and there's one sure way to find out. It also makes sense of this." He grabbed a folder from the corner of his desk and plopped it down in front of Sarah with a thud. It was about two inches thick and filled with loose sheets of paper. "This is why I had you come in."

"What is it?" she asked, wiping her eyes with the tissue.

"Don't rightly know. We found it in Dr. Summer's house with your name on it. I figured it must belong to you. I took a look, just to make sure there was nothing in there that might be connected to our investigation but it looks to be a lot of scientific stuff." He slid a sheet of paper across the desk along with his pen.

The moisture in Sarah's eyes made it difficult to focus on the print. "What's this?"

"You need to sign for it. You're free to take it with you, just don't let anything go missing. Our investigation isn't over, so we may need to get it back. Depending on how things turn out, it may need to be logged in as evidence."

"Evidence? What? For a hit and run?"

A man wearing latex gloves stepped up to the desk. Hugh stood and pushed his chair back to give the forensic technician room.

"When you run over someone and leave them to die, that's a crime. We'll probably go for manslaughter, but it could be worse. We didn't find any skid marks, which suggests the car didn't try to stop. It might be that Dr. Summer was run over on purpose, which would make this a vehicular homicide. You need to open your mouth. The man here needs to swab the inside of your cheek."

Detective Irons' partner, Eduardo Rodriquez, wasn't there for the interview. He'd lost the coin toss and was out buying lunch. He climbed from his unmarked police car, a no frills gray Chevy sedan, and pulled a bag of deli subs from the seat, slamming the door behind him. He liked Sundays. He could always find a place to park.

He turned and headed toward the station but pulled up short. *Is that what I think it is? A shiny black BMW!* He stepped around to the front of the vehicle. Paint chips from Dr. Summer's body showed the offending car was a BMW with Black Sapphire paint. *Sure thing, the grill's crumpled. Holy Mother of God. The perpetrator has come to turn himself in!*

He sighed, *this is a very good thing.* Their caseload was already more than they could handle. *Bet that car cost fifty grand.* The rich were a pain in the butt. "*Save your ticket. I play golf with the mayor.*" If the man turned himself in and had good legal representation, he'd probably walk. The scales of justice were unevenly balanced.

But what if the guy wasn't there to turn himself in? What if he was a lawyer or a judge, or someone with another reason for being there? *They think they're above the law, like it don't apply to them.* He set the bag with the subs on the car's hood and fished in his pocket for a pen. Pulling a handkerchief from another pocket he flicked several pieces of paint from the damaged grill and folded the sample inside. The guys in the crime lab would tell him if the paint was a match.

Could be a lucky break. He slipped the handkerchief into his coat and took a step back to read the license, then grabbed his pen and jotted down the number. If the man had come to turn himself in, booking would have a record of it. If not, he'd use the plate to locate the vehicle's owner. Then he'd wait a few days and just when it seemed the case was going cold, produce the evidence and claim dogged police work had led him to find the car. He grabbed the sacks of food, grinning as he made his way inside.

The nurse stepped into the corridor and waved Dr. Philips over. "Doctor, can I get you to take a look at this patient?"

The man paused and stood with his arms folded over his clipboard. "What?"

"I have a child without a doctor that needs help."

"A child, you say?" He stepped into the room and saw the boy lying on the bed. His eyes were closed. He appeared to be resting peacefully. "Whose patient is he?"

"No one's. He was left in emergency in a coma. We don't know who he is, let alone how to contact his parents."

The doctor leaned over and gently lifted one of Buddy's eyelids, then the other. "Yep, he's in a coma alright, but what's that to me? He's not my patient."

"But he's not anyone's patient, and he needs looking after."

"Right, but I can't recommend treatment without someone's waver. I could be sued. You need admin to approve it under their indigent program. If the hospital wants to assume liability, fine, but I can't treat a patient without someone saying it's okay. My insurance won't allow it."

Sarah found Aaron where she left him, still pacing the floor. She didn't know why but it made her feel better. Being asked to come down here had kept her from thinking about Buddy, and having a friend there to support her was an added blessing. Clouds with silver linings. She'd been gone half an hour but it appeared he hadn't sat down. She caught his eye and saw a look of concern and for the umpteenth time considered how she might have misjudged the man.

"How did it go? You all right?"

There was that question again. How could she be all right? It was taking every ounce of her strength to hold herself together. She nodded and folded the file she was carrying over her bosom looking down as they walked.

Aaron accompanied her back to the car and helped her climb inside. He settled in behind the wheel and started the engine.

"Could you do me one more favor?" she asked. She needed a shower. Her skin itched, her hair hung limp and oily, and her Army jacket did not fit the occasion, but this couldn't wait.

"What's that?"

"Could you drive me to the church? I need to let my pastor know about Buddy." She looked at her watch. "The service is over but he should still be there. I have to start making arrangements for the...you know."

Twenty-Two

Thus says God the Lord, He that created the heavens, and stretched them out; He that made the earth, and that which comes from it; He that gives breath unto the people on it, and spirit to those who walk therein. —Isaiah 42:5

SARAH SNUGGLED the covers around her neck and tried to ignore the woodpecker in her head, *tap, tap, tap, tap, tap.*

"Sarah? Sarah! Are you in there? Wake up. *Knock, knock, knock.* Open up. It's me, Beth." *Knock, knock, knock.*

Sarah heard the words, but they sounded surreal, like something spoken in a dream. She wanted to open her eyes but hesitated, unwilling to yield her serenity. She rolled, pulling the blanket over her head to stifle the noise and keep out the light. *Light? Morning?* Her eyes snapped open. Snowball was barking. She leapt out of bed dragging the blanket half way across the room. She'd overslept. Thank God for Beth. She had to get Buddy ready. *Buddy?* Her pace slowed as she opened the door.

"Sarah...*Sarah?* Hey girl, what's wrong?" Beth dropped a backpack full of books to the floor. Snowball was sniffing at her heels. She reached down to pick him up.

Sarah turned and went back into the room flopping on the unmade sleeper sofa. She looked up, her eyes glassing over. "He's gone," she said. "Buddy's gone."

Beth's eyes darted around the room, her mouth opening. Her lips were full and her eyes large and round. "Oh no, not baby Buddy. Not now." She placed Snowball on the bed and sat down.

Sarah felt Beth's arms envelope her, a warm blanket of comfort. They sat silently, Beth holding on as they rocked back and forth.

Snowball jumped down and began sniffing Beth's shoes. Sarah shuddered. She tucked her head to blot her eyes on her arm—*too many tears. Would they ever stop?* Her sleeve felt wrinkled and damp. She'd been sleeping in the same clothes she'd worn yesterday. She must be a sight—hair hanging limp and greasy, dark shadowy eyes, dried tears streaking her face—an unsightly mess. She folded her arms and stood, breaking free of Beth's embrace. "We're planning to hold the funeral tomorrow, if I can get everything arranged." Looking down, she swept the carpet with her toe. "I...uhm...I guess I'd better get ready or I'll be late for work," she said.

"Yo girl, you can't be serious? You're *not* going to work today."

Sarah nodded, her head bobbing in short little jerks. "I have to. I'm still on probation. I don't want to lose my job." She wiped her eyes on her sleeve and then realized what she'd said and how insensitive it must sound. "Oh, Beth, I'm sorry, I didn't mean...I'm sorry...I guess without Buddy, you'll be out of a job too, I..."

"Stop it, girl. You just stop it!" Beth scrambled off the bed. "Plenty of people need daycare. I'll find work. This isn't 'bout me; this is about you. You're in no shape to play scientist or whatever it is you do. And no one's gonna 'pect you to. Jus' call and tell 'em what happened." Beth's chocolate face held a frown, her long braids jangling as she shook her head.

Sarah took a deep breath, the air shuddering in her chest. "No, I have to go in. It's what Buddy would want." She turned and headed for the bathroom, running her fingers through her hair to untangle the mess. "Maybe I couldn't save him, he's with Jesus now; I know he's happy; but dozens like him die every day. I have to try and save as many as I can." She opened the medicine cabinet, avoiding the mirror while looking for her toothbrush. "Besides, I can't just sit here. I have to keep my mind occupied or I'll go crazy."

"What about the arrangements? If you want I can help."

Sarah wadded a tissue in her hand and approached Beth again. She'd put off looking for a gravesite while Buddy was alive because it seemed creepy—especially since Buddy was with her most of the time. Aaron had listened, said he understood, and then insisted on doing everything himself. She was distraught, unable to think let alone manage details, and he was persuasive so she'd reluctantly agreed. She pulled Beth into her arms clinging to the comfort it brought. "Someone's already on it, Beth, but thank you…ah… oh…" She stood back wiping her eye with the tissue. "…there is one thing if you wouldn't mind. You think you could write the obituary? *Sniff.* I don't want Buddy's passing to go unnoticed and you knew him better than anyone…"

Hurry was not a word generally associated with laboratory work. Everything had to be done in a precise, orderly fashion. Cultures required time to grow, notes needed to be taken and results verified two or three times, tests needed to be repeated ad infinitum, and clinical studies, especially where humans were concerned, could take years, so there was no logic to the snit Jen was in when she cornered Dr. Jaeger outside his office. He removed his coat and stood on his toes, placing the fringed leather jacket on the hook behind the door. Jen had a bur under her saddle about something. He could see it in her eyes.

"And what can I do for you, Dr. Carlson?" he said, indicating with a hand that she should take a seat across from him.

Jen sat, but she remained stiff, not relaxed, another sign that she was stewing about something.

"Dr. Jaeger," she began, "I know you haven't been my boss very long. If you had, you'd know my nature is to always get along. Go with the flow, that's what I always say. Truth is, I rarely complain about anything."

Carl rocked back in his chair. He didn't want to hear some woeful tale about not having the proper resources to do the job. Budgets were tight. But listening to employee grievances came with the territory. He wiggled in his seat, his hands fidgeting with the strings of his tie. "But..." he said.

"It's just that, I know you want to give the new girl a chance. I understand that, and it's only fair, but the truth is, it isn't working. So far she's disrupted our work so many times we're falling behind. And now this morning she isn't even here. And I don't know where she is because she hasn't called. You asked me to take her under my wing and help her. I tried, honestly I did, but she's not interested in being part of the team. She just wants to work on her own little project, the one Dr. Summer gave her. We can't operate this way. It's not efficient. In fact, it's counterproductive."

Carl puffed out a breath and struggled to set himself aright. He leaned forward placing his elbows on the table with his fingers laced, twiddling his thumbs. His lips puckered as he nodded. "You say she didn't show up and didn't bother to call in sick?"

"Right. She has a phone. It's not like she can't touch base."

"*Hummmm*, okay, I hear what you're saying. Leave it with me. I'll have a talk with her. By the way, did you see the article in the paper over the weekend?"

Jen shook her head. "Article, what article?"

"Appears Dr. Summer got himself killed."

"Killed? Dr. Summer?"

"Yep, sure looks that way. Newspaper said he was crossing the road Friday night and got hit by a car." Carl folded his arms across his chest and leaned back with a cynical smile. "I guess I should feel worse than I do, but the old coot was trying to get his chair back, so the way I see it, he got what he deserved."

Jen shook her head, her lips pinched.

"Oh come on, Dr. Carlson. Q was a dinosaur. You know we're better off without him. I mean, think about it, would you really want him for a boss again? You couldn't go to him with your concerns the way you just came to me. He wouldn't listen. Not me. I'm a team builder and being part of a team means sticking up for each other, pulling the same plow, so to speak." Dr. Jaeger leaned forward again, placing his elbows on the desk with his fingers laced in front of him. "So here's what we're going to do. I'm going to help you fix your little problem, and then if I ever get in trouble, you, out of loyalty, are going to help me. That's called pulling the load together. Sound like a fair deal?"

Sarah sat in her van with the heater on and engine running. She didn't like wasting gas and she was late but it was too cold to do it outside so she stopped just short of where the attendant could take her keys and bowed her head. "Please. Lord, give me strength." She took a long, slow breath and exhaled. Inside the lions were circling, but God could shut the lion's mouths. She pulled up and opened the door, feeling the chill as she handed the guard her keys.

She wore a pair of faded jeans and calf high lace up boots to keep her legs warm. Her heavy plaid jacket was zipped up, a bulky woolen scarf circled her neck, and she had a leather cap with fuzzy brown earmuffs on her head, but even with all that she still wrapped her arms around herself and shivered as she ran for the door. *Burrrr.* It had to be near freezing. *And God, Snowball's going to be alone in the apartment today. Please help him be alright.*

Sarah turned the corner, twirling the scarf from her neck. She hated to use her son's passing as an excuse for being late, but she had to let them know. And she had to do it while maintaining a semblance of professional composure. Maybe they'd just notice she'd been crying, and ask. That would be easiest. She swallowed, her eyes beginning to fill again. *No, not now.* She stiffened her face. *I can do this.*

Jen was standing in the middle of the aisle looking at her watch. "Good afternoon, Miss Hunter. Glad you could join us." Sarah passed her by, ignoring the remark. It was going to be harder than she thought.

May sat on a tall lab stool looking though a microscope. Larry was over by the coffee machine reading the morning paper as he poured a refill. She was only two hours late. Larry's coffee breaks tallied more than that. She unzipped her jacket.

"Dr. Hunter, can I see you for a minute?"

Sarah turned to see Dr. Jaeger beckoning her from his office. She took a deep breath. *Uh-oh, here it comes. Please God, I have to let him know. Help him understand. And please don't let me cry.*

She made her way over, her heart aching in her chest. She raised her chin and arched her shoulders. She had to stand tall and face her boss's rebuke for being late, and then tell him she needed a day off for the funeral. He was already seated as she entered the room, his round belly busting through the buttons of his cowboy shirt, the strings of his bolo tie hanging to the side.

"Could you close the door and take a seat please?"

Sarah nodded. She turned, pushed the door till she heard it click, and then sat down leaning forward with her elbows on her knees, rubbing her fingers together.

"I'm not one to mince words, Dr. Hunter. I call it like I see it so I'm not going to beat around the bush, no sir, that's not my style. Here's the thing, I've had numerous complaints about your work…"

What? Sarah's mouth opened in silent protest. *Complaints about my work?* She was late, yes, but her work was exemplary.

"…running around like a fox in a hen house ruffling a lot of feathers, and I can't have that," Carl continued. "I need my team pulling together. Therefore in the interest of the whole group I'm afraid I'm going to have to let you go."

What? Was she being fired? She must not have heard right. She began shaking her head.

"Technically, you're still on probation so we don't owe you a thing but I spoke with HR and they've agreed to give you two weeks severance, which is more than generous. Here's your letter of termination." Dr. Jaeger took an envelope from his desk and handed it to Sarah. "You've got a good resume, and there won't be any black marks on your record, so you should be able to find another position without much trouble. I'm sorry it didn't work out." He stood and extended his hand indicating the meeting was over. "I wish you good luck," he said.

Sarah tried to stand but had to support herself with the arm of the chair. She blinked but couldn't hold back. The tears burst from her eyes in a flood.

Carl balked, clearly not expecting an emotional response. "Hey, don't do that. Hey, come on." He spun around looking for a tissue but he couldn't find one and by the time he turned back, Sarah was gone.

Her legs were in retreat, moving as fast as possible without breaking into a run. The world was a blur, distorted images seen from underwater. Her eyes caught a fuzzy image of Jen standing to the side with her arms crossed, "See ya, wouldn't wanna be ya," but she ignored the remark and kept going until she was out the door and running as fast as her boots could take her away.

Mutations Don't Make a More Beautiful You
The Journal of W.L. Summer

Evolution requires we accept the idea that material bodies through random events evolve into increasingly complex structures. To accomplish this one must assume that organisms think. In order to gradually become more sophisticated an organism must know what's good so it can keep positive changes and what's bad so it can discard negative ones. But organisms don't have mechanisms for self-evaluation. All evolutionary changes happen strictly by accident.

In theory, evolution takes place via mutations in our DNA. There's no thought or purpose behind mutations, they happen randomly, so let's look at a few simple examples and see how this plays out. There are taste buds on our tongue. What accident do you suppose caused them to be there? The tongue didn't know there was anything to taste. A random mutation in our DNA could just as easily have resulted in our tongue being covered with hair. What about our teeth? What accident caused them to be different than the bones in our arm? According to evolution, there wasn't any thought behind this change. The mutation was accidental. Without a plan how do we explain the evolution of pairs? We have perfectly matched eyes, ears, teeth, hands and feet that all supposedly evolved through a series of accidents. The odds against one perfectly organized system evolving are astronomical, but two evolving simultaneously and ending up exactly the same—unthinkable, especially since accidents generally bring chaos not order. A billion automobile accidents might make a mess of the freeway, but it won't result in the creation of a lunar space probe. You can't have accident after accident result in billions of perfectly designed species with exceedingly complex brains, eyes, skeletal, circulatory, and nervous systems.

Why do people try to defend such nonsense when it's clearly impossible? Why not just use our God given logic and admit that our bodies are fearfully and wonderfully made?

Twenty-Three

Have you not known? Have you not heard? The everlasting God,
the Lord, The Creator of the ends of the earth, neither faints nor is
weary. His understanding is unsearchable. —Isaiah 40:28

ARON SLOGGED down the corridor dragging his feet like they were made of lead. Another dismal morning, one where the clouds weighed heavy on his shoulders. He'd gone through the garage looking for Sarah's van, but didn't find it. She was supposed to be at work this morning. Getting through the night must have been harder than she'd anticipated.

He swallowed his disappointment. He'd have to let her know about the arrangements another time. The body would be released by the hospital and picked up by the funeral home for direct burial. The memorial service would be held at gravesite. Sarah had opted not to have a funeral, per se. There was no one to invite. She had no family and other than a few couples in her support group, she hadn't had time to make friends. Eliminating the funeral meant they wouldn't need a viewing which meant they could save money on embalming. The Casket would remain closed. The funeral home would deliver Buddy to the cemetery where those who wished to come could pay their last respects.

It was the least expensive way to go. Sarah had insisted on a no frills internment. Why pay for things she couldn't afford when

Buddy wasn't around to enjoy them? In her view, Buddy wouldn't be in the box; he was in heaven. The rest was just dust.

The concept troubled Aaron but he honored her request. A simple casket was purchased, along with a plot of ground for Buddy's final resting place. The price was still over seven thousand dollars. He didn't have that kind of money. No matter how much he made he always found a way of spending every penny, and he knew Sarah didn't have the money either. He'd be disowned if she ever found out, but he'd gone into his mother's emergency fund. She'd given him signing authority with the proviso that he never use it except in the case of extreme necessity. It wasn't the kind of thing he'd use for fixing a car, though the thought had crossed his mind, but what else was the death of a child if not an emergency. He hoped Sarah could arrange a quick loan and replenish the account before his mother found the money missing.

Aaron unbuttoned his tan cashmere overcoat, brooding about God as he walked down the hall. He couldn't imagine someone as pure and innocent as Buddy fading into nothingness, nor could he imagine life beyond the grave. Physics argued against the hereafter. Life was over for little Buddy. His body would be buried and consumed by the elements. His smile was gone, never to be seen again.

But what about his spirit? That was the great unknown. Every civilization, every culture on the planet had ultimately come to believe in some kind of God, if for no other reason than it argued for an afterlife. There had to be a possibility. Where did life come from in the first place? Somehow the merging of a man's seed and woman's egg brought thought and breath and being. And if the combination of these materials could become sentient life, wasn't it at least possible that when those same materials were released from the body that the life portion, the thought, or being, could continue? The answers to such questions were elusive.

He rubbed his eye as he turned the corner entering the main laboratory. He'd become misty just thinking about Buddy. The kid's death affected him more than he realized.

Jen was waving at him. She looked excited, like she couldn't wait to let him know about some new milestone they'd reached. Any breakthrough should be cause for celebration, but he wasn't in the mood. He almost hoped it wasn't true. It was too late for Buddy.

He wandered in, slipped his coat from his shoulders and tossed it across the back of a chair. Jen was on her way over. He needed to ask if they'd heard about Sarah but sensed he should wait and let Jen share her news first.

"Aaron, where have you been? So much has happened I don't know where to begin..."

"Maybe I should be the one to explain."

Both heads swiveled around as Dr. Jaeger approached. The stout barrel of a man wore a plaid cowboy shirt with pearl snap buttons and a string tie with a miniature silver skull—that of a Texas longhorn—for a slide. He waddled over, the cuffs of his denim pants dragging on the ground behind his boots.

"Explain what?" Aaron said.

"About the death of your friend."

"Oh, so you heard."

"Yes-sir-ree, and I know none of us would spit on a man's grave, but you gotta admit the world's a better place without him."

Aaron squinted, shaking his head. "What are you talking about?"

"Dr. Summer. You know, how he got bushwhacked by a car."

Aaron's lips flattened forming a straight line; his eyes reduced to slits. "That's cold. The man should be honored for the good he achieved. Anyway, I thought you were talking about Sarah."

"Sarah?"

Aaron glanced at Carl then at Jen but their faces were blank. "You don't know? She didn't call and tell you? Sarah's little boy died over the weekend."

Jen's eyebrows rose. "Died. What? She never...She had a son? I didn't know..."

Aaron nodded, "Yes, a little boy with muscular dystrophy. That's why she was so bent on finding a cure, and why she sometimes ignored the rules."

Jen shook her head, idly flipping through the pages of her notepad. "She was always...so tense. No wonder..." She shot Dr. Jaeger a look, her eyes narrow and stern. "And you fired her. You fired a girl whose son just died. How heartless is that?"

"You fired her?" Aaron said.

Dr. Jaeger glanced at Jen. He shuffled his feet shifting the weight from one boot to the other. "But you said...I mean, no one told me she..."

"Don't look at me," Jen countered. I just said she was late." She spun on her heel and walked away, but Aaron could see she was shaken.

The sun tried in vain but just couldn't penetrate the fog. It was one of those mornings when color is reduced to a few shades of gray. Sarah meandered along the wharf feeling the moisture on her cheeks. She tugged at her plaid jacket, snuggling into its lining but it didn't help. The material was damp and the cold seeped through and settled on her skin. She wrapped herself in her arms and shivered.

Overhead, seagulls screeched hoping to be tossed a morsel of food, but she didn't notice. Nor was she paying attention to the dog tugging at the end of its leash. What she saw instead was Buddy. She felt the warmth of his small body meshed against hers as they sat on the trolley, his smile exploding into a million giggles at the clanging of the bell. She saw him on the boardwalk, his eyes wide with anticipation as mimes and jugglers performed their art, and his excitement as they explored the treasures found in the curio shops of Pier 13. She heard his voice echoing in Ghirardelli Square announcing loudly that peppermint chocolate was his favorite drink in the whole wide world.

Maybe she shouldn't have come. There were too many memories of things she needed to forget but she couldn't just sit around the apartment staring at the walls. Everything reminded her of Buddy. She'd walk by his wheelchair and tears would start to flow, heat a bowl of soup and realize she'd made enough for two, or turn on the TV and find herself watching his favorite show. What was she supposed to do?

That's why she needed her job. Of course she needed money, she had to return the van and buy a car, and she needed to pay the rent and buy food. She desperately wanted to find a cure for Duchene's, the lethal version of MD that took Buddy, she wanted to save other mothers from feeling the grief she now felt, but what she really needed was something to occupy her mind, to keep it from constantly mulling over things she couldn't change. God had taken her son, and her father, and now her job. How could He be so cruel?

She wanted to respond like Job—*The Lord gives and the Lord takes away*—but she wasn't sure she could praise the Lord, not yet, not right now. *Lord give me strength.* She wanted to be happy for Buddy, happy because she knew he was free of his wheelchair, free to explore heaven without braces or crutches or being carried in her arms—but she was still on earth, trapped in the circle of life: a time to be born and a time to die, a time to mourn and a time to dance. Perhaps she couldn't see it but somewhere a mother gave birth to another child, somewhere kids were at play, and somewhere another mother's heart was breaking. Life just went on, but God was everywhere, in, and among, and through it all. It wasn't much, but she took solace in that.

She found a bench and sat down facing the water. Snowball leapt forward, barking, *arff, arff, arff, arff, arff,* nearly ripping the leash from her hand. A lone pelican launched itself from a wood piling and disappeared into the mist. A fog horn sounded out across the bay. The ocean sucked, sloshed, and gurgled against the pier.

"Snowball, don't! Leave it alone." She reined the dog back, pulling him into her arms to scratch his head; his fur was as moist as the weather. Another problem—should she keep the dog, or find it a new home? And then there was Aaron—one question after another. She could no longer deny her feelings, but she was treading a dangerous path. Turn to the right and she might end up courting an unbeliever, turn to the left and she could end up miserable and alone. Maybe it was wrong, but she needed him.

So where did that leave her? She was an orphan, alone in the world without a job and, once she returned the van, no way of finding one. She should probably go home to South Dakota. The university had offered her a position as a post doc before she left, but she'd wanted to find her father. Maybe it was still open. It was either that or sit on the sidewalk begging money with the rest of the homeless. Her eyes began to fill—*again*. She couldn't even afford a decent funeral for her son. She'd told Aaron she'd pay for the casket and plot, but that was before she lost her job. What would she do now? Tears meandered down her cheeks but this time she couldn't say whether they were for Buddy—or for herself.

Twenty-Four

For we know that if our earthly house, this tent, is destroyed, we have a building from God, a house not made with hands, eternal in the heavens. —2 Corinthians 5:1

TWO DAYS and a thousand tears had already passed, but now was the appointed time to cry. Not even the coldest heart would deny a mother the right to weep at her son's funeral.

The small gathering shuffled around a mound of dirt removed from the earth to make room for Buddy. After so many days of fog and rain, they were blessed to be standing under a cloudless sky, wrapped by the sun's invisible warmth. Sarah could not have asked for a nicer day. The grassy lawns and stately palms looked refreshingly green, though the trees still lacked a full bounty of leaves.

The site's location was an elevated plane nestled among hills that rose and fell off toward the ocean. They were south of San Francisco, overlooking El Camino Real. Sarah didn't like having to go so far, but all the graveyards within city limits were filled long ago. It had fallen to the town of Colma to meet the need. So many cemeteries had been established in Colma it was said the town's population numbered more dead than living.

Sarah stood in front of a hole carved out of the ground with precision, a perfect rectangle with square sides like a giant mouth waiting to swallow her son. The small half-sized casket rested on a chrome apparatus of pipes, rollers and belts that would lower Buddy down to a place from which he would never return—*ashes to ashes and dust to dust.*

Aaron was standing on her left dressed in a black Calvin Klein suit made of hand-finished wool so smooth it shone in the light. His shirt was a Brooks Brother's white cotton accented with a black silk tie.

Sarah didn't begrudge Aaron for dressing up. The occasion of her son's passing called for looking his best. She wore a new black outfit herself, a skirt and matching blouse she'd bought at Walmart. It was a purchase that, without a job, she probably shouldn't have made but convinced herself it was okay because she didn't feel right about wearing something cobbled together from her existing wardrobe. Decorum was expected at a funeral.

Besides, that didn't mean all her clothes were new. Proper mourning required a veil so she'd gone to her neighborhood Goodwill and bought a black hat with a cloak of webby material that now covered her face. And her tall, black lace-up boots, which she slipped on over black nylons, were from the existing finery of her closet.

On her right stood Beth, whose tears also flowed freely. The two women were locked arm in arm, each supporting the other. Behind them stood a few folks from her support group who had come to pay their respects, each of them knowing they too would one day be standing there mourning a loss of their own.

For a man with a ponytail, Sarah had to admit Pastor Bob was also looking rather chic. He'd nixed his Levis in favor of a black suit, but shunned the formal tie opting instead to wear a black T-shirt under his coat. He looked solemn as he opened his Bible and began to read:

"'But I would not have you be ignorant, brethren, concerning those who are asleep, that you sorrow not as others who have no hope. For if we believe that Jesus died and rose again, even so those also who sleep in Jesus will God bring with him.' First Thessalonians 4:13 & 14."

He closed his Bible holding his place with a finger and looked up to search the faces of his small audience. "Aren't those wonderful words? Our brother, Buddy, wasn't without hope. If you ever talked with him, you know he trusted in Jesus, and according to God's word, that means he has the assurance of eternal life. We may not see him again until we ourselves cross over, but you can trust in the promise of God that he'll be waiting for us when we get there. Let me read you another passage, this time from First Corinthians, chapter fifteen."

It was obvious Pastor Bob wasn't comfortable speaking in tight spaces. He was a man who liked to move when he preached but here he was confined by the arc of people surrounding the grave. He turned one way while flipping through the pages, and when he found the passage, turned back again. "Ah, here we are. Let's begin with verse thirty-five. 'But some will ask, how are the dead raised up, and with what body do they come?'" He looked up catching Sarah's eye as if this was important for her to know. "That's a fair question, isn't it? I mean it would be kind of nice to know what's happened to Buddy, wouldn't it? Now skip down to verse forty-two for the answer: 'So also is the resurrection of the dead. It,' the body, 'is sown in corruption; it is raised in incorruption; it is sown in dishonor; it is raised in glory; it is sown in weakness; it is raised in power; it is sown a natural body; it is raised a spiritual body…So when this corruptible shall have put on incorruption, and this mortal shall have put on immortality, then shall be brought to pass the saying that is written, 'Death is swallowed up in victory. O death, where is your sting? O grave, where is your victory?'"

He looked up, his smile warm enough to melt butter. "Brothers and sisters, friends, I submit to you that Buddy has left this body of corruption behind and taken on a body of incorruption, he has left this mortal world and taken on immortality, no more wheelchairs, praise God!" He raised his fist and shouted, "O death, where is your sting? O grave, where is your victory?"

Sarah slipped a look at Aaron wondering if he was getting any of this. If he was, his face didn't show it. He had a look of boredom, or maybe he was just trying to look solemn for the occasion.

"The hard part isn't for Buddy. He's outta here, the hard part is for us, because we're gonna miss him…"

There was consolation in the warmth of the sun, the feeling that winter had passed and they'd finally moved into spring. It could have been cold and rainy. The previous week had its share of dismal weather but today the sun was shining and the damp on the newly mowed lawn smelled sweet. Sarah felt the black material of her blouse absorbing heat, warming her skin right down to her soul—*thank you Lord!* She held two things in her hand: a single long stem rose and an envelope containing the only letter she'd ever received from Buddy's father. She felt it appropriate to lay both on the coffin before it was lowered into the ground. The rose was a symbol of Buddy's life—*we bloom, we grow, we wither, we die*—and the letter because…well, just because she wanted Buddy to have something from his father and it was all she had.

She still hurt about that. Brian had promised so much, and delivered so little, but it wasn't fair to sum their entire relationship up in one letter, and especially one that didn't mention the time they'd spent together, or that he missed her and couldn't wait till they saw each other again. It was simply a missive about how dry the desert was: his sore feet, the inedible food, and the incessant heat. Sarah shuddered. She could only hope he'd been killed overseas, not because she wished him evil, but because it was easier to think of him as dead than to think he'd come home and not bothered to even call.

She did have one thing to thank him for. With her mother gone, and finding herself alone trying to raise a sick child while going to school, she'd turned to the church and in seeking solace had found Christ. If that's what it took to acquire the kind of contentment that came only through a relationship with Jesus, it was worth what she'd had to endure. But she did wish God would have allowed her to keep Buddy.

"If there's anyone here that doesn't know Christ," Sarah snapped out of her revere. Pastor Bob was summing up. "I want to invite you to stay after the service so I can pray with you. Or you can do it on your own. All it takes is that you call upon God, let Him know you believe Christ died to pay for the wrongs you've done, ask His forgiveness and let Him know you receive Him as Savior and Lord. God didn't make it hard, but He does require we do it His way. Praise God, Buddy knew this, and that's why I know we're going to see him again."

The pastor nodded to someone standing to his right. A girl Sarah recognized from the church moved to the front and began to sing a cappella.

"One day when heaven was filled with His praises,
One day when sin was as black as could be,
Jesus came forth to be born of a virgin,
Dwelt among men, my example is He!

"Living, He loved me; dying, He saved me;
Buried, He carried my sins far away;
Rising, He justified freely forever:
One day He's coming—O glorious day!"

Sarah swallowed the lump in her throat. She couldn't hold back her tears, nor did she try. Her lips quivered as she began to hum along with the soloist, not loud enough to be heard but enough to affirm her agreement.

"One day they led Him up Calvary's mountain,
One day they nailed Him to die on the tree;
Suffering anguish, despised and rejected;
Bearing our sins, my Redeemer is He."

She wanted to throw her hands in the air and with tears streaming down her face sing loudly: *We shall rise, hallelujah we shall rise. We shall rise hallelujah we shall rise. When the trumpet sounds and he calls us home, we shall rise...* but such joy didn't belong on the face of someone in mourning and it would be ill mannered to interrupt.

"One day the trumpet will sound for His coming,
One day the skies with His glory will shine;
Wonderful day, my beloved ones bringing;
Glorious Savior, this Jesus is mine."

Her son would be there and she was content with that. But what about Aaron? It was likely he disagreed with everything the pastor said. She had to steel herself against the disappointment that would come when they discussed the memorial service and guard against making the same mistake she'd made with Brian. She wasn't emotionally strong enough for a relationship. Maybe that was the problem. She was worried about her relationship with Aaron when she should be concerned about *his* relationship with Christ.

She caught Pastor Bob looking at her. His head gave a quick nod. It was time. Letting go of Beth's arm, she took a step forward and laid the flower and the letter on the coffin, then swung around and glanced up—*What?* Off to the side, dressed in black slacks and a sweater too tight for the occasion, was her nemesis—the embodiment of Cruella DeVil—but this girl had tears pouring down her cheeks—*Jen?*

The Sum of the Parts Are Equal to the Whole
The Journal of W.L. Summer

Molecular machines and other biological systems frequently need to have all their parts working at the same time in order to function. But according to evolution, organisms are supposed to improve over long periods of time by weeding out unnecessary or redundant parts while maintaining those which add benefit. If an organism requires all its parts to be in place before it works, then the parts have to arise simultaneously, but the process of evolution doesn't account for that.

A commonly cited example is the flagellum, a microscopic organism with a tiny propeller, a paddle, a rotor and a motor powered by acid that moves bacterium around. This tiny machine has over forty parts, none of which can function unless all the other parts are already in place. If any part is damaged or missing, the motor doesn't work, which discounts evolution because until all the parts are in place the motor has no purpose. Natural selection would see each individual component as pointless and weed it out before the whole assembly could come together.

Another example is the human eye. The eye is composed of numerous parts, all of which must be in place in order for the eye to work. If any part of the eye is missing the eye becomes useless. In this respect, the evolution of the eye is a non-start because in order to see, every part of the eye must function simultaneously but every part is so vastly complex, its own evolution would take billions of years.

However, if these systems were designed and built by a superior intelligence, well, that's another story…

Twenty-Five

He stretches the north over the empty place, and hangs the earth upon nothing. —Job 26:7 The sea is His, and He made it, and His hands formed the dry land. —Psalm 95:5

DETECTIVE Rodriquez patted his hair. He wore it swept back from his forehead in coal black waves, oiled and shiny, with sideburns to help widen the look of his narrow face. He stepped back from the mirror to straighten his tie and dust the dandruff from his jacket. Someday he would be lead detective. Maybe sooner than anyone thought. He grinned and gave himself a thumbs up—*looking good*. He plowed through the door of the men's room, returning to his desk.

Sitting on a pile of unopened letters was a large manila envelope with a flap held closed by brass tabs. The report? Must have just been dropped into his basket because it hadn't been there a few minutes before. Eduardo reached for the packet and held it up, anxious about seeing what was inside but needing to control his excitement. The test might prove negative. He pushed back the tabs and slid the document into his hand as he held his breath. *Yes! The paint chip is a match.*

A quick plate search had given him the name of the vehicle's owner, a Mrs. Rose, but an inquiry revealed the car was on loan to her son. A cross-reference database showed the boy worked at CellMerge Inc. and CellMerge was where the deceased had worked so there was a connection. Now he had the final piece of the puzzle—the proof. All he had to do was make the arrest without involving his partner so he could avoid sharing the credit. He looked up and saw Irons heading toward him with a coffee in hand.

They had already contacted the area's BMW dealerships and requested lists of anyone who purchased a vehicle in the past few years. Then they'd wasted two days calling every body shop in town. Lucky for him the car hadn't been left for repair or it would have been game over. Hugh would have made the arrest.

This was Eduardo's time. He had the name of the suspect, Mr. Aaron Rose, he had Mr. Rose's address—a condo in the Sea Cliff district, some of San Francisco's most prestigious real estate—and he had proof that Mr. Rose's car killed Dr. Summer. All he had to do was find a way to leave without making old Ironball suspicious.

"What's that?" Hugh asked. He pulled his chair back and sat down, careful not to spill as he pushed paper around to clear a place for his coffee. Steam wafted up from the rim. He scooted forward and leaned in to take a sip, his big hands making the mug look small.

Eduardo slipped the report back into its envelope and tossed it into a drawer. "It is nothing, jis a proposed settlement from the lawyer of my soon to be ex-wife." *Brilliant!* "Speaking of which, I need to take off for a few hours. My lawyer has drafted a counter offer and wants to go over it with me."

Hugh shook his head. "I feel your pain. A woman starts out stealing your heart and ends up stealing everything else. Sure, go ahead. I have a ton of paperwork to do. It'll give me a chance to clear my desk."

Eduardo smiled and stood reaching inside his coat to make sure he had his weapon. The cold metal welcomed his fingers. He adjusted the leather holster. It was warm outside. It would be better if he could lose the coat but he had to wear it to conceal his gun. Now if he could only think of a way of explaining how he was able to make the arrest when he was supposed to be with his lawyer… but, not to worry, he'd figure something out. "Alright, catch you later, amigo."

It was a twenty minute drive to the tri-towers of CellMerge. Eduardo found a parking space in the visitor section and went inside. The floors were a gleaming black marble surrounded by walls of gold tinted glass. Palms grew in gigantic pots toward the twenty foot ceiling.

The uniformed security officer behind the granite counter snapped to attention when Eduardo removed his wallet and flipped it open presenting his badge.

"Detective Eduardo Rodriquez with the San Mateo Police Department. I need to speak with Mr. Aaron Rose," he said.

The guard typed the name into the company's directory and reached for the phone, dialing Aaron's department while letting Eduardo know he was thinking of going back to school to major in police science and one day hoped to enter the academy. "Just a second," he raised his index finger as he turned back to the phone. "Alright, I'll let him know." He looked at Eduardo again. "Sorry, but Dr. Rose isn't in today."

"Did they say where he was?"

The desk jockey shook his head. "I didn't ask."

Eduardo leaned in, placing his elbows on the counter. "You want to be a good cop, you gotta ask lots of questions. Call back and see if there's someone who knows Mr. Rose's whereabouts. Better still, get his supervisor out here and I'll talk to him myself."

It was probably only five minutes but it seemed more like a half hour before the doors opened and a short man with a goatee entered the lobby. He was wearing a cowboy shirt that had become untucked because it was too small to fit around his gut. His round wire glasses looked smudged as he stepped forward with his hand outstretched. "I'm Dr. Jaeger. You the one looking for Dr. Rose?"

Eduardo took Carl's hand. It felt mushy, like a bag of boiled peanuts.

"Detective Rodriquez," he said. "Yes, do you know where he is?"

"What's it about?"

"I'm not at liberty to say. Police business. I just need to ask him a few questions."

Carl wavered for a moment, shifting his weight from one boot to the other. "Probably on his boat," he said.

Eduardo raised his chin. His lips were knotted, his cheeks sucked in.

"He and another one of my staff called in to say they were going to a funeral, which they probably did because there was a funeral to attend but that would have lasted only a few hours and they're still gone. A day like today, I mean look at it out there, perfect day and he has a boat he loves to float so if I was a betting man, I'd put my money on them being out on the water which is a real problem for me, leaving me short handed like that, but anyway, that's about all I can tell you."

Detective Rodriquez flipped his wallet open and produced a card which he handed to Dr. Jaeger. "Thanks for your help. If you see him, would you have him give me a call? It's important."

"Yep, you betcha, not a problem."

"By the way, you wouldn't happen to know where he keeps his boat, would you?"

The yacht rolled back and forth on the swells making it hard to walk the deck in a straight line, but Jen hadn't been drinking, and neither had Aaron. He'd wanted to drive Sarah home but she insisted on having Beth take her back to her apartment saying she needed time alone, and that left him with Jen, the only other person he knew at the funeral, and it was a beautiful day, one that shouldn't go to waste, and he did want someone to talk to, so there they were, riding the tide on an ocean blue as winter, with a sun so warm it felt like summer. Small whitecaps sloshed against the hull as the boat rocked back and forth on the breeze.

They sat beside each other on the white vinyl cushions that formed a U shaped couch at the boat's stern. Jen had her arm in his, holding his hand with her head resting on his shoulder.

"I have to admit I was surprised to see you there," he said.

"I confess I'm a bit surprised myself, but something inside made me go." Jen slid her hand up and down Aaron's arm. Her touch was warm. A tear rolled down her cheek falling onto his hand.

"What's that about?" Aaron said, feeling the drop wet his skin.

Jen rolled her head back and forth on his shoulder. "I don't know. I guess…I'm just melancholy, that's all." She sighed and then added, "I…I lost a child once."

Aaron pulled back. "You?"

She nodded. "Yes, not the same way, but I still hurt from it. I had an abortion."

"That's not the same thing."

Jen sucked in a breath and let it out with a sigh. "I know. That's what everyone tells me, but it hurts all the same. They told me I'd just eject some fetal material into a pan and it would be over. They were supposed to take it away quickly. I wasn't to see anything but the lady helping me, she wasn't a doctor, at least I don't think she was, but she got called out for a minute and there it was. I could see it, arms and legs, and it was my child, torn in pieces, and it hit me that I'd killed my baby." Another tear followed the first. "I don't even like Sarah but when I heard she lost her son, it kind of…you know, I just felt different, that's all. And to think he died of MD. I couldn't sleep last night knowing I'd just gotten her fired…"

"You didn't fire her. That was Dr. Jaeger."

"I know, but I went to his office and complained about her being late and he wanted me to say how much better it was with Dr. Summer gone and I…I went along, and that's why he let her go…and I'm thinking about how bad I am sometimes, and how

I killed my baby and…and I…" Jen raised her head off Aaron's shoulder. "Do you think there's a hell?"

Aaron was gazing out over the ocean where the blue sky and green sea dropped off toward the horizon, or maybe toward infinity. God? If God made the universe, then who made God? He knew time had a beginning, but maybe God preceded the beginning of time. Maybe He existed in a place where time didn't apply, a place without beginning or end. Maybe God just was. Is there a hell?

"I don't know. To be a hell there has to be a heaven and to be a heaven there has to be a God, and I'm not there yet. I try, I mean I'd like to believe but it seems a bit naïve. I don't know, I guess I'm conflicted. Dr. Summer came to the conclusion there was a God, and he's no dummy, and if you could have met Sarah's kid, Buddy, he had incredible faith. Like he didn't fear death at all. In his mind, he was just going to Jesus, but it doesn't work that way for me."

"I used to be Lutheran."

Aaron squeezed her hand and let go bringing his arm out so he could rest it on the back of the seat. The horizon held a thin white veil of clouds, the fragrance of ocean salt filling the air. "And…?" he said, prompting her to continue.

"I don't know. I used to believe in God but over the years it kind of just went away."

Aaron picked a piece of lint from the cushion and flicked it into the water. "Well I used to be Jewish," he said. I guess if anyone should believe in God it would be me."

Jen looked up. "You're not Jewish."

"Yes I am."

"To be Jewish you have to be born a Jew and you're…"

"Our family name is Rosenthal but my dad had it shortened. He and Mom were non-practicing anyway and it got in the way of business. He said goyem are funny about doing business with kikes, and Dad wasn't going to let anything get in the way of business."

"No way, but you never said anything."

"It never came up."

The air fell silent. Jen picked at her fingernail. The ocean rolled rocking the boat. A light breeze rippled her hair. "I did it," She finally said. She looked at Aaron, her eyes like liquid glass.

"Did what?"

"I said that prayer the preacher said to pray." She turned her head to stare out over the ocean. "I don't know if it'll do any good. When I think about, you know, some of the things I've done, I doubt God would want me, but I did it all the same..."

Eduardo scooted away from the curb, his tires spinning on the loose gravel as the car lurched into the street. Mr. Rose hadn't been at home either. He'd pounded the door loud enough to wake the dead. And he'd checked the garage for the car but it was gone.

There was one more place to try, the marina, but the thought troubled him. He hadn't known about the boat. If the suspect tried to escape using the roads he'd notify the Highway Patrol and put out an APB. Sooner or later someone would spot the damaged vehicle and the man would be brought to justice, and he'd still get credit for gathering the evidence before going to trial. But how do you catch a boat? There was the coast guard, but they didn't have the resources to check every craft on the water. Besides, once Rose took his boat beyond the three mile limit they wouldn't have jurisdiction. Then he could cruise the coast either up to Canada or down to Mexico and escape.

Sarah sat with the curtains drawn clinging to Snowball. The little dog was like a warm blanket covering her dark soul, a friend in time of need. Beth had wanted to stay and be a comfort, but Sarah insisted she leave. She wanted time alone with God.

She had prayed and asked forgiveness. God had taken Buddy. That was His choice. She didn't like feeling resentful. *As high as the heavens are above the earth are My ways above your ways.* Nor did she want to hold it against Brian whom she was tempted to begrudge for not being there—the father who never was. She shouldn't have feelings for the man, not after all this time, but she knew, even as she laid his letter on their son's grave, that she did.

Sarah shook her head. There was a house to clean and she needed to start looking for a job. She got up from the sofa and went to the kitchen, set on doing the dishes. Her movements were slow and mechanical, the routine requiring little thought. Life must go on. Covering the strainer with a rubber disc to keep the sink from draining, she cranked on the screeching taps. Water in an uneven flow filled the sink, bubbles growing up around the sides, tiny prismatic orbs glowing like rainbows. Her dishes hadn't been washed in several days.

She took a plate, one of the chipped set of flowery dishes she'd purchased at the thrift store, and began to scrub. There weren't many to do, since she had to force herself to eat, but she hadn't rinsed anything either so the food felt like it was held on with glue. By the time she finished the bubbles had dissipated and the water was gutter gray. Isn't that the way love is, lots of colorful bubbles at first until they burst and everything turns murky? Brian was her first, and only, and the father of her child, and now God had taken them both, and she knew His will had been done.

She dried her hands on a towel and made her way back to the living room. The balance of things that summed up her life with Buddy—a TV, some scattered books, a few drawers containing his clothes, the wheelchair—rested in the shadows. How could so little mean so much?

She began sifting through the mess. There were many things to do, clean the house, prepare a resume, find a home for the dog—she couldn't keep it, her apartment didn't allow pets—but Snowball was a friend, a comfort in time of need, how could she let him go? She looked around. She didn't have strength to begin. At least she could write a quick email. She picked up her laptop and flopped onto the sofa, taking Snowball into her lap as she flipped the computer open. The dog nuzzled her arm encouraging her to scratch its head.

From: Dr. Sarah Hunter <sarahhunter1989@gmail.com>

To: Dr. Michael Hudson

Dear Dr. Mike.

Sorry I haven't kept in touch. I've been busy trying to get settled in, but to be blunt, things haven't worked out. Truth is, I'm homesick. I was wondering if there's any chance the post doc is still open. I don't think San Francisco's where I need to be.

Let me know,

Sarah

Sarah let the cursor waver over the send button. Dr. Mike was a good researcher, and they got along fine, but she always felt uneasy when he pressed in a little too close while looking over her shoulder. His warm breath and the smell of his stale English Leather were creepy. She was the student, he was the teacher; she didn't need him breaking that trust. She used the mouse to drag the message to her draft file. She could always mail it later.

Twenty-Six

Where were you when I laid the foundations of the earth? Tell me, if you have understanding. —Job 38:4

EDUARDO PACED back and forth on the boardwalk, a man with lots of time and no place to go. He mopped his brow with the sleeve of his coat as he looked across the Pacific at the bright red tomato of a sun. His stomach rolled. He'd gone all day without eating.

It had been a frustrating afternoon, waiting, hoping, yes, even praying to the Blessed Virgin that his ship would come in, but one vessel after another had motored into the marina and, so far, no Mr. Rose. He was probably half way down the coast making his escape. Eduardo cupped his hand over his eyes. Another boat was heading toward the docks. He'd wait for this one, but it was getting dark. It would have to be the last.

The yacht was a sleek low profile motor craft. It cruised past the first platform, then the second. Eduardo held his breath, *Yes*, it was heading for a slip on the far side of the marina, right where it belonged. The twin diesel engines gurgled as they churned the water leaving a trail of white foam. It had to be him. It was hard to make out in the thin light but he was sure the words on the back of the boat read, "Rover Moon." That's what the guy back at CellMerge said the boat was called.

He looked at his watch. Tying off the boat should only take a few minutes. This might work out better anyway. He could say he'd been to his lawyer in the morning and then swung by to make the arrest. And he'd concocted a good story to make his little bit of luck seem like a lot of hard police work.

Two people were moving down the gangway heading his direction. There was no reason to expect trouble but it would have been better if the perp were alone. He reached under his jacket for his weapon and held it at his side until they'd cleared the gate, then stepped out from the shadows.

"Dr. Rose?"

The man turned, startled at hearing his name. "Yes."

Eduardo raised and pointed his gun.

"Ahhhh helllllllllp! We're being robbed," Jen screamed.

"Turn around and place your hands behind your head. Shut up Lady! I'm a police officer."

Aaron started to comply but hesitated. "What's this about?"

"Just do it!"

"Helllllp! This man's trying to rob us! *Helllllllllllllp!"*

"Shut up! This ain't no robbery." The detective addressed Jen but kept his firearm trained on Aaron. "I said turn around and lock your hands behind your head." He took one hand off his gun and slowly reached into his vest pocket producing a wallet which he flipped open. "Here, lady, check the badge."

Aaron did as told. Eduardo freed a pair of cuffs and moved forward, snapping them on Aaron's wrists, one at a time.

"Aaron Rose, I'm placing you under arrest for the murder of Dr. Wallace Summer. You have the right…"

"What? Wait a minute, there's been some mistake."

"Save it for your lawyer, bobo."

· * ★ 🌐 ★ * ·

Sarah picked up a shirt and held it to her nose drinking in

the faint scent of her son, then folded it into the waiting box. She was almost done. Buddy hadn't owned much. She looked into the drawer and found one last pair of socks hiding in the back. Over by the door sat a wheelchair, a portable fold-up bed and five other boxes filled with clothes and books, videos and DVDs, all of Buddy's earthly possessions.

It hadn't struck her as odd before but now, with everything in one place, she wondered about the things that were missing. *Toys.* Buddy had none. As his condition progressively worsened, things that amused him when he was younger and stronger were left idle and ultimately given away. His life had become a routine of trying to manage one breath after another just to stay alive. It wasn't much of a consolation, but the realization did make letting go easier.

She sighed, feeling the air in her chest flutter as she swept a strand of hair from her eyes. The apartment was starting to look organized. It surprised her that she'd been able to do anything at all. The dishes were dried and put away; the wheelchair was parked by the door, ready to be given to someone in need. She'd called and got permission to keep the van a bit longer, just until she could find another job and buy a car of her own. The box at her feet was half empty but there was nothing left to put inside. Everything was packed. She picked it up and set it by the others.

That was it. She wiped her hands on her pants. The bed was made, the room vacuumed and dusted, the bathroom neatened up and the toilet cleaned, all clutter picked up and put away. She'd even pulled back the curtains and opened the window to let in fresh air, though it was time to close it again. The evening was getting cool.

There were a few things she'd decided to keep. First and foremost was the photo album. Too bad she'd never taken a picture of Brian but back then her cellphone didn't have a camera. She was certain he'd come to visit her as soon as he got leave and they only

191

had a few days together so she figured there'd be plenty of time for that later. Buddy never got to see what his father looked like.

She went to her dresser and opened the album, turning the pages, she and Buddy in MacDonald's, his favorite restaurant, celebrating his sixth birthday with him wearing a silly paper crown and a smile as broad as his face, and one at two years old where she was holding him in front of Mt. Rushmore—she'd taken him there before she realized Brian wasn't coming back—and a more recent picture taken on a gray winter's day showing Buddy in his wheelchair with Beth taking him out for a stroll in Golden Gate Park, treasured memories of their life together. A tear formed in her eye. She wasn't through grieving yet, but that was okay, her healing would come. It was just a matter of time. She closed the book and placed it back on the bureau.

The black skirt and blouse she'd worn to the funeral were now powdered with dust. Her closet still needed work, and so did her wardrobe...

Knock, knock, knock.

Snowball darted for the door barking, *arff, arff, arff, arff, arff, gurrrrrrrrrrrr.*

Aaron? She ran to the bathroom mirror and flicked her hair setting it in place.

Knock, knock, knock.

"I'll be right there." Her face was a mess but she didn't have time to make it better. She hurried to the door flinging it open.

Aaron sat at a table in a room with just four empty walls and a mirror. They'd brought him in and left him alone, ostensibly to consider the consequence of his actions and ripen him up for a confession. He'd seen enough cop shows to know there were people on the other side of that mirror watching him. If the TV programs depicted real life, he could expect two cops to enter any minute, the good cop, and the bad cop, one to act like he was there to help, and the other to pronounce him guilty, and threaten him with all the horrors he would experience as soon as they put him away.

What he couldn't grasp was why he was there at all. The officer who made the arrest said it was for the murder of Dr. Summer, but that was ridiculous. It was probably best to not say anything until he had representation. That's what TV lawyers always told their clients. The police were notorious for twisting things around and getting you to say things you didn't mean. How was he supposed to afford a lawyer? He'd just burned through his mother's emergency fund, and she was off climbing the Himalayas where she couldn't be reached.

The door opened and Aaron looked up at the man who had arrested him. The file he carried went *wafump* as he slapped it down on the table. He was thin and swarthy, of obvious Spanish decent.

"Evening Mr. Rose, my name's detective Eduardo Rodriquez."

Aaron nodded. "I guess you already know my name," he said.

"That's right. In fact, I know a lot about chu, but before I get into that I have to let you know you don't have to talk to me without your lawyer present, but I promise it will go better for you if you cooperate."

"I'll do what I can." Aaron assured him.

"That's good. You seem like a bright kid. I just hope you're smart enough to do the right thing. You're being charged with a very serious crime but there's a bit of latitude in the way we lay the charges, and much of that depends on you. At the very least you've committed a hit and r…"

"But I didn't…"

"There you go hurting yourself. You should be trying to gain my trust. I mean, you don't have to confess, whether you do or not is strictly up to you, but we know you did it. We have proof.

193

What has yet to be determined is, were your actions the result of an accident, or intentional. You could be looking at manslaughter or homicide depending on two things." The detective brought his fingers up and counted them off. "One is how cooperative you are, and the other is, of course, where the evidence leads."

Aaron felt his whole body twitch. He scooted forward. "You can't be serious. What evidence?"

Rodriquez drew the file in toward himself and removed a photo which he slid across the table. It was a close up of the Beemer's bent bumper and grill. "Your car, I had it impounded. The paint is a hundred percent match for paint chips left on Dr. Summer's body, and this," Eduardo slid a second photo across the table to Aaron, "is a close up showing several threads of Dr. Summer's coat caught in your grill. Perhaps you can start with an explanation."

"That's ridiculous," Aaron said, pushing the photo back across the table with his fingertips. "I wasn't even around. I was out with Mr. Landon. You can ask him."

Detective Rodriquez made a note and looked up. "And who is Mr. Landon?"

"President of CellMerge. Go ahead, call him, he'll vouch for me."

"And what time did you and Mr. Landon part company?"

"I don't know, I guess it was about seven. I think he was meeting someone for dinner."

"According to the autopsy, Dr. Summer wasn't killed until around eleven, so you had several hours to get there. Perhaps you can explain what you did in the meantime."

Aaron slouched in his chair and folded his arms. "I think I'd better see a lawyer," he said.

Sarah held the door open unable to find her tongue. The sun at Jen's back cast her in silhouette but the tall shapely figure with backlit yellow hair was unmistakable. Already Sarah questioned Jen's showing up at the funeral. Her tears may have been real but Sarah couldn't help thinking she was there more to protect her interests than to pay last respects. Jen didn't even know Buddy; she just wanted Aaron within reach. And now she was standing in the doorway. What was she supposed to say?

"Well, are you going to invite me in?"

No. She wanted to slam the door and walk away but decency forbade it—*If your enemy is thirsty, give him something to drink.* She took a step back pulling the door open wide.

Jen sauntered in with her hands stuffed in the pockets of her coat. "*Hunh,* so this is where you live," she remarked. "I suppose it suits you." As she turned, her eye caught the wheelchair, the roll-away bed and the stack of boxes on the floor. Her ponytail was draped over her shoulder, her pink lips compressed flat. She wore a white leatherette jacket over a thin black sweater. The jacket fit tight around her waist where it was zipped, but was spread open at the top to frame her bosom and it had a furry collar that fluffed up under her cheeks. Her skintight denims rode two inches above her ankles where she had high-stepping white spiked heels. She glanced at Sarah.

"What's the matter, cat got your tongue?" She brought a hand with white fingernails up to scratch her nose. "Look, you don't like me, I get that. Can't say as I care much for you either..."

Sarah was still in her drab black outfit, the one she'd worn to the funeral. *How pathetic.* But it didn't matter, she couldn't compete with Jen even if she'd come home and changed. Fashion wasn't her thing. *I don't care much for you either. Right, but who dissed who first?*

"...I mean, you said you wanted to be left alone so Aaron and I took his boat out for a cruise and it was really nice, just being on the water on a sunny day and getting to talk. There were things I didn't realize. You and I aren't so different you know, at least in some ways, and we have the same taste in men, though Aaron is far more interested in you than he is in me, which is something I *totally* don't get. No offence, but he's way out of your league, but that's not why I'm here. It's that I need you to do me a favor..."

Whatever this was about, Sarah wasn't up for it. She was too tired and too stressed to decipher the incoherent ramblings of someone who made her feel like a bug. It wasn't enough that Jen ridiculed her at work, or that her constant harassment was probably the reason she'd been fired, now she was standing in her living room bragging about stealing Aaron and sailing off into the sunset. The door was still open letting in the cool air. Maybe she'd take a hint...*A what? She wants a favor?*

"...Our mutual friend's been arrested and he's going to need our help but I have to be at work tomorrow and since you don't, I mean, sorry about that, but it wasn't my decision, though I know I didn't help any, but since you have some free time now I thought maybe you could look into seeing if there's anything we can do..."

Sarah shook her head. "I have no clue what you're talking about. You barge in here babbling on about who knows what without any respect for the fact that I'm trying to mourn the loss of my son and..."

"I know and I'm sorry about that but I've been trying to tell you, Aaron's been arrested and he's going to need help and I couldn't think of anyone else to turn to. Maybe it will take your mind off things. I don't know..."

"Wait. Stop. What do you mean Aaron's been arrested?"

"They think he killed Dr. Summer."

"What?"

"Yeah, crazy, right? I mean, I know he said some things about him being old and maybe a bit flaky, but murder?"

Sarah reached over to close the door but air circling through the open window ripped the knob from her hand and slammed it shut with a *bang.* "*Ouch,* sorry." She grimaced and shrugged. "Have a seat," she said, pointing to the sofa. "So, what's this about?"

It Really Matters that Matter Can't Think
The Journal of W.L. Summer

It's generally held that the eye began as something called an eyespot or photoreceptor protein on a single celled organism. Because the intensity of direct light was unpleasant these so called eyespots gradually shrank back into concave depressions to find shade. As the cavity depressed further the opening became smaller until eventually there was only a small opening which, like a pinhole camera, allowed for the distinction of shapes. A layer of transparent cells eventually formed over the opening to keep out foreign objects and protect the fledging eye from harmful radiation. This layer ultimately divided itself into two layers which increased the viewing angle and resolution. Then, as the space between the layers widened, they took on a convex shape, which provided refraction. Two more layers eventually split off the front of the eye, one transparent and one opaque, forming the cornea and iris.

This is nonsense. The eye is actually an outgrowth of the brain, (some would say the brain is an outgrowth of the eye) but either way both are necessary for sight. The trouble is there's nothing orchestrating this development. Matter can't think. It has no way of determining what's good and what's bad, whether too much light hurts or is beneficial. Matter can't initiate cause and effect.

The evolutionary paradigm states that changes happen by accident. If a change is beneficial it survives but if it's bad or weakens the organism it's eliminated. However, when you read about the evolution of the eye you get the feeling the eye, or brain, knew what was needed and developed mechanisms to bring about the necessary changes. This would have required an evaluation process that didn't exist. The brain couldn't have realized a need to see and then coordinated the formation of the eye because while in darkness the brain didn't know what sight was. And the eye couldn't have determined that it needed a brain to analyze the images it received because it didn't know what thought was. The most rudimentary form of eye, the photoreceptor protein on a single celled organism, couldn't know it was receiving too much light and pull into a hole for protection. It had no way of determining whether light was harmful or not. If it was exposed to too much sun, it would simply burn up and die, not sit around thinking about where to find shade. That's called survival of the fittest. That's evolution.

Twenty-Seven

That they may see, and know, and consider, and understand together, that the hand of the Lord hath done this, and the Holy One of Israel hath created it. —*Isaiah 41:20*

EDUARDO SAW Battleship Ironsides cruising his way. He swung his feet down off the desk, his mind tingling with anticipation. Now was the moment he'd waited for. He wanted to seem casual and nonchalant, but he was too excited to pull it off. He'd been in the station since seven, wired on caffeine, unable to stay home and rest. He hunched over and began shuffling paper like he was hard at work. His heart flittered as he imagined himself telling his story and receiving the credit due. Outwardly his face bore a look of serious contemplation, but inside he was smiling ear to ear.

Hugh shrugged off his coat and draped it over the back of his chair. His collar was open and his tie hung loose. He plopped down with a huff, his desk notably cleaner than it had been the day before.

"Where were you yesterday? You said you'd only be gone a few hours?" He leaned back and slid a drawer open, pulling out an empty mug which he set on the cleared desktop. He looked up at his partner.

"We got him!" Eduardo said, his face breaking into the smile he could no longer contain.

"Got who?"

"Dr. Summer's killer. I arrested him yesterday."

"What?"

"I arrested the man who killed Dr. Summer."

"Yeah, yeah, I heard that." Hugh waved his hand dismissively. "What's the story?"

"Remember how we ran that list of local BMW owners. I decided to take it home and cross reference it with their employment records to see if I could find a connection and sure enough, I found the name of someone with a BMW that worked at CellMerge, the same place the vic previously worked. I say to myself, this can't be a coincidence so I go to the man's condo and guess what? There's a black Beemer in his carport with the front bashed in, so I take a chip of paint and bring it back and have forensics run an analysis, but I decide to hold off saying anything until I'm sure because I could still be wrong. I didn't want to get the dogs barking up the wrong tree. Anyway, the report came back yesterday and it turned out to be a match and since I was already out, I decided to go ahead and make the arrest."

Hugh leaned back, crossed his feet and stretched out with his fingers laced behind his head. "So you trespassed on private property without a warrant and stole evidence. Good luck with that. They'll throw it out in a New York minute."

Eduardo balked, his mouth hanging open. His eyes were blinking rapidly. Then shaking his head he blurted out, "No, no, I mean the car was parked on the street out front of where he lives, on public property. Sorry, I jus' didn't say it right."

Hugh puckered his face. "Okay, so you notified patrol and had them pick up the guy."

"No, I did it myself."

"You brought him in yourself? Alone? What for? You should have let patrol handle the arrest."

"I would have, but I was talking to someone that knows our

perp and he tells me the guy's got a boat and that he's out sailing and I get to thinking, maybe he's gonna split for Canada or Mexico and get away, so I decide the smart thing to do is to take action."

Irons shook his head. "Smart is never going in without backup. At the very least you should have called me. I would have met you there."

"He's just a punk rich kid, didn't even put up a fight. Anyway, I didn't think he'd be armed, probably doesn't even own a gun. If he did, he would have used it on the vic."

Hugh shook his head. He leaned in placing his elbows on his desk, hands folded. "'Didn't think' has got more good officers killed than any two words I know. You sure you went through academy? You're breaking every rule in the book. I'll be lucky if you read him his Miranda."

"Of course I read him his rights and then I brought him in and booked him. I tried to get a confession but he lawyered up."

"Kid's already got a lawyer? *Sheeech*."

"I don't know. Probably does by now. He was calling one when I left."

Hugh shook his head and began rubbing his knuckles. "Okay, show me what you got?"

Eduardo nodded excitedly. "Like I said, I have absolute proof his car killed Dr. Summer."

"And…"

"And what?"

"It's one thing to find a smoking gun, but another to place it in the hand of the shooter."

"So?"

"So the fact that someone used this particular car to run over the doctor doesn't necessarily mean your suspect was the driver. What about motive and opportunity?"

"Yeah, yeah, plenty of opportunity. He was out having drinks with another big shot," Eduardo pulled his tablet in close to check his notes, "a Mr. Landon, the president of CellMerge, but that ended about seven and he can't account for his whereabouts after that. Just says he went home and crashed, and he's got no one to corroborate his story."

"And motive?"

"Don't have anything there yet, but I haven't really started my investigation. I'm sure when I start digging something will come up."

Hugh's lips formed a scowl. "Better hope so, amigo. These rich folks like to sue. You just may find yourself facing a lawsuit bigger than the one you got from your wife."

Sarah couldn't imagine Aaron locked up with a bunch of mindless miscreants. She didn't like using the word "jail" because the image, by association, brought to mind a cage filled with skin headed, body pierced, bulked up, tattooed felons, and since the people answering the phone referred to it as a "correctional facility," that's what she decided to do. But a rose called by any other name still smelled like a rose and a lockup by any other name was still a jail.

She began by making a call to the sheriff's office in San Francisco and from there was referred to one facility after another but no one had an intake record for an Aaron Rose until she queried the Maguire Correctional Facility in Redwood City, which made sense when she thought about it. Dr. Summer had been killed outside his home in Redwood City, though it was the San Mateo Police who originally called her in for questioning.

The kettle on the stove whistled.

She pushed herself away from the table, the chair squeaking on the linoleum as she struggled to her feet. The dozen steps to the sink were a wearisome mile. Her bones ached from lack of sleep.

Buddy would make noises, sometimes just a groan, or a sudden sip of breath, but they were sounds she was accustomed to hearing, sounds she had trained herself to listen for. The absence of his murmurings had kept her awake, and the longer she was awake, the more she thought about him and that just led to more tears and less sleep.

She reached for a mug. The cupboard had been painted at least three times. Impressions of old chips could be seen under the surface of the newer layers. The tap groaned and the pipes thudded against the wall as she rinsed the cup. It was her habit to rinse everything before using it, even things that were supposedly clean because of the number of insects she'd found in the cupboard. She dreaded looking into her cup and finding a dead bug.

Most of her dry food was sealed in plastic bags, even things that came in boxes. The tea was no exception. She undid the Ziploc and removed a bag of Red Rooibos, her tea of choice because it contained no caffeine, though upon reflection, caffeine was something she could use right now. She filled her mug with hot water and, with the teabag steeping in the vapor, made her way back to the table. Now that she knew where Aaron was being held she needed to find out whether or not she could see him.

Jen had been right; keeping her mind occupied was therapeutic. She couldn't think about Buddy without crying, but she was able to avoid that drama as long as she was focused on helping Aaron.

Jen? Weird! The last thing she would have expected was for Jen to darken her door, *darken* being the operative word, yet she'd not only been reasonably civil, she had bordered on being downright nice. She suggested they work together and keep each other informed about the developments and discoveries they each made. Aaron was wrongfully accused, on that they both agreed, and if they could put aside their differences, they might be able to help. Jen volunteered to keep her eyes open for anything unusual at CellMerge while suggesting Sarah work things from the outside.

Sarah agreed. Something had to be done and while she needed to get her resume together, she had time to look into, at least superficially, the evidence that landed Aaron in jail.

The real surprise came as Jen was leaving. Standing at the threshold she'd smiled at Sarah and said: "Hey, I don't know, maybe you and I can be friends," and when Sarah, too shocked to respond, didn't say anything, she'd added: "You look good in black. It offsets your hair. In fact, I like your outfit, a bit less bizarre than the stuff you usually wear. You should try dressing like that more often." Then she high-tailed it out the door with her high heels clicking the pavement and her white jacket disappearing behind the black curtain of night. Sarah was left to wonder how a colorless dress that she herself had called drab had caught the attention of a fashionista like Jen.

She clicked her mouse, scrolled down to find the number again, and realized it was probably stored in her cell's memory. She should have thought to ask about visiting hours when she was talking to the lady earlier. She picked up her phone, hit redial, and got the same voice.

"Hi, I just called a few minutes ago, asking about Aaron Rose… yes that's right…*un-huh*…yes, well I was wondering if there's any way to see him?" She reached for her pen and began to write. "*Un-huh*, what's that? Yes, that's very helpful. Thank you so much. I'll be there."

Sarah spun around glancing at her watch. *Ouch*, if she didn't get moving she'd be too late.

Aaron stood in the echoing chambers of the San Mateo County Court before the monolithic bench of Justice Bertrand Osgood. His palms felt damp and his stomach fizzed like a balloon filled with seltzer. He looked over his shoulder and saw the seedy underbelly of society, greasy malefactors with stringy hair, yellow teeth and arms inked with blue body art. He was having a hard time believing *any* of this was real. He couldn't help thinking that once he explained himself, the judge would cast a disparaging look at the prosecutor and dismiss the case.

Across the aisle a lawyer from the district attorney's office sat with his briefcase open going over his notes. Behind him was a gallery of onlookers, friends and loved ones of those who, like Aaron, would be brought up one at a time to have their cases reviewed by the judge. He'd already scanned their faces. No one was there for him. He stood alone.

Surely by now Jen, who wasn't known for holding onto gossip, had shared everything that had happened. His friends at the lab would be nibbling on every detail. Couldn't they take just a few minutes from their work to see how he was doing? He just wanted someone to talk to and it didn't matter if it was a friend, a loved one, or even his mother, though she was, in some ways, at both the top and the bottom of his list. Everything she offered had strings attached—*You can have the car, but I'll hold onto the pink slip*—consequently, she never tired of reminding him that he was forever in her debt—*You need to listen to your mother. Remember, bad little boys lose their toys.*

But now, though he hated to admit it, he needed her. If she were there, she'd hire the best law firm money could buy, a mega-national with hundreds of offices coast-to-coast and lawyers billing five-hundred dollars an hour. They would leave no stone unturned in providing for his defense. With unlimited resources at their disposal they would research every possible case with a bearing on his and show clear precedence for his acquittal.

A bailiff moved to the center of the room. "The Court of San Mateo County is now in session, his honor Judge Bertrand Osgood presiding. All rise."

Aaron's hands were clammy, his heart popping like flip-flops on hot cement. He stood alone, lacking the presence of an attorney, and without his mother's money, little chance of finding one.

The judge entered. He was a stocky man, or maybe it was just the billowy motion of his long black robe that made him appear so. His hair was thick and wavy but it was receding leaving him with a high forehead and his reading glasses were perched on the end of his nose. He climbed into a chair behind the bench where he opened a folder, scanned the document inside and then summoned the bailiff. The court officer moved to the bench, accepted some papers from the judge and handed them to Aaron.

Judge Osgood looked at Aaron. "Will the defendant please state his full name for the court?"

Aaron was trying to speed read the document. It appeared to be a statement of the charges filed against him. His head was shaking in disbelief as his eyes met those of the Judge. "Aaron Jacob Rose," he said.

Judge Osgood glanced at the prosecutor. "Is this the person identified in the charges?"

The attorney looked up. "Yes, your honor."

The judge adjusted his glasses and read from the folder. "The defendant has been charged with one count of felony hit and run causing death." He brought his chin up to address Aaron again. "The defendant has the right to plead guilty or not guilty. The defendant has the right to have an attorney present at all times during these proceedings." His eyes went to the prosecutor. "And the defendant has the right to require that the prosecution prove beyond reasonable doubt that the defendant committed the offenses of which he is accused." Then his eyes drifted back to Aaron. "Do you understand these rights?"

Aaron nodded. "Yes, your honor."

"Fine. Does the defendant have an attorney?"

"Not at present, your honor. I was hoping to find a lawyer but in my current situation I don't have the money to hire one."

The judge leaned back in his chair, his bottom lip protruding. "I don't want to drag these proceedings out. I'm going to appoint the defendant a lawyer for now. The defendant can request a change of counsel at any time. Mr. Frisk, would you be so kind as to stand with the defendant."

A man seated at the side of the courtroom stood and made his way over to Aaron. He was young, about Aaron's age, with his hair combed forward and brought to a peak above his forehead. The polyester blue suit he wore looked like it had come off the 80% off clearance rack. His hands were empty. *Shouldn't he at least be carrying a briefcase or a few law books or something?*

"I'm going to assume the defendant wants to confer with his lawyer before entering a plea…"

"That's not necessary, your honor. "I'm innocent. I don't even know why I'm here."

"The judge looked at him sternly. "You're here because of the charges filed against you. I thought I made that clear."

Oh oh, not a good start. "No, I understand, I think."

"What is it, you think, or you know?"

"No, I guess I know, but I didn't do it. I'm innocent."

"That's for the court to decide. The plea is ether guilty or not guilty. How do you plea?"

"Not guilty."

"Let it be known that the defendant has entered a plea of not guilty. I highly recommend that from now on the defendant wait to speak with his lawyer before making statements. Judge Osgood turned his head toward the man seated at the prosecution table. "Roy, are there any arguments for bail?"

Uh-oh they're on a first name basis.

"Yes, your honor, we've taken a look at the defendant's background and have determined him to be a flight risk. He comes from a wealthy family capable of whisking him out of country, and there's the matter of the family boat which the defendant has access to, enabling him to flee across the border into Canada or Mexico. We would like to recommend the defendant be held without bail."

The judge frowned. "A bit extreme for a hit and run."

"Your honor, the state has not had time to properly build its case but we have evidence to suggest there may be grounds for upping the charges to vehicular homicide. I think the fact that the defendant has the means to flee and could likely face charges of premeditated murder warrants denying bail."

The judge looked back at Aaron's lawyer, and nodded. "Mr. Frisk."

"Your honor, without conferring with my client it's hard to respond. I assume he has no priors or it would have factored into the prosecution's argument and without priors the presumption that he's a flight risk is ludicrous."

The judge nodded. "I'm inclined to agree. But since, as has been pointed out, the Rose family has means, I'm setting the bail at one-hundred-thousand."

Aaron gasped. "Your honor, I don't have that kind of money."

Judge Osgood leaned in toward Aaron placing his arms on the bench. "Are you saying your family's destitute, that you don't have a boat or other assets you can use to post bail?"

"Yes, but they belong to my mother, not me."

"Then I suggest you talk to her."

"No, your honor, I can't. She's on some kind of unplugged retreat. They don't allow tablets or cell phones or anything. I have no way of communicating with her. That's why I'm accepting the service of a public defender. Until she gets back, I'm broke."

"Then I guess you'll just have to wait until she gets home to post your bond. Roy, I'm inclined to fast track this so if you're going to up the charges I suggest you do it quickly, and Mr. Frisk, in consideration of the fact that you haven't had time to prepare, I'll hold back for at least a month, but then we're going to trial. If you find yourself in need of an extension, I suggest you petition me in chambers." With that the judge slammed his gavel down ending further discussion.

Aaron shook his head. He had a public defender named Frisk who wore a rumpled, ill-fitting suit that didn't scream success. It made him wonder where the man went to school—*Yale? Harvard?* or was he an ambulance chaser with a law degree from a school advertised on the back of a matchbook cover: "Earn your degree on-line." His stomach curdled.

The lawyer handed him a card and said he would stop by the jail later to begin discussing strategy. At least that was something. The bailiff took him by the arm.

Aaron felt the knot in his stomach tighten as the bailiff placed a hand on his shoulder and turned him around. No bail, no freedom, just another day of isolation, staring at the walls with nothing to do. This was wrong; he hadn't done anything. He recoiled, jerking away, but felt the grip tighten around his arm. Mr. Frisk stood to the side to let him pass.

"I'll be in to see you soon as I can," he muttered as Aaron stumbled by. Aaron twisted his head around to respond and as he did caught a glimmer of hope, the first he'd seen since they'd slapped the cuffs on him the day before. Standing at the back of the room, dressed in the same clothes she'd worn at the funeral—*was Sarah.*

Twenty-Eight

All things were made by Him; and without Him was not any thing made that was made.—John 1:3

TINY CLIPPINGS of auburn hair hit the floor surrounding the chair in which Sarah sat. She hadn't had a professional cut in years. The indulgence felt good. She reveled in the sweet sensation of having her scalp massaged with shampoo, the mild scratching of the comb on her skin, and the tickle of hair being lifted and trimmed—just a little, mind you, to eliminate split ends.

While Buddy was alive, she'd stayed away from beauty parlors. She wanted to avoid the furtive glances he'd receive, the silent speculations about what might be wrong with her son. He deserved better. Besides, she didn't need the extra expense. She had taught herself to cut his hair, and then had learned to cut her own, which was easy since all she had to do was clip her hair so that it flared out at odd lengths around her neck.

This was a little different and she hoped her haircutter was up to the challenge. While reviewing memories of her life with Buddy she had come across photos taken during her university days and was reminded of how much better she looked with the long full waves of her russet hair shining on her shoulders. Other than the convenience, she couldn't remember why she'd cut her hair in the first place, but now, as part of her life change, she'd decided to grow it back.

There was no rational to it. She would have thought the death of Buddy, along with the murder of Dr. Summer and the loss of her job would have caused her to crawl into a hole and stay. Instead, the dissolution of so many pieces of her life seemed to create an urging within to shed her former persona and start anew.

An apron tied around her neck prevented loose hair from finding its way onto her clothes. She slipped a finger into the collar and scratched where it itched. Beneath that apron was a new outfit, a dark blue skirt that actually fit her slim figure and a white button up shirt with lace trim accentuating the short sleeves and collar. Maybe she couldn't afford it, especially since she was still without a job, but part of the change called for a whole new look. She had Jen to thank for that. Funny how one little comment could make such an impact. *"I like your outfit. You should try dressing like that more often."*

Maybe it was the failing economy, or maybe the fact that clothes could be produced cheaply in places like Pakistan and China, or maybe it was that every store she walked into seemed to have everything on sale with a few clearance items marked down to practically zero, *whatever*, but she had walked into a bargain bonanza. One of her chief reasons for purchasing her wardrobe at thrift stores was the economics but she was finding new clothes in stores where she could put together things that actually matched for a pittance. She would have to clean out her closet. The one in her apartment wasn't much bigger than a shoebox. The five new outfits she'd purchased would practically fill the space. All those "bizarre" loose fitting corduroy pants, and woolen plaids, and floppy hats, and colorful belts were about to be recycled. Out with the old and in with the new.

The process was cathartic, but that didn't make it easy. She would be working her way through a rack of clothes and turn to look for Buddy and not finding his chair nearby, once again feel the ache in her chest and have to force herself to press on. She had to learn to function without her son. He was gone and he wasn't coming back.

It was important to look her best while interviewing for a job, she told herself. She had two weeks severance and the next payment on her credit card wasn't due for a month. If looking professional increased her chance of landing a position, it was worth every penny.

The hairdresser spun Sarah's chair around and handed her a mirror so she could see both front and back at the same time. She had evened up the odd lengths while keeping her hair long enough to rest lightly on her shoulders, and topped it off with a bit of wave and enough highlights to make the hair shine. Yes, indeed, worth every penny.

"That's great," she said. "Thank you so much."

Jen turned to see if Dr. Jaeger was still in his office. He was, still leaning back in his chair with his cowboy boots propped up on his desk, reading a magazine. *The little dweeb.* He had vowed to be an active participant, the kind of manager that rolled up his sleeves and worked with his team. He wasn't giving her time to snoop around.

She didn't know what she expected to find. If the man had half a brain, he wouldn't leave incriminating evidence lying around, but she had to at least try. Aaron's car had been used to kill Dr. Summer, but Aaron didn't do it so someone else had to have used his car and framed Aaron in the process. The only one she knew who loathed and feared Dr. Summer enough to do that was Dr. Jaeger. He was practically giddy about Q's death. But having suspicion was one thing, finding proof was another.

She didn't have much to go on, in fact she had zip, but her instincts were good. If Dr. Jaeger wasn't guilty, wouldn't he have expressed outrage when she shared how Aaron had been arrested for the crime? *How dare they suspect one of my best researchers*—but instead, he'd smiled and said, "That boy juices up like a tick on a hound. Dang straight, poor old Wally stepped into a drunk's line of fire." It was like he wanted to blame Aaron. And when Sarah called to let her know about the arraignment and she asked Dr. Jaeger for an hour off so she could attend, he'd callously said, "That train has left the station. You gotta wave bye-bye 'cause it ain't comin' back." Then he'd walked off in a huff muttering about her wanting to leave him more shorthanded than he already was. Served him right. If he was so worried about staffing, he shouldn't have fired Sarah.

May Ling was bent over her microscope trying to analyze a serum containing the enzyme telomerase. Jen wanted to confide in her but she wasn't certain whose side she'd take. Larry on the other hand could be bought, but he was fickle and would only be loyal as long as she showed him favor. The trouble with approaching him right now was that for reasons she couldn't explain, she'd decided to tone down the sexy look—at least for the day. She was wearing a turtleneck sweater and denims. Okay, her pants were tight, she didn't own any that weren't, but except for her hands and face, her skin was covered. Shouldn't men like her for her brains? *Silly question.* It didn't matter that she had a PhD from Stanford. As far as men were concerned the only thing important was her body, not her mind, but that was going to change. Sarah hadn't used sex to get Aaron's attention, so it could be done, but even as she thought it she realized it would be easier to get Larry on-side if she were wearing something a little more provocative. And she needed him. He was close to Aaron. They were friends. He might have insights she didn't possess.

She didn't have to look far to find him. He was in the break room standing over the coffee pot. *Where else?* His corpulent body looked like a white potato dressed in a lab coat. Larry needed supervision. He needed someone like Aaron making sure he was getting his work done. As long as Jaeger remained cooped up in his office, Larry was likely to stand around eating donuts all morning.

"Hey, Lar."

Larry turned, his eyes roaming her body. "Hey, Jen, what's up?"

Jen reached in to fill her mug feeling oddly exposed. "Can you believe they arrested Aaron?" she said, holding her cup in front of her with both hands. Steam rose to the occasion wafting up under her nose.

"Yeah. Bummer, huh?" Larry stuffed his mouth with a donut, his cheeks blossoming out. His mouth was a gob of pasty white dough. "It was probably an accident but I've never seen Aaron so drunk he couldn't handle himself, and I question what he was doing on Dr. Summer's street in the first place." He licked powdered sugar off his thumb and fingers. "Course, he'd been there once or twice with that Sarah chick, so there was something going on, but by himself, at eleven at night? It just doesn't compute."

"No, it doesn't," Jen said. "He sure didn't act guilty when they arrested him. He was as surprised as I was. It doesn't make sense. I drove over to Sarah's to see if she knew anything..."

"Sarah? Our Sarah? Dr. Hunter?"

Jen nodded. "She couldn't believe it either. We started piecing things together and..."

"Excuse me. You went over to Sarah Hunter's house? Ohmygosh. Is she in the hospital? How bad was she hurt?"

"Cut it, Larry. She's not as bad as you think. Anyway, she told me why she and Aaron went to see Dr. Summer. It had to do with her work but the conversation ended up being more about that paper that got him censured awhile back. The point is, she said Dr. Jaeger found out about it and took it to the company president and that's why Dr. Summer got fired. That's when they put Dr. Jaeger over us but recently Dr. Jaeger told me he thought Q was trying to get his old job back and the next thing you know, he's dead."

Larry pulled the donut back from his mouth. "You can't be suggesting Dr. Jaeger had anything to do with it?"

"I don't know. I just know Aaron didn't, and if he didn't, who did? Besides, remember the night Dr. Jaeger took us to that cowboy bar? You told me Jaeger said the world wouldn't be safe until Dr. Summer was six feet under. And then I was in Dr. Jaeger's office the day Sarah got fired and he was going on about how Q deserved to be run over because he was trying to get reinstated. He even thought he might run into some problems and said if I would support him he would support me and the next thing I know Sarah is running out of the lab crying. I think he actually fired her because he thought it would make me happy."

"And like, you weren't?"

"Of course not! Okay, maybe Sarah's a little weird, like she dresses like a munchkin and doesn't do her hair, but I didn't want her fired. Anyway, that's a side issue. The point is Dr. Jaeger was worried that Dr. Summer might be trying to get his old position back. That gives him motive. The question is, how far would he go to get Q out of the way?"

"So you think Jaeger did it."

"I don't know but I intend to find out and I'm going to need your help."

It wasn't a private room. Another bed was situated on the other side of a curtained wall occupied by a thirty-something recovering from an appendectomy. Dr. Philips could hear the nurse encouraging the patient to get up and walk.

He raised Buddy's eyelids one at a time, confirming he was still comatose. *Hummm.* The boy wasn't in good shape. He needed looking after. His wrist was nothing but skin and bone. Dr. Philips felt for a pulse, counting while watching the second hand of his watch. The nurse threw the curtain back looking startled.

"*Oh*. Sorry Dr. Philips. I didn't know you were here."

"Just thought I'd check in on our patient. How's he doing?"

"Fine, I guess. There hasn't been any change."

"Is he being seen by a doctor?"

The nurse hesitated, taking a deep breath and exhaling audibly. "No, I'm afraid not."

"Why?"

"I spoke with Lillian Bradshaw, she's the VP, she said to keep the patient comfortable but not to get a doctor involved unless it was necessary. The hospital has to absorb the cost, you see, and with budget cuts and all…well, we had him in the ICU but without a medical history all they could do was make sure his circulation and respiration were okay…"

"Did they do a CT scan?"

The nurse flipped through the boy's chart. "Yes, his brain activity appears to be normal. There's no apparent head trauma and he seems to be stable so they have me monitoring his vitals and rolling him onto his side every few hours to prevent bed sores but that's about it."

Dr. Philips crossed his arms and brought a hand up to rub his chin. "I shouldn't be doing this, but I want you to run a complete blood count on the boy. I didn't notice how thin he was before."

"But I can't…I mean, Lillian said not to. Who's going to pay for it? There's no insurance."

The doctor frowned. "There's something else going on here and my first thought is leukemia. This boy's wasting away. He's skin and bone."

"But why would his parents abandon him? I mean they just left him here. Wouldn't they want to see he's being looked after?"

"I don't know. Could be any number of reasons. Maybe they're out of work and their insurance lapsed. Leukemia is an expensive disease to treat. I'm wondering if he's supposed to be receiving chemo somewhere. Lack of treatment could have weakened him to a state where he slipped into a coma."

"But his hair?"

"Depends on how long it's been since his last treatment. It's pretty short. It may have started to grow back. I want you to get right on this…" The nurse was shaking her head. "Have them send the bill to me. It's just a blood test for Pete's sake."

Aaron was led to a room he hadn't been in before. It was similar to the place where he'd been interrogated, small and windowless with nothing but a table and chairs, only this one lacked a mirror which meant he wasn't being observed. Same cream yellow walls though, just like every other room in the prison. *The place lacks imagination*, Aaron mused.

A uniformed guard stood at attention by the door, his buzz cut hair giving him a serious demeanor, the baton at his side ready to crack heads at the first sign of trouble.

The door opened and attorney Eric Frisk entered. Aaron gave him a quick glance and started to turn away but at the last second saw he was accompanied by Sarah. He jumped up but the guard forced him back into his seat. He winced at the officer's grip on his shoulder. The man had biceps made of steel.

"The prisoner will remain seated at all times," he said.

"You can remove the cuffs," the lawyer added.

"You sure?"

Eric nodded. "He's not going anywhere. And please, wait outside while we talk."

The guard removed Aaron's manacles one at a time and left the room closing the door behind him.

Aaron flexed his shoulders and rubbed his wrists trying to get comfortable in the metal folding chair. He was glad to be free of the chains but still embarrassed to be in his orange prison pajamas. He offered Sarah a fainthearted smile.

"You two know each other, of course," Eric said, laying his briefcase on the table. He took a seat and Sarah, following his lead, did the same. The lawyer's hair was still spiked up in front. His skin was smooth and his chestnut eyes were warm as a sanguine puppy. A good looking kid, if not handsome, depending on who was doing the review. But *Sarah*, Sarah looked great. Aaron couldn't put his finger on it but something was different. Maybe it was her hair, yes definitely, her hair was smooth, longer and not sticking out, her makeup distinct but not overstated and she was dressed like a model.

"Sarah tells me you're friends. By way of explanation, she approached me after your arraignment and offered to assist me in preparing your case. Since they don't afford me the luxury of having an assistant, I took her up on it, so unless you have an objection I'll probably have her with me at most of our meetings."

Aaron shook his head. "No objection at all."

"How have you been, Aaron?"

Aaron's expression turned serious. "Really? You want to know how I've been. What about you? Are you okay? I wanted to call, but under the circumstances."

"I'm okay. I'm taking it one day at a time, and God is good. I think He has me working on this just so I won't have time to think about Buddy. What about you?"

"Yeah, well let me tell you, it's hell. I'm locked in a box that smells like a gym locker and made to eat processed food, all because these idiots think I killed Dr. Summer."

"Did you?"

Aaron frowned. "How can you even ask?"

"Because I need to know. I still think he may have been my

father. Did you kill him, I mean even by accident?"

The lawyer looked askance, apparently peeved that Sarah was asking the questions and probably also taken aback by the idea that Dr. Summer might have been her father.

Aaron shook his head. "No, Sarah, I did not kill Dr. Summer. I've gone over and over it but there's no way."

Eric opened a legal pad and clicked the button of his pen. "Are you sure, because they think you were so drunk you just don't remember? And bear in mind that I'm your lawyer. We, and I'm including Sarah in this because she's my assistant, have attorney client privilege meaning what you say stays in this room. But I have to know the truth, even if you think it will incriminate you. My job is to defend you to the best of my ability but I can't do that unless I know everything, understand?"

Aaron sat back in his chair. Eric had a briefcase, and not just some cheap plastic knockoff but a burgundy leather case. At least he had the trappings of a lawyer, which was more than he'd had in court.

"The truth shall set you free, huh? Well, the truth, the whole truth, and nothing but the truth, is this: I had a meeting with the president of CellMerge, that's the place where I work, and I had a few drinks." Aaron's eyes shifted to Sarah wondering how she'd respond to this, but it had to be said. "I'd been out late the night before with the man I report to, Dr. Jaeger, and I'd been pretty looped that night too. When I had my meeting with Mr. Landon, that's the company president, I was already exhausted and I hadn't eaten anything so when Mr. Landon started insisting I have one after another I'm thinking this guy's a flaming alcoholic trying to sneak in a few before dinner but I figured what can I do? So I just kept drinking and yes, I got tipsy. I could barely walk to my car. I shouldn't have tried to drive. Mr. Landon wanted to call me a cab, but I insisted I was okay. I don't remember much after that. I just remember waking up the next morning sprawled out on my bed with my clothes still on and one heck of a hangover."

"And you didn't notice any damage to your car the next morning?"

"No, see the thing is, when I parked my car I pulled straight in and the next day when I approached the car it was from the rear, so I didn't have a chance to see the front. I stopped at a restaurant for breakfast but again, I parked straight in. Then I went to CellMerge and met Sarah and we went out for dinner but she drove." His eyes glanced over at Sarah and then back at the lawyer. "I didn't see the damage until later that evening when I took a cab back to the office. That's it. That's all I know, except they say the paint chips on Dr. Summer's body came from my car and a tiny fragment of his suit was caught in the grill so they think my car was used, but how that happened I don't know. The real question is, why would I kill Dr. Summer? He hadn't done anything to me. In fact, ask Sarah, we got along fine."

Eric was still writing, a southpaw with a funny way of gripping the pen, holding it in his fist rather than with his fingers. His elbow arched over the pad. "Can you think of *any* reason they might have for you wanting to kill Dr. Sumner," he said without looking up. "Did you get a bad review, maybe you were passed over for a promotion, anything like that?"

"No, nothing."

"Okay, so they don't have motive, that's good. Now all we have to do is establish reasonable doubt."

Seeing the Forest Through the Trees
The Journal of W.L. Summer

The entire human body: skin, bone, hair, cartilage, tendon and teeth, is made of collagen, or rope like structures that connect and hold our cells together. Except in one place—the cornea of the eye. In the eye the twine like material becomes a grid so that rather than being opaque, it becomes transparent enabling us to see. To say this change in the collagen's structure came about by a series of random accidents, defies reason. How would the collagen know the cornea needed transparency when matter has no thought or purpose?

The cornea acts like a window in front of the eye to admit light and keep out foreign objects. It bends the light enabling it to pass through the pupil which changes size to manage the amount of light hitting the lens. The light then continues through the lens where images are focused to a sharp point on the retina. All of these systems, cornea, pupil, lens, and retina are engineering marvels making accidental development a non-start.

Once light hits the retina, a million and a half neurons each take a separate piece of the image up the million and a half fibers of the optic nerve to the brain where the pieces are reassembled in perfect order and sequence. Each eye sees a flat two dimensional image but the brain merges and overlays the images to create one three dimensional picture. Then it takes this image, which is upside down, and inverts the pixels to make the picture appear right side up.

The human eye also contains one hundred thirty million receptor cells: one hundred twenty-four million rod shaped, to differentiate between light and dark, and another six million that are cone shaped which distinguish between the eight million variations of color.

It's difficult to imagine even the most skilled team of engineers designing such an intricate and beautifully organized system, let alone to believe that without thought or purpose trillions of random accidents took place that just happened to end up becoming a fully functioning eye. Of course the same could be said of every part of our body, or for that matter, of every organism on earth.

But we don't have one eye, we have two, each of which begins as a node on our brain and grows from there. Are we to believe both eyes evolved independently but somehow followed the same evolutionary path and with all their complexity, ended up exactly the same, or do we assume once the first eye completed its evolution it somehow cloned itself and became two? Either idea is absurd.

And what about the number of different kinds of eyes required by birds, insects, fish, reptiles and mammals, all of which are designed for a specific purpose but all of which supposedly came about by accident?

As men of science, we would do well to remember the old cliché about not being able to see the forest for the trees. So often we stand lost in a forest of evolutionary thought, seeing only the trees, or individual evidences that support our beliefs, without standing back to look at the whole forest of information that challenges our point of view.

Twenty-Nine

...O Lord my God, thou art very great; thou art clothed with honor and majesty. You who cover Yourself with light as a garment: Who stretches out the heavens like a curtain. —Psalm 104:1-2

THE GUARD cranked the handcuffs down and pushed Aaron's shoulder to get him moving. *Ouch!* "Hey." *Such hostility.* Aaron stumbled forward rubbing his wrists while thinking about adding this guy's name to the suit he was planning to file against the city for false arrest. They had no right to treat an innocent man this way.

The guard grabbed Aaron's arm, pulling him to a stop while they waited for someone behind a bulletproof window to key the electronic lock. The metal gate creaked as they moved through, and clanged shut behind them. The hand on his back pushed him forward. It was the hand of an angry man—little tolerance and no patience—the hand of a glorified babysitter looking after belligerent overgrown children who hadn't been taught to behave.

Aaron shivered then rubbed his arms waiting for the guard to get the door open. It didn't make sense. Maybe Dr. Summer wasn't the most popular scientist in the community but Aaron couldn't think of anyone who would want to hurt him.

He wondered how Sarah was holding up. She seemed okay, but he could only see the surface, not what was going on inside. She had every reason to be miserable and yet she seemed to be putting her own feelings aside and had gone out of her way not only to attend his arraignment, but to actively seek a position on his legal team—if you could call one lawyer and his volunteer assistant a team—but she would be working to get him out. Just that was enough to get him through the day, and the promise that she'd be back tomorrow would get him through the night.

But the real surprise came when Sarah said she was collaborating with Jen. Sarah and Jen together? Who would have thought? Or was it just the calm before the storm? Jen might not act so kindly when, at the end of the day, he chose Sarah over her.

The guard pulled the door back and stood aside allowing Aaron to enter. *Oh no!* Sitting on the bunk at the far side of the room holding a book in his lap was another inmate. He was wearing the same orange scrubs as Aaron, but his skin was blue. The guard, sensing Aaron's reluctance, pushed him forward and slammed the door behind him. *Bang!*

Aaron sucked in his breath, his heart palpitated, his hands beginning to sweat. For the first time since being arrested, he felt genuinely afraid. There wasn't one inch of the man that wasn't covered in tattoos. His arms had demons and dice and swastikas and crosses and the flames of hell burning up toward a neck circled with alternating bands of chains and razor wire. Covering his cheeks were the prongs of pitchforks that pointed in toward his nose and his shaved head looked like a hybrid between a cactus and a coral reef. He looked up and smiled and when he did, Aaron could see his teeth were filed to points like the canines of a rabid dog.

"Hi uh, sorry, is this your bunk? I can sleep on the upper one if you want. Don't matter to me."

Aaron backed up till his heel hit the door.

"Glad you're here. I don't like being alone. Name's Jethro, Jethro Bane, but everybody calls me Blade, you know, 'cause I like to play with knives, but I'm through with all that now so you can just call me Jethro."

Aaron held his breath half expecting Jethro to thrust out his hand—would a handshake make them friends and establish some kind of secret bond?—but the man just kept rambling on.

"I won't be here long though. Me and another dude were just brought in for sentencing. I hear mine tomorrow. I think his is tomorrow, too. Then we'll be taken to San Quentin, at least I will 'cause that's where death row is. See, I'll get the death penalty for sure, 'cause of the nature of my crime. From then on, I'll be in a cell by myself 'cause they don't allow inmates to share a crib on the row. What are you in for?"

He paused waiting for Aaron to answer but Aaron didn't know what to say. He took a quick peek out the window behind him to see if the guard was nearby, he needed to request a transfer to another cell, but the guard wasn't there. Would saying he was in for a hit and run mark him as a lightweight? He'd heard about the crimes that took place inside prisons. The strong sensed fear and took advantage of the weak. It wasn't wise to look intimidated. "They say I killed someone, but I didn't. I'm innocent."

"Yeah, I know, me too, bro. Everyone says that. Only I stopped kidding myself. I did the crime, now I gotta do the time, maybe even let them slip me the needle, but for what it's worth, I'm okay with that. I made my peace with God, know what I mean? You don't have to stand over there, bro." Jethro patted the mattress. "You can come over and sit down. There's plenty of room, or like I say, I can move upstairs." Jethro pointed at the bunk above his head with a blue thumb.

"Uh, no, I'm fine. I was, uh, thinking of doing some exercises, you know, to keep in shape. Mind if I do a few calisthenics?"

"No bro, knock yourself out."

Great, now what? Aaron rolled his shoulders craning his head around his neck. Who was he kidding? He had to sit down sometime. "Actually, there's not enough room. I just wanted to loosen up a bit, but there's no point, if you don't mind scooting over."

His fellow inmate smiled and slid to the side, his blue face dark as the grim reaper. "Cool. Hey, you look like someone who knows how to read. I mean, I can read a bit, but I'm slow so I like it better when someone reads to me, would you mind?" he said holding out his book.

Aaron reached out and took the soft cover volume. "Sure, I guess. What is it?"

A smile grew on the man's face. "It's a Bible," he said.

Sarah wasn't ready to give up her boots. They might be secondhand but some of them were originally from nicer stores than those where she'd just purchased her new clothes. Calf high lace up boots were never out of style. The hats could go too, she'd seen dozens of magazines where models wore knit caps and felt fedoras just like the ones she'd collected, but most of the fashions worn by models were never seen in places of work. She had to let go. Being unique was fun and had its place but now she wanted to fit in so, *plop, plop, plop*, the hats were in the bag.

She stood back, admiring her new wardrobe. The look she'd seen in Aaron's eye made getting rid of her old clothes much easier. He liked what he saw; she could tell by the way he kept returning for a second look, and a third, like his eyes were feasting on the new Sarah, that's what made it worthwhile.

She interlaced the handles of the plastic bag, tied them in a knot and set the bag on the floor by the rest of Buddy's things.

The flap of one of the boxes was open. She reached in and removed a faded red T-shirt holding it out to read the silk-screened message. The words were printed in yellow.

No Jesus, No Peace
Know Jesus, Know Peace

"Oh Buddy," she said, bringing the shirt up to her cheek. "Where are you, little man? Have you finally found peace? I know you have; I just wish you could be here." She used the soft cotton to dab the tear in her eye, and then folded the shirt and placed it back in the box.

She sighed, and made her way over to the stove. *How high, and deep, and wide the love of God.* The burner flared. She brought the kettle over the flame. Something odd occurred to her. She wasn't afraid, not that there was any reason to be, but she'd always feared being alone. The thought of not having someone in the apartment with her was terrifying, but here she was, and had been for the past several days, and while there was grief, she hadn't experienced the panic she'd so often felt.

The cup received the teabag and water. Steam circled around the rim as she went to the table. Snowball hopped into her lap as she sat down. She reached for the folder, the one her father left her. She still hadn't read it. A quick scan confirmed what the detective said. It was filled with page after page of personal notes and articles about the formation of Earth and its abundant life forms—*Creation.* Dr. Summer had stumbled onto the truth but there was no way to be certain he'd also found Jesus. She could only hope that one day she'd get to see him again. She stroked Snowball's ears. The dog nuzzled her hand and whimpered with contentment.

That's an idea, she thought. If she wanted to solve the murder she had to find a way to get inside the man's house. Yes, *murder* was the right word, because she knew Aaron hadn't run Dr. Summer down, not even accidentally. She could see it in his eyes. And if he didn't do it then someone must have taken his car and used it to kill the man, and that was murder. That detective—what was his name? She had his card in the folder. *There,* Detective Hugh Irons—he as much as said it was murder when he brought up the fact that the car hadn't stopped. If someone wanted Dr. Summer dead, there had to be a reason. The police must have overlooked something. Maybe there was a connection between his death and his being fired. That's what Jen thought. According to the memo, the company and Dr. Summer mutually agreed to go their separate ways, so why kill him after he was already gone? No, it was probably something totally unrelated.

It would help if she could get inside his house to look around but the chances of them letting her were slim to none. That's why she needed Snowball. Detective Irons already knew she'd inherited the dog. All she had to do was convince him she needed access to Dr. Summer's house to get information pertaining to Snowball's health: did he have rabies shots, was he on any kind of special diet, when was the last time he'd seen a vet? Irons might not buy it, but he'd already indicated their search of the property hadn't turned up anything, so what was the harm?

Snowball began to whine. *Ouch!* The dog scratched her leg as it jumped down and ran to the door, barking all the way. *Arff, arff, arff arff, arff, gurrrrrrrrrrrrrr.* The intercom speaker buzzed.

Sarah massaged her thigh, *owww, bad dog.* She looked at her watch and got up limping. Must be Jen. She would be off work by now. Probably wanted an update on her meeting with Aaron. She swung the door open—and gasped.

A beggar stood there looking for a handout. His clothes were filthy, his hair long and matted, and his beard unkempt. Speechless, her heart thumping, she stared deeper into the man's blue eyes—*Brian?*

Thirty

Before the mountains were brought forth, even before You formed the earth and the world, from everlasting to everlasting, Thou art God.
—Psalm 90:2

THE CLUB was rocking with sound. Cowboy Billy Bob and his Buckaroos were on stage playing boot-stomping white-lightnin' tunes while the dance floor pounded with city-born hillbillies scuffing back and forth under a bank of colored lights.

Jen had her cowboy hat on, a white one she'd brought from home. She leaned back against the bar with her boot heel hooked over the bar's foot rail and the frosty mug in her hand raised in salute. *Yea-haw!* Her long blonde hair flew out from under the rim of her hat as she shook her head, her firm figure accented by her skin tight denims. Her long sleeve shirt was blue cotton, over which she wore a white leather vest, and she had a silver belt buckle the size of an ostrich egg with the image of a cowgirl riding a bucking stallion.

"You didn't say anything about owning your own outfit last time we were here."

Jen looked down on her partner, an off-putting little man in a ten gallon hat who persisted in calling her his *date*. "You never asked," she said, shouting to be heard over the band. "Anyway, I'm not a weekend cowgirl. I bought these duds for a costume party a couple of years ago."

"Pretty expensive costume. Those boots alone probably set you back two or three hundred bucks."

"And your point would be…"

"It suits you."

"Yeah, sure it does. And what about you? You got more quotes than Will Rodgers and you dress like Hoss Cartwright but you live in the Bay and work in biotech which is the furthest thing from a ranch. You're just an urban cowboy. Bet you never even been on a horse."

Dr. Jaeger took a swig of his beer and set it on the bar. The brim of his hat was so large he couldn't see Jen without tipping his head back to where it nearly fell off. He grabbed its rolled edge and held it in place. "That's where you'd be wrong, little lady. I was country born and raised. My folks were simple people who owned a shoe repair shop in a small town just outside Rapid City, but my uncle actually had a ranch where I used to spend the summers mending fence and bailing hay. I've been on a roundup or two, and I've branded a few doggies, though I have to admit, I don't much care for the smell of burning hide."

Jen smiled and winked playfully. "And I thought you wore the boots and hat just to look tall."

"There is that." Dr. Jaeger crawled up on his bar stool so he and Jen could talk eye to eye without having to shout. The music of the Buckaroos blared on. "It's not easy being short, and I'm not saying I'm trying to compensate, but if when I look in the mirror it makes me feel better about myself, then I'd call it a good thing."

"Excuse me," a city Texan standing on Jen's right nudged her arm. "Can I buy the lady a drink?"

Jen smiled. She was liking this place better all the time.

"Sorry Jack. The lady's with me," she heard Dr. Jaeger say.

The cowboy stood at least a head taller than her boss, a lean machine, buff and beautiful. He crossed his arms and raised his chin. "Maybe, maybe not, but I wasn't asking you."

Jen swung around deciding she didn't like this cowboy after all. "He's right, Jackson, we're together."

"*Really?*"

"What? You think you're the flavor of the month? Suck it up cowboy, my man's got more than you'll never have."

"*Excuse me?*"

"Figure it out."

The cowboy smirked. "Wanna bet?"

"And I suppose you're rich too. A woman needs money, honey. My man treats me right. You gonna lay down the cash to take me to Cancun for the weekend? I don't think so. My man's a doctor. What are you, a courier, a mechanic, oh, I know, a clerk in a grocery store? In my book, good looks are only half of what it takes, and you, sir, don't measure up."

"*Woohoo*, guess she gotcha, Ronnie boy." A friend standing to his right slapped him on the shoulder.

"Shut up!" Ron flung the arm away. "You let your woman do your talkin' half pint?" he said shifting the attention back to Jaeger.

"Come on, let's get outta here." The friend grabbed his arm and pulled him back. "There're better watering holes than this." He managed to get Ronnie turned the other way and pushed him through a group of onlookers, dragging him off toward the door.

Jen placed her empty mug on the bar and slid it forward. She nodded at the bartender, "I need a refill." Then she said to Dr. Jaeger, "and since you're my date, you're buying." She gritted her teeth at the duplicity of protecting the man she was about to pump for information. If he was a killer, he didn't deserve defending, but she couldn't help feeling sorry for him. The obnoxious little jerk.

"You betcha." Dr. Jaeger swiveled on his stool and propped his elbows up on the bar. "Make it two, barkeep."

The band stopped playing and drifted backstage to take a break, emptying the dance floor. Cowboys and cowgirls were hitting the outhouse, and those who weren't, were hitting on each other. The conversation wasn't as loud as the music, but the room was still a cacophony of noise. Jen leaned in close to be heard. "I have a problem I was hoping you could help me with."

Jaeger nodded, resting his chin in his hands, stroking his goatee. His small round glasses made his eyes appear large as eggs. "Oh, What's that?"

"I'm having a problem with my online security. My Facebook and Yahoo accounts keep updating and want me to reenter my password, only between my bank, EBay, Amazon, Facebook, Twitter, my online store accounts and half a dozen others I keep forgetting which password to use. And they all want something different. Like one wants letters, some a combination of letters and numbers, a few want eight characters, others more, and on, and on, ad infinitum. I need to think of a password I can use that will satisfy them all, and one that's easy to remember."

Dr. Jaeger smiled. He removed his hat, wiped his bald forehead on his sleeve, and plopped the hat down on the bar. "Everyone has that problem. Not every site demands a combination of letters and numbers but I include both in all my passwords. It's more secure that way."

"But that makes them hard to remember." Jen pursed her lips. The lights from the stage made Dr. Jaeger's shiny head alternate green, yellow and blue.

"No it doesn't, not if you use the right kind of password. Lots of letters sound like words, like the letters A, B and C. Take ICU for example, those three letters spell out the words, *I see you*. And numbers sound like words too, 1 and 2 and 4 and 8 are all words. So when you combine them together you get passwords you can remember, like this one." He took a pen from his pocket, slid a bar napkin over, and wrote, CINOV84U. "Eight characters that spell out the phrase, *See, I innovate for you*. Since I'm a research scientist it fits and all I have to do is remember the phrase. Or how about the one I use for my email account?" He scribbled another string of characters on the napkin." O2BA104U, *Oh to be a 10 for you.* Catchy huh? You can work on dozens of these and have fun doing it." He flipped the napkin over and scrawled some more. "Here's one you might like, ICURA102, *I see you are a 10 too.*"

Jen was subconsciously shaking her head. Never in her wildest did she dream it would be this easy. She leaned over and planted a kiss on the top of Carl's bald dome. "Dr. Jaeger, you're wonderful. That's just what I needed. *Uh-oh*, I think I hear nature calling. I'll be right back." She rushed off, grimacing all the way. Kissing a murderer was like the kiss of death. She had to keep reminding herself that he was just a little creep she was going to put away.

She slipped her cell phone from her hip pocket and tapped in Larry's number as she made her way over to a dark corner on the far side of the room. He answered on the first ring.

"I got it," she said. "Write it down, it's all capital letters, are you ready? ...Okay here goes, O2BA104U. Okay read it back to me... Perfect...Don't worry about it. He's here with me so you won't get caught...For heaven's sake, Larry, just do it. If for some reason he insists on leaving I'll call, but he won't, not as long as I'm here. I want you to get every email from about a month before Q was fired till now...No, don't try to read them, we'll do that later. Just forward them to my address. And be sure to delete the forwarded copies. Got it? ...Okay ...What? ...No, I won't forget." She snapped her phone shut. *Boy the things I have to do.* The band was back onstage, the sound of drums, guitar and bass filling the room again. She fluffed her hair and did the *boot scootin' boogie* all the way back to the bar.

* * * 🌍 * * *

Sarah glanced around her small apartment thinking about the musty smell, the flakey paint, the stuttering pipes and thrift store furniture. At least it was clean, and Brian fit right in.

His hair was long and greasy and his beard a ragged mess. He wore soiled jeans and a flannel shirt that smelled like rotten fruit. She'd listened to his story, but it seemed so bizarre, so much like a novel, she found it hard to believe. She wanted to believe, she wanted to help him into the shower, and into some clean clothes, and into a job, into society, and into a new life—one that included *her*—and she didn't know why she wanted it, because his being there, just days after Buddy's departure, seemed wrong. If he'd shown up a week earlier, when he'd still had a chance of meeting his son, it would have been better. *Why now, Lord?*

It *was* possible that her letters never got to him, possible that he'd been transferred from one outfit to another and when a roadside grenade killed two of his good buddies, was left with a concussion that erased his memory. That for the past several years he'd been in and out of one VA hospital after another, while little by little pieces of his memory were restored. All but the one he carried closest to him about the girl whose face he could not forget, a beautiful face that haunted him, with a name he could not remember, and how after finally recalling his own name, and the place where he'd formerly lived, he'd made his way back to San Francisco where he wandered the streets hoping to reassemble the puzzle of his life until a few days ago when, while reading a newspaper he'd found in the trash, he'd seen an obit about the death of a boy named Buddy who was survived by his mother, a Sarah Hunter, whose face had sprung into his mind putting the final pieces together. A web lookup on a library computer had revealed her address and here he was, with apologies for showing up just when he knew she was probably grieving the loss of her son, but knowing he had to come as long as there was any chance of learning more about his former life.

Sarah glanced at her watch, almost eleven. The file she was planning to read lay on the table unopened, a casualty of the war between her emotional heart and her rational mind. She hadn't considered Aaron and what he was going through. If she was to be of any help, she needed to read that file before their meeting tomorrow, and yet she somehow knew she wouldn't because now her past had caught up with her present and was demanding her time.

"So, I take it you're married," Brian said wistfully, as though hoping to hear otherwise. His arm was slung over the back of the sofa, his feet outstretched and crossed in front of him, relaxed and in control as ever, right at home.

"What makes you say that?"

"You have…ah, sorry, *had* a son. That's what the newspaper said."

Sarah bit her bottom lip and nodded slowly, her breath fluttering in her chest. Throughout the telling of his story her one overriding thought was whether or not to tell him. It wasn't that he didn't deserve to know, but she wasn't sure about the timing. But he'd opened the door…

"You said you couldn't remember my name, only that you had a picture in your head of someone you thought you'd loved in the past. Now you know that person was me. Do you remember what became of our relationship?"

Brian's mouth puckered as he shook his head.

"It was after you left. You promised to return but I never heard from you again."

"Yeah, I know. I'm sorry about that, but…"

"That was thirteen years ago, Brian. Buddy was twelve when he passed. It's right there in the obit. Do the math."

Brian squinted, looking perplexed.

"He was your son, Brian. Buddy was *your* son."

They would be turning the lights out soon, but to Aaron's regret because something about the story he was hearing made him want to keep Jethro talking. This was the epitome of a messed up life, from bad to worse. Jethro was your typical Channel Six news story about the kid who was beaten by his habitually drunken father, who tried to defend his sorely abused mother and who out of desperation one day when he was fourteen years old, had taken a baseball bat to his old man and beat him to within an inch of his life.

Jethro had spent a year in juvenile detention for the assault while his dad went Scott free, and it had been a litany of drugs, heists, gambling, abusive sex, and running from the law ever since. The culmination of his nefarious deeds came to a head one night when he needed money for a cab.

He and his buds had been out drinking and joyriding around town in a pickup. When the driver rounded a corner so fast the tailgate flew open, he'd been ejected from the truck. Rolling across the asphalt he'd escaped with only a few cuts and scratches, but was huffing mad when they didn't stop and come back for him. They'd just hooted and hollered and waved goodbye as they bounced on down the road. He wasn't going to walk home. The lights of a twenty-four-hour mini-mart blazed in the darkness. He had a gun. All he needed was enough cash for a ride, but the robbery had gone sour. The small Chinese proprietor had given him the cash he demanded, but at the last minute reached under the counter saying, "I have something else for you…" Jethro saw something shiny and black come up and thought it was a gun so he shot the woman, but when he went around the counter, he saw she was holding a Bible. She was trying to say something so he bent down and heard her whisper, "Jesus loves you…I forgive you…Jesus…"

"Man, can you believe that? She's down there on the ground bleeding to death and she's sayin' 'I forgive you.' I started pacing the floor, man, like I covered my ears but she wouldn't stop and she just kept saying it until she ran out of breath and died.

"I was like, out of control, Bro, know what I mean? I was so loaded I didn't know what I was doing. I stumbled out of that place right into a wash of blue and red flashing strobes. I didn't know it but someone else had driven up while I was robbing the store and they saw me through the window and called the cops and when I tried to leave they had the place surrounded. They hit me with a spotlight blinding me and I was standing there with blood all over my clothes and that was it, game over."

Aaron leaned away from Jethro, not wanting to actually touch him. He didn't know how to process what he was hearing. He knew bad things happened, someone had killed Dr. Summer and was trying to blame it on him, but this seemed more repugnant. Maybe because Jethro looked like the embodiment of evil, or maybe because he actually was a cold blooded killer.

"So, now you read the Bible, like, what, it makes you feel better or something?"

"You didn't let me finish. See, here's the thing. While I was waiting for my trial, the woman's husband, Mr. Chen, comes by and wants to visit. Like he was asleep when all this happened. I found out later they both worked twelve hour shifts at the store to keep it open twenty-four-seven just so they could put their son through college, and I screwed the whole thing up big-time. At first I refused to see the man. I don't want to hear any crap about how I ruined his life. I don't want to see his tears or any of that. But he keeps coming back, day after day, so I finally give in and go listen to what he has to say, just to get it over with but he doesn't give me any lip. He just tells me the same thing his wife did, that he forgives me, and that Jesus loves me, to which I tell him he can go to hell, but he just shakes his head and says he'll be praying for me. Pray for me? Did you get that Bro? Man, I can't handle all the stuff that's going on, and he's going to pray for me.

"But that's not the end of the story. I can't sleep at night because those words keep coming back at me, so I ask the screw to bring me a Bible. The guards don't like trouble in the block and since the Bible is considered a book of peace, he's good with that. And I start reading but I don't get it, this Jesus dude seems kinda lame to me, you know like, 'blessed are the meek,' and stuff like that, but when I get to the part where he's murdered, that I get.

"And then the prison Chaplin comes by to see how I'm doin' and see if I have any spiritual needs, and man, he doesn't know what he's in for. I know he can't rat me out on account of him being a priest and all, so I give it to him straight and I tell him what I done, and I know God aint' gonna forgive that, and he tells me I'm wrong. He shows me where Jesus was crucified between two guys who were killers and thieves and Christ looks at one of them and says He's gonna take him into paradise with Him, and how if He can do it for that murderer, He can do it for me. That's it, man. That's all she wrote 'cause after that I'm crying like a baby, and I've been reading this book ever since. Anyway, that's my story." Jethro stood and wiped his designer blue hands on his pants. "Look, they're going lights out pretty soon. I think I'm gonna crawl upstairs and sack out."

Aaron yawned, then covered his mouth and stretched. "Yeah, I guess so," he said, scooting aside so Jethro could climb into the bunk overhead.

Jethro placed a hand on the top rail and looked down at Aaron, his face a blue stain, his teeth like daggers. "I killed an innocent woman that day, destroyed not only her life, but lives of a whole lot of other people like her family and friends, and I gotta pay for that. I'll probably get the needle, and I deserve it, but you know what? It's all good because I know I'm forgiven. I can't wait to run up to that lady in heaven and tell her how much I appreciate what she done for me. I'll probably ask her to forgive me again, but I know she already has." He straightened himself, arching his back like he was working out a kink. "Just food for thought, if you know what I mean." And with that he swung his leg up and hauled his gangly frame onto the upper bunk.

Aaron closed his eyes and shook his head exhaling a deep breath. That a man tattooed with demons and blood, and hellfire could be a man of God didn't wash. He was crazy, but at least his insanity had made him a better person.

Aaron had read the book *The God Delusion* while in college. It had circulated among students in the science department because it was written by an evolutionary biologist, Richard Dawkins, who maintained there was no such thing as a supernatural creator. He argued that believing in God qualified as a delusion because such belief went against a preponderance of scientific evidence. Whether the premise was correct or not, Aaron couldn't say, but it did make him wonder how Dawkins would account for the change in someone like Jethro. Food for thought. Maybe Dawkins should have written *The Evolution Delusion* because if Jethro's life didn't prove the existence of God, what did? This former wigged-out motorcycle bandit was ready to die if that's what God called him to do. And Buddy had been ready to die too, and he hadn't harmed anyone so it wasn't just about assuaging guilt. And Jen was working with Sarah and there was no accounting for that. Go figure. The metal pan of the bunk above him creaked as Jethro stretched. "Hey, you said you were into motorcycles. Ever hear of a Harley Blackline?"

"Sure, nice street machine, if you're into that."

"What do you mean?"

Jethro leaned over the edge of the bunk gawking at Aaron, his bulbous blue head looking like a giant purple cabbage. "You ride?"

"No, not yet, but I've always wanted to. Maybe someday, if I get the chance."

"Cool." Jethro rolled to the center of the bunk and lay on his back staring up at the ceiling. "I got a real sweet ride, a 1995 Harley Low Rider with front end extension, a six-speed tranny and a 1,500 cc engine that growls like a lion. I was never good at much, but there's one thing I know and that's how to dress a bike. The paint on my Baby shines like a crystal blue river, and there's so much chrome you can see your face smiling back at you from every direction."

"Sounds nice. You still got it?"

"Yeah, my mom and I are good on account of the way I tried to come between her and my old man. My baby's parked in her garage.

I left it there the night I was out joyriding. Man, I'd give anything to have taken my bike out instead, but I can't change what is."

"So you really believe in all that Jesus stuff, huh?"

"Damn right. Look I'm not trying to convince you or anything, I just know it works for me. Like there's a story in that book we were reading about this blind guy that Jesus heals on the Sabbath, which is some kind of holy day, and these religious dudes are freaking out 'cause it breaks their tradition. They're all hung up on trying to convince everyone that Jesus is a fake, so they say Jesus didn't come from God because only a sinner would heal on the Sabbath. And the guy looks at them and says, 'Whether the man is a sinner or not I can't say, but this I know, I once was blind, but now I see.' That's how it is for me. I can't prove anything about Jesus or God or any of that. All I know is, I once was blind, but now I see."

Mother Nature Doesn't Run the Copy Machine
The Journal of W.L. Summer

Evolutionary theory purports that original reproduction began with a simple division of cells. The first cell divided and we had two, then the two divided and we had four, and so on. At that point there was no male and female, just division.

Somewhere along the line we assume one of the cells separated leaving a seed with one part and an egg with the other. From then on, the half with the seed had to find the half with the egg to create progeny.

Where humans are concerned the two components necessary, one to create seeds and deliver them, and the other to receive the seeds and combine them with the egg for fertilization, had to evolve independently and yet become fully functional at the same time. Human reproduction could not occur until both sexes coupled and found they fit together in every morphological and physiological way.

The problem is, once the male and female elements were separate they would be on their own evolutionary paths and owing to accidents and mutations would be subject to change in an infinite number of ways. The odds of their being able to fit perfectly together would become astronomical and as such the evolution of the reproductive system would never occur.

But suppose for a moment that it did. Then you have to determine what evolutionary process resulted in the need to mate? Whether it's the musk given off by a dog in heat, or the titillating sensation enjoyed by humans, or the pollen distributed by bees, every organism needs to have a way of ensuring procreation. Evolutionists like to give Mother Nature credit for drawing the sexes together, but unfortunately Mother Nature (read that matter) doesn't think.

There's no purpose behind the accidents that occur in evolution. Matter didn't say, "I need to figure a way to get dogs together so I'll give the female a scent that attracts the male, but I can't do that with plants because they're stationary so there I'll use bees, however humans are intelligent, they understand the need for procreation, so with them I'll just make it enjoyable."

No, based on a series of random evolutionary accidents, it was just as likely sex would be painful as it was pleasurable, or harmful as it was beneficial, or that the male and female parts wouldn't fit together in the first place. The accidents of nature happen without thought or purpose, which is how we know reproduction, whether through copulation, pollination, or division, is a matter of design.

Thirty-One

I will lift up my eyes unto the hills, from whence comes my help. My help comes from the LORD, maker of heaven and earth. —Psalm 121: 1-2

LIGHT FILLED the cafeteria falling on rows of tables and chairs. Jen slid her tray down the chrome rails pausing to reach across the counter for a salad and diet ginger ale. She and Larry had snuck out early to avoid the noon rush but it wouldn't last. As they reached the hour the throng would grow quickly making it hard to hold a private conversation.

Larry trailed behind. For once he was ogling something besides Jen's derriere. His eyes were on the menu reading down the list of cheeseburgers, french-fries and carbonated drinks. Jen waited for him to flag the cook and order the bacon and cheese special, and supersize it please, but he surprised her and reached for a salad. *Go figure.*

The outside wall of the cafeteria was made entirely of glass looking out onto a courtyard with an enormous fountain. Jen made an instant decision. It was a sunny day with a temperature in the high sixties. They would eat outside. They didn't have much to talk about, but she was determined their conversation would remain private.

She made her way through the door holding onto her tray. Larry tagged along without asking questions, though he probably understood the need for discretion. She took a seat on a bench

244

feeling the cold cement soaking through her clothes. At least they were able to sit upwind to avoid the fountain's spray. And the sun was warm on her shoulders. She popped the plastic lid off her salad and coated the greens with a raspberry vinaigrette dressing.

Larry was trying to get his package of salad dressing open but his fingernails were too short to grip the zip-off tab so he had to resort to using his teeth. He spat out the piece of plastic and smothered his salad in Thousand Island, and then attacked the cellophane wrappers of the half dozen packages of saltine crackers he'd scooped onto his tray.

Jen began nibbling her lettuce and cucumber slices watching as Larry tried in vain to poke the prongs of his plastic fork into a slippery cherry tomato. The whole thing was ridiculous. You couldn't put Larry and salad in the same sentence without it becoming an oxymoron. *Odd*, she didn't recall seeing him with a donut that morning either. He finally succeeded in plopping the tomato into his mouth. "So, you got everything, didn't you?" he said, starting to chew.

"Yes, I checked and it was all there."

"And…"

"And nothing. I haven't read anything yet. I didn't get home until after midnight."

"That's not what I meant. Are you going to keep your end of the deal?"

Jen stared at Larry, unblinking, then closed her eyes and shook her head like he'd just said the most disgusting thing she'd ever heard. "You pig. You amaze me. You should be doing this to help your friend. Why don't we focus on that? Once Aaron's out there'll be plenty of time to settle up between us."

"Don't get weird. I just want to take you to dinner, and maybe a movie, no big deal." The fountain sent a huge flume into the air and a shift in the breeze brought it down a few feet from where they sat. "Think we should move?"

Jen braced herself, watching as the fountain returned to normal. "No, we're almost done."

"So you really believe Aaron's innocent?"

Jen nodded. "Don't you?"

Larry used a cracker to scoop the last bit of salad dressing from the container. He popped it into his mouth and licked his fingers because they held as much dressing as the cracker. "I don't know. They got his Beemer, and they're saying the paint's a match with the chips found on Q's clothes."

"That doesn't mean Aaron was driving."

"Yeah, but it doesn't mean Dr. Jaeger was either. Somehow I can't imagine that fat little porker stealing his car. I just can't see him crawling around under the dash trying to get it hotwired. I doubt he'd know what to do."

"You should talk."

"Touché, I can't hotwire a car either."

"No, I mean you calling Dr. Jaeger a porker."

"Hey, proportionally he's fatter than me, considering how short he is, besides, with me there's just more to love."

"Fat chance. Pun intended. No, it has to be Dr. Jaeger. He hated Dr. Summer, called him a dinosaur. We know he had something to do with getting him fired and then when he hears Q's trying to get back in he practically goes ballistic. It makes sense. I mean, was he upset when Dr. Summer turned up dead? Not in the least."

"I don't know, Jen, seems a bit of a stretch to me."

"And it's not a stretch to think Aaron did it? Okay, alright, listen, I could use a hand going through all those emails. You come by my place tonight and help out and if we can't find anything that supports my claim, I'll back off. Deal?"

She shouldn't have offered Larry anything. The goofy smile on his face told her he would have helped just for the privilege of being invited over.

"Deal," he said.

Sarah and Eric Frisk sat across from Aaron. It was the second time they'd conferred together in the pale yellow room with no windows or mirrors. The inch thick file was on the table in front of Sarah, her fingers running along its smooth spine as she waited for Eric to finish explaining the strategy he'd prepared. Brian was waiting in the van and it made her anxious. She wanted the meeting to be over.

All those years she'd thought he was intentionally avoiding her when, in a way, he'd actually spent the past several years tracking her down, though he didn't know who she was. As he'd put it, he'd finally found his way home.

They had stayed up until three with her doing most of the talking as she recounted story after story about the son they shared. She'd gone to the dresser for the photo album and had taken him through every picture on every page: Buddy as a toddler crawling across the living room carpet with toys cluttering the floor, she and Buddy feeding pigeons at the summer art festival in Pioneer Park, Buddy zooming down the sidewalk in front of their apartment on his tricycle, and all the fun they shared while he still seemed like a normal child, before his condition was diagnosed. Then as he became weaker, leaning on crutches outside the Dairy Queen with more ice cream on his face and hands than on the cone, and when his legs became so weak he could no longer walk, waiting at the edge of the street in his new wheelchair to see the floats go by in the Brookings' Fourth of July parade.

"He looks like such a neat kid. I wish I'd got to know him," Brian had said, and when she burst into tears, he'd nestled her under his arm and told her over and again how everything was going to be alright. It was just what she needed to hear.

Regaining her composure, though still unable to speak without sniffing, she'd completed her story by telling him how she'd come to San Francisco to find her father, but how it now appeared she'd lost him too. She could feel the warmth of his arms surrounding her. He'd kissed the top of her head and suggested maybe he'd been brought back into her life to fill the void. At least part of what she'd lost had been found. She no longer needed to be alone.

Another tear washed down her cheek. He'd reached for a tissue but she'd pushed him away and pointed out that he needed a shower and that it was three in the morning and she had to get some sleep. She'd offered him a clean washcloth and towel and sent him to the bathroom while she retrieved Buddy's fold-up bed and covered it with blankets so he'd have a place to sleep. It probably wasn't the best idea to let him spend the night but it was late and she knew she couldn't ask him to leave but she was very clear, what had happened between them was in the past. She was a different person now. As a Christian, she had made a commitment to never again become intimate with anyone until she was married.

He'd said he understood and sauntered off to the shower turning back to lean on the door and say: "You're a good person, Sarah. You're everything I envisioned, worth every minute of all those years I spent looking for you."

She had awakened him to the sizzle of eggs frying in the pan and the smell of waffles on the grill. Sarah had felt a tinge of excitement about the day even before the sun could be seen filtering through the curtains. It had been a long time since she'd fixed a regular breakfast for someone. As Buddy had become weaker he'd found it increasingly difficult to chew and she had succumbed to eating Cream of Wheat and applesauce but now she was delighting in the sizzle of the frying pan and was overjoyed to find the ingredients for making waffles still good and bug free.

Brian had climbed off Buddy's rollaway bed and dressed while she consciously kept her back to him, but then he'd gone over and placed his arms around her waist and kissed her hair, bidding her, "Good morning."

She'd spun around and pushed him away, but not harshly. "Let's take it slow," she said, relieved to smell soap on his skin, but noting that his clothes were still ripe.

"I thought you said you'd spent the last ten years pining away for me."

"I did, and it was twelve years, not ten. But that was then, and this is now. You can't expect me to just pick up where we left off. We need to take it one step at a time."

"Okay. Gotcha. But I want you to know it's not the same for me. With my memory gone, it feels like we just said goodbye yesterday." He ambled over to the sofa-bed, which Sarah had already folded back into a couch, and sat down. "Why are you up so early? I would have thought you'd want to sleep in."

She kept her back to him, sliding the eggs onto two plates and adding waffles on the side, then picking up one dish in each hand, turned to set them on the table. "I have an appointment this morning, one I made before you showed up, and now that you're here we have to do a little shopping."

Wearing her second new outfit, a long brown skirt and matching jacket with a cream colored blouse, clothes she'd purchased with Aaron in mind, she had taken Brian to the mall. Her credit card was heading for the stratosphere but she just couldn't bear to see him dressed so shabbily. At least she'd discovered where to shop and how to find good deals. Surprisingly, she found men's clothes even cheaper than women's.

Her final conquest came when she found a haircutter and convinced Brian to sit for a do-over. Gone were the shaggy beard and long locks. The new Brian came out looking every bit like the man she remembered. Her only regret was that Buddy wasn't there to see how handsome his father was...

"Did you have something for Aaron, Miss Hunter?"

Sarah's head snapped up. "Hunh?"

"Are you okay? You seem lost."

She straightened herself, sliding back in her chair, catching Aaron's eye—woeful, but at the same time, expectant. She couldn't deny she had feelings for him, but he was sitting across from her in orange prison scrubs and the question was, would he be released, or would he spend the next few years in jail? Brian or Aaron? A dilemma made even more difficult in knowing that neither man seemed to know Christ.

"No, I mean yes, I'm okay. And yes, yes, I have something." She slid the folder across the table to Aaron. "This is the file Dr. Summer left me, the one the police recovered."

Aaron reached out and pulled the folder across the table to himself. "What's in it?"

"I don't really know," Sarah responded, "mostly just technical stuff about the origin of life, many pages of hand written notes from his journal, and that paper he wrote but as you know, that's at least part of what got him fired. I'm hoping maybe there's some clue in there, something that might tell us why he was killed. I thought I'd have time to read it myself, but something's come up and…I really need to focus on looking for a job." Was that disappointment she saw in Aaron's eye, or confusion? He was bound to find out about Brian sooner or later, but she didn't want to hurt him, and especially not while he was in jail.

"Are you leaving the team, then?"

"No, of course not. I just don't have as much time to devote to it as I thought. In fact," she looked at her watch, "I'm afraid I have to bow out early." She scooted her chair back and stood. "Mr. Frisk, if you need anything, please don't hesitate to call, but, I'm sorry, I really must be going." And with that she went to the door and knocked for the guard to let her out.

"Wait!"

Sarah looked back over her shoulder.

"I need you to do something for me." Aaron took the pen Eric had been writing with and scratched down a number on the corner of the file. Tearing it off, he reached out, his eyes pleading with her to take it. "That's the number of my mother's cell phone. It's a private number known only by her closest friends so she usually answers. I don't know when she'll be down from the mountain and able to talk, but I need you to start calling now, and try again at least once a day until she picks up. Please. She needs to know what's going on."

Aaron held the folder under his arm as he shuffled back down the hall. He couldn't help but feel dejected. Yesterday Sarah was full of hope and promise but it was obvious something had changed. He'd glanced at her several times hoping to catch her eye but always she seemed distracted, off in another world.

He stood back as the guard unlocked his cell, and then stepped inside feeling as much as hearing the loud echo as the door slammed shut behind him. The room was empty. Jethro was gone, but he'd said his sentencing was today. The Bible was still there so he'd probably be back. No time like the present to start reading the file. He glanced around the tiny room and imagined life reduced to a bunk bolted to a cinderblock wall. He shuffled over, his feet feeling heavy as they scuffed the floor. He reached out to set the file down and saw a small piece of paper sitting on the mattress. The writing was atrocious with about a third of the words misspelled.

It felt like someone had punched him and for a moment he couldn't breathe. His eyes welled. He sat down, placed his face in his hands, and began to cry.

Thirty-Two

For your Maker is your husband, The Lord of hosts is His name;
And your Redeemer is the Holy One of Israel; He is called the God of
the whole earth. —Isaiah 54:5

AN ORANGE SUN, pinned to the sky behind the Golden Gate Bridge, caused the waters of the bay to shimmer with flecks of gold. It had been another cloudless day with temperatures in the mid seventies, warm enough to make one believe winter had been banished for good. Sarah glanced in her rearview mirror at the man seated behind her.

She parked the van feeling embarrassed. She didn't like having to ask Brian to ride in back, but the passenger seat had been removed and the space made to accommodate a wheelchair. Grabbing several bags of groceries she staggered inside, a light sheen of perspiration glistening on her skin. Her apartment felt musty and stale. She set her bags on the counter and rushed to open the window, ignoring Snowball's enthusiastic welcome. Gossamer webs clung to the rungs of the chairs around the table, exposed by the light. She reached down to pat the dog's head. She'd have to do a quick dusting, hopefully before Brian noticed.

Brian trailed in with a few parcels and set them on the couch. There was something about his lanky frame, perhaps the way his arms hung loose with his thumbs hooked in his pockets, that made Sarah see him as relaxed even when standing.

She went to the door and used her foot to slide the stack of boxes out of the way. Snowball danced around her ankles. "Calm down, dog, relax." She looked at Brian. "I should get these things to the Salvation Army. I just haven't had time."

"No, uh, why don't you leave it with me. I'll take care of it."

She could almost hear a southern drawl in his voice, a stalk of wheat hanging from his lips like a toothpick, laid back and easy. "It's no problem. The drop off isn't that far."

Brian raised his chin toward the wheelchair. "I was thinking of asking if you needed that. I have a friend who could really use it. Lost his legs in Afghanistan. He's been waiting to get one from the government but they're in short supply. He'd really appreciate it."

Sarah nodded, "Of course, if he can use it, I'd be honored. Anything for a vet. I just want it to go to someone in need."

"Great, because he and his family are desperate." He spun around, glancing at the clock over by the sofa. "It's only five. Would you mind terribly if I rushed it over right now? I know its kinda last minute, but it'd really make him happy. You should see him, he's too heavy for his wife to lift so he sits on the bed and watches TV all day. He has to wait until someone like me shows up to move him. It's really sad."

Sarah could relate to that. How often she'd wished for help with moving Buddy. If giving the man a wheelchair improved his situation, it was the least she could do, but she also knew it meant letting Brian use her van. She'd let Beth use the van to drive Buddy around. It was insured for other drivers. "I suppose. How long do you think you'll be?"

"Hour at most. I'll even run the other things by the Sally-Ann and get them out of your way."

Sarah picked up the dog and held its muzzle to keep it from licking her chin as she went to the kitchen for her purse. "There's something else we need to discuss," she said. "I let you sleep here last night, but I don't want my neighbors getting the wrong idea.

If they start seeing a man coming and going, *well*, you know how people talk. You need a place of your own. Have you tried finding a job?"

Snowball was licking her face. She set him down. Thrusting her hand into the leather bag she fished through its contents until she found her keys. She turned around to face Brian. He'd grown pensive, maybe even sad, the doleful look of a scolded puppy.

"It isn't easy on those of us who've given the most for our country," he said. "I can't find work because I don't have a resume. I can't even provide a family history, or list my past addresses or tell them where I went to high school, or if I even graduated."

Sarah moved toward him, her heart reaching out to the wounded warrior. "I can help you there, at least some. You graduated from Hawthorne High before moving to San Francisco. I don't know your complete employment history, but you were working as a pipefitter before you joined the Marines. You had just quit your job and were about to take a quick trip around the US when we met. You told me a lot about yourself so maybe when you apply I can help fill in some of the blanks."

Brian opened his arms. "You are truly amazing," he said, taking her in. "I didn't thank you for all the clothes. I couldn't have gotten a job the way I looked but that won't be a problem now."

They stood staring at each other. Her hands were on his shoulders, his around her waist. He leaned in to kiss her, but she turned her head away.

"Hey, what's the matter?"

She pushed him back and wiggled free. "I don't know. It's just that, well, one thing leads to another and with you staying here…I don't know, I just don't want to make another mistake is all, not that Buddy was a mistake, but you know what I mean."

"Tell you what, if that's the way it's gonna be, I'm gonna grab a newspaper while I'm out and start applying for every job I see. Then I'll get my own place and…well, whatever it takes to make you happy. Now that I've found you, I don't want to lose you again."

Sarah held out her hand with the keys dangling from a finger. "Take good care of the van. It's not really mine. I have to return it soon. You still have a driver's license, don't you?"

Afternoon shadows stretched across the road as Brian navigated the hills of the mission district. Entering the parking lot from 26th Street, he rolled past the gate and pulled up beside a truck where two Salvation Army employees stood ready to help him unload. He left the engine idling as he hopped out and went to the side door, sliding it open. The evening was warm, as it had been the past few days. Maybe they'd have an early spring. He brought an arm up to wipe his forehead. The new shirt was great, a deep purple with crosshatched lines of gray and mint green, but it had long sleeves. He stopped to unbutton the cuffs, rolling them back over his forearms to keep from getting sweaty.

The wheelchair had to be removed first to get it out of the way. He set it on the ground and started handing the boxes to the workers who walked back and forth from Sarah's van to their truck until the van was empty. Lifting the wheelchair back inside, he closed the door again, thanked the men for their help, and headed for his next destination. The sun had dropped behind the buildings but the sky held a dusky orange light, enough to let him know it wasn't yet six. Barry's would still be open.

He turned the van into a tight alley and drove around back to park. The asphalt was crumbling. Dirt and grease stained the pavement and weeds grew through the cracks. The power lines overhead were so low he could hear them *buzz*.

This was the second time he'd had to remove the wheelchair and it wasn't light, but he didn't want to bother with the ramp so he slid his shirtsleeves up and hefted it down. He grabbed the handles, spun the chair around and wheeled it to the back of the store, where he rang the bell.

The man who answered wore a black T-shirt with KISS Rock the Nation Tour silkscreened on the front. He was bald on top but had curly black hair wrapped around the sides. His arms were hairy. There was a big gold watch strapped to his wrist and a cigar clamped between his teeth.

"Well look at you. What happened, somebody give you a bath? What's that? Don't tell me you're bringing me more junk I can't use." Barry swung the door open wide, letting Brian and the wheelchair inside.

The walls were covered with shelving units stacked with TVs, stereos, GPS units, microwaves, laptops, old cell phones, and assorted other electronic gadgets.

"It isn't junk and you know it. Lots of people need wheelchairs and where better to get one than Barry's Pawn and Loan."

"Don't try to schmooze me." The man pulled his cigar from his mouth and tapped the end letting the ash fall to the worn linoleum. "That won't get you breakfast."

"How much?"

"Ain't worth nuthin'."

"Just tell me how much. I need to score. I'm starting to get the jitters. How much?"

"Best I can do is thirty bucks."

"Thirty? No way. These things cost a couple hundred at least."

Barry reached out taking hold of the chair, turning it this way and that, and stooped over for a closer look. A head of ash fell on the seat but he swept it away. "Maybe if it had a motor it might get you a hundred but not a manual rig like this. Nobody wants 'em. Thirty's my top offer."

"Come on, Barry, thirty won't get me any juice and you know it. I'm hurtin' here."

"So, come up with some collateral."

"You already got my Colt. That's an heirloom."

"So, what else you got?"

Brian thought for a moment. "What if I can get you a TV, and maybe a stereo. If I promise to get you those will you front me a little blow. You know I'm good for it. Have I ever let you down?"

Barry hesitated and then shook his head. "Unless you're talkin' big screen HD, I ain't interested. Look at all this junk. My shelves are packed and I can't move any of it," he said, waving a hand around the room.

"Okay, look, I got a friend with money, like she's a doctor or something. She went out and bought me these clothes without batting an eye…"

"Yeah, why'd she do that?"

"Because she knows me. We have history. I read about her in the paper and I remembered her name, it just came back to me out of the blue, so I went to her place to see if she could help with my memory thing. She's cool. She even wants to help me find a job."

"Yeah, right. Good luck with that."

"Here's the thing. She's got credit cards. I can lift one and buy a few things. You give me something to get through the week and I'll bring in enough to cover it by Friday."

Barry twirled the cigar in his mouth, squinting as smoke spiraled up to the ceiling. "Okay, tell you what, you get me a card and we'll do business. Who knows maybe you'll even cover the loan and get your weapon back." He walked to a desk piled high with paper and pulled a notepad from the drawer. "This is my marker," he said, scrawling a short note. "Give it to Cueball and he'll fix you up." He held the note out between two fingers but when Brian reached for it, pulled it back. "You blow this and your girlfriend won't recognize your face the next time she sees you, understand?"

"No worries. And, hey, I'll take the thirty bucks for the chair."

Sarah was singing as she set the table, which, when she thought about it, surprised her. She hadn't felt like singing since...well, it was like when God took Buddy, He'd taken her song, but now it was back again. *La, la la, la la.* The tune was familiar, but she couldn't quite remember the words. Would she be the future Mrs. Brian Johnson? God never closed a door without opening a window. He had taken Buddy, had He given her Brian? *La, la la, la la, la la.*

She'd swept the cobwebs from the chairs and closed the window again. Everything looked ready. The only thing left was to make the call. She'd never met Mrs. Rose. What would she say? She found the phone in her purse, felt her heart tremble, and dialed the number. Two rings, three...

"Hello."

"Oh, you're there."

"Yes, who is this?"

"Uh, hi Mrs. Rose, this is Sarah Hunter, I'm a friend of Aaron's. He asked me to give you a call."

"Because he doesn't want to call me himself, or is he just too busy?"

"No, it's not like that. He can't, he..."

"And why not?"

"That's what I was about to say. He's in jail and he doesn't have calling privileges, he..."

"I think you're breaking up on me. It sounded like you said my son's in jail."

"I did. But he didn't do anything. He's been falsely accused, but he doesn't have any money and he needs help. He was wondering if..."

"Who are you?"

"Just a friend."

"I know most of Aaron's friends. Who are you?"

"I'm sorry Mrs. Rose. Aaron just asked me to call..."

"Are you that new girl? The religious one."

"I…I don't know. I'm a Christian if that's what you mean."

There was silence at the other end. Sarah searched for something to say but Mrs. Rose spoke first. "Well, Sarah, Aaron's just going to have to get himself out of this one. I'm on a cruise halfway up the Nile. Tell that son of mine if he wants my help, he needs to follow my advice."

"I'm sorry, what?"

"Just tell him, dear. He'll know what I mean."

"Alright but I think he'd like to hear from you, if you could just…hello, hello?" The line had gone dead.

Sarah shook her head. *Weird.* She slipped the phone back into her purse and went to check the oven. The meat was done, the smell of onions and garlic watered her mouth, and the table was set with white linen that glowed rosy in the evening light. Now she just had to get herself ready. She glanced out the window. *Oh no, he's here.*

She ran to the bathroom checking herself in the mirror. Snowball jumped up and scooted away. Her makeup looked good. The eyeliner and mascara made her green eyes seem greener and her lipstick made her lips full and inviting. She used her fingers to fluff her hair. It was starting to grow and it suited her. Perhaps the effort to improve herself hadn't been in vain.

She took a step back. The cream blouse and brown skirt had been replaced with blue denims and a white top, a more casual look for a relaxed evening. She tucked in her blouse, sliding a finger around her waistband to smooth the material, and went back to the kitchen. The oven was off, but warm enough inside to keep the meatloaf and potatoes hot.

The door opened and there he was looking every bit the man she'd fallen in love with all those years ago. The lean dark denims fit like a glove, and that classy deep purple shirt with the cuffs relaxed and folded back on his wrists, the woodsy shoes, a cool classy look that reminded her of—*Aaron.* It suddenly occurred to her that she might be subconsciously trying to turn Brian into someone else.

"Something smells good," he said, as he sauntered in heading straight for the kitchen.

She'd been thinking about him all day. If he tried, she'd be tempted to let him kiss her. She turned away. "How'd it go?" She said, wiping her hands on a towel.

He nodded. "Fine. My friend really appreciated your gift."

"That's great. Were you able to find the Salvation Army drop off?"

"Of course. They took everything, no problem."

"Cool. Might as well go wash up. Dinner's ready. I'll start putting it on the table."

Brian ducked into the bathroom. The taps *screeeeeched* and the pipes thudded. She grimaced and turned back to the counter serving up two generous portions of meat and potatoes. Snowball sat at her feet whining. She crumbled off a piece and set it in his bowl. The dog leapt forward with its tail wagging, devouring the morsel in one quick gulp. "You're a *good dog*, Snowball. Good dog." Snowball bounced against her leg, whining for more, but she wasn't about to start feeding him scraps. It wasn't her dog. Snowball belonged to... She glanced around the counter and grabbed a paper towel to dab her eyes. *Not again.* She straightened herself and swallowed the lump in her throat, trying to put on a good face and prevent Brian from seeing her meltdown. "I hope you like meatloaf," she called, but her voice was full of gravel.

"Love it." Brian stood at the bathroom door wiping his hands.

She cleared her throat. "Good, sit down, everything's ready."

"You Okay?"

Sarah nodded and went to her chair, standing until he joined her at the table and then took a seat trying to avoid eye contact without seeming rude. He picked up his knife and fork and started to dig in.

Sarah folded her hands in her lap, waiting. "You mind if I say grace?" she said.

Brian set his fork and knife down. "No, fine, go ahead."

Sarah bowed her head and closed her eyes. "Dear Lord, thank You for loving us and watching over us. Please help me as I struggle to get over Buddy, and thank You for sending Brian to help. And thank You for the food we're about to eat. Please bless it in Jesus name. Amen."

She glanced up. Brian was sitting there with his eyes open, waiting politely but not joining in. She tipped her head toward his plate. "It's okay, you can start now," she said.

Brian dug in ravenously, putting Snowball to shame as he inhaled bite after bite. "You must be hungry," she said. She could understand how he might pick up a few bad habits while living on the streets.

He pulled the fork back from his mouth and grabbed a napkin to wipe his lips. "Sorry. I guess I'm making a pig of myself."

Sarah continued cleaning her plate until Snowball bolted for the door, barking. Brian looked up. The intercom sounded. "Now who could that be?" Sarah hadn't had this many visitors in as long as she could remember. She scooted her chair back and started for the door but it flew open before she got there. Larry and Jen charged in without waiting to be invited. Snowball began doing figure-eights around their legs, trying to get a good sniff.

"We got it," Jen said, waving a piece of paper as she passed by.

"Excuse me," Larry said, squeezing around Sarah.

Jen looked up. "Oh sorry, are we intruding? I didn't know you had company."

Sarah went to close the door and came back to the table. "No, we were just finishing up." She began stacking plates and carrying them to the kitchen placing them in the sink. "This is Brian." She returned to the dining area and placed a hand on his shoulder. "Brian was my son's father but we'd lost touch. He saw my name in Buddy's obit and looked me up. We were just reminiscing, that's all."

Sarah saw Jen's eyes wander over to the extra bed and then back to Brian. She stepped forward offering Brian her hand. "Well, Sarah, you do have good taste in men. I'll give you that. Hi, I'm Jennifer, and this is Larry," she said, glancing back at the big guy dressed in a golf shirt and shorts. "We work with Sarah over at CellMerge. Or at least we used to."

Jen was wearing a pair of denims, not baggy, but not the bellybutton-showing skin tight ones she usually wore, and she had on a T-shirt that hung loose on her torso. *Thank God for small favors.* Sarah noted the flirtatious smile and soft batting of her eyes as Jen held Brian's hand. She was probably wishing she'd worn something a little more sensual. "So what's this about," she said.

Jen went and grabbed Larry, pulling him into the room. "Have we got a story to tell. I told you I was going to do some snooping around. Well, I went to Dr. Jaeger saying I needed to talk to him about something private and suggested we go out for a drink." Jen raised her hand and flipped her palm forward, "like he was going to say no, anyway, while I kept him busy, I had Larry go through the computer in his office and look what we found."

"You broke into Dr. Jaeger's office?"

"Not exactly. After he agreed to go out with me, I stuck a wad of tissue into the strike plate thingy on his door. That way the door wouldn't lock when he closed it, and then I distracted him when he was leaving so he wouldn't notice. All Larry had to do was walk in, sit down at his computer, and forward the emails. I had the real work; I had to coax Dr. Jaeger's password out of him, which I thought was going to be impossible but, truth is, he made it easy. I couldn't believe it, but that's another story. Anyway, look what we found." She held the paper out for Sarah to read.

From: Dr. Carl Jaeger <drjaeger@cellmerge.com>

To: Jack Landon

Subject: Dr. Wallace Summer

Thank you for seeing me this afternoon. I was surprised, but also pleased to find we're in complete agreement. Dr. Summer's termination was not merely justified; it was the right, if not only, course of action to take.

However, in light of recent events that suggest he may be staging a coup, I would advise remaining vigilant. We either do whatever it takes to prevent his return, or stand by and watch as he undermines our board's decision. I've already decided which I'm going to do. I trust you have too.

Sincerely,

Dr. Carl Jaeger.

Sarah looked up. "Wow, this is great! You mind if I borrow it? There's another meeting tomorrow. Detective Irons wants to question Aaron but he's had to wait until Aaron's lawyer could be present. I was going to stay out of it, but this is too good to pass up."

A King Is Known By the Robe He Wears
The Journal of W.L. Summer

Darwin believed we would eventually find fossils of every transitional form needed to prove his theory. It was a reasonable expectation, providing evolution was true. The problem is, we've been searching more than a hundred years and haven't found one irrefutable example.

Science textbooks are filled with colorful illustrations showing the transition from monkey to man. Unfortunately, none of the pictured transitional forms really exist. In the real world there are simply men and apes with nothing in between. On the homo sapiens side you have Homo Erectus, Peking Man and the Neanderthals, all of which were originally touted as missing links but were subsequently classified as fully human and as such don't qualify as transitional forms.

Java Man is supposedly a candidate. The illustrations show him as having a sloped forehead with thick eyebrows, a flat nose and broad big toothed mouth, but all that was found of Java Man was a skullcap and three teeth. The subsequent drawings are the product of someone's creative imagination. Piltdown Man later proved to be a fraud, turned out to be a four-hundred year old skull with an orangutan's jaw attached. Nebraska man was based on one tooth that later proved to be from a pig, and from that we got Pithecanthropus, the forerunner of man. Nutcracker Man later proved to be an extinct ape.

Ardipithicus Ramidus is composed of several teeth with a handful of bone fragments some of which were found nearly two hundred feet away from the teeth in one direction and the rest about seven hundred feet away in the other. Most of the teeth were broken and the few that remained intact pointedly resembled those of a chimpanzee. That didn't stop us from classifying this as man.

Lucy, the skeletal remains found by Dr. Leakey, had more bones than the others but she ended up being classified as an australopithecine, a distinct animal group separate from man and apes.

The Times, London, quoted Nigel Hawkins as saying, "Few sciences produce such abundant returns from so few fragments of fact as paleontology."

As scientists, desperate to prove what we believe, we've become accustomed to seeing what isn't actually there. We have a king walking around in his underwear and we're trying to convince the world he's dressed in fine apparel. The day is coming when some brave scientist is going to point and say, "The king has no clothes."

Thirty-Three

Thus says the Lord, your redeemer, He that formed you from the womb, "I am the Lord that makes all things; that stretches forth the heavens alone; that spreads abroad the earth by myself." —Isaiah 44:24

ARON SAT on a steel folding chair in an orange jumpsuit with his elbows on his knees and his hands clasped. Perhaps it was just the fluorescent lights bouncing off the pale yellow walls that made his skin appear grey, but Sarah couldn't help but think he looked ill. His head was bowed and hanging low, his sallow cheeks were unshaven, and his hair was flat on one side and stuck up on the other.

It was enough to make her forget her own pain and reach out to him with compassion, and not because misery loves company, as those prone to clichés might say, but because only those who endured pain themselves could fully empathize with the misery suffered by others. She wished she hadn't told him about her conversation with Mrs. Rose, but he'd forced the issue.

"Did you get hold of my mother?"

"Yes, I caught up with her. I think she was on a cruise or something. The reception wasn't very good. All she said was if you want her help, you need to follow her advice. I asked what she meant but she said you'd know. That's about it. The line went dead after that."

Aaron had slumped into his chair and hadn't spoken since.

The sound of the door opening made Sarah look over her

shoulder. A uniformed guard stood to the side as Eric entered carrying his briefcase which he placed on the table. His pointed hair looked like the crest of a bird.

"Morning Aaron, Sarah," he said tipping his head to each in turn. "Glad to see you're both already here. I want to go over a few things before we meet with the detectives." He slipped his suit coat off and draped it over the back of a chair and with a hand holding his tie against his chest, sat down.

"I'm glad you're here too. I have something to show you." Sarah reached down to retrieve her purse and removed an envelope which she handed to Eric.

"What's this?"

"Read it," she said.

Eric tugged the letter from the envelope and shook it open, his eyes scanning the page. "Interesting, where did you get this?"

Aaron looked up. "Get what?"

Eric slid the piece of paper across the table to Aaron. "I don't know what it proves, but it is interesting."

"What it proves is that someone else had motive. You said that's the weakest part of their case. Aaron didn't have any reason to want Dr. Summer dead, but this proves someone else did, someone who by their own admission was ready to make sure Dr. Summer, who'd recently been fired, never got reinstated."

Aaron was nodding, his face now looking like the sun on a landscape after breaking through the clouds. "She's right. *Dr. Jaeger.* Unbelievable. He'd do it too. The dude's crazy. Me and Larry and Jen were out with him before all this happened and he was saying how a man should be free to do anything he wants, even murder, if the situation warrants. I'll bet he was thinking about killing Dr. Summer even then. It just makes sense. I can see him trying to pull this off."

Eric leaned over, took the letter from Aaron's hand and held it out to Sarah. "The question remains, where did you get this?"

"I personally didn't. It was Jen Carlson and Larry Lofter. They're friends of Aaron's. They somehow got into Dr. Jaeger's computer and found it there."

"Well, I sure hope they had his permission, otherwise it's inadmissible."

"But it does give the police a reason to start looking at someone else."

The door opened again. Detectives Irons, wearing a frumpy brown sports coat and wrinkled tan slacks, along with Eduardo Rodriquez in a starched blue suit with crisp white shirt and tie, walked in. Sarah could tell the suit was new. It looked just off the rack. They each nodded curtly and took seats around the table. Eric leaned in toward Aaron and whispered in his ear. "It's best if you let me do the talking. I'll let you know when it's okay for you to answer."

"I see we're all here," Detective Irons said.

Rodriquez tossed a folder on the table, his eyes bouncing from Sarah to Eric to Aaron. "Good, let's get down to it. You're accused of a hit and run causing death, but that's not what you did. You used your car to kill a man. That's vehicular homicide." *Whapppp*, he smacked the file with the flat of his hand. "We know you did this thing. We have proof." He leaned back. "But if you're willing to cooperate and sign a confession, we'll see what we can do to get the homicide charge off the table."

Detective Irons reached out and took his partner by the arm. "Wait a minute, Ed, we're getting ahead of ourselves. Let's hear what the kid has to say."

Sarah glanced at Eric whose mouth curled slightly. He too realized the detectives were playing good cop, bad cop. Funny, she would have thought they'd use Irons for the bad cop, he had the muscle. Rodriquez didn't seem strong enough to squeeze a confession out of anyone.

"My client," the lawyer said, "has already stated his innocence. I've given you the transcript of our initial interview. He's already told you everything he remembers about that night. I've spoken with him several times since and I assure you nothing has changed, so unless you have something new to offer…"

Eduardo smirked. "We don't need anything new; we have the car."

"Arguably for the hit and run, but you're using homicide as a bartering chip to get a confession when the charge is absolutely baseless. You'll have to do better than that."

"He didn't even slow down, ran right over the old man without looking back. I think we can convince a jury that no one does that unless it's on purpose."

"I doubt it, but for the sake of argument, even if you could, you'd have to show motive. My client had no reason to kill Dr. Summer. In fact, as I will demonstrate in court, they were friends."

Detective Irons frowned. His hands were on the table, his pencil tapping out a cadence on the yellow legal pad in front of him. "Save your arguments for the courtroom. All I want is to hear Mr. Rose tell me what happened."

"And hopefully trick him into saying something you can misconstrue and use against him in court. Sorry, that's not going to happen."

"It's not like that. It's just, I wasn't part of the first interview. Maybe if your client explains himself, I can help."

"Right. Sorry, you have the initial report. You'll have to make do with that."

"There is something you're missing."

All eyes went to Sarah.

"If that car didn't stop or slow down, as you said, then it follows, as you also said, someone wanted to kill Dr. Summer. I can't for the life of me imagine why, but I can offer you this." She took the printed email and slid it across the table to Detective Irons. "Apparently, there was someone at CellMerge, and maybe even more than one, who wanted Dr. Summer out of the way."

Irons scanned the note and passed it to Eduardo who was

craning his neck to read from the side.

"My partner here has already interviewed Dr. Jaeger and cleared him, haven't you, Ed?"

"Where did you get this?" Eduardo said, tossing the paper back at Sarah.

"That's not important, but what is, is that Aaron, I mean Dr. Rose, didn't have any reason to kill Dr. Summer, but there is someone who did."

Irons turned to his partner. "What did Dr. Jaeger say when you interviewed him? Did he have an alibi?"

"Alibi? No, I mean, I didn't interview him. There was no reason to; we have our man."

"And that was the extent of your investigation," Eric challenged. "One man. You focused your entire investigation solely on my client without exploring any other possibilities?" He took the email, flipped it over and began writing on the back.

Detective Irons rolled his eyes and shook his head. "Okay, maybe we need to broaden our scope a little," he looked at Eric, "but if that email was obtained illegally I can't use it to get a warrant so we'll just have to go with what the man says, and if he has an alibi it's game over. We'll be holding onto your client because he's already been arraigned and until proven otherwise, he's still our number one suspect, understood?"

Brian stood on the sidewalk fanning the air. A car had skirted the corner too fast spinning road dust onto his brand new shirt. The unseemly weather made him moist and he didn't want dust sticking to the material. He took a whiff under each arm to reassure himself and stepped into a bright red telephone booth. A reminder of days gone by, it was probably the only one left in San Francisco, but it stood outside an Old English pub where it served as a novelty. He was lucky the phone still worked. He didn't have a cell.

It was time to meet with Barry. He had the card and was ready to go on a shopping spree to cover the debt he owed. That was the deal. He wanted it over and done.

He wasn't sure where he was headed with Sarah. It wasn't her looks. Her friend Jen was nicer looking and probably had a better figure, though he couldn't say for sure because of the baggy T-shirt. But Sarah was sweet, that's what it was, she was sweet, and naïve, and trusting. There was a goodness about her he found attractive. He retrieved the handset, found the change swimming at the bottom of his pocket, and reached up to feed the phone. The dial tone hummed. The sky on the other side of the fogged glass looked like a smear of grey mustard. He took a deep breath and dialed.

Aaron tried to shake himself out of his funk. It wasn't fair to say he was on his own. Maybe his Mom wasn't coming, but Eric seemed to know what he was doing, though how much time he'd spend on jurisprudence remained to be seen. And Sarah was getting things done. Even Jen and Larry were helping so, technically, he had a team of people working for him.

But Sarah was the one that mattered. He welcomed the opportunity to tell her about Dr. Summer's paper and the abundance of information compiled by hundreds who had walked away from naturalism. Not that he was ready to join them, at least not yet, but the evidence was compelling.

He rubbed his wrists to keep the cuffs from chaffing. The email she'd found was magic. Just when he was at his lowest point, feeling abandoned by his mother and totally alone, she'd brought him back to the top by giving the detectives a reason to expand their investigation.

The door opened to a room with a long counter separated by cubicles, each with a chair and a phone. His police escort prodded him forward. The thumping in his chest accelerated as he passed one after another waiting to see Sarah's face. The officer pointed to an empty station and Aaron stepped inside, disappointed to see the person waiting on the other side of the glass wasn't Sarah after all. It was Jen.

She looked different. Her hair was rolled in a bun with a pin holding it in place. He'd seen her do that before, especially on hot days when her hair lay on her back like a blanket, but it wasn't warm in here. And her blouse, a regular short sleeve shirt with a collar, was buttoned above her cleavage so that her breasts remained hidden even when she reached for the phone. Give her a pair of black spectacles and she'd qualify as a librarian. *Really?*

Aaron picked up the phone on his side.

"Hey Aaron, how have you been?"

The glass was smudged causing Jen to look slightly out of focus and her voice coming through the speaker was tinny. He raised his eyebrows and shrugged. "Can't say I haven't been better."

She smiled and nodded. "Yeah, well, what can I say? Anyone ever tell you, you look good in orange?"

Aaron glanced down at his jumpsuit. "Mother would be proud."

"I'll bet."

"So what brings you here? I don't suppose you came to see the latest in jailhouse fashions."

"No, just wanted to see how you were doing. I'm working with Sarah to get you out."

"Yeah, I heard. How's that going?"

"Great, as weird as it might seem we're getting along. Did she show you the email Larry and I found on Dr. Jaeger's computer?"

"She did. She was here for a meeting with me and my lawyer this morning and based on that piece of new evidence the police are thinking of widening their investigation."

"Really?"

"I guess I owe you."

"You're welcome. Hey, don't worry about it. We just want to help. Did you hear about Sarah's other good news?"

"What news?"

"Oh, if she hasn't said anything I should probably wait and let her tell you herself."

Aaron sighed. "Jennifer..."

"Okay, but you didn't hear it from me. Anyway, you know she had a son, the little boy that...well anyway, his father tracked her down, they were lovers once but I guess something happened and they went their separate ways only now he's back and they seem to be working things out."

"What do you mean?"

"I was at her place last night and met him. Nice guy, good looking too."

"And they're getting back together?"

"Well, she didn't actually say, but you can tell. Haven't you noticed how she's got a whole new look and she's going around all goo-goo eyed? He's even staying there, like they're living together. I guess that speaks for itself."

Aaron slumped back in his chair, crossed his arms and dropped his chin. His mouth puckered.

"Oh, but don't worry. I know she's still committed to helping you," Jen said.

Thirty-Four

...And to make all men see what is the fellowship of the mystery, which from the beginning of the world has been hidden in God, who created all things by Jesus Christ. —Ephesians 3:9

ARON FELT sick. His stomach wrenched, twisting like a rag. He tried to blink the dryness from his eyes but they scratched and burned refusing to yield moisture. The sound of stale air channeling through the prison's ventilation system had kept him awake most of the night, its continuous drone inflicting a low grade headache. His mother had abandoned him leaving him to rot in jail and Sarah was so busy schmoozing her ex-boyfriend she didn't have time to see him. He felt the walls closing in, pale yuck walls coming closer and closer pressing him like a vise.

The world outside was filled with children, running, laughing, and playing. Birds, animals and all manner of men were free to come and go as they pleased, but for him, days aboard the Rover Moon with the wind combing his hair as he bounded through the waves, were over. If the police had their way, these four walls would be his home. His only fresh air that which he could suck up during a daily walk around the prison yard.

What chance did he have? His rookie lawyer was going head-to-head with an overzealous cop and a mountain of indisputable evidence. He sat on the bunk in his cell with his elbows on his knees, the unopened Bible on the bed beside him. Jethro had left it with a note saying: "Hey dude, I got my sentence. They've decided to send me to heaven. How cool is that? I'm leaving this with you 'cause I figure you need it more than me." Aaron's arm ached with tiredness as he pulled the book into his lap. Was there really a God? If so, it was beyond his grasp. Maybe his problem was that he wanted to quantify God, to reduce Him to a being he could understand. What if man was too small to fathom God? It was certainly possible. He couldn't even understand the complexity of man—the five hundred trillion neurotransmitters in the brain that facilitated thought, or the hundred thousand miles of blood vessels needed to deliver oxygen, or the billions of chemical letters in every DNA molecule that served as the blueprints for life. He was beginning to see how Dr. Summer came to the conclusion that these things couldn't just happen by accident.

He'd ignored Dr. Summer's paper when it was first published, giving it about as much credence as missives written about conspiracies and UFOs, but now he had to admit the case for evolution wasn't as strong as he'd originally thought.

What did that make him, no longer an atheist but still agnostic, one who couldn't say for certain whether God existed or not? He didn't like being ignorant. He wanted to know for certain one way or the other. After all, he was a Jew, one of God's people. Einstein was a Jew and he believed in God. Did that make him gullible? Weren't the Jews the ones to whom God was supposed to have revealed Himself? Shouldn't he have some kind of special insight?

He was ready to concede that life was more than just the body, it was the result of having a soul, or thought, or conscience, the ethereal part of man that set him apart from plants and animals. Dr. Summer pointed out that non-material things like thought and consciousness couldn't evolve, because evolution necessitates having something material to start with, something to build upon. The conclusion was that such could only come from God. But who was

God? And why bother to create something so infinitesimally small and insignificant as man? What purpose did it serve?

Buddy said to know God you have to know Jesus, but Judaism labeled Jesus as a false teacher. Jethro shared a story about that, how Jesus had healed a blind man on the Sabbath which the scribes said a righteous man wouldn't do. But like the man said, if Jesus weren't righteous, how could he heal anyone? He found himself yearning to believe what Buddy seemed to take for granted, that Jesus was the way to God. That little boy had great faith, enough to stare death in the face without blinking. And what about Jethro, who claimed God had turned his messed up life around? What stronger evidence could there be for the existence of God than for a wacked out psychopath to suddenly become a doting puppy? Or maybe it was Sarah. She shared the same faith—but he wasn't doing this for her. He wanted to be clear about that. This was for himself.

He flipped the Bible open and started reading, not any particular place just where his eyes fell on the page. It was a story about some guy named Peter who was in prison until an angel showed up and set him free. He felt goosebumps prickle his arms. His face began to flush, his eyes welling with water.

Aaron closed the book, the overflow streaming down his cheeks. His lips parted, his breath caught in his throat. *Enough!* "God, whoever you are, show yourself. Jesus, if you're real...help me..."

Sarah looked around, nervous that someone might be watching. Her mouth was dry, her heartbeat loud as a drum. It was only the second time she'd ever been to Dr. Summer's house and the other time he'd let them in. Neighborhood watch programs were probably in effect.

This was an upscale neighborhood with ocean view homes on large lots and landscaping done by professionals. Automatic sprinklers were watering lawns up and down the block. The trees were Monterey Pine, Blue Spruce and White Birch. Dr. Summer's house was an English Tudor with a sharply angled roof of wood shakes, grills in the windows, and a flagstone walkway with a coach lamp. She stood on the porch with narrow walls and tall shrubs concealing her from view on the left and right. Her main concern was that someone might see her from across the street.

There was a yellow crime scene ribbon across the door and a sign prohibiting entry. She didn't know if the sweat she felt on her forehead was from the heat or from nerves. Probably both. What would Pastor Bob think? It seemed hypocritical to attend church in the morning and break into someone's house in the afternoon. At least she had an excuse, or a reasonable explanation to give if she got caught. Dr. Summer had left her his dog. She wasn't there to take anything, she just wanted to find out what kind of food the dog ate and see if she could learn who the dog's vet was.

She glanced over her shoulder and, assuring herself she was alone, reached down and lifted the corner of the mat. Nothing there. She tried it again with another corner but still nothing. Finally she rolled the mat back until she could see completely underneath but the key wasn't there. *Rats.* She stood looking around. Wasn't much in the way of decoration on the porch, no potted plants to hide a key under, no ceramic animals. Her eyes went to the top of the doorframe. It was wide enough. She reached up letting her finger swipe the top edge. *Bingo!* She felt a key. She pulled it back and inserted it into the lock. The door swung open. Ducking under the tape she slipped inside and quickly closed the door, locking it behind her.

Heavy shades were drawn over the windows making the room dark, but that was a good thing. If she couldn't see out, people couldn't see in. It took a minute for her eyes to adjust. She didn't know what she expected to find, but the more she saw, the more she realized the impossibility of the task. Books and magazines and newspapers and journals were stacked everywhere. She didn't remember it being this bad, but then the only other time she'd been there was at night and the lights in the living room were out.

She began by searching for Dr. Summer's computer. Dr. Jaeger had left incriminating evidence for Jen and Larry to find. Maybe Dr. Summer had received a threatening email or something else that might solve the mystery of his death. She checked the counters and tables in the kitchen. Dishes were piled on the sink and unwashed pans sat on the stove. Notes, old newspapers and past due bills were strewn everywhere. The coffee was now completely evaporated and caked to the sides of the pot. The computer wasn't there. He wouldn't leave his laptop sitting on top of a pile of magazines. It had to be on a flat surface somewhere. She turned and started down the hall toward the bedroom.

The house had been locked for several days and with outside temperatures soaring, the room was hot and musty. Perspiration was seeping through her blouse. *What's that?* She froze, listening, but heard nothing except the sound of her heart continuing to pound. She pulled the moist material away from her skin and treaded softly down the hall.

One of the bedrooms had been converted into an office. A desk was over by the window under a pile of paper but the laptop wasn't on it. Maybe in the drawer. As she got closer she saw a clearing in the dust where it was obvious the computer had sat. Of course, the police would have taken it. They would be looking for evidence too.

A red light on the phone was blinking. Someone had called and left a message. Without thinking she pushed the play button and listened. The caller identified himself as Mr. Fishman. It was the man Dr. Summer had been trying to reach. She scrambled for a pen and wrote down the number, then grabbed the handset and dialed.

The call was answered on the third ring.

"Hello."

"Is this Mr. Fishman?"

"It is."

"Oh hi, uh, my name is Sarah Hunter. I used to work for Dr. Wallace Summer at CellMerge."

"Un huh. Okay, what can I do for you, Sarah?"

"Uh, well, I guess I'm calling about Dr. Summer's death…you have heard Dr. Summer was killed, haven't you?"

"I have. I received an email a few days ago. A tragic loss."

"I know. I was wondering if you knew anything about it. Dr. Summer asked me for your number and I thought…oh, I don't know what I thought. The thing is, the police think Dr. Rose did it and he didn't and they've got him in jail but he's innocent."

"What makes you say that?"

"I don't know. I guess I don't have any proof but I worked with Dr. Rose and I know he wouldn't do such a thing. He had no reason to, and the police haven't been able to establish a motive. I think he's being framed…"

"I agree."

"You do."

"Yes, I do. I think there's something else going on. I received a call from Wallace a few days ago. He had to leave a message but from what I gathered he seemed pretty upset. He claimed he had information showing the company was defrauding its investors which he was ready to make public and the next thing I know he's dead. I can't help but believe there's a connection. I've still got the message if you'd like to hear it…"

Sarah set the phone back in its cradle and did a happy dance, her feet pounding dust from the carpet as her hands balled into fists pumped the air. *Yes Lord, yes Lord, thank you, thank you, thank you!* She froze. There was a sound, like someone shaking the front door. Looking through a crack in the blinds she saw a police cruiser sitting in front of the house with its lights flashing.

Brian looked at his new watch. It wasn't much, just a cheap timepiece, but Sarah insisted he needed one and bought it for him. He couldn't very well say no. She was ten minutes late already. His eyes watched the window at the front of the café. It was a busy intersection with throngs of people milling up and down the street. He picked up the menu and lay it down again. He'd already decided what he wanted—burger and fries. It was one of the least expensive entrees, and she was paying—*again*. Hopefully, one day when all this was over, he'd be able to pick up the tab. He glanced up and saw Sarah heading down the aisle toward his table.

"Sorry I'm late," she said.

She looked nice, better if she could nix the red hair, but he'd fix that later. Her fingernails and lipstick were coordinated and her eyebrows were brushed dark to accent her green eyes.

"I was beginning to think you might not show."

"Me," she said, pointing at herself, "I always keep my word."

"So, how'd your day go?"

Sarah placed her hands in her lap and sighed. "Good and bad I suppose. I visited our son's grave. That was tough. I probably shouldn't have, you know, I need time to heal, but it's hard not thinking about him when he's been a part of my life for so long. But I had a good cry and I'm better now."

Brian reached across the table with his palm up waiting until she took his hand. "Why didn't you let me know? I would have gone with you. It kills me that I never got to meet him. What was his name again?"

"Buddy, and it was a spontaneous decision. I felt I had to go, and I couldn't call because you don't have a phone. You have to call me, remember?" It wasn't a lie, not entirely. He didn't need to know she'd stopped at the cemetery on her way back from Redwood City.

Her brush with the law had been close, but she didn't want to talk about that.

"Right, Buddy. Sorry, my mind is so messed up. What kind of dad can't remember his own son's name?"

Sarah pulled her hand back, placing it in her lap. "I was just thinking the same thing."

"Don't hold it against me. Half the time I'm lucky to remember my own."

Sarah nodded and smiled thinly.

A waitress stopped and set two glasses of water and two napkin wrapped place settings on the table in front of them. "Can I take your order?" she said.

"No, I haven't had a chance to look at the menu."

"No worries. Take your time. I'll be back in a few." She spun around and headed back toward the kitchen.

"I did have one good thing happen, though," Sarah said. "I found out something that might get my friend out of jail."

Brian took a sip of water and set the glass down. "This friend, you really like him don't you?"

"What do you mean?"

"I mean, is he *more* than a friend?"

"We're close, but I'm not sure that's any of your business."

"I think it is. I'm your son's father don't forget. In a way we're kinda married. I still think you should be letting me stay with you."

Sarah picked up a fork and began polishing it with her napkin avoiding eye contact. "That's not going to happen, Brian. Just because you popped into my life out of the blue doesn't automatically make us a couple. That may come, but it'll take time. I've still got things to figure out…"

"So he *is* more than a friend. Are you sleeping with him?"

"Brian!" Sarah looked up sharply.

"No, I mean let's get this out. I need to know. You said you'd waited for me all these years. Well, here I am."

"It's not like that."

"Okay, what's it like? Tell me. You want to know what I did all day? I filled out job applications. Soon as I find a job I plan to get my own place and I'm hoping we can pick up where we left off. Is that what you want? I need to know we're on the same page."

"Brian, calm down, you're starting to raise your voice."

"Look, I'm no one's fool. You got eyes for someone else, I'm outta here. Me or him, what's it gonna be?"

"Settle down, please. You're embarrassing me."

"Well, I wouldn't want to be an embarrassment. Let me know if and when you decide." Brian got up, tossed his napkin on the table and stormed out leaving Sarah to wonder if all men were idiots, or just the ones she was attracted to.

Brian knew he'd blown it but if he hadn't walked out, things would have come apart. Rule number one, when you feel the heat, walk away. What was it about women that always pushed his buttons? He'd never met one with the good sense to back off, but that was no excuse. He'd have to call and apologize. *Later*. Right now he had business to take care of.

"You got the card?" Barry said, holding out his hand. "Let's get this done. You're ruining my only day off."

Brian fished in the pocket of his shirt and retrieved the small rectangle of plastic. It was a VISA with the name Sarah Hunter embossed on its face. He handed it over.

"Sweet." Barry went to his computer and sat down. The stubby cigar smoldering in the ashtray smelled like a wet fire. He reached for the mouse and with hairy fingers moved the device around to awaken the screen. The bodacious watch was gleaming on his wrist. The website had a Samsung 52" HDTV for a price of $999.99. "Looky there, it's on sale. This one purchase is going to clear your debt, Kid." He clicked the Shopping Cart icon, went to Checkout and began setting up an account in the name of Sarah Hunter giving her a user name and password and filling in her credit card number, expiration date and security code. He used her current mailing address to match her credit card records, but for a shipping address he chose an empty tenement he held under a bogus name. Click *Continue,* click *Purchase Now,* click *Finish,* and done. "I took advantage of overnight delivery so I should get it tomorrow and you'll be off the hook."

"But won't the cops track the package to where it was delivered?"

"Sure, but as soon as we get it we plan to clear the place out. Too many bums live there now. It's overcrowded."

"So when do I get my Colt back?"

"Soon as I get my TV."

"But I need it now."

"Sorry, it doesn't work that way. The lady could get a call asking if she made the purchase. Sometimes credit card companies check these things, and if she doesn't verify they'll cancel the order."

"What then?"

"Then I don't get my TV and you don't get your gun, and I'll send someone around to collect for the blow I fronted you." Barry held the card up between two fingers. "If I were you, I'd get this back into your girlfriend's purse ASAP. Hopefully she'll never know it went missing. And be prepared. When the bill comes in she's gonna scream bloody murder, but just stay cool. She'll claim she never bought any freakin' TV and the credit card company will believe her, reverse the charge, and file an insurance claim. Happens all the time. People scam the banks, the banks make their insurance companies pay and no one gets hurt."

Necessity Is the Mother of Invention
The Journal of W.L. Summer

We should have a wealth of evidence to demonstrate the slow evolution of every living organism on the planet. We have an abundance of extinct animal fossils, everything from trilobites to dinosaurs, and we have modern fossils, but there isn't anything to demonstrate how one animal, through successive changes, became something else.

To explain the missing links we've had to invent theories like the "Cambrian Explosion" which purports the sudden appearance of various species, and "Punctuated Equilibrium" which says animal groups exhibit little evolutionary change for centuries until some event causes a split which results in two distinct species. Neither idea can be observed or tested. They're simply notions put forward to compensate for the lack of transitional forms in the fossil record.

Commenting on Darwin's tree of life, Paleontologist Stephen Gould summed it up this way: "The evolutionary trees that adorn our textbooks have data only at the tips and nodes of their branches; the rest is inference, however reasonable, not the evidence of fossils."

Fellow evolutionist Collin Patterson agreed when he wrote, "Fossils may tell us many things, but one thing they can never disclose is whether they were ancestors of anything."

Paleontology isn't my area of expertise but if after a hundred years of searching you can't find what should be there in abundance it's probably because it was never there in the first place.

Thirty-Five

...And swore by him that lives forever and ever, Who created heaven, and the things that are therein, and the earth and the things that are therein, and the sea and the things that are therein. —Revelation 10:6

MORNINGS WERE the hardest. Sarah would awaken before dawn and in the stillness realize she was subconsciously listening for the sound of Buddy's breathing. She would pull herself from bed, take Snowball in her arms and with a blanket wrapped around her shoulders pace the room just to keep her mind distracted. There was agony in knowing she'd have to start the day without hearing the voice of her little man. She was the mother, she was supposed to encourage him, but no matter how sick or feeble he became, in his unwavering faith he had always ended up encouraging her.

She thought about calling Aaron, *oops*, not Aaron, Brian, but she couldn't call Brian, he didn't have a phone. Aaron either for that matter. She needed encouragement. She was no longer employed, and there were no prospects on the horizon. She had no money in the bank and no income. When it fell due, she wouldn't be able to pay the rent, let alone her credit card. And she hadn't worked long enough to collect unemployment.

She snuggled the little dog against her cheek and felt his warm tongue licking her face.

"It's just you and me now, Snowball. We've got to make it through this together." But she knew even as she said it, it wasn't true. She had God. Jesus always carried her through the difficult times. It was just that it seemed harder without Buddy. *Why did you take him Lord? Why have you left me alone?*

* ★ ★ 🌍 ★ ★ ·

Detectives Irons and Rodriquez sat in the cramped quarters of Dr. Jaeger's office. Hugh had to lean forward to keep his knees from plowing into the front of Carl's desk. The pint size cowboy slouched in his chair. He wore a white lab coat but it wasn't buttoned. Underneath, his jeans rose over the crest of his belly crowned with a silver buckle. The tail of his shirt was half out.

Irons twisted in his seat trying to get comfortable. Eduardo should have already interviewed Dr. Jaeger and everyone else at the company connected to Dr. Summer. Focusing on one suspect was sloppy police work. This was the rookie's chance to redeem himself so Hugh let Eduardo do most of the talking.

"I assure you, it's just a formality."

"But I thought Dr. Rose was already in custody, guilty as a fox in a hen house. I heard his car had Wally's DNA on it. Doesn't that prove he did it?" Dr. Jaeger squirmed, lifting himself on his elbows.

"He is, and it does, but we have to cross every T and dot every I. The defense is going to try and point fingers at anyone who might have had motive to hurt Dr. Summer. It's a tactic. They want to throw seeds of doubt at the jury. All they have to do is get one juror to think it might have been someone else and we lose. We know you had issues with Dr. Summer, that you thought he was incompetent and wanted him fired. You also benefited from his removal by being the one they appointed to take his place. Maybe it's all coincidence, but it gives the defense a chance to point a finger at someone other than the accused. So I ask you again, where were you on the night of the twenty-first."

Dr. Jaeger pulled his desk calendar in toward his gut. *Humpruh.* "That was a Friday night. There's only one place I'd be on a Friday night. The Corral. I'm always there on Friday nights. Go ahead, ask anyone. I'm regular as rain." He slouched back into his chair again.

"And they'll vouch that you were there on the twenty-first?"

"I can't speak to the twenty-first specifically, but I can tell you they'll say I'm there every Friday. One girl in particular. I'm a big tipper. This girl told me if I ever missed a Friday, she wouldn't be able to pay the rent. She was joking of course, but she would notice if I wasn't there, and I was, because I'm there every Friday."

"And what about the email you sent Mr. Landon where you said you wanted to get rid of Dr. Summer at any cost? I think you suggested doing whatever it takes to prevent his return. How do you explain that?"

Hugh shot Eduardo a look of strong disapproval.

Carl's eyes grew wide, filling the frames of his glasses. He unclasped his hands from his stomach and leaned forward. "What email? How do you know about that?"

Hugh waited until they were outside. The sun was shining on a beautiful cloudless day, but the warmth only served to fuel his rage. Eduardo might be a good street cop, but he sucked at being a detective. "That's it," he said. "I'm going to the chief and have you taken off this case."

Eduardo shook his head. "Relax Bro. I only got him thinking. No harm, and I'm not going anywhere. This is *my* case. I'm the one who found the evidence and made the collar, remember?"

Detective Irons stopped and grabbed Eduardo's shoulder spinning him around. Latching hold of his tie he pulled him in so close Eduardo had to lean back to avoid the spittle from Hugh's mouth.

"You little piss ant. Don't get smart with me. Now I'm going to tell you how this is going to play. I'm going to the Chief and I'm going to tell him we've got a scheduling conflict and you're not going to object because if you do, I'll tell him the truth, that you're prejudiced against the boy and…"

"Whoa, no way…"

"Shut up! You think I can't read? You said you took the paint sample from the car while it was parked in the street but the kid's transcript says he parked in the garage, which is what you said too until I called you on it. That's gonna come out in discovery so your evidence will probably be thrown out and there goes your case. And you lied to me about cross referencing BMW owners with CellMerge employees to find this guy. I did a search of my own and found out his mother owns the car. You just made that up. Then you focus on this one suspect alone. You don't even interview anyone else. And when we find another possible suspect, you go and tell the guy you know about an incriminating email. You know what he's gonna do? He's gonna delete it, which is exactly what you want. That's obstruction and evidence tampering. Man, you want this kid so bad you can't have anyone else look guilty, can you?" Irons loosened his grip on Eduardo's shirt. "I'll tell you this, if what you did gets back to the Chief, he'll have your badge."

Aaron looked different, perhaps calmer. He sat in his chair with one leg crossed over the other leaning back, the lines of stress visibly softer. *Why?* "So how are you doing?" Sarah asked pulling a chair back to sit down.

Aaron smiled. "Good, I guess, as much as can be expected."

Sarah nodded.

"Jen stopped by."

"Oh?" Sarah's stomach tightened.

"Yep, wanted to see how I was doing. She told me your good news."

Sarah looked at Aaron, her brows raised. She did have good news. Fishman had evidence showing why someone else might want to hurt Dr. Summer, but Jen didn't know that. She hadn't had a chance to tell her. And she didn't want Aaron knowing about it until she had more to go on. "Oh, what news would that be?"

"About Buddy's father. She said you two are back together."

Oh no. She sighed and closed her eyes. "Look Aaron, I..."

"No, hear me out. I'm okay with it. Whatever makes you happy. I mean, you know this God thing. I've been trying to figure it out and..."

Sarah's face blossomed. "You found Jesus?"

"Well, no, it's not like that. I mean...I got hold of a Bible, and it does help."

"So what's holding you back?"

"I don't know. It's just...I mean, I know it works for you but I'm not so sure about me. I guess I'm still searching..."

The screen of Dr. Philips' computer was filled with the faces of missing children. He'd spent hours sorting though dozens of databases within the various jurisdictions of California. If this boy was a missing person, he wasn't in the system.

He glanced at the folder lying open on his desk. The report had come back. The boy's blood count was normal. He didn't have leukemia. That didn't mean he was well. He could be suffering a host of other diseases but at least leukemia had been ruled out. He needed to find this boy's parents. It was likely they already knew what the problem was, and if not, at least they could consent to the hospital running a few more tests.

It was a long-shot, but there was one other thing he could try. He removed a business card from his drawer and held it up debating whether or not to make the call. His eyes went to the phone, *now or never*; he picked it up and dialed.

"Cal Miller," the voice answered.

"Cal, this is Dr. Philips. I don't know if you remember me but you had your film crew in here about a year ago and..."

"Sure, Doc, I remember. We did a segment about that new laser surgery technique you were using. How have you been?"

"Fine, just fine. Ah, say, I was wondering if you could do me a favor."

"I'll try."

"Here's the thing, we have a boy here and he's sick and needs treatment but we don't know who he is or where he came from. He was just dropped off at the hospital in a coma. The problem is the hospital doesn't want to treat him until we get authorization from a guardian. I was wondering if you could put a picture of the boy up on the nightly news with the hope that someone might recognize him and give us a call. I'm afraid if we don't talk to someone soon, the boy could die."

"Sounds serious. Okay, no problem. Always happy to do a public service piece. You got a photo of the boy."

Dr. Philips reached for his cell phone. "I do, just took it an hour ago. I can text it if you want."

It was the same café as the day before but since Brian had abruptly walked out and they hadn't had the chance to enjoy a meal together, they'd agreed to try it again. The booth had hardwood benches and lacquered tables. Antique road signs, farm implements and nostalgic posters covered the walls and ferns hung in areas of light to give the room life.

Brian had called Sarah and pleaded with her to meet him, promising he'd be on his best behavior. He took a huge bite of the double cheese and bacon burger leaving streams of mustard, catsup and greasy juice running down his hand. He set the burger down and wiped with a napkin. "Sorry," he said with his mouth full. "I haven't eaten in a while."

Sarah noted he was still wearing the purple shirt she'd bought him, only now it was wrinkled. She was glad to be sitting across the table. He was starting to smell like he hadn't showered.

"Where did you stay last night?" she asked, poking at the chicken divan she'd ordered.

Brian shrugged and frowned. "Around."

"Around where?"

"Does it matter?" He shoveled a fry into a pool of catsup and plopped it into his mouth.

"Please, just tell me you're not sleeping on the street."

He frowned. "Of course I'm sleeping on the street. Not that you should care. You're the one who threw me out."

"I didn't throw you anywhere, but you can't stay with me. You should respect that. I'm trying to help you Brian. I *want* to help, but there are certain lines I won't cross, and sleeping with someone before I'm married is one of them."

"Kinda late for that don't cha think?"

Sarah nibbled on a bite of lettuce. "Why can't you stay with your friend, the one you gave the wheelchair to? You don't have to sleep on the street. There are homeless shelters. How's the job search going? I hate to say it, but frankly, Brian, you need a shower. And you need to wash those clothes." She reached down, grabbed her purse and removed a few bills from her wallet. "I think the YMCA has showers," she said. "Here, use this to get yourself clean. You never know when someone might want you in for an interview. You need to be ready."

"Is that what I am to you Sarah, a charity case? Keep your money, I don't need it." Brian stood and placed his napkin on the table. "Thanks for the burger; it was good. Oh, and I didn't want to say anything but I'm very close to landing a job. In fact the next time you see me I expect to be fully employed. There, I said it. I wanted it to be a surprise but now it's out."

"Brian, sit down. Please, finish your meal."

"I didn't come here to be insulted, Sarah, but don't get me wrong. I'm not mad or anything. I just need a little time to sort this out. Let me call you in a few days. If things work out the way I plan, I'll be buying you lunch, not the other way around." And with that Brian walked away leaving Sarah to eat alone for the second time in two days.

Perhaps it was better that Brian left when he did or Sarah might have been tempted to have him sit in on her meeting with Larry and Jen. She'd seen the way he'd eyed Jen. The thought had crossed her mind that they made a cute couple, though Jen's educational level was so far above Brian's it probably wouldn't work, but that was true of herself as well and she was seeing him, so...

Jen's hair was tied in a ponytail and she wore a pink T-shirt. Sarah didn't dare ask, but she was pleased to see the change, though she knew better than to let down her guard. Jen could revert back to her old self at any minute—*Dr. Jekyll and Mr. Hyde—the Incredible Hulk—Jen Carlson.* There were too many hurts to believe the transformation was permanent.

She had made the bed into a couch so Jen and Larry would have a place to sit. Now she poured coffee, setting the mugs on a tray along with a saucer of donuts, the powdered sugar kind Larry was so fond of. Returning to the living room she offered them to her guests.

They each took a cup. Jen set hers on the lamp table by the couch and Larry, because there wasn't a second table, held his in his lap. Sarah continued to stand in front of him holding out the plate of donuts but he waved her off. "No thanks," he said, "I'm on a diet."

Sarah turned and rolled her eyes, making sure Larry didn't see. She set her coffee on the dining room table and grabbing a chair spun it around so she could sit facing the group.

"Thanks for coming guys, and sorry about making you take your lunch so late but I had a meeting I couldn't get out of."

"No problem," Jen said. "Jaeger can't fire us if he's in jail, which is where he's going once we get Aaron out. Speaking of which, did you guys know Aaron was Jewish?"

"Ya think?" Larry said. "His name's Aaron. What gave it away?"

"Yeah but Rose...I guess it used to be Rosenthal but his dad had it changed. I hope that doesn't turn you off Sarah, but he told me so himself."

"What? Why?"

"I heard you were a Christian that's all."

"I am, which means I follow Christ, and Christ was a Jew so..."

"Was not, Christ hated Jews. They killed him."

"Christ doesn't hate anybody. And yes he was a Jew. He was born in Bethlehem, a Jewish town in Israel, of Jewish parents, Mary and Joseph. They worshiped in the temple and..."

"Okay, maybe, but He became a Christian."

Sarah shook her head. "He didn't become anything. He was Christ, which is just a Greek word that means Messiah. He was the Jewish Messiah, but for the most part they rejected him. Those who remained faithful and followed Him they called Christians. And that's what they still call those of us who follow Him today."

Larry puffed out his breath. "Hey you guys, we didn't come here to talk religion. We're supposed to be figuring out what to do about Aaron."

"You're right. Let's get back to Aaron. By the way, I talked with him earlier and I got the feeling he may become a Christian too."

"Now that's just plain crazy. A Jew can't be a Christian. It goes against the code," Larry said.

"Sure they can. Most of the first century Christians were Jews. That's how it all started. The Jews are God's chosen people. Nothing makes God happier than when one of His own takes His Son, Jesus, as their Messiah."

"Can we just get back to Aaron. This whole conversation's off track."

"Wait, I just want to say one more thing." Jen interjected.

"What?"

"I am too."

"You're what?"

"A Christian. I told Aaron about it the other day just before he got arrested. Maybe that's why he's thinking about converting."

"*Scheeech.* This is crazy," Larry said.

"No, it's true. I just wanted to get it out. Anyway Sarah, you called this meeting. You made it sound urgent. What's up?"

Sarah took a sip of her coffee and pulled it back, fanning her mouth. "*Ouch.* Be careful, it's hot." She set the cup down. "Okay, first off, if that's true, Jen, I'd like to talk to you about it, but we can do that later. What I called you here for is there's been a new development. You know how you guys got into Dr. Jaeger's office. Well, I thought what if Dr. Jaeger also wrote an email to Dr. Summer, maybe even threatening him. I figured it wouldn't hurt to find out, so I drove out to his house and took a look around."

"You broke into Dr. Summer's house?"

"No. I found a key and let myself in. You should have seen it. I'd only been there a few minutes when this police car pulls up and two officers start banging on the door. I don't know if they got a call from a neighbor or what, but I think I must have tripped a silent alarm because they went around checking the doors and windows to make sure everything was secure and then left. Scared me to death. Anyway, I didn't find anything. I think the police already have his computer, but while I was there I did notice someone left a message on his answering machine and I decided to listen. It was from a Mr. Fishman. He's on the CellMerge Board of Directors..."

"You're an idiot," Larry interrupted. "You don't break into a house in broad daylight. Everyone knows that. You're lucky you're not sitting next to Aaron in jail. We'd be having to get both of you out. As for Mr. Fishman, far as I know he's one of the company's biggest shareholders, and also very rich. The way I hear it, his wife has muscular dystrophy. He's invested heavily in our company hoping we'll find her a cure."

Sarah nodded. "Really? That's interesting. Anyway, I called Mr. Fishman and it turns out he received a message from Dr. Summer before he died, which he let me listen to. It appears Dr. Summer thought our board was involved in attracting new investors by telling them we hold patents that actually don't exist, which constitutes fraud. Dr. Summer was threatening to expose the hoax which would give someone a reason to shut him up, and that's a motive for murder. I asked Mr. Fishman what he thought but he'd been in Europe, out of the loop. He said he'd already booked a flight back to the states but at this point he couldn't say whether Dr. Summer's allegations were true or not, so I figure the one way to find out is for me to take a look at Mr. Landon's files myself."

"Our CEO? That Mr. Landon?" Larry sputtered. "Wait a minute. I see where this is going and no thanks. It's one thing to break into the office of a hick like Carl, or even Dr. Summer, but you get caught in Mr. Landon's territory and you could end up doing serious time."

"Larry, you are such a whuss." Jen leaned over and punched him in the arm. "Big as you are and you're scared as a baby."

Larry set his cup on the floor and crossed his arms and legs. "You bet I am. You don't know the power this guy holds."

Sarah shook her head. "I know what you mean, Larry. I'm not so brave. Sneaking into Dr. Summer's house scared me to death.

That's why I'm not asking you to do it. All I want is for one of you to sneak me into the building because I don't have access, and maybe do that trick with the lock so I can get into his office. I can take it from there."

"Right. You know how much security they got in that place? They got a guard at the front desk twenty-four-seven and every night he makes trips around each floor checking things out. He's bound to figure something's up."

"We don't need you Larry," Jen said. "I jammed Carl's door. I can do this one too. And you're not going in alone, Sarah. If nothing else, I'll stand guard."

"*Scheeech.* You girls are crazy. We're all going to jail. Move over Aaron old pal, here we come." He sat there with a scowl on his face and arms folded, then spoke again. "Oh, what the heck. I don't like working for Carl anyway. Count me in."

Jen reached up to tickle Larry's earlobe and then whispered in his ear, "My hero." She turned back to Sarah. "When do you plan to do it?"

"I was thinking maybe, tonight."

Thirty-Six

You forget the Lord your maker, He that stretched forth the heavens, and laid the foundations of the earth —Isaiah 51:13

LARRY AND JEN ran toward the building, Larry huffing and puffing with Jen grabbing his arm to pull him along. They wanted to get back before anyone noticed how long they'd been gone. The thirty minute drive to Sarah's, plus the time it took to discuss a plan, and the drive back had taken more than the hour allotted for lunch. The sun still blazed in the sky. Jen had her card out and swiped it before Larry could catch his breath. She grabbed his shirt and pulled him inside. His face was red and stippled with sweat and his temples throbbed, but he managed to keep pace as they hustled down the hall.

They entered the lab and stopped. Larry leaned over with his hands on his knees, panting. "If Jaeger says anything, *uh huh, uh huh,* tell him your car was in the shop and *uh huh* we went to pick it up."

He couldn't care less whether Carl liked the excuse or not. With Aaron in jail and Sarah fired, the company couldn't afford to let them go. With the exception of May, they were all that was left of the group. He could see the Chinese scientist taking notes on the other side of the glass. As always, she had stayed at her station, diligent in her work.

They went back to their posts, picking up papers and shuffling petri dishes to look busy. Larry, still dripping sweat, slipped into his lab coat and hustled off to the coffee room to fill his cup. Jen followed a few minutes later. She'd purposely walked by Jaeger's office, but he hadn't looked up. He was leaning back with his cowboy boots parked on his desk reading a magazine.

Larry turned as she made her way over, her own white coat buttoned top to bottom. In her hand was a roll of duct tape. She ripped off a six inch strip and affixed it to the inside of her arm, then pulled her sleeve down to cover it.

"What's that for?" he whispered.

"I can't stuff tissue into the lock. It's too easy to see. Instead I'm going to cover the strike plate with tape."

"And that won't be seen? Besides, how we supposed to gain access to Mr. Landon's office."

Jen shook her head. "The elevator I guess, how else?"

"That's not what I mean. How are you going to get that piece of tape over the lock on his door when you're not even supposed to be in that part of the building?"

"Don't you worry my little butterball, I got it all figured out."

"Really? Care to share?"

"No, you just be ready to run on my signal."

"Ready to run...what are you talking about?" But Jen had already turned away and was heading down the corridor in the direction of the ivory tower.

"Could ya be a little more specific? *Scheeeesh.*" Larry shrugged and headed back to his station looking around for something to do but uncertain about where to start. He felt someone standing behind him and turned to see May.

"I don't know what you two are doing, but it's affecting my work," she said. "We're supposed to be a team but lately all you do is tell secrets. I haven't seen anything I can process or analyze in days."

She was little more than five foot tall, shorter even than Jaeger, and only chest high on Larry. Her jet black hair shone like a silk curtain. "Sorry about that, May. I guess we're kinda handicapped with Aaron being in jail. He's the one who kept us working in a coordinated..." Larry flinched, startled by the shriek of a fire alarm. It started in the hall but resonated outward tripping other alarms until the entire campus was filled with the screeching sound.

Dr. Jaeger's feet rolled off his desk. He stood and reached up to grab his cowboy hat and coat. "Oh for Pete's sake," he muttered as he headed for the door.

Larry peered through the glass watching him leave. "It's probably another false alarm, but I guess we better get out of here," he said to May.

Her hands were on her hips, but she threw them in the air and walked away shaking her head.

The elevator stopped with a *ding*. Jen ducked around the corner, waiting for the president, his secretary, and several vice presidents to exit, then she hopped inside and pushed the button for the top floor. She wasn't surprised when she stepped into an empty foyer. The company's research involved the use of toxic chemicals and their health and safety code required that strict procedures be followed in the event of a fire. Everyone, even the president, had to exit the building. The security narcs at the front desk would be obligated to leave the building too, so she wouldn't be seen on camera. She went straight to the president's office. She'd never been there before, so she couldn't be absolutely sure, but with floor to ceiling doors of solid oak, who else's could it be? She didn't hurry. No one would be allowed back into the building until the fire department had been there and cleared the area. They wouldn't find a fire, but it would take at least an hour to examine every floor.

She heard voices. Two men in business suits rounded the corner heading for the elevator. They saw her and stopped.

"I uh, Jack sent me back to grab his coat." She clenched her teeth and felt her stomach tighten. She hoped they didn't notice.

The elevator *dinged* and the doors opened. "Hurry up, we'll hold it for you."

Jen shook her head. "You go ahead, I have to grab a few things. I'll be down in a minute."

The men stepped inside. The doors were starting to close. "Better hurry. You know the rules..."

Whew, Jen wiped her hands on the sides of her smock and tried to calm her breathing. She opened the door to Landon's office, peeled the tape from her arm and slipped a small pair of scissors from her pocket to cut a piece the size and shape of the latch plate.

The silver tape was a good match to the brushed metal. In the soft glow of the vestibule's lights she had to focus to see it was there. When Landon left for the day he would close his door but the lock would fail to engage. She turned, headed for the elevator and rode it down to the lobby. She wasn't surprised to find a few stragglers still making their way outside. She mingled in and slipped out unnoticed.

Sarah strolled the beach until the red lava sun poured into the inky black sea and darkness overspread the sky, and then headed back following footprints washed away by the waves. She had walked the shore for miles lost in thought, praying to her Maker, desiring to know about things she didn't understand.

Did God judge Corrie ten Boom for breaking the law when she hid Jews from the Nazis? And what about God's servant David? He feigned to be the friend of King Achish and then went on raiding parties killing the King's own subjects. This would be her second trespass. Could doing wrong ever be construed as right? They weren't going to steal anything, not even a paperclip, they were after the truth and the truth was something you couldn't steal.

Larry and Jen had returned to the office leaving Sarah alone. She should have used the time to prepare her resume, but she'd sat down at her computer and instead found herself writing an email apology to Danny. She'd inadvertently had him test Snowball's hair against her own. She owed him an explanation. No one deserved to be treated that way. She could only hope he had a forgiving heart.

She sat down squishing sand between her toes. Moonlight danced on the water making the whitecaps glow. White gulls bobbed on the ocean like tiny sailboats reflecting the moon's light.

Here I am again, Lord, wondering what to do. You've given me Brian. You know I prayed he'd return, like for twelve years I prayed and now he's here and I'm confused. He has a temper, Lord. I never saw that before, but after what he's been through, maybe...

Sarah gazed out over a horizon she couldn't see. Several stars glimmered in the evening sky, the brightest of the bright. It reminded her of the first evening she'd spent with Brian, except here the zillion lights of San Francisco dimmed the luminescence of the stars. When she and Brian were in the desert, there wasn't a city for a hundred miles. It was like someone had taken a brush and dipped it in a bucket of white paint and flicked it at a black wall. Billions upon billions of white dots. She scrunched the sand with her feet.

The wind picked up flicking her hair about her neck. She shivered. It was getting cool. She wasn't meeting Jen and Larry until later on, and that was assuming Jen had been successful in her mission—*please God*. Sarah stood, grabbed her flip-flops and dusted sand from the seat of her pants. Without the sun, winter hung in the air. She wrapped her arms around herself and began her trek back to the van.

From the freeway, the CellMerge tower rose out of the ground like the gold statue of Nebuchadnezzar. The night air was cold and damp in sharp contrast to the warm weather she'd enjoyed throughout the day. The smell of the ocean still clung to her skin, but she wore a sweatshirt hoping Jen and Larry wouldn't notice. She rubbed her arms, her anxiety building.

They waited until eleven before heading back to CellMerge. It was the latest they felt they could come without drawing suspicion. They had to use an employee card to access the facility and the entry would be recorded but they could explain being there as long as it wasn't too late.

No one said anything as they scurried down the corridor that led to the lab; the clapping of their shoes on the linoleum was enough to make them fear being heard.

Jen placed a large purse on the counter inside one of the glass cubicles.

"You sure you want to do this?" Sarah whispered.

Jen straightened herself and unbuttoned her heavy overcoat, folding it over a chair. The old Jen, dressed in hip hugging denims and low cut blouse, was underneath. She loosed her hair and let it fall around her shoulders. "You bet your sweet bippy I do."

Sarah shook her head. "I can't thank you enough. Larry and I will give you five minutes before leaving the area. We'll need at least a half hour. You sure you can keep him occupied that long?"

Jen glanced at Larry. "He's a man isn't he? Don't worry, I know how to hustle." She opened the briefcase-size purse, removed a bottle and splashed a few drops of scotch on her face and shoulders like perfume. Then she brought it to her lips and took a swig, washing it around in her mouth before spitting it in the sink. She capped the bottle and slipped it back into her purse, handing it to Sarah. "I'm ready," she said, and with that she turned and staggered down the hall.

Jen stumbled into the front lobby looking confused. "Hey, tish isn't my cubicle."

The man at the security console glanced over his shoulder, then swiveled around in his chair. "Can I help you?"

Jen knew she had him. He was staring at her chest instead of looking her in the eye. She meandered to the front and placed her elbows on the smooth surface of the granite counter. The guard wore black rimmed glasses and had a mop of curly hair. She looked down on him making sure her breath was accentuated. "I'm loshed."

"You're what?"

"I'm loshed. You know, I can't find my way…" at that she burped and covered her mouth. "Oh, *tee, hee, hee.* Sorry."

"I know you. You're the girl from the party. The one with the flower in her teeth. I wondered what happened to you."

She laughed again. "*Tee, hee, hee*, ya shure, thass me." She feigned like she was trying to salute. She stuck her chest out and pulled her body rigid as she snapped her hand to her forehead, but the motion threw her off balance and she ended up toppling over backward.

The man jumped out of his seat and hustled around the console, dropping to his knees. "Are you alright? Hey lady, you okay?" He took her hand. "Lady, wake up."

Jen's eyes popped open. "Where am I?"

"You're in the lobby of CellMerge. I think you passed out."

"Ohhhh, gee, that's right. I gosh work to do. Who are you? Oh yeah, I know, you're that cute little cop…the one I danch with. How come when I smile yoush ignore me?" Jen brought a hand up taking hold of his tie.

"Me? No, I don't…I mean…"

"Don't play games with me." She pulled the tie in. "I alwich said you was hanshum."

His face was so close she could feel his breath. She brought his head down and kissed him full on the mouth.

Sarah and Larry rode the elevator up in silence. Both wondered if Jen had been successful. There was no way of knowing for sure, they could only hope, but if anyone could pull it off it was Jen. The elevator doors opened with a *ding* that in the silence sounded like a brass bell. They swallowed hard, and went to Mr. Landon's office, hearts thudding softly as they passed under a camera. If they were being watched there was nothing they could do about it now.

Larry reached out. "Here goes nothin'." He grabbed the door handle and gave it a tug. It swung open to the right. "Man, I'm glad they don't use deadbolts." He removed the tape Jen had placed over the latch and balled it up stuffing it into his pocket, closing the door behind them.

Larry went straight for Mr. Landon's desk. "I don't see a computer," he said.

"Check underneath."

He stooped over. "Nope, nothing under here either."

Sarah bit her lip. "Rats. He probably has a laptop and took it with him."

"Now what?"

"Hopefully we'll find something in his files." Sarah nodded in the direction of a row of lateral cabinets.

"We can't go through those. It would take too long. You said you wanted to download his emails to a flash drive."

"I said we were going to search his office for evidence. You didn't think you could get into his computer anyway. Come on. We gotta at least try." Sarah moved to the wall and reached for the drawer. She pulled it back but it pinched the tips of her fingers and held fast. She grimaced. "They're locked."

"Okay, I guess that's it then. Let's go."

Sarah was taking short quick breaths, her heart palpitating. "Just a second. Maybe he left the key in a drawer."

"Not likely. We can't leave Jen too long. Come on."

Sarah ignored him and sat down in Mr. Landon's cushy leather chair trying the drawers one by one. They were all locked. "Okay, I guess you're right. *Dang.* What a waste. Maybe there's something in his secretary's files but I doubt they're unlocked either. Her eyes fell on the single manila envelope in his mail tray. It was probably nothing but she reached for it all the same. It was sealed, but only by the tip of the flap. The envelope was stamped "Confidential" in bold red letters. It had to have been dropped in the basket after Mr. Landon left for the day. Sarah slipped her finger under the flap and lifted gently. The glue gave way. Inside were several documents along with a two page letter that appeared to have been written by a lawyer. The writer's signature was followed by a J.D. which as far as she knew stood for Juris Doctor, a professional Doctor of Law.

"What's that?"

"*Shhhhh*, just a minute."

"Come on Sarah, we gotta go."

"We will," she said, "we will, but not until we've copied everything in this file."

Scaling the Mountains of Ignorance
The Journal of W.L. Summer

I began writing these notes on a personal level to justify my reasons for rejecting the theory of evolution. However, it now occurs to me that I might want to expand and add to them. There is so much more to be said, enough to fill several books, should I choose to take it that far. At the very least I should write a technical paper. I know many of my peers would find my thoughts of interest. Cosmologists in particular since they, more than others, know the universe had a beginning, and Origin of Life scientists, many of whom already reject the random chance scenario.

I fully expect to receive criticism. I know the larger part of the scientific community refuses to believe there's a God, but it's not science that deters them. The immense complexity of every form of life on the planet demonstrates how we couldn't have evolved by accident. No, it's that to admit we were wrong, to accept the existence of God, would require submitting to His authority, and that's something people generally are hesitant to do.

Sadly, with all we've learned there's not much left to stand on. I suspect when all is said and done, the likes of Darwin, Huxley, and Dawkins will be relegated to the dustbin of history along with those who argued that the earth was flat.

Cosmologist Robert Jastrow showed unique candor when he said: "For the scientist who has lived by his faith in the power of reason, the story ends like a bad dream. He has scaled the mountains of ignorance; he is about to conquer the highest peak; as he pulls himself over the final rock, he is greeted by a band of theologians who have been sitting there for centuries."

Everyone should climb that mountain. The view is fantastic and the air crystal clear.

Thirty-Seven

For by Him were all things created that are in heaven and on earth, visible and invisible, whether they be thrones, or dominions, or principalities, or powers: all things were created by him, and for him.
—Colossians 1:16

IT WAS almost midnight but Aaron couldn't sleep. He slid the sheet of paper into the folder, tilting his head back to stare at the ceiling. Collectively, Dr. Summer had written more than sixty pages of notes and he'd read them all. Dust curled and blew around the air channeling through the vent. He stretched and rubbed his arms to ward off the chill.

He couldn't argue with the reasoning. He doubted anyone truly believed that everything sprang from nothing, let alone the billion upon billions of stars that became our universe. Difficult too was that life just happened, that matter somehow got zapped by energy and sprang to life. And could software simply write itself? Science had no explanation for the billions of lines of code in a molecule of DNA. Nor could it explain the origin of thought, enabling man alone to become self-aware, and yet, even with all this, he felt a resistance to believing that the universe and everything in it was created by God. *Why?*

It was said everything came about by accident but everything that could be observed looked like part of an exquisite plan. In some ways he could see how it took as much faith to believe the theories of men as it did to believe in the existence of God. It all boiled down to presupposition. Evolutionists began with the premise that God didn't exist so they looked for ways to prove how life could invent itself. Those who chose to believe in God looked for evidence of design. And both relied on faith to bolster what they believed.

He felt a war going on inside, a struggle he couldn't define but was engaged in nonetheless. To accept the beliefs of Dr. Summer, or Jethro, or even Sarah, would mean he'd be ostracized by his peers. Like Dr. Summer he'd be shunned, thought a fool, no longer worthy of respect. He had a promising career ahead. He chuckled to himself as he sat staring at the walls and bars that imprisoned him. *Right.* What was there to lose? What was holding him back? He grabbed the folder again searching through it to find a note Dr. Summer had scribbled on a small piece of paper. He held it up staring at it in the dim light. "What does it profit a man if he gains the whole world and loses his own soul?"

* * ★ 🌐 ★ * *

Larry slammed his shoulder into the double doors throwing them open. "Jen! You in here. Where are you?"

Sarah followed behind. They were now in the main lobby where visitors and guests entered the building, but since they'd come through the interior, they were on the back side of the security console. Four small black-and-white monitors mounted under the counter scrolled though scenes picked up by cameras placed throughout the building. One was on the floor they'd just left. The camera was pointed at Mr. Landon's office, but the guard who was supposed to be watching was absent.

There was a scuffling on the other side of the console followed by a muffled voice: *"Get off me, urguhhh."* A man popped up with a curly fob of hair dangling across his forehead. His shirttail was out and his glasses askew. He straightened the glasses but his hands were visibly shaking. A bead of sweat rolled down his cheek.

"Hey, what are you doing?"

"Me? I…I don't know, I…"

"I'm looking for my girlfriend, Jen."

"Larry, baby, is that you?" Jen sounded winded like she'd been in a struggle.

Larry stomped around to the other side of the counter. "Jen? What are you doing down there?" His eyes hardened as they bore through the security guard. "What are you doing with my girl?"

"I…I…I'm not doing anything. She wouldn't…hey, I didn't know she was your…I mean she came in here like she was lost or something and she fell. I tried to help, that's all…"

Larry reached down and pulled Jen to her feet. Her hair was disheveled and her lipstick smeared but she was fully clothed. "Hey Babe, did this man hurt you?"

Jen stumbled forward and rested her face on his shoulder. Her head rolled back and forth as if to say, no.

Larry brought his hand up to embrace her.

The man fumbled nervously, trying to tuck in his shirt.

"You're lucky I don't bash your head in," Larry said, his face flushing red.

"Hey man, I didn't do anything. I swear. She came on to me."

"That true, Babe?" He tried to push Jen back far enough to look her in the eye, but she just shook her head.

"Okay, look, this is my fault. I shouldn't have let her wander off. She's kind of, you know, but she wouldn't stay in the car. I was trying to keep an eye on her. I guess I got carried away talking to May about our research; we've both been kind of busy and had a lot to catch up on. Look, okay with you if we just forget the whole thing? We don't need the boss knowing Jen was in here like this, and I'm sure you don't want anyone knowing you left your post. Let's just say it never happened. You good with that?"

"Sure, Man, sure, whatever you say."

Larry, Jen and Sarah pushed through the door. The cold air reddened their cheeks as they hustled across the dark parking lot. The breath from their mouths turned to steam.

"There you go, telling everyone I'm your girlfriend again," Jen said, lacing her arms in front of her. She turned back to face the building. "Wait, I need my coat."

"You're a girl, and you're my friend, what's the big deal? It worked didn't it?" Larry took Jen's arm pulling her along with him. "But no, your coat stays where it is. We're getting the heck outta here."

"Why did you call me, May?" Sarah interjected. "Now that security guy has her name. I don't want her getting in trouble."

"*Scheeech*, guys, lighten up. I couldn't call you Sarah because you don't work here and that dude probably has a list of persona non grata. If he rats us out, May will just swear she was never here, but he won't because he knows Jen will accuse him of molesting her."

Jen shivered and leaned in toward Larry who put his arm around her helping her pick up the pace. "And he was. Good thing you guys came when you did. That creep was all hands. *Ough* and he tongued me. Made me want to puke. I don't think I could have kept it up much longer."

"Maybe you should have. You were supposed to be drunk. Puking would have seemed quite natural."

"Good point. *Ahhh*, you're warm. I guess fat has a purpose, but don't stop the diet. I think its working. How'd you guys make out?"

Sarah hefted the large purse up to see. "I think we got him. We won't know until we get the chance to read everything, but I think we hit the jackpot."

"So, you think Landon did it?"

"Don't know. Maybe. At least we've got another suspect."

· ＊ ★ 🌍 ★ ＊ ·

George stood at the door of Sarah's apartment. His plane had touched down at SFO and rather than head straight for his hotel, he'd sent Sarah a text letting her know he was in San Francisco and looking forward to their meeting. It was after midnight so he wasn't expecting a response. It surprised him when she replied.

"No time like the present," she wrote, and added that if he wasn't too tired she and two other employees of CellMerge were going over something he needed to see. He smoothed his camel overcoat and reached for the door, ringing the bell. A dog was barking on the other side.

The door opened. The light was at her back so the features of the girl facing him were hard to see, but she had a friendly voice. "Mr. Fishman? Come in, come in."

"And you must be Sarah."

"I am. Just set your bag over there and take your coat off." Sarah turned and led George into the apartment. George rolled his carry-on to a stop just inside the door. He tried to ignore the dog sniffing his cuffs as he glanced around the room. The setting was sparse, typical of a person struggling to make ends meet. He could relate. His mother had worked two jobs so he could go to school. Two other people were standing next to a mismatched dining set, a stocky man and an attractive blond. The table was littered with paper. He turned looking for a place to set his coat. His eyes caught a picture of his hostess kneeling down beside a young boy in a wheelchair.

"Can I get you anything, coffee, tea, a glass of water?" Sarah said, looking back over her shoulder.

"Water would be nice." He walked over and picked up the photograph.

"Just set your coat on the sofa," Sarah called as she opened the refrigerator to remove a plastic bottle.

"Nice picture. Is he yours?" George turned the framed photograph to face Sarah.

Sarah paused. She took a breath, smiled faintly, and nodded. Her eyes seemed to moisten.

"Yes," Larry piped up, "but he passed on recently." He reached out, took the frame from George, and set it on the coffee table again. "She's still carrying the weight," he added, tilting his head toward Sarah.

"Sorry, I didn't know."

"No worries."

Sarah reentered the room with a glass of water in hand. "My son's not dead," she said. "He's just moved off this planet to be with God." Her eyes were misty, but she was holding back the tears.

"I understand. Was he...I mean, I don't mean to sound presumptuous..."

Sarah nodded, her head bobbing up and down in quick little jerks with her lips pinched together.

Larry stepped forward extending his hand in an attempt to change the subject. "Name's Larry, Larry Lofter and this is Jennifer Carlson. We work at CellMerge, in the research department. Used to work for Wallace Summer—I understand you knew him—but, *ah*, he was let go and, as you probably know, ended up dead. Are you up to speed because I can explain everything but there's no point in telling you what you already know. What we want is to get Aaron Rose out of jail. They think he's the one who killed Dr. Summer but we know he didn't."

George shook Larry's hand, the difference in their skin as evident as the difference in their size. George was tall and thin, Larry of medium height and husky. George's hand was dark coffee, Larry's doughboy white. He could guess what they were thinking. They weren't expecting him to be black. Didn't matter that he was wearing one of his nicest suits, the custom tailored brown twill with a red silk tie, or that he owned more of CellMerge than the company president.

"I knew the board had agreed to let Dr. Summer go," he said. "They called an emergency session and held the vote while I was out of town so I couldn't do much about it. As to Dr. Summer's death, Sarah and I talked about it and I'm inclined to agree, he may have been murdered. That's why I'm here. I have a recording of Dr. Summer saying he was about to blow the whistle on the company president, Jack Landon, over false information he was feeding shareholders. And now I understand you may have come up with something else. So if you want to get right into it, I'm all ears, though I want you to know Miss Sarah, if there's anything I can do..."

Sarah handed George the glass of water, the ice cubes rattling as she shook her head. Her eyes went to the photograph. "I'm good. God knows what He's doing, and I...well, I guess I just have to accept that. Everything's spread out on the table. We've been going through it but if we're going to do anything we'll have to act fast. It looks like Mr. Landon is planning to leave the country." She reached for the letter and offered it to Mr. Fishman.

"Yeah, you should see what this twerp's been up to," Jen chirped.

George nodded. His bottom lip jutted out as his eyes scanned the page.

Dear Jack

Enclosed are the final papers pertaining to the sale of your house. I know it's not as much as we hoped for but with the market being what it is and the urgency placed upon your broker to move this property, I'd say you received a pretty fair offer. That said, I am pleased to report that escrow is now complete. A deposit, minus all closing costs and legal fees, has been made to your checking account in the amount of $3,205,483.83.

As you requested, I also looked into your agreement with Tecnologias Celulares of Rio de Janerio. I made several attempts to reach Dr. Silva to enquire about the security of the CellMerge shares entrusted to him for safekeeping. Each time I was told he was unavailable. On my third attempt I was put through to a Mr. Figuiera who informed me that Dr. Silva had been hospitalized. Mr. Figuiera would not speak to me regarding your position in Tecnologias Celulares and cited security measures that prevented him from sharing private information with a third party. As you know we anticipated this, but I did promise to try.

Lastly, I have witnessed your letter of resignation. I admit I'm saddened by this but I respect your decision and trust it's in the best interest of all concerned. I will hold it until I receive instructions from you regarding the timing of its delivery. Here's wishing you good success in all your future endeavors.

In matters of law, I remain faithfully yours,

Jonathan Kramer, J.D.

George looked back at Sarah. "Indeed," he said. "About six months ago Jack made a presentation to the board recommending we invest in Tecnologias Celulares but we declined. The Brazilian economy was too volatile and the company's financials weren't good, but we did agree that if he wanted to invest some of his personal shares he should be allowed to do so." George tilted his head slightly. He could see they weren't cluing in. "It has to do with Jack's compensation package. He gets an excessive salary, which is something I personally voted against, but he also has the prospect of earning a million shares of CellMerge, though he doesn't get the shares up front. They come by way of a bonus of one-hundred thousand shares each year for ten years, providing certain financial criteria are met. And even those are held in escrow until the company's shares cross the thirty dollar mark.

"It's a pretty common practice. We have to protect the company because when a principal sells his shares he's required to file a report with the SEC and that sends a signal to the market. Other shareholders note the sale and become jumpy. They assume the president must know something and that it must be bad or he wouldn't sell. They begin dumping their own shares and that sends the company into a downward spiral which reduces capitalization."

George glanced at the letter again. "Anyway, we didn't think letting Jack invest in a small company in Brazil would do any harm so we voted to release some of his shares early. Tecnologias Celulares is another biotech. His interest in the company was positioned as putting feelers out for a possible acquisition. If CellMerge later acquired a majority position in Tecnologias Celulares, then their growth would only mean additional profit for CellMerge. We limited the investment to two-hundred and fifty-thousand shares, authorized the transfer and let it go at that.

"Now I'm trying to read between the lines here, but I suspect he really didn't invest in this company at all. That was just a ruse to get his shares released and out of the country. This letter suggests he had someone down there put them aside for him. And since Tecnologias Celulares is a privately held company, they aren't required to publish their financials so we had no way of knowing. If I'm correct in my thinking, Jack has someone, probably this Dr.

Silva, sitting on his shares until he gets the stock price up, which he's done by saying Dr. Summer received a patent on some proprietary process we don't actually have, and now he's ready to cash in. There was a spike in our valuation when he made the announcement, but now he has to sell before word gets out that Dr. Summer's patent isn't real and everything comes crashing down. You can also see why he'd want Dr. Summer out of the way. If Wallace had gone public as he threatened, it would have ruined everything. But Jack knows he'll be found out soon enough, which is why he's making his move now. You got a calculator?"

Sarah nodded. She went to retrieve one from the kitchen and returned handing it to Mr. Fishman.

"Thank you," he said as he began punching numbers. Let's say Jack still has the two-hundred and fifty-thousand shares we thought he'd transferred to Tecnologias Celulares. At our current share price of twenty-seven dollars that would be…six-million seven-hundred-and-fifty-thousand, and if he combines that with what he sold his house for, it's…just about ten million. Not a bad amount to retire on.

Fishman smiled and shook his head. "I got to hand it to Jack, he's a lot craftier than I thought. I doubt any of you know this because the board wants to keep it under wraps but aside from the recent announcement, which is a momentary blip, the company's been on shaky ground for some time. We haven't really produced any new cures and the market is getting nervous. CellMerge is a young company and everyone understands that research takes time, but after ten years, investors, including myself, are beginning to wonder. A few weeks ago our share price dropped to a low of fifteen dollars and one of our investment consortiums threatened to dump its shares, which would have killed us. Then Jack let it out that we'd received patent approval on a new proprietary process developed by Dr. Summer and that started a rally which eventually brought us to where we are today."

"But it's a house of cards," Larry offered.

"Exactly, and Jack has to act fast. If those shares weren't really invested in Tecnologias Celulares, then he's got quite a nest egg down there. He can resign, sell the shares while they're at their peak, and disappear with his ten million dollars to spend the rest of his life on some remote island living like a king."

"Boy that's one piece of nasty work. Good thing we got that." Larry nodded at the letter in Fishman's hand. "It's time to bring that turkey down."

"Not so fast. I'm not going to ask how you came by this," he held the sheet out to Larry, "but I'm pretty sure Jack didn't give it to you. You can't use stolen information. You'd be admitting to a crime. You're the ones they'd arrest, not Jack. And the police couldn't use the information if it was obtained illegally."

Sarah took the back of a chair with both hands gripping tightly. "That's insane. I've heard that twice now and it makes no sense at all. Criminals are running around free because the police can't use the evidence people give them." She turned the chair around and slumped into it. "Now what are we gonna do?"

George sighed. "I don't know. It's one thing to know about a crime, but a whole other thing to prove it."

Thirty-Eight

For the invisible things of Him from the creation of the world are clearly seen, being understood by the things that are made, even His eternal power and Godhead; so that they are without excuse.
—Romans 1:20

THE SIRENS screaming through the city could be heard for several blocks. One cruiser veered off down a narrow alley that led to a parking lot in back. Another pulled up in front with its lights painting the storefront red and blue.

Across the street people peered from windows while those on the sidewalk stopped to see what the commotion was about.

Two policemen emerged from the car. A third unmarked unit slid to a stop, its blue strobes flashing against the store's window. A man in street clothes climbed out and went to confer with the two uniformed officers before they went inside.

The patrol car that turned down the alley pulled up facing the rear entrance making sure no one escaped out the back. Two policemen hopped out and stood behind the cruiser using it as a shield, their guns at the ready. It only took a few seconds before several people burst through the door.

"Halt! Police. Get your hands in the air where we can see them."

Three men stumbled to a stop bumping into each other. *Busted.* They raised their hands limply, begrudging the effort. The largest of them, a burly man with a cigar clenched in his teeth, cursed profusely.

The plain clothes officer swung the screen door open. "You gentlemen care to step back inside?"

The man with the cigar shrugged and turned, pushing himself through the door followed by his two cronies.

The officer nodded. "Barry, nice to see you again. You still got my Colt? You know I carried that old 45 with me all through the war. I sure would hate to lose it."

Barry removed the cigar from his mouth and leaned forward to spit on the floor. "So you're a cop?" he said, flicking a loose piece of tobacco around on his tongue.

"Yep, 'fraid so. Been playing you for narcotics, but thanks to the little purchase you made with that stolen credit card, now we got you on grand theft too." Brian wrinkled his nose. The air reeked of stale cigar smoke and sweat. Two soiled sleeping bags were tossed in a corner. "Man, did I ever tell you it stinks in here?"

"I take it the card wasn't really stolen."

"Nope. Just a card the bank set up for the sting. I need you to get rid of that cigar and turn around with your hands behind your back."

"If it wasn't stolen you got nuthin' on me." Barry said, dropping the cigar to the ground and snuffing it underfoot.

"Might be the case if you hadn't taken possession of the allegedly stolen property, but you did. Spread your legs apart please."

"This is entrapment!"

"We'll see."

One of the other officers snapped the cuffs on Barry's wrists and began to pat him down.

"But you know what the nice thing is? I've been working this gig for six months and I still didn't know where your distribution center was. Then, after you sign for the delivery and leave, your flunky has us bring the TV inside and tells us to put it in the back and guess what we find. Yep, we got your meth lab, a half dozen kilos of cocaine and a computer with all your contacts and sources. You really should hire smarter people. Barry, I'm placing you under arrest. You have the right to remain silent…"

Brian was feeling good. He'd had a shower and put on a fresh charcoal-gray suit over a sky-blue dress shirt with an open collar. The wind was whipping his hair as he drove his MX 5 Miata convertible with the top down. The day was brisk under a canopy of blue cloudless sky. The chill made his cheeks rosy but it didn't dampen his spirits. He had a new arrest to add to his record—one that could only advance his career, and a date with *Sarah*. He brought his hand up to rub his chest.

The Miata took the crest of a hill too fast and landed hard on the other side. Not good for the suspension. He hit the brakes and downshifted through the five speeds of the manual transmission, the engine mellowing to a low growl as he came to a stop at the light.

This was it. Tonight he was going to seal the deal. She was resisting, but only because she saw him as a lowlife, a street person, a hapless victim of lost memories with no hope for a future. Who could blame her? A girl needs security.

He looked to his right and saw a reflection of himself in the building's windows. *Looking good.* He ran his fingers through his hair smoothing it out. The car was washed and waxed, its stormy blue mica paint gleaming in the evening sun.

Tonight the wrapping came off. He was finally free to tell her who he really was, and all he'd accomplished. Okay, so she was a PhD, a bit nerdy, but cute in a way. He reached out patting the passenger seat headrest. He'd ridden the rocket past street cop into vice. He was going places too, and he wanted Sarah along for the ride. Maybe he could get her to dye that hair. Blond would be better, and if she wore it long, like when they first met, and maybe with a little curl—*perfect*. If he was lucky he'd get a chance to take her back to his apartment. Without her nosey neighbors for an excuse, she'd be powerless to resist.

The light turned green. He jammed the car into first and put the pedal to the metal unleashing all hundred and sixty-seven horses. The wheels spun as he lurched forward, the rear of the car fishtailing. The squeal could be heard echoing off the buildings. He eased off the throttle. They'd ticket a regular guy for a stunt like that. Oh, but he was feeling good, and he couldn't wait to see her again. Besides, he'd left late so she was probably already there. He didn't want her to leave. He hit the gas and shifted again as he zoomed around the car on his right, weaving in and out of traffic.

He did wish he could have invited her to meet him at a nicer restaurant but he couldn't. This had to be a surprise. He was going to walk in wearing his finest and baring a wallet full of cash. He'd blow her away. That other guy was history. He almost felt sorry for him, *almost*, but the guy brought his grief on himself. *You do the crime, you do the time.* There was no future for Sarah there. Move over, here comes Brian.

He turned the corner. The low angle of the sun cut between the buildings hitting him square in the eyes. He eased off the gas slowing until he caught a shadow and could see again. The coffee shop was just ahead and it looked like there was an empty space right in front. *Perfect!*

Dr. Philips made his rounds checking in on his patients. It was important that he be there to answer their questions and address their concerns. In some cases he had good news, the surgery went well, or the results of the tests were encouraging, but for some he had to deliver the news that the cancer had metastasized spreading to other parts of the body. Then, after assuring them there were still several options open, he would smile and let them know they were in this together. Keeping a positive attitude was half the battle.

But however important the life and death struggle of those under his care, he couldn't help but think about the patient in room 402. The boy was still in a coma and he was powerless to help until a parent or guardian stepped forward and gave their permission.

He slipped into the room quietly, not wanting to disturb the patient in the neighboring bed who looked to be asleep. A curtain partition separated the two. He reached up to draw it back and stopped, puzzled. He turned and went back into the hall to find a nurse.

The woman at the desk was new, or at least he hadn't noticed her before. "What happened to the boy in room 402?"

The nurse scanned her computer screen. "Looks like he was released this morning."

"Released? To who?"

"Says here his mother came and got him."

A grin sprouted on Dr. Philips face. It had actually worked. Someone had seen the broadcast and had come to claim their child. "That's wonderful," he said, "though I wish she'd have left the boy here. I think he needs further treatment, and I doubt she has the ability to care for him while he's in a coma."

The nurse scrolled down a page. "Apparently that was discussed but the mother assured the hospital that she has a nurse to look after the child and that he'll be in good hands."

"Really? Then why was he left here in the first place? *Hummm.* Alright, I guess it doesn't matter as long as he's being taken care of."

Sarah sat at a heavy wood table with swirls of grease revealed by the light from the window. So many things were happening it was hard to keep track. She looked at her watch. Brian was late. She only had a few minutes, just time enough for a quick bite, and then she had to scurry home. She picked up her spoon and looked it over. It appeared to be clean, so did the fork and knife. She laid them back on her napkin and took a sip of water. The grill was sizzling. Several customers were seated on swiveling stools at the counter. A light haze of smoke wafted up from the burners in the kitchen.

A blue sports car pulled up but the glare from the windshield prevented her from seeing the driver and besides, Brian would be on foot. She glanced at her watch. Where was he?

She was pleased that he'd called. There were things they needed to discuss, but she had to tiptoe softly. Brian was fragile, still trying to piece his life back together.

A man seated himself at the table pulling her from her thoughts. *Brian!*

"Sorry I'm late," he said, slipping into the seat opposite her, "traffic was a nightmare."

"No problem. I've only been here a few minutes."

"Did I surprise you?"

"What?"

"You looked startled."

"*Oh.* A little perhaps. I was just thinking about our son."

Brian nodded.

A waitress approached and handed them menus. "Today's special is broiled cod with a seafood rice pilaf and your choice of clam chowder or salad for seven dollars and that comes with coffee or a soft drink."

Brian waved her off. "Your burgers are great. I want the one with everything on it, bacon, cheese, the whole works."

"That'd be our bacon cheese bonanza. And you?" she said turning to Sarah.

"I'll just have a salad."

"Spinach, Caesar, Garden?"

"Spinach."

"French, Italian, Ranch, or Thousand Island?"

"Ranch," Sarah said, handing the menu back to the waitress. She looked over at Brian. "Where'd you get the suit?"

He reached up taking hold of the lapel, rubbing it between his thumb and finger. "Like it? It's mine. Actually, I have a closet full of them."

Sarah raised an eyebrow.

"What do you think of the car?"

"What car?"

"Mine. Right there." He looked out the window lifting his chin. "The blue Mazda. You didn't see me pull in?"

Sarah glanced over, then back at Brian. "But you don't own a car, I mean…"

Brian raised his hand cutting her off. "I know, I know, but if you give me a minute I can explain." He hesitated but when Sarah remained silent, ventured on. "Okay here's the deal. Buddy's obit appeared in the paper while I was in the middle of an undercover operation. I'm a cop, Sarah. I'd been working to bring down a man who's responsible for a lot of the drugs in this city and my cover was a vet who had lost his memory and was down and out of luck. You just fell into it, that's all."

Sarah shook her head. "You're a cop?"

Brian smiled, his eyes warm as he reached across the table for her hand. "Detective, yes, but I couldn't tell you. You don't know how bad I wanted to, but once you go undercover you can't even tell your best friend, not even if they recognize you on the street. You have to stay in character, and maintain your cover at all times. Your life depends on it."

Sarah could feel the pulse in Brian's fingertips. Her skin tingled as she searched his eyes. A girl could do worse. Infatuation's bubbles were surfacing again. "You mean you don't live on the street?"

"No, in fact I have a condo not far from here which I'm hoping to show you after we eat."

"And all this time...wait a minute, you never lost your memory?"

"No, that was all part of the sting. It's what I told the guy I just arrested so I had to use the same story with you. But no, I remember everything about our time together. That's why...well, that's why it was so easy for me to fall for you again. And I have, at least I think I have. All I know is, I haven't felt this way in years."

Sarah pulled her hand back. "But why didn't you contact me when you got out of the service? Why did you stop sending letters?"

Brian shook his head and shrugged. "I don't know. When you're in a hot zone, and believe me, that's where I spent most of my time, all you really think about is how to survive. I watched fellow soldiers, some of them good friends, step on land mines and get blown apart; I saw an armored personnel carrier loaded with men take a rocket to the side and evaporate, one pal of mine asked a man for his I.D. and the man blew himself up taking my friend with him. I was only twenty feet away. I mean it was hell over there, but no regrets. We were doing it for the right reasons. We were serving our country. I was just one of the lucky ones that got back alive with everything intact."

"But what about afterwards? Why didn't you contact me then? I waited, Brian. We had a son I couldn't even tell you about, but I waited for you believing you'd get in touch with me as soon as you got home. I finally gave up. I started telling Buddy you were dead."

"I know. I should have. I just got home and kind of picked up where I left off, except I knew I didn't want to be a pipefitter so I enrolled in the academy and here I am."

"And you've lived alone all this time and it never crossed your mind to give me a call?"

"Not exactly. I mean I did end up meeting this girl and we got married but we shouldn't have because we were never in love…"

"You're married?"

"No…yes…no, I mean, not exactly. It's complicated. I had a relationship on the side, which really didn't matter because my wife and I were already in the process of getting a divorce, but the girl I hooked up with got pregnant so when my divorce went through I married her, but it was a disaster, out of the frying pan into the fire. Everyone knows you shouldn't marry on the rebound, so anyway, I'm in the middle of getting divorce number two, which is why I'm so glad I found you again, because I've had time to think about it and I've come to realize you were the one I was meant to be with all along."

"Boy or girl?"

"What?"

"Your child. You said your second wife got pregnant. Did you have a boy or girl? I want to know if Buddy has a brother or sister."

"Girl. I have a daughter, but I don't get to see her. My wife has a restraining order on me. Claims I hit her, but I never did. I swear. I lose it sometimes but I'd never hit a woman." Brian reached out to take Sarah's hand again but she jerked it back. "You have to believe me."

"Actually, I don't." Sarah stood, grabbing her purse and coat from the seat.

"Sarah?"

She was looking down on the man she'd spent years thinking she was in love with and now realized she didn't even know.

"You just told me everything about you is a lie. Why should I believe you now?" and with her coat across her arm and her bag slung over her shoulder, she headed for the door leaving Brian to pick up the tab. Her only regret was that she hadn't ordered something more expensive.

*　★　★　🌍　★　★　·

What the? Jack's arms flailed in the dark struggling to find his phone. *Bllllleeeeeeeeppppp.* He pulled himself to a sitting position and checked his watch, four in the morning for cripes sake. *Bllllleeeeeeeeppppp.* He reached over snapped on the lamp and grabbed his cell from the table pulling it to his cheek. "What?" He barked. "What? Slow down and speak English. What?…If this is some kind of joke I don't appreciate it…Then you've got the wrong number…Yes, this is Jack Landon…who is this?…Look do you know what time it is? …What? …You did what? I didn't authorize that. Where's Dr. Silva?"

Mr. Landon's silk pajamas rustled as he climbed out of bed. He slipped his bare feet into slippers and began pacing the hardwood floor with the phone to his ear. "Now listen here, and you listen good. I want you to stop selling and stop right now, you understand, *comprender?* You tell Dr. Silva I'm flying out right now and I expect to see him, so you have him there…I don't care. Drag him out of the hospital if you have to…Yeah, yeah, right, everyone's got a cure for cancer. All I care about is my money! You just tell him to be there."

Thirty-Nine

Thou art worthy, O Lord, to receive glory and honor and power: for Thou hast created all things, and for Thy pleasure they were created.
—Revelation 4:11

HIGH UPON Mount Corcovado the giant image of Jesus known as Cristo Redentor looked down upon Jack with its arms open wide ready to receive the wayward child. But Jack wasn't buying. He'd seen it before, a one hundred and thirty foot tall tourist attraction celebrating the weak and superstitious, nothing more. He did not believe in the absolution of sin. He didn't believe in sin, period! He squeezed his hand into a pocket and withdrew a roll of antacids peeling one from the foil wrapper and popping it into his mouth. His ulcer was acting up again.

His cab wove in and out of traffic. The smog was as thick as the fog back home burying the sun in a sweltering sky. South of the equator it was summer where the temperatures topped a hundred and the days languished for sixteen hours. Jack wiped his brow with a handkerchief. He was impatient. He hadn't planned on making his final move so soon but the crisis pushed his schedule ahead. Counting the time it took him to clear his calendar and the eighteen hour flight, it had taken nearly two days to get here.

Maybe after all this was over, he'd relax and look around. Brazil was worth taking time to see. Postcards in every store showed verdant rainforests filled with brightly colored macaws and butterflies. Coastal waterfalls fell into rivers that surged into the ocean where peaks jutted up like giant blue teeth. Rio was a jewel in Mother Nature's crown.

The taxi sped along the waterfront where tourists sat under straw umbrellas sipping caipirinha while listening to a gentle samba. He envied them. Maybe someday he'd be able to kick off his shoes and walk the sands of the famous Ipanema Beach with the sun rolling off his back—but not now. He was there to get this mess straightened out. His future depended on it.

His cab pulled to the curb. The words were painted on the building in huge orange letters that read, "Tecnologias Celulares." He reached for his wallet and paid the driver in American dollars because he hadn't had time to convert his US currency into Brazilian Real.

Jack pulled himself from the cab, sweat streaming down his face. His coat was moist. He brought his handkerchief up to mop his brow again. The temperature was something he'd have to get used to. He'd directed his lawyer to place his letter of resignation in a sealed envelope and leave it with his secretary. She would hold it until he called and gave specific instructions for its distribution. There was no point in going home. He'd given it his best shot, now he had to wait and see how everything played out.

The taxi pulled away leaving him standing alone in front of the building. He shook his head. *What a dump.* His watch probably cost more than the entire facility. He took a step forward assuring himself there had to be a mistake. Selling CellMerge shares to shore up Tecnologias Celulares was pointless. The company was in the tank and everyone knew it. They were heading for bankruptcy. Dr. Silva only stood to make his commission if Jack personally sold the shares. Any other way and the company would still go under and Silva would get nothing. He wouldn't risk letting that happen.

This place is a disaster, he thought as he pushed through the door. The building was old and in desperate need of paint. It was a conversion job, a row of small shops that once lined the street now joined into a single building with each of the former establishments becoming either a laboratory or office space.

A woman sat at a reception desk polishing her nails. Her hair was black, typical of Brazilian natives, but her fair skin made her look European. Jack approached the counter and produced his card. "My name's Jack Landon. I'd like to see Dr. Silva."

The girl's face grew somber. "I'm sorry Senhor," she said, handing back the card, "Doctour Silva ees not here."

"Okay, look, I need to see whoever's in charge." Jack shoved the card back into her hand with a force that suggested he wasn't taking no for an answer.

"I…um…hokay, I think Doctour Rodgers is in. I see if I can reach him. You like to take a seat?"

Jack turned looking back over his shoulder. The only two chairs in the lobby looked like they'd been salvaged from a condemned school. "No thanks, I'll stand." He listened as the receptionist spoke with someone over a telephone intercom.

"Doctour Rodgers ees very busy but he say he need to see you, if you can wait."

"Your English is quite good. Where did you learn it?"

"My papai was Brazilian but my mamae ees American. She came here on vacation and they fall in love. I learn both languages, no? But they no last so my mamae, she go back to America. I need to see your cell phone." The girl held out her hand.

Jack patted his coat pocket. "My cell phone, why?"

The girl leaned in whispering conspiratorially. "Ess something big going on back there, all very hush, hush. They not let anyone inside without identification."

"Oh, you mean you want to see my driver's license."

"No. Senhor Rodgers ees firm. He say he know you whould be coming. We don't get many visitors but they make an exception for you. But Senhor Figuiera, he say no one goes in there unless it ees the man he talked with two days ago. I must look at your phone to see if that call was made to you."

"This is ridiculous," Jack said, but he surrendered his phone.

The lady began scrolling through the phone log but after a few seconds looked up frustrated. "I sorry, I no see our number here."

Jack huffed through his nose with a force that sent a note flying off the girl's desk. She scrambled to retrieve it. "I think the phone only stores its history for a day or two. Anything beyond that and you'll have to call my provider to get a printout."

The receptionist shook her head. "They only take a request like that from you."

"This is ridiculous. Where's Dr. Silva. He'll vouch for me."

The girl looked down fidgeting with her cuticle. She picked up a bottle cap brush and began applying another coat of polish to the nail. "Doctour Silva was in hospital," she said without looking up, "but he no longer can help. He die yesterday."

"He what? Oh for Pete's sake. Gimmie that phone." Jack used the speed dial. The call had to be routed through a network and took several minutes but he eventually got through. He was in no mood to be told the report would have to be mailed. His patience was growing thin. Several supervisors up the chain, he finally found one that promised a log of his call history would be emailed to the receptionist within minutes.

He slid the phone back into his pocket. "Sorry you had to hear that," he said. I don't usually get upset but those guys are idiots."

"Ess hokay. I deal with telefhone companies too."

"You think Rodgers will see me now?"

"Not till I see the report. He say not to bother him till then."

"Oh for Pete's sake. What kind of name is Rodgers anyway? Doesn't sound Portuguese."

"Doctour Rodgers is American." Leaning forward, she lowered her voice again. "He only here because he was caught with narcotizar while in college and can now no find a job."

"That instills a lot of confidence."

The girl shrugged and held up her hand to inspect the work she'd done on her nails, all red and shiny. "Maybe, but whatever big secret they got back there, he the one who make it. He was at the Universidade in Michigan but they kick him out before he complete his PhD so he bring everything with him and finish here. He say they are going to regret the day they no let him graduate." The girl blew on her fingers to dry the polish. A new email popped up on her computer. "Here," she said. "Give me won minute and I see." She began scrolling. "There," she said. "That's our number. You the one who they call." She held up a finger with a glossy red fingernail. "Un segundo. I let Doctour Rodgers know." She picked up the receiver and punched in a number. "Doctour Rodgers, I have your confirmation...Yes, positiva. Hokay, I tell him." She hung up the phone and looked at Jack, smiling. "He be right out."

Jack followed the infamous Dr. Rodgers down a long corridor. The man didn't appear capable of discovering anything. In truth he looked rather dull with glasses too small for his face and something resembling a rug sprouting from his head. His beard and eyebrows were bushy and in desperate need of a trim. They'd sent him to meet with a Muppet.

They passed through several rooms that formerly housed individual shops. Two appeared to have been converted into laboratories filled with testing benches, microscopes, and Pyrex flasks—but where were the people? They were supposed to be on the verge of a major breakthrough. The place should be bustling with activity. Other sections were crowded with desks, computers and file cabinets, but again, except for the occasional straggler, the rooms were devoid of life. *CellMerge on a Sunday*, he mused.

The Muppet stopped at the end of the hall and waved Jack into a room with a scarred laminate topped table surrounded by folding metal chairs. *Don't tell me this is the boardroom.*

"Please have a seat," Dr. Rodgers said. He shut the door, set the file he was carrying on the table, and pulled a chair back for himself. The room didn't feel air conditioned, though it had to be because it was much warmer outside. Jack removed his coat and draped it over the back of a chair before sitting down. He stared at the man seated across the table from him, sizing him up: brown eyes framed by granny glasses, a bushman's beard and a mop of dark unruly hair. Dr. Silva was dead. He had to trust someone. Might as well be the American. At least there wouldn't be a language problem.

"Okay," he began. "I know you're busy. I don't want to waste your time, or mine. Under normal circumstances I would deal only with Dr. Silva, but I understand he's no longer with us, so I'll have to confide in you. You look like a man who can keep a confidence. Am I right?"

Dr. Rodgers leaned back crossing his arms defensively. "I was wondering the same about you. You have nothing compared to what I have. You want to trade secrets, fine, but what I have must not leave this room. We can't afford any leaks."

Jack brought a hand up, his lips pursed in a straight line, his eyes squinting. "You have no idea what I've got, or how important it is. I'm the president of CellMerge. We buy companies like this and eat them for breakfast. You think you've got a cure for cancer, stand in line, so does everyone. It takes years to prove the efficacy of a new drug and I'd rather not wait. I have money on the table right now and I'm here to collect. I recently invested some two hundred and fifty thousand shares from my personal portfolio into this company. I need to know what happened to those shares. Two nights ago I received a call from a Mr. Figuiera who I really couldn't understand because he was talking so fast, but he seemed to imply the company had sold my CellMerge shares. Now I really don't think that happened because Dr. Silva wouldn't let it happen, but I need to know those shares are safe."

Dr. Rodgers shook his head imperceptibly. "I think you need

to speak with Mr. Figuiera. I'm a scientist. This isn't my area of expertise."

"I'd rather not. Look, the fewer people I let in on this the better. Just level with me."

Dr. Rodgers inhaled and let out a sigh. "Mr. Figuiera already knows. Besides, what does it matter if they were sold? You hold a piece of Tecnologias Celulares, tit for tat, we're even."

"Come on, Tecnologias Celulares isn't worth squat. This company's about to go belly up. The Shares in CellMerge are at a peak right now."

"Then why did you bring them here?"

Jack shook his head. "Look, do I have to spell it out? I had a problem selling my shares stateside, insider trading rules and all that. Dr. Silva agreed to have me transfer the shares to him and then I'm supposed to hand in my resignation and retire. I move down here and sell the CellMerge shares. Dr. Silva, of course, gets a nice commission and everyone's happy. If you want, I'll pass the same deal on to you."

"Wouldn't do any good."

"Why not?"

"When Dr. Silva was admitted to the hospital, our president, Senhor Figuiera, sold the CellMerge stock to a private party."

"What? What private party? He can't do that! Those shares are mine."

"That's the way I hear it. Senhor Figuiera only found out about your arrangement with Dr. Silva a few days ago and when Dr. Silva passed, he did what he felt he had to."

Jack slammed the table with his fist causing Dr. Rodgers to jerk back. "That son of a…"

"But…but he only did what he had to do to save the company. Like you said, we were going down. We owed everybody. The sale didn't even clear our debt, but it did get the creditors off our back, at least for now."

Jack slumped in his chair. "No way. This isn't possible. That was my retirement." He reached for his antacids, removing them from his pocket. His hands were shaking. Two tablets dropped to the floor before he succeeded in getting one into his mouth. His mind flashed back to his resignation letter. He'd have to make sure it never got delivered, but what was the point? He couldn't go back. They were bound to learn about the phony patents sooner or later. He'd be arrested and CellMerge would go bust.

"You're not broke, if that's what you're thinking."

"What?"

"You're going to be rich."

"What do you mean?"

"My research." Dr. Rodgers slid the file across the table. "You think Senhor Figuiera would try to save a sinking ship for no reason? I've been working on this for years but I haven't talked about it because stuff like this is easy to steal. My former professors would love to get their hands on it, as would a million other people. In fact, this stuff is so sensitive I couldn't even let Dr. Silva know how close I was, but this is one cure that works."

"Yeah, right."

"No, seriously. What I've done is polymerize radioactive isotopes into a pill that's lethal to cancer. A person takes the pill and the molecules are released virtually killing cancer cells on contact. That's the simple version. I mean the isotopes are lethal to healthy cells too so the trick was to find markers or identifiers common to all cancers that through polymerization could be combined into a molecule that's only attracted to cancerous cells."

Jack had begun to flip through the file while listening. One line caught his eye: *Proven efficacy 100%.* "How much testing have you done on this?"

"Years worth. I mean I was only allowed to work with mice while in the States, you have to go through reams of red tape to get approval to test on humans, but it's different down here. I've worked with more than two dozen volunteers and in every case we've had one hundred percent success. Regardless of the kind, six weeks after starting the pill, the cancer's gone."

Jack looked up. "Who else knows about this?"

"Right now just you and Senhor Figuiera. I had to tell him because he was in the process of putting the company into chapter eleven but your contribution saved us from that. Figuiera says once this gets out we'll get offers from the likes of Pfizer, Glaxo, Abbot, you name it. What do you think those companies might pay for a pill that cures cancer? Do you have any idea what that might be worth? Billions. Like I was saying, you're going to be rich."

Jack reread the words, *Proven efficacy 100%.* It couldn't be. He looked at Rodgers again. Delusional, or genius, which one? Senhor Figuiera was betting on it being genius. A chance like this came only once in a lifetime. He reached for his coat and removed his phone. "You got reception in here?"

"Yes. Why?"

Because I've got another three mil I want to invest."

"Oh, *ah.* You have to remember we're a private company, you can't buy shares over the phone."

"Then, what? There has to be a way."

Dr. Rodgers looked troubled, thinking for a moment and then slowly nodded. "Our current investors don't know anything about this. They think we're on the verge of bankruptcy. That's why we're keeping a lid on it. Figuiera and I have been buying the others out at rock bottom prices, but we're out of money. I don't see why we can't cut you in."

It took three tedious hours of waiting before the lawyer for Tecnologias Celulares had the completed paperwork in Jack's hands. By then he had finished his roll of antacids and was looking around the floor for the two he'd lost. They'd ordered in lunch, moqueca capixaba, a dish of slow-cooked fish, tomato, onion and garlic, topped with cilantro, but Jack couldn't eat. It was all he could do to carry on a conversation with Dr. Rodgers about the handcuffs the FDA always seemed to put on business.

Jack reviewed the contract carefully, trying to take slow deep breaths. His hands trembled, the pages flicking as he read. He checked his watch. It was only three. They had plenty of time to get the names of both parties on the document but he was antsy. He couldn't help feeling any delay might result in the whole thing slipping away. "Where's Mr. Figuiera? Shouldn't he be in here?"

"Sorry, he's not able to join us. If you don't like the deal just tear it up. Senhor Figuiera won't mind. We only agreed to let you in out of respect, because you saved the company, but if you want to back out, be my guest."

It wasn't about liking the deal. The deal was fine. If Tecnologias Celulares had a cure for cancer, Jack wanted as big a piece of the pie as possible. *No risk, no reward,* he reminded himself. He reached for his pen, signed three copies of the agreement and slid them across the table to Dr. Rodgers, who picked them up with a smile, patted them neatly into a stack and headed for the door.

Jack didn't like being left alone. His stomach churned, making him grimace. He searched the floor for the elusive antacid. He'd already found one, but the other remained at large. Doing what's right shouldn't be so stressful. CellMerge had been good to him. He took satisfaction in knowing he'd kept the company afloat as long as possible. *Wallace?* Well, that was unfortunate, but it was self defense. If he hadn't stopped Wallace, Wallace would have stopped him. And the boy was too inquisitive. Besides he had rich parents. They'd bail him out. No harm there. Being at the top meant making tough decisions. That's what they didn't understand. It wasn't his fault. It was his research team who'd failed to deliver on their promise. Ten years and they hadn't come up with a single cure. Shareholders expect their shares to increase in value. He was forced to make claims just to keep them happy…The door opened—*Fishman?*

"Hey Jack, how you doing?"

"What? George. What are you doing here?"

George slid a folio across the table. "I'm just here to make sure you get the maximum return on your investment."

Jack flipped the file open. The contract was there, but instead of Mr. Figuiera's signature, it had been signed by George Fishman."

"What's this?"

"Your copy of the agreement to purchase a minority share of Tecnologias Celulares for the price of three mil."

"I can see that, but why does it have your signature. Where's Mr. Figuiera?"

"I don't know any Figuiera. As to why I signed that, it's because I own Tecnologias Celulares. I bought the shares of all the principals forty-eight hours ago. Your shares in CellMerge were used to pay down what I could of the company's debt." George hooked his thumbs in his pockets and stood looking down on Jack with a toothy grin.

"This is crazy." Jack hesitated, but slowly a smile crept across his face. "Why you old fox. I don't know how you did it, but I want to thank you for cutting me in. I always said you were smarter than you loo…I mean, imagine buying these suckers out just before they announce a cure for cancer."

"Beg your pardon. What cure for cancer? The only thing this company has is debt which I just about cleared with the sale of your shares. I'll use the remaining three mil to satisfy the rest of their obligations and then I'm shutting the company down."

"What? Are you…" Jack rose from his chair and gathered the papers putting them back into the file. "Son of a…you conned me. I'm going to have you arrested for fraud. You and that Dr. Rodgers and…and everyone else involved."

"Dr. Rodgers? Who's Dr. Rodgers? And what fraud? Selling something that doesn't exist to secure investment capital is your game. I just followed your example."

Jack grabbed his stomach, gripping it in his hand. He closed his eyes grimacing. He'd been played. There were no witnesses, no one to back up his claim. All he had was a document that said he'd just purchased a piece of Tecnologias Celulares along with his authorization to transfer three million from his bank into the company. His stomach burned. "I don't believe it. I just don't freaking believe it. Why, George? Why would you do such a thing?"

"Why? Because Wallace deserved better, that's why, and because you're a crook. Oh, and I have another small surprise." George reached back and opened the door allowing a third person to enter the room. "This is Alan Polanski. He's an agent with the SEC. He'll be escorting you back to the U.S. to be indicted on charges of fraud, stock manipulation and a half dozen other miscellaneous crimes. If you're lucky, you may be out of jail in time to enjoy your ninetieth birthday."

Forty

...Thou art the God, even Thou alone of all the kingdoms of the earth; Thou hast made heaven and earth... —2 Kings 19:15

THE PLANE was rounding the crest of the planet bringing the sun into view, its rays spreading across the horizon like a fan. They were coming out of darkness into light.

Jen turned off the movie and yawned as she looked around the cabin. *Flying first class, the only way to go.* She snuggled into the soft leather wondering if she should take a quick nap. Larry had his eyes closed. She didn't know if he was sleeping or just relaxing but it didn't matter, he deserved a little R&R. Mission accomplished. They were almost home.

Across the aisle Mr. Fishman was awake, typing something into his laptop. Probably a report. Last night he had taken them to Porcao, a Brazilian steakhouse with a name that meant "Big Pig" because it was *churrascaria de rodízio*—all-you-can-eat. Surprisingly, Larry ate only one modest helping disappointing Mr. Fishman who chided him for not taking advantage of his generosity. They were there to celebrate their victory. They had run a flawless con. Mr. Landon was in cuffs and on his way back to America. Jen melted into the subtle upholstery thinking about how Mr. Landon would be flying economy, not first class. She smiled. Funny how things had changed.

Larry's eyes opened. "You're awake," he said.

"Yeah, but I slept most of the night. Watched a good movie too, and saw the sunrise through the porthole. Kind of awesome when you think about it, being up here with the earth so far below," she yawned and stretched again. "I'll sure be glad to get home."

Larry glanced at his watch, then back at Jen. "Won't be long now. You know what, you look good as a brunette."

"Yeah, maybe, and you should grow a beard, makes your face look thinner. Anyway, don't get used to it. I may be a bottle blond, but I'm blond for a reason."

"Oh, what's that?"

"Blonds have more fun."

"Yeah, right."

She reached out and lightly punched his shoulder. "Hey, you did good back there," she said, bringing her hand up and putting it under her head like a pillow.

"You didn't do so bad yourself. I wouldn't know Portuguese from spinach but you could have fooled me. Got right into the character."

"Ah Doctour Rodgers, my papai may not be from Brazil but my mamae ees from America so it ees only half a lie, no? Too bad we couldn't get the creep on murder charges, too."

"Six of one, half dozen of another. He's going to jail all the same. George says he won't see the light of day for many years to come."

"I guess, as long as what we've got is enough to get Aaron out."

"It better be. They have no reason to think Aaron would want Dr. Summer dead, but they have plenty to suggest Mr. Landon would. I think it's a no-brainer."

"Except we don't have enough evidence to prove it."

Dr. Philips passed room 402 with a smile, pleased to know the boy had made it home. Being a doctor had its rewards. There were times, of course, when he had to deliver bad news, but overall it seemed they were winning the battle. He was seeing more and more of his patients walk away cancer free. He had to remember to call the family. Something was causing the boy to waste away and if it wasn't leukemia, they needed to find out what it was.

His cell phone rang. The hospital frowned on their use. They were concerned that wireless signals might interfere with medical devices, but recent studies had shown otherwise so he, like many other doctors, kept his cell phone turned on. The advantage of being able to be reached by a patient in an emergency, or receiving critical test results faster, far outweighed the supposed drawbacks.

He stepped into the stairwell and slipped the phone from his pocket checking the display. The caller was a Gordy Hyndman, not a name that sounded familiar. The phone continued to ring as he trundled down the stairs picking up the pace. Level two had a courtyard where patients could enjoy the sun and a little fresh air. The phone was ringing for the fourth time as he pushed through the door leading outside. Reception would be poor in the stairwell and besides, he didn't want to break the rules if he didn't have to.

"Dr. Philips," he said, sucking in his breath to keep from sounding winded.

"Yes, hi, uh, this is Gordy Hyndman. We haven't met but I got your name from a card I found stapled to some papers my wife brought home from the hospital a few days ago." The clatter of a saw screeching and clanging pipes sounded in the background.

"I'm sorry. What did you say?"

"There's a problem you need to know about. There's been a mistake."

"I'm having trouble hearing you. Are you in your car?"

"No, I'm at work. It's a metal fabrication shop. I can't call from home. Let me step outside and find someplace quiet."

Dr. Philips waited. The ringing chains, pulleys and gears were cut off by the sound of a door banging shut.

"Is that better?"

"Yes, that's good. What did you say your name was?"

"Gordy, Gordy Hyndman."

"Okay Gordy, what's this about a mistake?"

"My wife brought a boy home from your hospital. But he's not our son."

"What?"

"I don't want her in any trouble, she's just confused, but our son died over a year ago and she can't accept the idea. Still says he's coming home any day, but it's not like that. He was in a boating accident, fog thick as pea soup, you know? Our son went overboard and drowned…"

Dr. Philips nodded. He recalled the story. The tragic accident had been in the news for several days.

"…The thing is, the Coast Guard got involved and they tried to find Jimmy but they couldn't and because we didn't have a body my wife refused to believe he was dead. She has the crazy notion that our son will come home someday, and then the other night we were watching the news about how they were looking for the parents of this boy and I see her smile with a kind of glazed look in her eye, but I don't say anything because I know what she's thinking and I don't want to encourage her, but then I come home from work and she's acting funny and I notice her sneaking off into our son's bedroom so I follow her and, well, she has the boy in there, but this kid's not our son.

"You gotta understand, my wife's a good person, and I don't think she's crazy. In all other ways she's perfectly fine except this one thing. And now we got this boy and I can't convince her he's not Jimmy and I don't know what to do. I tried to explain, I really did, but now she's saying I got rid of our son once, and now he's come home and I want to get rid of him again. So, yeah, I guess she's a little off. Anyway, I've been trying to think of what to do and I finally found your card and I thought I'd better call."

Dr. Philips took a long slow breath and let out a sigh. "I'm sorry about your son, I truly am. I remember reading about it when it happened, but if this boy is who I think he is we need to get him back to the hospital. Is he still in a coma?"

"Yeah, that's another thing. Betty's been trying to feed him but he can't eat, like she pours soup down his throat but he keeps gagging it up. I'm afraid the boy's gonna choke."

"Okay. I really appreciate your calling. I'm going to send an ambulance over to pick up the boy. Give me your address."

"Sure, but don't come right now. I worked an early shift. I get off around one. If you have someone come around one-thirty I'll be there. Otherwise I'm afraid my wife won't let you in. She's kinda like a mother bear protecting her cub."

"Right. Perhaps I'll have Public Safety attend to make sure things don't get out of hand."

Sarah took in the room, same dull yellow walls, no art, or plants, or comfortable furniture, a space designed for lulling one to sleep. She sat in a folding metal chair at a table across from Detective Irons. It was the same interview room where she and Aaron's lawyer, Eric, had passed along the information Irons used to reopen the investigation. "Thanks for seeing me," she said. "I promise I won't take much of your time. I have something that proves Dr. Rose's innocence."

Detective Irons nodded. "I'm all ears. You never know, sometimes the most trivial piece of information changes everything."

"Good, only this isn't trivial. The first thing you need to know is that Jack Landon, the president of CellMerge, has been arrested."

Hugh made a pretense of looking around, his shoulders turning with his head like they were locked together. "That's news to me. I don't recall booking him."

Sarah's auburn hair flicked against her shoulders as she nodded. "Not by you. He was arrested by an agent of the SEC. He'd been telling company shareholders that CellMerge had obtained patents that were never actually granted, patents originally applied for by Dr. Summer. He was trying to pump up the price of the company's shares so he could cash out. Dr. Summer found out about it and was threatening to expose him which gives Mr. Landon a motive to want Dr. Summer out of the way, don't you think?"

The detective slouched back in his chair crossing his arms over his thick chest. He pursed his lips and nodded slowly.

"He'd written a letter of resignation to the Board of CellMerge and jumped a plane for Rio where he had some of his CellMerge stock stashed away. I mean, he knew sooner or later someone would check those patents and realize they'd been duped. It was only a matter of time. So here's a man with a motive to kill Dr. Summer who suddenly flees to Rio to avoid being detected. That's got to be proof of his guilt."

Detective Irons inhaled and puffed out a lungful of air. "It might prove he's guilty of breaking some SEC regulations, but it doesn't mean he had anything to do with the death of Dr. Summer."

Sarah reached for her purse and plopped it on the table, its buckles clanking on the simulated wood. "Yes, but there's more," she said, retrieving the file she'd brought. "We got hold of his cell phone records and they show he called Dr. Summer on the very night he was killed." She pulled the file out and handed it to Detective Irons. "The call was made to Dr. Summer around ten PM, about an hour before he was run over. It looks like Mr. Landon made the call to lure him out of the house."

"And you got these, how?"

"Got that covered. We asked if we could check his phone logs and he gave us permission so it should be usable as evidence in court."

"He gave you permission?"

"Well, he didn't exactly know how we planned to use it."

"You'd make a good detective, Miss Hunter. Unfortunately, it's still circumstantial. His lawyer will say he was just calling Dr. Summer to remind him about something. We have to weigh that against the fact that the car used in the crime belonged to Dr. Rose."

Sarah's mouth opened, but Hugh raised his hand. "Hold on, don't get in a twist. I've got my own investigation going. I interviewed Dr. Jaeger again but aside from his Texas swagger I doubt he has what it takes to pull this off, at least not alone. That left me with Mr. Landon who coincidentally, had met with Aaron Rose earlier that night, which seemed suspicious. But according to Dr. Rose, he went home after that so I had to wonder how Mr. Landon got access to the car.

"I decided to go back and interview the guard at the parking garage. When I let him know what I was looking for he suddenly remembered a day when he walked in and found Mr. Landon with a set of keys that belonged to your friend, Aaron. Mr. Landon made some excuse about grabbing them by mistake but according to the guard Mr. Landon doesn't park his car in the garage, nor does he leave his keys there. He has reserved parking at the front of the building. The guard says he remembers Jack being nervous. He even dropped the keys and when he tried to put them back on the peg, his hands were shaking.

"I suspect he lifted those keys to have a copy made. But once again that's just circumstantial." Detective Irons leaned forward and removed a sheet of paper from the folio in front of him. "But this isn't. I asked our forensics team to go back and look at the car again, and this time pay attention to more than just the grill. Guess what they found?"

Sarah shrugged shaking her head, then sipped in her breath, held it, and edged forward in her seat.

"Hair, found on the driver's seat. Gray hair. Hair not belonging to Dr. Rose, and pipe tobacco. Your Aaron doesn't smoke a pipe does he?"

Sarah continued shaking her head but a smile crossed her lips.

"Because Mr. Landon does, and the kind of tobacco we found matches the kind of tobacco he smokes. I don't think his pipe was lit or your friend would have noticed the smell but he might have held it in his teeth, or maybe a fleck of loose tobacco fell off his coat onto the seat, but however it got there, we found it. We haven't been able to run Mr. Landon's DNA to prove whether or not the hair is his because he isn't in the system, but if he's in the custody of the Feds I'm sure they'll provide us with a sample at our request. I'm betting it was his hair, and if so, we have proof he was in that car.

"So here's what we have. A man accused of fraud leaves the country but gets arrested and brought back to face charges. The basis of the fraud, as we now know, is that he was telling investors the patents Dr. Summer applied for had been granted, when they actually hadn't. Since this involved tarnishing Dr. Summer's good name, it's reasonable to assume Dr. Summer wanted the matter cleared up, which made him a threat, so our suspect comes up with a plan. He lifts Dr. Rose's key and makes a copy, then he invites Dr. Rose out for a few drinks and either drugs him, or gets him so drunk he can't remember anything. He waits until he's sure Rose is asleep, and then drives to his condo, borrows the car wearing gloves so as not to leave fingerprints, and drives back to Dr. Summer's house where he parks and calls Dr. Summer, which we now have phone records to prove. When Dr. Summer comes out, he runs him over, drives the car back to Dr. Rose's, parks it in the garage, gets into his own car and drives home leaving Dr. Rose to take the fall. But he makes the mistake of leaving behind a small amount of evidence that proves he was in the car. There you go. We have means, motive, and opportunity. That's called building a case."

"So you really think you've got him?"

"Absolutely, and murder takes priority over fraud so I think the SEC will release him into our custody. He'll stand trial here first, and I know what you're thinking. You want me to grab my keys and go get your friend out of jail. I tell you, I'd love nothing better but unfortunately it doesn't work that way. Aaron's been arraigned so we have to go back to court and have the prosecuting attorney dismiss the charges. But it shouldn't take more than a few hours. We'll have your man out soon as possible, hopefully by this afternoon. I promise."

Detective Irons picked up a pencil and began tapping the tabletop with the erasure. "*Ummm*, I have something else for you," he said. He reached over slipping an envelope from the folio and handed it to Sarah. "You were wondering if Dr. Summer was your father. Sorry, but the DNA screen came back negative."

Sarah bit her lip. "But… my mother…the article…I was sure he worked at CellMerge."

"You can read the report for yourself. It's conclusive, though I'm not sure you'll like what you find, but if you're looking for the truth, it's in there."

Forty-One

Have we not all one father? Has not one God created us? —
Malachi 2:10

THE CALL came at precisely one-thirty. The ambulance
was dispatched and the two-man crew fastened their
seatbelts, hit the lights, and raced out of the fire station
with sirens blaring, though there was no life or death emergency. It
was merely a transport, but that didn't diminish the buzz of racing
through traffic while everyone else had to stop. The glass of the
buildings on both sides reflected a rippled image of the red and
white bullet speeding by.

The distance wasn't that great. Almost every part of San
Francisco could be reached within minutes as long as traffic wasn't
an issue. They rounded the corner and pulled to the curb finding
a police car already parked and waiting. The EMTs hopped down,
went to the back of the van for a gurney and rolled it up the
driveway into the house. They weren't prepared for the firestorm
they found inside.

"You get the heck out of my house! Get out! Get out now!" The
woman stood pointing toward the door, her face flushed and awash
with tears.

"Betty, please, you have to let these men take the boy."

"You're not taking my son."

"Betty, can't you see? This isn't our son." The man tried to put his arm around the woman but she threw him off.

"You stay away from me. Stay away. You're in on this. All of you. Why are you trying to steal my boy? Get back!"

The paramedics stood in the doorway unable to move. The woman was wacko. They needed to get by her to get into the room, but she needed restraining and that was a job for the police.

"I want you all out of my house! Right now! You have no right to be here."

"Betty, honey, these men want to help. The child needs to be in a hospital. He's not eating and you can't feed him, you know that, and if he doesn't eat he'll starve to death. Let these men take him to the hospital until he wakes up and then when he sees you he'll tell them who you are. You want Jimmy to be healthy don't you?"

The woman closed her eyes, her tears flowing out from beneath her lashes. "No, I want my son. I just want my son." *Uh, huh, uh huh, uh huh.* She stooped over and buried her face in her hands. Her husband put his arm around her shoulder moving her away from the door.

The police officer motioned to the EMTs ushering them into the room quickly. As they pushed the gurney up to the bed Gus glanced over and stopped. "Hey, I know this boy," he said.

Jen and Larry sat behind closed doors in the hallowed halls of CellMerge where no expense was too great for comfort. The chairs were deeply padded and the table solid oak. One wall featured a large plate glass window that let them see into the lab. May Ling was trying to carry on the work by herself but Jen could tell she was frustrated. A dozen other people milled about the floor working on various assignments.

The other three walls were decorated with nicely framed motivational posters: an American flag being planted on the moon and a surfer riding a wave so large it made his surfboard look like a Popsicle stick. Message: courage and perseverance lead to success. There was even a potted plant, which seemed to do amazingly well under the fluorescent light.

Sarah had called to let them know their efforts weren't in vain. Aaron would be released later that day. Aaron's lawyer had convinced the prosecuting attorney to get the item on the judge's afternoon docket.

Jen was thrilled. She wanted to be there. She looked at her watch, wondering how Mr. Fishman was making out with the board. He had spent the better part of his flight preparing for the meeting. It was his responsibility to convey everything that had happened and the impact it was likely to have on the corporation. He'd placed a call to each board member, and followed it up with an email to ensure they understood the importance of the emergency session. They were sequestered in the corporate boardroom, for how long no one knew, but George had insisted that Larry and Jen stay put. They were admonished to not talk to anyone until he'd had a chance to debrief them. Unsubstantiated rumors would spread through the company like wildfire. They needed to handle the news of Mr. Landon's arrest with discretion.

Carl swaggered by peering in the window, clearly upset that Mr. Fishman was keeping his employees from their work. Jen caught his eye, but he turned his head away feigning disinterest.

"It must be driving Dr. Jaeger crazy. He has to be wondering what's going on. I mean, we're gone all week and then we get back and are told to just sit here." She glanced at her watch and turned to Larry. "At least Aaron will be out in a few hours. They should just let him go, right? I mean, they know they've got the wrong guy. Why does it have to take so long?"

Larry puckered. "I'm sure they're doing all they can. So, was he happy? You spoke to him, didn't you?"

"Duh, what do you think? Of course he's happy," Jen said,

swatting Larry's shoulder. "Wonder what Fishman's doing in there."

"Don't know," he said, "but I do know this, the company's shareholders aren't going to be pleased. George thinks our stock value could drop as much as fifty percent. More if things really go bad. He said they'll have to hire a PR firm to put a good spin on it, but they're already in trouble and if they lose too much capitalization, they'll be forced into bankruptcy and then we'll all be out of a job. But that's a worst-case scenario."

Jen pouted, crossing her arms as she leaned back in her chair.

"Hey, I said it was a worst-case scenario. It probably won't happen. Cheer up. We have reason to celebrate."

"We already did," she said, looking over at Larry. "We had dinner with Mr. Fishman, remember?"

"No, not that. I'm talking about me. I stepped on a scale. I've lost eight pounds. At this rate, in six months I'll be looking good."

"Good for you!" Jen said. Light returned to her face.

The door opened and George Fishman shuffled into the room. He was wearing a dark blue suit with a white shirt and butterscotch tie. He slid his hands into his pockets, his long arms elbowing out, his smile white as polished ivory. "Hey guys," he said. "Thanks for waiting. Sorry I took so long."

"So what's the verdict?" Larry piped up.

"Well, it's good, all good. I can't tell you everything, but I can share some of the highlights. Number one: we'll be doing as much damage control as possible. The entire board is committed to saving the company, even the investment group that was threatening to leave, but there's going to be some changes. First off, we'll be looking for a new president but until we find one, I'm stepping in to take the helm. I don't want the job permanently, it's not my forte, but until we find someone, I'll be running things. And I did manage to get both Sarah and Aaron reinstated with full back pay..." Mr. Fishman's eyes looked through the window at the rotund little man pacing the floor with his cuffs dragging behind his boots, "...and we'll probably be letting Dr. Jaeger go."

"No, don't!" Jen's protest surprised even herself, but for reasons she couldn't explain she found herself feeling compassion for the man. He was just a messed up little dude, hurt and hardened by the unfairness of life. "Everyone deserves a second chance. Maybe you can just watch him and make sure he doesn't get us off track."

Mr. Fishman frowned. "Jaeger wanted Dr. Summer gone as much as Landon did, but we'll see. As for you two," his eyes swept back and forth between Larry and Jen, "I appreciate the integrity you've both shown. I like people with determination, a sense of what's right, and the ability to get things done. I have to believe God brought this team together for a reason and I suspect it's because He wants us to find a cure for this awful disease." He glanced out the window again. "I'll explain to Carl where you've been for the past few days, and why. He'll understand..."

"I doubt it," Larry said.

"Doesn't matter. He reports to me now. That is, if I decide to let him stay. In the meantime it's Friday. I want you two to take the rest of the day off and get an early start on the weekend. You deserve a little R & R. Only I have to ask you to keep a lid on what's happened. We'll be meeting with our PR firm to develop a strategy for presenting it to our employees but until we do, let's keep things hush, hush. We have a long road ahead and I'd like us to start out on a positive note if we can."

Forty-Two

He has shown you, O man, what is good; and what does the Lord require of you but to do justly, to love mercy, and to walk humbly with your God. —Micah 6:8

SARAH SAT on a park bench outside the courthouse with a small white poodle lying at her feet. The sun was brilliant, the sky blue, and the air crisp and cool. She snuggled into her sweater and turned her face up to catch a few rays. A dove cooing in a nearby tree brought a song to mind and she began to hum.

She was three hours early, but she had nowhere else to be and she couldn't bear sitting around alone in her apartment. The sun warmed her cheeks, the sweet smell of the ocean wafting through the air. The courthouse was just off Highway 101, not far from Bair Island with its sandy meandering trails. She thought of taking Snowball for a walk, but keeping him on a leash would be hard, and she didn't want him chasing the herons, egrets, and terns that made the marsh their home.

The song in her heart made its way to her lips:

> "Oh Lord my God, when I in awesome wonder,
> Consider all, the worlds Thy hands have made..."

Her purse began ringing, the sound of her cellphone muffled

by the soft leatherette. She reached inside hoping it was Lawyer Frisk letting her know they'd be starting early. She looked at the display but didn't recognize the number. She brought the phone to her ear.

"Yes, this is Sarah Hunter…What? Say again…What? What mix up? No, that's impossible, I buried my son…What?" Sarah's face clouded. She pulled the phone down, tabbed to her messages, and stared at the photograph the caller had sent. *Buddy?* Her face went pale.

Sarah jammed the van into park, the front tires bouncing against the curb. She let the window down a notch. It was cool outside. "Stay!" she barked, holding the dog back as she threw open the door. She jumped down, slammed the door and took off running for the hospital's entrance. *Buddy alive?* No way. It wasn't possible.

A man was already talking to the receptionist. She couldn't wait. She ran down the corridor with her shoes clapping the floor, the sound echoing against the pale green walls. *He said room 402. Can't be hard to find.* The elevators were just ahead. She hopped in, pushing the button, and then pushed it again for good measure, and when the doors didn't close, pushed it again. Stepping back, she could see the numbers ascending—*one, two*—the elevator stopped. She stood back waiting for the man in hospital greens to exit and leapt forward pushing the button with as much fervor as before.

A nurse was blocking her way as the elevator doors opened. "Where's room 402?" she said, her voice clipped, betraying urgency. The nurse pointed stepping aside, "Just down the hall on the right," but Sarah was on the move before the words left the woman's mouth.

She plunged into the room and stopped short, placing a hand against her breast. There was Buddy, lying in a bed with wheels and rails surrounded by monitors with numbers and green wavy lines, his arm taped to an IV drip. A rollaway tray had the remainder of what appeared to be a breakfast, scrambled eggs, orange juice, a cup of applesauce with a plastic spoon. His eyes opened. He smiled faintly as he struggled to sit up. "Mom," he said.

In the hallowed halls of justice, where the ladder of law has no top and no bottom and the scales are evenly balanced, a small cadre of men convened to right an injustice.

The courtroom was the same, same dark wood paneling, same heavy wood fixtures. Aaron looked back over his shoulder, smiling at Jen, then glanced around the room. He was hoping to see Sarah, but it appeared she couldn't make it.

He stood before the court wearing the clothes he'd been arrested in. His hair was combed and he still had his beard, trimmed short and neat. He liked the way it looked but he knew his mother wouldn't let him keep it.

Eric stood to his right, though it was just a formality. The charges were being dropped. The lawyer's hair towered to an apex in front asserting youthfulness but he carried a briefcase and wore a suit lending an air of dignity to his office. The prosecutor finished reading his statement and glanced up at the judge.

"Your Honor, with respect to the aforementioned new evidence which now leads us to conclude this crime was committed by another party, we move for dismissal of all charges brought against Dr. Aaron Rose and request his immediate release."

The judge turned to Eric. "I don't suppose there's any objection."

"No, your Honor," Eric said.

"Very well then, the court apologizes to you sir," he said, looking at Aaron, and then back at the prosecutor, "and admonishes the office of the District Attorney to henceforth be more thorough in their investigation before bringing an indictment before this court. All charges brought against Dr. Aaron Rose are hereby vacated. You're free to go." And with that the judge brought his gavel down hard.

Aaron turned and embraced Eric. "Thanks. You did a great job. I really appreciate it."

Eric stepped back and shook Aaron's hand. "Here's where I'd like to say I'll send you a bill, but lucky for you the state's picking up the tab."

Aaron chuckled and turned to leave but Detective Irons stood in his path. The detective put out a hand and Aaron, wary but wanting closure, responded in kind. "I don't expect you to understand but I was just doing my job," Irons said. "I'm glad it didn't go any further than it did," then he stepped back as Jen squeezed in and jumped into Aaron's arms...

Sarah checked her watch. She was a half hour late but it couldn't be helped. Her son had to come first. She drew the door back slowly not wanting to interrupt the court in session. Tipping her head in, she froze, then jerked back sharply and let the door softly close again. She turned and stumbled off toward the front of the building. *God why do you do that? Lift me up only to drop me again?* She swallowed the lump in her throat, her chest on fire. Her fingers fumbled in her purse searching for her phone. There was nothing holding her here, and she needed a job. She scrolled to her email drafts and paused, hesitating only for a moment, and then tapped the "Send" key.

It was a sunny day, as it should be when a man is set free because it implies God is smiling.

Jen was at the wheel of her Corolla, its metallic silver paint sparkling in the sun. Aaron sat beside her, making small talk but not as happy as Jen thought he should be. "What's the matter, you seem a bit down. I'd think you'd be thrilled to be out of jail."

"I am," Aaron said, rolling his head as though working out a kink in his neck. "I guess I'm just tired. It's hard to get a good night's sleep on a prison cot." A Bible lay in his lap, the one Jethro had given him. "Hey, you mind if we take a detour before we get to my place? It's on the way."

"I suppose. What do you have in mind?"

"Not much. There's this guy I met in jail. He wrote me a letter asking me to look in on his mom."

"You want to do that now?"

"I don't know, seems as good a time as any."

Jen pulled her long blond hair around, draping it over her shoulder. She tilted her head. "Where do I have to go?"

"Right up the freeway. Jethro said she lives in the projects."

They drove without talking for awhile. The cityscape swept by in a blur like an image seen from the window of a fast moving train.

"Did I tell you my mother finally called?" Aaron said, breaking the silence.

"No, you failed to mention that. What did she have to say?"

"She wasn't happy, got really upset when I told her about the car. Not so much that I was in jail or that I might be there for life. I don't know, maybe she figured she'd hire some fancy lawyer to get me out. She asked about you."

A faint smile played on Jen's lips. She waited for him to continue.

"She wanted to know if you and I were dating."

"And…" Jen said.

"I told her I'd just spent the past week in jail. Kind of hard to carry on a relationship behind bars."

Jen looked over, trying to catch Aaron's eye. "You kissed me in the Courthouse."

But Aaron continued staring straight ahead. "No, you kissed me. And my response was robotic, not romantic. Look, Jen, I…"

"No, don't say it. I get it. Really."

The car grew quiet. Jen reached up fidgeting with the visor, twisting it down to block the sun. The freeway became a glut of five o'clock traffic turning the cars into one slow-motion caterpillar inching across the causeway that connects South San Francisco with San Francisco proper, but the traffic began to loosen again as they approached the other side.

Following Aaron's instructions, Jen found herself driving through a neighborhood even seedier than the one in which Sarah lived. The streets were lined with ramshackle two-story tenements. Most were in dire need of paint and a few had their windows boarded over. She was trying to negotiate a hill littered with newspapers, food wrappers and broken bottles alongside a wall covered in graffiti. One scribble read: "Fallen Soldiers RIP" and another: "God help us all." She passed a car with shiny chrome rims and bright blue paint with the rear window smashed and bullet holes piercing the fender. A tree had a cross stapled to it with plastic flowers and a framed photo, probably a picture of some mother's son killed in a street fight. "You sure this is right?" she said.

"Yep."

They watched the scene go by, passing a store with iron bars over the windows. A group of youths in hoodies and dark glasses loitered outside.

"They call it the Sunnydale projects, but it doesn't feel very sunny," Aaron said.

Jen pulled up to a curb strewn with weeds and broken glass. "This is the address, but I'm not sure I want to get out. No wonder your friend was so messed up."

"Yeah, no, I don't blame you," Aaron said. "Look, if you're

uncomfortable, stay in the car with the doors locked. I'll go in and see how Jethro's mom is doing. I won't be long."

"No, I'm good. Let's go." Jen reached for the door and threw it open, her white slacks whispering as she stepped down.

They made their way to the porch. Jen rubbed the goosebumps that suddenly appeared on her arms. The doorbell was missing though there was a hole in the wood where one had been. Aaron knocked. A few moments passed. They stood self-consciously looking over their shoulders to see if they were being watched, wondering if anyone was home. They were about to turn and go when the door opened a crack.

"What do ya want? If you're selling something, go away. I ain't got no money."

"Mrs. Bane? My name is Aaron Rose. I was in jail with your son. He asked me to look in on you."

There was a long pause, then the door slowly opened. The woman looked like she'd been living out of a shopping cart, hungry and homeless. Her baggy eyes were runny and red. The lines in her face were deep and her hair matted gray. The pale blue dress she wore was soiled and faded.

"Jethro wrote me about you. Said you was good to him."

"I doubt I was as good to him as he was to me. I owe him a lot."

"Well, don't just stand there." Mrs. Bane stepped back as Aaron and Jen entered. "I ain't much for entertaining, but make yerselves comfortable."

The room smelled like mildew and cigarettes. A collapsed gray couch sat along one wall, threadbare with tuffs of cotton poking through. Several pictures were thumbtacked to the wall, all of them photographs in cheap plastic frames. Aaron stopped to look.

"That was Jethro when he was a boy. He wasn't always a bad kid. I wish I could've done better by him."

"Your son loves you, Mrs. Bane. You must have done something right."

The old lady swallowed. Her marbled eyes were moist and puffy. "Never told him I loved him. Don't know why, I just couldn't say it."

"You still can."

She shook her head. "No, it's too late for that."

"Why? They have visitation. If you need a ride, I can take you."

"My son didn't make it. The fool got religion and got it bad. Just couldn't keep his mouth shut about it. Felt he had to tell everyone but there're some just don't want to be told. Way I hear it, he was talking about his Jesus and got himself shanked. He bled out before the guards could get through to save him." She ran a hand through her hair as though trying to brush it out.

Aaron took a step back turning from the wall, his eyebrows furrowing. "Jethro's dead? Oh no. Oh, Mrs. Bane, I'm sorry, I didn't know." He shook his head. "Man that's crazy, but it kinda makes sense. I got the same thing from him. I thought he was nuts at first but, you know, now I think maybe he was right."

Mrs. Bane's face puckered. She went to the counter for a pack of cigarettes, lit one and used the red tip to point at Aaron. "Don't tell me he got to you, too. My son was a fool and it got him killed. He wasn't perfect, but at least he survived. All Jesus ever did was make him weak. They said he didn't even try to defend himself. Just died with a stupid grin on his face." She brought the cigarette to her wrinkled lips and blew a stream of blue smoke into the air, looking toward the door.

"I'm sorry, Mrs. Bane, I didn't mean to offend. It's just, well, I mean, Jethro left me his Bible and I've been reading it and it says sometimes you have to lose your life to save it. That's what I think Jethro was trying to do."

Jethro's mother took a long pull on her cigarette, her watery eyes squinting. "That's the biggest load of crap I ever heard. Now you're getting me all upset. Why'd you come here anyway? I didn't ask for no company. I just want to be left alone."

"I'm sorry, I…"

"I'm not up for entertainin'. I'm tired. I think you should leave. I need to get some rest."

Aaron shrugged. "If that's what you want, but I didn't mean to offend." Aaron glanced at Jen tilting his head toward the door and then began walking. He was reaching for the knob…

"Wait! Jethro said if you ever showed up I was to give you something. This way." She turned and shuffled through a side door leading to the garage, her pink slippers picking oil off the cement floor. "There," she said.

Standing in the middle of the room was the meanest, cleanest, most dressed out Harley Aaron had ever seen. "You take it and go. I don't want that thing around no more."

"I don't understand."

"Jethro was never going to ride again. He knew that. He told me to give it to you. Already signed the transfer of ownership. It's in the saddlebag. Now, take it and get out of here. And don't come back." Mrs. Bane flicked a head of ash from her cigarette, placed it back in her mouth and went to open the garage door, the thin plywood creaking on its hinges.

Aaron gasped. "You sure?"

"Just go. Hear me? Git." She plucked the cigarette from her mouth and dropped it on the ground crushing it under the rotation of her dirty pink slipper.

Aaron glanced at Jen. She brought her shoulders up and shrugged, her lips forming an inverted smile. He placed his foot under the kickstand moving it out of the way and pushed on the handlebars rolling the bike out into the light.

Jen followed alongside, her flowing hair drenched with sun. They'd hardly made it to the driveway when the garage door slammed behind them. Aaron rolled his eyes but brought his leg around to straddle the Harley. One crank and the bike sprang to life. *Rumble, rumble, rumble.* "Sweet, but I'm not sure I should take it."

"Why not? She doesn't want it and your friend won't be needing it and he wanted you to have it."

"I suppose. What the heck, climb on. Let's go for a ride."

Jen took a step back. "Wearing these?" she said. "I'm not getting my pants dirty on that greasy seat. Besides I have the car. How 'bout I go home and change and meet you at your place in an hour?"

Sarah had barely entered the hospital when her phone buzzed. Someone had sent her an email. She retrieved it without slowing down, her gait quick and purposeful. Buddy was waiting.

From: Dr. Michael Hudson <dr.hudson@sdsu.edu>

To: Dr. Sarah Hunter

Subject: Your message

Sarah, good to hear from you. Yes, the postdoc is still open. I've been interviewing candidates but haven't made a final decision. I promised the dean I'd pick someone this weekend. You know you're my first choice; I made that clear when you left, but I can't risk tendering your name if you're not here so if you want the job you need to be on campus by Monday latest. If that can be arranged, let me know.

Kindest Regards

Mike

Sarah stopped, inhaled deeply, and closed her eyes. Her skin felt tense and prickly, her heart thumping loudly in her chest. She opened her eyes, looked at her phone, and tapped, *Reply.* She began composing her response.

From: Dr. Sarah Hunter <sarahhunter1989@gmail.com>

To: Dr. Michael Hudson

Subject: Your message

Thank you, Dr. Mike. I accept. Buddy and I will be on the next flight out. See you Monday.

Regards,

Sarah

Sarah slipped her phone back into her purse and continued walking, picking up the pace again. She needed time with her son. He'd fallen asleep earlier, giving her a chance to run by the court and pick up Aaron. With his car impounded, she assumed he'd need a ride—but she didn't know about Jen.

The nurse had said the doctor wanted Buddy in the hospital overnight for observation. She would stay by his side, though she'd have to make a dozen arrangements by phone. The van would need to be returned. She also had to let her landlord know she was leaving and turn in her key. Her last month's rent was paid in advance and the furniture was his so that wasn't a problem. And she had to book airfare, unless, of course, the doctor said Buddy wasn't well enough to travel, then all bets were off. Sarah made her way to Buddy's room to tell him the good news. They were going home.

She entered with her shoulders back and chin held high. It was the right thing to do. Buddy was alive! *Thank you, Lord!*

A doctor was standing beside Buddy's bed, his arms wrapped around a clipboard. He looked up as Sarah approached.

Buddy's eyes brightened. He struggled to sit up and Sarah rushed over to help.

"No Mom, I can do it."

"I know. You're amazing…" a tear washed down her cheek. "I can't believe…" Her hands began fluffing his pillow and straightening his hair.

"No, I mean, I don't think I'm sick anymore."

"So you're Buddy's mother," the doctor said. "I'm Dr. Philips."

Sarah looked over and saw the Doctor offering her his hand. She took it shaking it cordially. "Sarah Hunter," she said.

"You've got quite a boy there, a real trooper. We've been having a nice chat. You know he was in a coma when he first got here, just woke up earlier today."

Sarah nodded. "We thought he'd…well…we thought he'd passed on," she said, another tear coursing down her cheek.

"So I'm given to understand. I've been trying to manage his health. He's malnourished and I suspect…"

"Buddy has Muscular Dystrophy."

"The doctor frowned and looked at Buddy again. "That's what he said but I checked his enzyme levels and his CK came back normal. I also did a follow up muscle biopsy. The tissue shows degeneration, but it seems to be contained. In fact there appears to be new growth around the damaged areas. Frankly, I'm not sure what to make of it…"

Forty-Three

Thus says the Lord who stretches forth the heavens and lays the foundation of the earth, and forms the spirit of man within him.
—Zechariah 12:1

THE ROVER MOON roared through the swells, breaking waves and washing the bow in foam. The yacht wasn't made for speed, but speed was an elixir, so Aaron gave it all she had.

Clouds languished off the horizon illuminated by threads of coral light. He liked being out at dawn, he liked the solitude, though Jen made privacy impossible. She had called the night before wanting to come over. He'd begged off saying he was tired and that he wanted to get up early to take the Rover out for a spin and she'd just sort of invited herself along. He leaned on the throttle.

"*Whooooeeeee,*" Jen screamed, standing behind him as he managed the helm. Her long blond hair was streaming in the wind, the white scarf around her neck flapping like a flag.

Aaron looked around as though noticing her for the first time. "Aren't you cold?" he asked, easing back on the throttle.

"Don't slow down. I don't mind. It's fun." The yacht hit another swell knocking her off balance. She grabbed his shoulder hanging on. She wore comfort fitting white slacks and a white T-shirt with an embroidered nautical crest. The thin silk scarf and high heel sandals completed her outfit, but they weren't doing much to keep her warm. According to the boat's thermometer, it was a cool fifty degrees outside. A pair of large white sunglasses were perched on her brow.

"You must be freezing," he said.

"I'm okay."

Aaron leaned forward to check the compass. The boat slowed to an idle and swayed, rising up and down on the swells. He locked down the wheel and headed for the U shaped couch at the stern.

Jen followed and sat down beside him. "I guess it is a little chilly." She rolled her shoulders and rubbed her bare arms looking around at the table, the awning, the bell outside the wheelhouse clanging in the wind.

Aaron stared out over the horizon. "I talked to mother last night," he said. "She took the Beemer away. Says she doesn't want me hot-rodding around. She never did like that car. She wants me to get something sensible, a nice four door mush-peddle, you know, lots of comfort but no guts."

Jen brought her hair around front, combing it through her fingers. "There are a lot of great cars out there; I'm sure you'll find something, and you still got the bike."

"No. She thinks motorcycles are for lowlifes. She told me to get rid of it, said I had to choose between it and the Rover Moon."

"Serious? Wow, can she do that? I mean, wasn't it a gift from your friend? How can she make you get rid of it?"

"My mom can do anything, including cut me off. It doesn't pay to go against her. The price is too high."

Jen took his hand in hers. "So that's why you're in such a snit."

"What?"

"You've been acting weird all morning, standoffish, like you're mad at me or something."

Jen scooted closer, rubbing up against him to get warm. He looked over catching her eye—eyes brown as the earth, hair blond as the sun. "Jen, I have to be straight with you. It's not about my mom, or even the boat, it's about Sarah."

"I know, I…"

"What?"

"*Duh.* Really? I wasn't coming-on to you." She gripped his hand tightly then her eyes drifted out over the horizon as she relaxed. "Truth is, Larry and I have a thing going, nothing serious, at least not yet, but I've found there's a lot more to him than meets the eye."

Aaron shot her a sideways glance.

"You know what I mean," she swatted his arm. "He's nice. I mean, we went to dinner and, he's fun, you know? Anyway, he's not bad looking and he's trying to lose a few pounds, and besides, I'm not blind. I know you have a thing for Sarah."

Aaron nodded. "Truth is, I do, but she's back with Buddy's father so there's no point…"

"What?"

"You know, the guy you met at her apartment. You're the one who told me about it."

Jen shook her head. "Nope, that blew apart. She found out he was married…"

"Huh?"

"The guy's a sleaze. His wife's got a restraining order against him. What a creep."

Aaron reached for his iPhone but as he began scrolling got a message that read: *No service.*

"Too far offshore to get a connection?"

"Must be. Dang it, I need to talk to Sarah."

"It's a bit late for that. Don't you read your messages? She accepted a position at her old school. She has to report for work on Monday so she had to leave right away. Said she'd be in touch once she got settled in and fill us in on the details. I didn't even get the chance to tell her Fishman got her reinstated."

Forty-Four

But they that wait upon the Lord shall renew their strength; they shall mount up with wings as eagles; they shall run, and not be weary; and they shall walk, and not faint. —Isaiah 40:31

THE PLANE was gliding through the clouds, the moisture on the window blurring Sarah's vision. She couldn't see beyond a few yards. It was something she wouldn't miss about San Francisco—the dismal gray.

She inhaled, deeply, trying to relax. It was Sunday afternoon. It had taken that long to put everything together, but in all that time, Aaron hadn't called. *Que sera, sera, what will be, will be.* She turned to her son. "How you doing, little man?"

Buddy looked up and smiled. He would need a wheelchair for a while; the muscles in his legs were atrophied, but Dr. Philips felt there was a good chance, over time, and with proper diet and exercise, he might recover full use. Sarah promised to enroll Buddy in physical therapy as soon as they got settled and with that, the doctor had signed his release.

Buddy smiled, but it waned quickly. "I'm okay."

"This is the first time you've been in a plane. Pretty cool huh?"

"Uh huh."

"You want to sit by the window?"

Buddy shook his head.

"Doctor said he thinks you'll be able to walk again."

"I know, it's just that…"

He didn't need to finish. She shuddered inside. She couldn't deny it hurt.

She crossed her legs and reached to catch her Bible before it slid to the floor. She had begged God to bring Brian back. She would not do that with Aaron. Lesson learned. When God wants something to happen, it happens. Best to ask and leave it with God, even if you don't like the answer. If she'd done that with Brian she might still have fond memories instead of resentment.

She'd had to tell him. As Buddy's father, he had a right to know. When the nurse came to change Buddy's bedding she'd slipped out to make the call. She owed him that. The precinct switchboard had transferred the number to Brian's cell where against a background of happy-hour noise she'd explained Buddy's survival.

"Let me get this straight," he'd responded. "The son you told me is dead is really alive, and you're taking him with you back to South Dakota. Look, if this is about child support, I'm not buying. Have a nice life, Sarah." And with that the line had gone dead.

At least she could say she tried.

The jet broke through the coastal clouds filling the porthole with light, the tip of the wing reflecting a golden glow as they banked left bringing the plane around to a northern heading. For a moment Sarah saw the immensity of the desert and in the far, far distance, the Black Hills of South Dakota. A lone vehicle moved up the road reflecting light like a bead of water on a gossamer web.

A dozen years ago she and Brian had crossed that highway. She'd thought she'd been in love, and so too with Aaron. So why was she still alone? Her eyes began to burn, but she blinked it back. She had Buddy…and Snowball. The little dog was housed in the tail of the plane. At least Buddy would have a friend at the start of their new adventure.

She reached over and tousled her son's hair. God was so good. She was sitting beside a living breathing miracle. It was more than a healing. In a very real way God had raised Buddy from the dead. The sun streamed in, beaming with the brightness of a new day.

She'd tell him about his grandfather, eventually, but it could wait for now. How he'd react was anybody's guess. The man was so off putting—*a cowboy with a saddle and no cattle*. They had nothing in common, she wasn't sure they'd ever get along, but he *was* her father, of that she had absolute proof.

"Are you sad, Mom?" Buddy asked, his eyes rolling up to meet hers.

She placed her arm around his shoulder and leaned in to kiss his cheek, then released him, shaking her head. "No, darling. Why would I be sad? I have you don't I?"

"Yes, but…"

"Then I have everything I need, and that makes me very, very, happy."

Sunday afternoon, the second day of his journey. The road that crossed the Wyoming prairie stretched farther than the eye could see, the dotted white line ripping under his wheels like film through a projector. The wind chaffed his skin, his legs vibrating with the engine's roar. The sensation was that of standing on the bow of the Rover Moon looking out across the main, its vastness making him feel small. He didn't know how many miles he'd traveled; and frankly didn't care. The sky above was cobalt blue and the air crisp and pristine.

He wore a short beard, and a seasoned leather jacket that furled in the wind. Finding that particular coat on a rack of recycled clothes was a sign, of that he was sure. He couldn't have found a more righteous way to demonstrate his decision.

He brought his wrist around, remembering as he did that his Rolex was in a pawn shop back in San Francisco. He smiled. Time was of no concern, and the money was needed for the trip. Only those in prison had reason to count the hours.

One day, in the realm that lay beyond, he would thank Dr. Summer. The man had helped him escape, not from a jail of steel bars, but from the imprisonment of his mind. The shackles of a baseless ideology had prevented him from searching for truth.

A tiny silver bird screamed overhead, a jet with a contrail like a plume of white feathers. It would land before he crossed the border into South Dakota, but its passengers, trapped in that ball of tin, couldn't feel the freedom he now felt, and he'd arrive all the same.

And Sarah? Well, Sarah was a flower of uncertainty with petals sailing on a breeze—*she loves me, she loves me not.* He was resolved not to rest until he held those petals in his hand and knew one way or the other.

The engine roared, its drone like music making him want to sing. *Hallelujah!* His fingers curled around the throttle giving the bike an extra burst of gas. There wasn't a cloud to be seen, nothing to block his view, only the fullness of creation—endless miles of earth and sky. He surged toward the never ending distance with the sun at his back shining on the patch of his motorcycle jacket, an emblem with threads of gold that pictured a man kneeling at the foot of the cross.

Epilogue

Which in his time He shall show Who is the blessed and only potentate, the King of kings, and Lord of lords. Who only hath immortality, dwelling in light which no man can approach unto. Whom no man hath seen, nor can see, to Whom be honor and power everlasting. Amen. —1 Timothy 6:15-16

One year later

On the west end of Golden Gate Park where the sun falls into the ocean and trees shimmer in the yellow afternoon light, a small group of people gathered to celebrate a birthday.

Aaron sat beside Sarah on the grass. The kite, the one he'd purchased at a Chinese curio shop more than a year ago, hovered over the ocean like a small piece of red origami bobbing on the wind. Off to his left a bike with more chrome than a '57 Chevy stood on its kickstand sparkling in the sun. The color of the recently added sidecar wasn't a perfect match, but it was close enough. He rolled onto his stomach, his worn and faded denims feeling warm on his legs. The hood of his sweatshirt caught a gust of wind.

"I'm glad we're doing this," Sarah said. She reached out to pluck a dandelion but stopped short. A butterfly landed on the yellow flower, its wings shining in the light slowly rising and falling, and then departed as quickly as it had come. "Did you see that?" she said, stretching out on her side to face Aaron.

He nodded. "Cool."

"You two better get over here and get some of this food before it's gone," Larry called.

"Like you're going to eat it?" Jen chided. "There's enough here for an army. Go ahead, fill your plate."

"I will *mon chéri*. Just pass the salad." Larry thumped his stomach proud of the lean machine his low cal diet and daily regimen of power walking had produced.

The table was spread with a picnic lover's feast. There were hot dogs and burgers, squeeze bottles of condiments, onion buns, potato salad, chips, and of course, a salad of lettuce, tomatoes, onions, olives, and green peppers. Larry had brought the salad as his contribution to the party. Sundry colas and lime drinks, both diet and regular, were in the cooler. But the centerpiece of the table was a chocolate birthday cake.

"I'm not waitin'. That son-in-law of mine's slow as a lizard in winter. We'll starve to death before he gets here. Those better be all beef weenies."

"One hundred percent."

"Good. Cowboys eat cow. May Ling, you and Beth wanna to go first? I usually wait like one pig on another but my daughter says I need to work on my manners. Ain't that right, Sarah?" he called over his shoulder.

May Ling looked at Beth, smiled demurely, and picked up a paper plate.

"Can I get you a pop? I'm getting one for myself. I can get one for you too if you want." May Ling nodded and Danny grinned like a moon struck puppy. Beth grabbed a plate for herself. "Better get it while we can."

Dr. Jaeger grabbed his ten gallon hat to keep it from being blown away. His boots were buffed to a spit saddle shine. He waddled over to the table. "Hey George, you heard the bell. Come and get it."

George stood a few yards off in the shade of a Monterey Pine that rustled in the breeze. His wife was seated beside him in a wheelchair. She smiled as he squeezed her hand. "You go ahead, dear, I'm not hungry."

"You know you have to eat to keep up your strength."

"I'm fine," she said.

"Don't argue or I'll sic your nurse on you."

"Beth won't bully me. She's one of the sweetest people I know. And she's a caregiver, not a nurse, waits on me hand and foot. It almost makes being sick worth it."

"You can thank Sarah for that. She's the one who found her." George slipped his hands into his pockets grinning broadly as he tipped back on his heels. "They're a good bunch aren't they?"

"Yes, they are. I can't understand why you want to leave."

"I told them it was only temporary when I took the job."

"But the board wants you to stay."

"The board thinks I'm responsible for boosting our share price."

Florence leaned back tilting her head to look up at her husband. "But you are, aren't you?"

"No, and you know better. It was Sarah's work that got the market excited again, that and our virus group coming up with a new flu vaccine. All I did was sit back and take the credit."

"It's credit where it's due."

"Let's just agree to disagree," he said.

"I'm telling ya George, these folks look hungry enough to eat a horse. Better hurry up."

"You'd best wait until I say the blessing or God's gonna strike you dead, and then you'll know for sure whether He's real or not."

"If He strikes me dead, then I'll believe."

"If He strikes you dead, it'll be too late."

"Least I'll go to hell on a full stomach."

Aaron helped Sarah to her feet. Yanking the stick from the ground he began winding in the string, dragging the kite back down to earth. The ocean was rolling toward the shore dumping wave after endless wave on the sand. Gulls and sandpipers darted in and out of the surf. It all seemed to make sense, earth, sky, and sea working together in perfect harmony, the product of design.

"You know you should have invited your mother."

Aaron glanced at Sarah, her long auburn hair flowing in the wind, the glossy color looking even richer in the late evening sun. "Really? My mother. The woman who refused to come to our wedding. The woman who for nine months wouldn't take our calls. You know she only talks to us now because she found out you're pregnant."

"I know, but she's still your mother."

"She's going to spoil our child. You know that don't you?"

"We'll have to make sure she doesn't."

"We can't afford to give our kid the kind of things she can. She'll take advantage of that. You wait and see."

"I guess we'll cross that bridge when we come to it." Sarah watched a pelican dive into the foam, come up with a fish, and fly off into the setting sun. The wind was whipping the waves into a froth. A gust sent her hair wind-milling about her face. She brought a hand up to hold it back and slipped her other arm through her husband's. He continued winding the string around the stick. The kite dipped and bobbed and spun as it was forced to yield.

Sarah felt a thump and brought her hand to her stomach, her fingers rubbing the bulge of her tummy. She thought for a minute and then reached into her purse for a small pair of cuticle scissors.

"Hey, what are you doing," Aaron said as she pulled the string toward herself but it was too late. She cut the line and let it go.

"What's that about?" He held up the stick but the string hung loose, no longer attached to the kite.

"All Buddy's life he was tethered to something, his wheelchair, his bed, even to me. It's his birthday. It's just symbolic, but I thought it would be nice to set him free."

Aaron placed his arm around Sarah's waist pulling her in until her head rested on his shoulder. The kite was sailing out over the deep green sea caught on a current of air that lifted it higher and took it further away with the passing of time. They waited holding each other, watching the tiny red dot shrinking over the ocean until it slipped into the dusky yellow haze and disappeared.

But the gesture was lost on Buddy. He'd become bored with the kite a few minutes after it was launched. In the shade of a huge oak with its branches overspreading the ground like a giant umbrella, a small white Poodle was prancing back and forth ducking this way and that trying to catch up with, and maybe even get ahead of the laughing and dodging and very energetic—*thirteen-year-old boy.*

A Final Word from the Author

This was a difficult manuscript to write, one that took volumes of research, and while I would like to thank everyone whose book, CD or website helped shape my writing, owing to space limitations I'm unable to provide a complete bibliography. Suffice it to say: "If I have seen further, it is by standing on the shoulders of giants."

That said, many of the ideas put forward in this book are God given and while I strived to ensure accuracy, any errors that may appear are my own, for which I apologize profusely. I am, after all, a novelist, not a scientist.

One of the most difficult issues I faced was trying to hold the reader's interest while stopping the action to provide scientific information. I considered removing these segments, but the theory of evolution is failing, and people need to know. I did reduce their original number by about a third, but I determined to leave the rest in. A critique by four women, Linda Anderson, Sunny O'Donovan, Kathleen Moore and the love of my life, my wife Kathryn, helped me decide what should stay and what could be taken out. Thank you ladies, your help is greatly appreciated.

Finally, while I'm sure most of my readers already believe in God, there are some who may not. If while reading you came to the realization that God does exist I am truly pleased, but knowing there's a God is not enough. Salvation comes through His Son. It's as simple as ABC: Admit you haven't lived up to God's standard of perfection. "All have sinned and come short of the glory of God."— *Romans 3:23*. Believe, or put your trust, in Jesus for your salvation. "For God so loved the world that He gave His only begotten Son, that whoever believes in Him should not perish but have everlasting life."—*John 3:16*. Confess Jesus as Lord. "If you confess with your mouth the Lord Jesus and believe in your heart that God raised him from the dead, you will be saved."—*Romans 10:9*.

I trust I'll see you in heaven. Sincerely,

Keith R. Clemons